SUMMONERS:
THE AWAKENING

By

~ Judith Laszlo ~

A Creative Light eBook

Cover art by Ksenia "Snowskadi" Mamaeva, http://snowskadi.deviantart.com/

Typeset and Ebook produced by ebookpbook.com
mobi ISBN: 978-0-9891717-0-0
ePub ISBN: 978-0-9891717-1-7

Also By Judith Laszlo

Summoners Series
Summoners: The Awakening
Summoners: Shards of Evil (*coming soon*)
Summoners: Rise of a Dark God (*coming soon*)

The Wilds of Asatiria
Heart of the Black Crystal Forest (*coming soon*)

TABLE OF CONTENTS

ACKNOWLEDGMENTS

To Judith G, Jennifer, Nichole, Michelle, and Amanda,
Thank you for your encouragement, prayers, edits and
constructive criticism.
A special thank you to Melissa Favara for her diligent editing.
And to my loving husband Michael,
Without your constant vigilance, coaxing and the day to day
reminders, this book would never have gotten so far!

-1-

DEMON XENOPUS

B rek arrived at the massive doors to the summoning hall, cradling his sack of filched goods and taking great pains not to make any sound that would wake his master. Crouching on his left shoulder was the gray, leather-skinned imp that had appeared at his window but three nights ago, promising him the very thing that he most desired. "It all begins this night," the imp's squeaky voice whispered into his ear. "No longer will you be just an apprentice!"

"Yes! You will make me the Grand Summoner!" Hesitating for only a moment, Brek applied his weight to the right side of the heavy double doors; the one he knew would offer less complaint. He slipped inside and pressed his back against the door, wincing as it gave a short groan when it closed. Brek hurried forward into the massive room with its domed ceiling looming high over his head; the only sound was the echo of his leather boots across the midnight blue tiles. He passed between a set of pillars that lined the circular hall, each one displaying elaborate dragons, fairies, unicorns, and other such magical beasts carved into its surface. It was as if they were all staring down at him, and he felt a pang of guilt.

Since the day he turned sixteen, Brek felt that he should perform a summoning himself. That day had come and gone, and his master, the Grand Summoner Estat, had shown no indication that he would allow him to do so. Then the imp had come, calling himself Ecnair and explaining to him that he could help Brek achieve all he desired. Brek had not wanted to trust the imp at first, but the strange creature convinced him of the truth. That his master had not felt he was ready, and only wished him to remain as he was, a simple apprentice forced to clean the many rooms of this great tower and labor over other dull tasks. His only reward was hours of difficult studies. He often felt alone and overworked. He deserved more than that, Ecnair had declared.

Nearing the middle of the room, Brek came upon the first of five braziers. He paused to rummage in the sack, fishing out a flask of lamp oil, a torch, and some flint and steel, using the latter to ignite the oil-soaked torch. After a moment it flared to life and he snatched it up, dipping it into the prepared basin; the oil and coal set fire, allowing Brek to see the other four braziers, all five marking the tips of a giant star within a circle carved into the floor. He proceeded to set flame to each one, then returned to the sack, extracting the rest of the stolen tools that he would need to perform the delicate process.

"Tonight you become the King of Demons!" the imp piped. "No more waiting, no more pointless lessons. You have learned all you need know from him. You will be the most powerful summoner in all of Asatiria!"

Fueled by the imp's words, Brek worked faster, pulling a red candle and a roll of parchment from the sack and placing the candle in the center of the star. He unrolled the delicate parchment, examining his own rough sketches of the intricate symbols used to summon the demons his master called the amarill. "I copied these symbols from my master's book as you instructed." He said, recalling the plans that Ecnair and himself had made. They would call up a strong amarill and with it; he would run Estat from the tower, making it his own. Then he could do as he pleased, perhaps making himself rich as a king, able to have servants. He would never have to clean another cobweb again. Maybe he could even marry any princess of his choice from any kingdom he pleased? The imp had assured him that by having such powerful beings under his control, these things could be accomplished. Ecnair's only stipulation was that he would be allowed riches of his own and that was more than fair.

"Good, good," the imp cooed. "And did you find a proper and powerful subject to summon?"

Brek's eyes fell on one of the symbols on the page that resembled a large serpent with bullhorns. "Yes, it is called Malstraun." He spoke the name with care, and the imp cocked its head. "He is the one who speaks often with my master." Brek had never seen Malstraun in its true monstrous form. It had most often come to his master in a human form. The thought of using Malstraun against his master was much too compelling.

"Hurry then! We are wasting time!" the imp coaxed.

Brek rolled the parchment and tucked it under one arm. He then lowered the torch to the candle, lighting it and chanting in the mystic language of magic that Master Estat had taught him. The flame of the candle flickered and danced in response to his strange words, turning from a soft yellow to an angry crimson. Brek straightened from his crouching position and lowered his torch to the crimson flame of the candle, chanting once again as the torch came in contact with the flame; like a hungry tiger, it consumed the yellow glow until the torch's blaze was as crimson as its own. Pausing to smile in triumph, Brek turned and lowered the reddened torch to touch the etching of the star on the floor. The indent ignited and spread throughout the entire symbol; even the flames in the braziers succumbed to the fierce ruby glow and became matching flares feeding the entire room with their light. Throwing his torch out of the huge circle, Brek returned his attention to the rolled parchment and a chunk of soapstone chalk that he fished from a pocket in his robe. Stepping over the burning lines, he knelt in the blank space at the top of the star. There he drew the symbol representing Malstraun upon the smooth tile, but his hand was trembling, and he paused from the symbol to shake it, jostling the imp.

"What are you doing fool?" The imp growled. "Your symbols are sloppy! Are you sure you are doing it right?"

Brek continued the drawing. "Of course it is right," He snapped. "I copied it exactly!" It was true his master's hand was steady and eloquent, outrivaling his own, but he had reminded Brek that with constant practice, he could become so himself. He had spent a full turn of the hourglass practicing last night on spare parchment. Standing, he nodded at the finished product, satisfied that it would do its job. Next, he crossed over the lines, entering the space in the right arm of the star. There he scrawled a new symbol, one that would lure Malstraun to the portal from wherever he resided. Continuing around to the legs in the star, he drew symbols for binding, controlling and the gateway. These came to him without effort, as they were the symbols Master

Estat first taught him and required him to practice often. Brek found the exercises tedious and dull. Master had never allowed him to practice the summoning himself, but permitted him to watch as he summoned lesser creatures from other planes of existence. The final marking, placed in the remaining arm of the star, represented Malstraun's weakness, the most important tool to containing its power. Placing the chalk back into his pocket and dusting his hands on his robe, Brek backed out of the star, its carved lines still burning with red flames. The imp wrung his tiny-clawed hands, appearing pleased with Brek's work.

"Is it ready, then?" Ecnair's voice was eager, its body leaned forward.

"Yes, I must now recite the spell." He glanced at the grand doors over his shoulder with a tinge of nervousness and fear of what he was about to do. Then he examined the words written on the bottom of the parchment and turned to face the glowing star. In his most authoritative voice, he spoke the final incantations of the spell. The drawn chalk symbols took on their own strange crimson glow and quivered. Was this how Estat's summoning had worked? He recalled the symbols taking on a life of their own, or did he imagine that? As he finished the incantations he waited, anxious for the results, his eyes darting from the door and back.

"What's taking so long?" grumbled the imp as it examined the symbols.

"I don't know…" But he had an inkling that the symbols were wrong somehow. Perhaps he could fix it? How? Before he could think of what to do, the entire room shook with a loud rumble and a pillar of crimson and gold light erupted from the etched star, stretching to the ceiling high above and forming angry red clouds. Brek jumped back, his eyes locked on the glowing pillar's base, ready to behold his new pet Malstraun. This was not how it went with his master. Was it still going to work? There came a noise like the rumbling of many carriages along a cobbled road. Two deep green tentacles swept their way out of the boundaries of the pillar of light, dissolving the crimson and gold into smoke. Once the haze cleared it revealed a frightening reptilian beast that towered above him almost 15 feet. Its head was almost lizard like, with large eyes, the pupils black as onyx. Its neck as thick as its body, the thin front legs ended in long clawed fingers and its hind legs folded under its thick, shiny torso like a frog. The tentacles grew from its back and acted like an extra set of arms moving about as if searching for prey. Was this Malstraun's true form?

The creature's eyes oriented on Brek and he backed away a few steps. It studied him, and he prayed that the binding symbol was working.

"And what do I have here?" The demon's voice was deep, sinister. It echoed through the hall with a haunting effect. As it spoke, the demon turned within the circle to get a better look at Brek. "A mere pathetic human?"

"Y…. you are not the one!" Brek stammered, taking a few more paces back. This could not be him, for Malstraun knew of Brek. "You are not the one I wanted! How can this be? Who are you?"

"Not the one?" Spoke the demon in a rather bored tone. "I dare say if you were trying to summon a specific demon, you should not have drawn your symbols so sloppily. And as for who I am, I am called Xenopus."

"What does it matter? This one is as good as any is it not?" The imp flexed his leathery bat wings. "He will serve our purpose well enough."

The demon smiled in a far too pleasant way, revealing a set of shining sharp teeth. Brek stepped back again coming against one of the room's pillars, fearful of this creature that was not Malstraun. At that moment one of the double doors was shoved open and striding into the room came a tall man wearing a dark blue robe; though his long hair was white, he was barely past his twenty-fourth year. Though he was young, his features held a kind of wisdom attained by years of dedicated study. Brek cowered as he drew even with him and stopped, for it was his master, the Grand Summoner Estat.

"What is the meaning of this, Brek?" Estat's gaze snapped about, his stern eyes upon him, and the commanding voice caused him to flinch. Never had Brek seen the calm and collected man appear so angry. "Do you realize what you have done?" His eyes flitting to the demon then back to Brek. "I strictly forbade you to summon because of..." His sentence broke off and Brek realized he had caught sight of the little imp.

"He's too late! You can command the demon!" The imp whispered.

"Estat! I...I..." He looked from Xenopus and back to his mentor. Command the demon? Then he'd done it! He took new courage as the imp's words took hold. "I no longer need to study from you! Look what I have summoned," He stepped away from the pillar and waved a hand at Xenopus. "A great and powerful demon no doubt. And here you have said I was not ready!"

"Fool!" Estat spat, "That is a being of evil! You made a foolish mistake in your symbols and have created a gateway of access for any demon to cross!"

Xenopus' demonic chuckle made the very walls quiver. "Don't listen to him Brek, you did well in summoning me, I shall make all your dreams come true. I am under your complete and utter command."

"Truly?" Breks' eyes widened in amazement, "Then I have done it! I will become the Grand Summoner!"

"Don't listen to that rubbish!" Estat faced the demon. "He speaks lies to you so as to gain your trust and use you for his own ambitions."

"I will give you anything you wish. Forget being Grand Summoner, what about Emperor of this land? With my help, you can have it all."

Brek smiled as he realized the power he held; the demon's power.

Estat must have realized this as well, for his features grew stern. "You are a fool, and so too am I, for believing I could teach you what I know. It would seem I made a great error in my judgment of your character." As he spoke he strode forward, his features showing no fear.

"I am not a fool! I am Brek the Grand Summoner, and.... soon to be the Emperor of the entire kingdom!" He called back. He could feel his world growing even now, the things he could do, the riches he could possess!

"Quickly! You must not let Estat reverse the spell!" the imp cried.

"Stop him!" Brek commanded of the demon without thinking.

Estat had opened his mouth to speak, slipping his hand into a pocket of his robe just as Xenopus opened his enormous mouth. A great ball of white-hot light gathered there and shot like the bolt of a crossbow towards Estat, who abandoned his words and instead withdrew and flung a tiny red marble from his pocket. It struck the side of the pillar and burst into tiny shards of glass. The sphere of ivory hit Estat square in the chest, and he was thrown back through the open door to the hall from whence he had come.

"Well, my master," purred Xenopus "now we shall begin your plans to rule over all."

Brek could feel his eyes widen as he stared at the doors of the hall. Had it killed Estat? Was that what he wanted? He hesitated, wondering if he should go to him, but then the demon's words tore his gaze away from the doors "Well, yes, I suppose we should but…." He lifted his gaze to Xenopus, intimidated and fearful of him once again. The demon must have realized this too, and without a word shrank his form down until it was only a head or so taller than Brek. Then, with a swirling of green smoke, he reformed his shape into that of a human. He retained a greenish tint to his skin and the ever-moving tentacles upon his back, and his short hair held the dark green color along with some elaborate clothing. Though Xenopus still towered over him, Brek's fear diminished and his hopes and dreams, all the steps he had planned when this moment came, returned to his thoughts. What did it matter if Estat were dead or alive? He could have anyone he wished at his side to keep him company, someone who could even love him.

"First, I want a princess." He said, his mind fixing on the part of his new life that would make him most happy.

"A princess? What kind of request is that? Surely you should be planning how you will overthrow the current Emperor of this land." Xenopus suggested.

"Later," he said, new confidence rising within him. "Right now, I want a bride, an otherworldly princess! Yes that's it, a woman born of another world. All will be in awe over my abilities, my power, even the Empress at my side!" His excitement grew. Oh what great things he would do!

Xenopus let out a sigh of boredom. "Very well master, an other worldly princess you shall have."

He was almost surprised to hear the demon accept this task, but why not? He was its master; he held its power almost as if it were now his own! Brek began to pace about the floor, imagining what his new bride would look like. The imp upon his shoulder remained quiet, and he wondered if perhaps it was contemplating their next move. It did want its riches, but that could wait. After all, such things took time, right? "Do be sure she is beautiful." Brek added as an afterthought.

"Of course lord, nothing but the best for you. I shall go and retrieve you a beauty beyond the realms of this world." With a wave of his hand, and the tentacles about his back dancing in unison, a dark tear appeared in the air beside him, and in the next moment, Xenopus had stepped through the rift and was gone.

~2~

INTO A LAND OF LEGEND

Ralley stood before the door in her flannel sheep-covered pajamas and fuzzy white bunny slippers, holding a stuffed purple elephant. "Would you hurry up Mel? You've been in there for hours!"

The door to the bathroom opened, revealing a tall girl in a blue prom dress, her washed and steam curled blond hair bobbing around her. "Alright, alright, no need to shout. Someday you will be dressing for your senior prom night dear sister, and it will be the most important night of your life."

"Humph! That's still two years away and besides, you won't have anything to worry about; you probably won't be here to need the bathroom!"

Melanie giggled and stepped away from the door to twirl around, the lacy bottom of her prom dress billowing out. She looked back to Ralley and lifted her bare arms to either side to show the decorative beading on the front of the spaghetti strapped top. "So what do you think?"

Her annoyance easing off and a smile creasing her face, Ralley looked her sister over a moment. "You really do look beautiful sis but…" Her smile faded.

"But?" Her sister asked, still smiling.

"I just don't see why you want to go to the prom with Eric." Ralley said the name as if it gave a bad taste in her mouth.

"What's wrong with Eric? He's the cutest senior in school! Blue eyes, blond hair, we're the perfect match; we will make prom king and queen easy! Don't get me wrong, he's a little rough around the personality department, but he's a jock, and we all know popular jocks are the ones that get prom king."

"That's just the problem, Mel. You're so concerned about how great he looks with you that you don't see how much of a jerk he is. He's going to break your heart, just like Dan, Greg, Peter and that guy you went out with for a week, Bic, or whatever his name was." She shrugged.

"Vic." Her sister corrected. "Oh don't be ridiculous, Eric is very thoughtful and he cares about me. Besides, you don't need to worry about me, you should be hunting down that Brad guy who keeps following you home." Melanie spun about and surveyed the six pairs of shoes displayed on her bed. "Should I wear the blue ones to match the dress, or the white ones to match the lace? Or maybe I should be dramatic and wear the red ones to match the corsage and my scarf?"

"Brad?" The name burst from her mouth like sour milk. "He's a total prick! He crashed the computers in CAD class and screwed up everyone's work! He likes to put pencils up his nose to make his buddies laugh and he picks on the freshmen." Ralley gave a shudder of disgust at the thought of him. All boys sucked, and Melanie's past boyfriends were proof enough to solidify her opinion, not to mention the annoying Brad and his apparent need to walk home with her every day and talk about who deserved to get beat up.

"Hmm… I really like the red ones, but they might be too much…" Her sister said, tapping her chin as if this decision were the most important one.

"Hey, are you listening to me?" Ralley snapped, one hand on her hip.

"Oh… sorry, I think you two would be fine together. Could you help me put this necklace on?" Glad to just let the subject go, Ralley tucked the purple elephant under her arm and followed Melanie to stand before the long mirror where she held the necklace up. As Ralley took the ends and clicked the clasp together, she sighed. "What's the matter, Ralley?"

"Oh… it's nothing really, I was just wondering if I would look half as good as you in a prom dress." But for her the thought was out of the question. There was no guy she could think of on this planet she would want to go out with, and her own hair was shorter than Melanie's, and a dull brown.

Melanie turned as Ralley finished and smiled. "Don't you worry, you will look even better than me. You just need to lose the dopey elephant and stop being such a child all the time; you're going to be a junior in September for goodness' sake! It's high time you stopped acting like a kid and realize you're seventeen."

Ralley stuck her tongue out. It was childish, but at least she wasn't 19 and acting like her mother. "Yeah right, Mellon head." Before Melanie could grab her, Ralley darted off down the hallway and ducked into the bathroom. She giggled and held her stuffed elephant up. "Now I can brush my teeth and get some sleep!" Ralley said, smirking at it. "Don't worry, I don't think you're Dopey," she added, but before she could take a step towards the sink she heard Melanie's piercing scream. She felt her heart skip a beat and she clutched the purple elephant in a tight, fearful grip, frozen in place. Melanie screamed out again, breaking the moment of paralyzing fear, and she spun around and threw open the door, racing out into the hallway to Melanie's room. "Mel, what…." But her words were cut short at what she was now seeing. Melanie burst into frightened tears as she tried to pull away from a tall man with dark green hair who held her arm in a tight grip. He wore strange but expensive looking green clothing, which gave his skin a sort of green hue. Frozen once again with fear, Ralley could only watch as the stranger pulled her sister toward an inky black hole that floated off the floor a few feet away.

"W…where are you…. taking my sister? Who…who are you?" Ralley swallowed hard, wishing her legs would move, wanting to reach out to Melanie and pull her away from him, but her arms were clamped around the purple elephant and her knees felt as though they would never bend again. She wanted to scream for her father, but she was too scared to even do that; it was like one of those dreams where no noise would come no matter how loud you tried to shout. The stranger only laughed, the sound echoing in the room. He grinned as if he enjoyed her sister's whimpering and sobbing, her eyes were shut tight, her free hand clawing at his. The stranger stepped into the floating black hole, dragging Melanie along, tears streaming down her face. "NO!" screamed Ralley in a desperate attempt to stop him, but when her sister began to disappear into the darkness Ralley forced her legs to move, leaping forward, screaming out and flinging an arm out to grab her. But she was too late. Her hand grasped nothing as she tripped forward and fell headlong into the dark hole. She yelped out as she did a somersault, getting a brief look at the bedroom beyond, but she was floating away from it, as if she were falling through space. She clutched her elephant, gasping in fear, not knowing whether she was going to hit the ground, or if there was a ground.

She heard a shout from the direction of the bedroom... her father? But then darkness filled in the image and nothing more was heard, leaving her floating, perhaps falling, through the darkness. After only a few moments she regained herself, her fear receding somewhat as she realized that she was not falling, but floating through this place of nothingness. She realized that she could breath just fine. "M...Mel? Mel, where are you?" Her words did not echo but they were loud here where there were no other sounds. She reached an arm out and began to try and feel her way to something solid, perhaps a wall, or a floor, but there was nothing. She could not even see her own hand. "Oh please, someone, anyone! Is there anyone here?" She waited but no answer came, no sounds of any movement. It was worse than sitting in detention. Once again, fear swelled up inside her. How long would she be in this place? Where WAS this place? Who was that stranger and what did he do with Melanie? How long had she been here? She began to wonder if she were suspended in time; perhaps time had stopped around her.

As hopelessness filled her heart and tears came to her eyes, she pleaded to the darkness, "Someone, anyone, please help me, please! I need to find my sister, if there's anyone out there, please help me!" Ralley blinked away her tears and watched as a dim red glow from somewhere behind her illuminated the droplets floating away. Surprised, she tried to twist herself around to see where the glow was coming from. Perhaps it was the way out? But as she turned, the red light was gone, and instead there appeared to be a strange creature made of a yellow light. It was so bright here in the darkness that she had to half shield her eyes from it to allow her squinting gaze to adjust. Unsure of what this thing was, she hesitated to call to it though it noticed her and began to run her way. As it approached she could see its four legs moving, but they were not touching any sort of ground and they didn't even make noise. "Wait…. what are you? Are you here to help me?" In answer the thing began to change, it became a man-shaped golden light that reached out and took hold of the arm she held in front of her. Before she could protest, the gentle grip pulled her forward as a bright tear in the darkness flared up around them. She peered up, catching a glimpse of the man-things gentle face and soft blue eyes before the brightness of the light forced her eyes closed. There was a sudden gut-wrenching feeling as if she were on a roller coaster careening down toward earth. Her eyes still shut, she felt a wave of dizziness wash over her.

-3-

ESTAT'S DILEMMA

Estat wheezed, his throat burning, his head and chest throbbing with pain as he recovered consciousness. How could he have let this happen? he thought. Estat rubbed his eyes and opened them, seeing only white spots of light. He rubbed them again, but no matter how much he blinked, he could see nothing. What was this? Was he blinded? Slamming his fist, he tried to vocalize his displeasure, but sound would not come. As he realized he was mute as well, a moment of panic gripped him. His hands felt about for some reassurance that he was still moving. Yes, his body, though pained by every movement, was still functioning. Estat forced his nerves to return to their faithful calmness as he began to sort out what to do. Not far, he heard the voice of Brek, his apprentice. "No," he thought, "former apprentice." He forced his aching body to move, crawling in the direction of Brek's voice. Estat bumped his head on a wall and hoped they did not hear. Unable to curse, he sat back rubbing his head and running his fingers along the surface he had just blundered into. It was the gilded doors of the summoning hall; he knew by the feel of the etchings his fingers ran along. He listened as Brek and the demon spoke of kidnapping a princess, and then he felt a prickle of energy and the demon Xenopus' presence had dissolved. At least that was working; his sense of magic had been with him for as long as he could remember.

Estat could hear Brek pacing, his boots making soft thuds and he was mumbling to himself, or perhaps to the imp. He wondered where the imp had come from. Such creatures were always up to no good and often out to please themselves. At least his messenger had been released; he recalled the moment at which he threw the marble casing against the pillar. No doubt they were too intent upon him to see the tiny red glow that would have flitted from the broken pieces and, he hoped, out the nearest open window. He prayed to Austia that it would find help.

Feeling the prickling sensation again, Estat brought his attention back to the summoning hall. The nausea told him the evil demon Xenopus had returned, but now there was another magic presence; slight, pleasant.

"Exactly as you requested my master, a princess worthy of your eminence." Xenopus intoned, sounding as if he were Brek commenting on what he deemed was a boring lecture.

"What have you done to her?" Brek's voice demanded.

"She has fainted, you buffoon." There was a brief pause. "Master, we should now direct our attention to maximizing my power so that I may be of more assistance to you when you take over the kingdom." Xenopus said, his voice returning to a honeyed coo.

"Put her in Estat's, er, my room!" Brek commanded.

Estat clenched his fist, determination and anger washing away the last of his shock. Brek will not get away with this, his thoughts raged. Hearing their footsteps as they approached the doors, Estat hurried as best his aching body would allow along the wall and came to a pillar half built into the structure. He slid behind it.

Estat listened to their footsteps as they passed through the doors to the hall. Brek's footfalls stopped. "Where is he? He is still alive?" Estat could hear the fear rising in Brek's voice.

"He will no longer be a threat to you master. He may have survived my blast, but he will undoubtedly feel the effects for the rest of his measly life." Xenopus' evil chuckle echoed through the stone hall as they continued on.

Estat sunk to the floor, pain surging through his head and chest. He waited there, resting, fading in and out of consciousness, thoughts flitting through his head in a hazy half dream of what he could do to stop Brek and the demon. He must get to his study. He could not allow his former apprentice to get his hands on any more of the summoning materials or the precious information held within. He was not sure how long he sat there, but when he came to this conclusion, a new purpose rose within him. Estat knew he must get there before Brek thought of it. Crawling along the floor, he groped about for the staircase. After a moment or two of painful searching, he came upon the edge of the stairs and with care began to descend to the library.

Prince Talon sat in the large window of his bedchamber, the knee of his bent leg supporting his arm while the other dangled down the side of the outer wall. The sun had not yet touched the trees of the distant forest, so he continued to watch for his father's hunting party to arrive. They had been gone from the castle since the sun had reached its peak, and if his father did not return soon, he would be forced to appear before the citizens. This was one of Talon's least favorite tasks, for he would be required to listen to their petty squabbles and act as judge to solve their problems. He would rather have been practicing his swordsmanship with Master Regence in the courtyard. Three floors below he could see his mother, the Empress, sitting on the lip of the fountain in the royal gardens with various ladies in waiting, one of them braiding her golden hair with small purple flowers. He watched her a moment before returning his gaze to the forest far beyond the outer walls of the castle. Talon's spirits rose as he saw the distant movement of a large hunting party making its way from the tree line and along the farming roads. In moments he was navigating his way down the winding flight of stairs from his bedchambers and out into the courtyard where his mother turned to greet him.

"Talon my son, I see you are in high spirits. I take this to mean your father is making his way homeward?"

"Yes, I am on my way to inform Master Regence myself that I shall be attending his lesson this eve."

The Empress laughed softly. "Then be off with you, and give Regence my greetings."

With a quick nod he strode past her and made his way to the outer turrets of the keep where his master teacher lay in a patch of grass, his feet propped upon a rock and one of his favorite plumed hats covering his face. With only a slight pause, Talon changed his pace to a noiseless step, sneaking up on his master with the grace of a cat and drawing a small knife at his belt with practiced ease. With knife poised in one hand, the Prince reached with the other to lift the hat from the quiescent man's face, but as his hand but brushed the plume, he felt the pressure of cold steel against his inner thigh.

A chuckle came from under the hat, and Master Regence lifted it away to give him a coy smile. "Your royal clothes are so noisy, my student, when next you sneak up on me, you would do well to cast aside such garments."

"But then you would simply hear the grass under my feet, or the birds as they startle from my approach. Perhaps even the very air would make noise in my passing. I fear that nothing I do can catch you off guard, Master Regence." Talon said with a chuckle.

"You flatter me Talon, but enough with that." With a simple backwards roll, sir Regence was on his feet and slapping the hat to his thigh, knocking the dirt from it before setting it atop his head. "You came to inform me that your father returns and I am to prepare to give you more lessons."

"Does everyone in the castle know my every thought this day?" Talon retorted.

"Your high spirits give you away my Prince. No student I have ever taught in my life thus far enjoys my lessons so much as you. I am truly honored to have a student who is so devoted to learning my technique."

"The honor is mine that you would teach me. I look forward to it as always, but first I shall greet my father and see what has fallen prey to his skill at the bow." With this he departed for the private courtyard and rear gates of the castle reserved for the royal family. What greeted him there shattered his good spirits and scattered them like dust to the winds.

His father's chestnut mare did not carry the Emperor, but pulled him through the gates upon a small cart that, were this a normal day, would have carried the bounty of the mornings hunt. Talon raced to his father's side, taking up the hand of the skilled bowman as he looked him over. The Emperors legs were bound from knee to ankle and the bandages were red with bloodstains. "Father! Are you all right? What's happened?"

"Peace my son…" His father soothed. "Is it here? Is it with you?" His eyes peered up at him with hope.

"Is what here?" Talon asked, feeling somewhat baffled.

At this reply his father's gaze dropped away in disappointment. His hand fell to his side and gripped an empty scabbard. "Take me to my chambers…" he said, his voice now heavy with the pain of his injuries.

"Father?" Talons eyes stared at the empty sheath. "Where…"

"The Blade Beast has left me, and it is not with you." His father spoke without looking at him. Before Talon could question him further, several servants rushed to help carry him away. Talon did not want to believe it. The Blade Beast… gone? Since he was but a child he had known of it. A powerful tool created by the seven gods to bring peace to Asatiria. It had taken the form of a great sword when his father had first laid a hand upon it. When one Emperor passed on, the Blade would seek out the next Emperor of Asatiria. There would be no contest, no quarreling, no tyranny. but why had it abandoned his father? And if so, why had it not come to him?

Talon turned to one of his father's fellow huntsmen, a tall, sturdy framed baron with a thick black beard. "What happened to my father? Where is the Blade Beast?"

"Strange black wolves, their eyes red with fury, attacked us, your majesty. Just as they arrived, the Blade Beast took the form of a small dragon and flew away to the south. The black creatures leapt upon the Emperor, knocking him from his steed. We rushed to his aid and fought the beasts off. A strange, thick fog confused the men, and those beasts would have had us all but for a howl that cut the air like a sword. It scattered them back to the trees. I can tell you for certain, Majesty, those were not normal wolves," the man said, fear behind his words.

"Did you manage to kill any of them?"

"No, your majesty. Though we filled their sides with arrows, they were still able to escape us. Our best tracker could not follow their trail." The huntsman paused a moment, frowning. "There is great evil upon us. Why else would the Blade Beast go?"

"Demons? Sorcery?" Talon asked, though he was more concerned that the Blade had left...and there was no way to know where it had gone.

"Perhaps so, your majesty. They did not shed blood that we could see, and neither did they falter when they ran from us, but run they did."

Talon gave a curt nod, dismissing him. His mother approached and whispered to the waiting handmaidens. He stood next to her until she gave her last direction. "Will father be well?"

"He is a strong man, and he will not let this slow him for long."

"Mother, I must ask that you sit in for me at council."

"What is this? I? And what is it you will be doing this eve that requires me to sit in for a future Emperor?" She asked with a delicate frown.

"The Blade Beast is gone, mother. Perhaps it may yet come to me, but until then, I have a hunting party to gather. Those beasts are still roaming about the woods. Perhaps they will not go far, and we can find them and destroy them before they become a danger to the people."

His mother gave him a look of surprise, but it left her moments after. "Your duty is here, as judge. If the beasts truly are injured, they will not be venturing out this night."

"Mother, this may be our only chance to destroy them; we must use this time to our advantage."

"The people need you here," came her patient reply.

"You will do just as well as I," retorted Talon, anger rising in his voice. "Action against those beasts is what matters more. If they are not destroyed, they will kill again."

His mother replied with patience. "I will not have my son, the prince, hunting a pack of injured beasts after dark."

"You will be judge in my place, for if I venture not into the woods, then I must hold council with the advisors on what actions shall be taken the following day." With that, Talon turned and stormed into the castle, leaving his mother to her thoughts. He was troubled by the Blade Beast's disappearance, but he was also hopeful that it may yet come to him.

That evening there was indeed a council held for the discussion of the events that day. After listening to the council drone on about the possibilities of what the creatures were, where they came from, and what should be done about them, his mind drifted off in search of his mother. She was likely speaking to an angry pair of farmers who were fighting over a flock of stray sheep, or perhaps a disgruntled trader complaining about a group of children stealing his apples. Her calm and caring tone would cool their hot heads, and allow them to solve their own problems. Talon often wondered why it was so necessary for royalty to settle the problems of the citizens. After the council had mulled over the information from the huntsmen, they agreed, much to Talon's annoyance, that hunting the beasts would be a waste of time. Finding the new Emperor was far more important, though the elders did agree that extra guards should patrol the woodland border to make sure that the beasts did not get too close to the outer villages or farmlands. Still, Talon was adamant about hunting these creatures down. Perhaps he could find his own way to resolve the matter despite what the council had decided, and then the Blade Beast would come to him.

-4-

Ralley Wakes

There was the sound of children whispering in excited tones, and for a moment Ralley thought that someone had left the T.V. on. She groaned and rolled to her side, her hand groping for a blanket, but she must have kicked them off the bed. Her pillows too were missing and her bed was lumpy and smelled of early summer grass. A rough jab to her hip made her sit up with a start and rub the sleep from her eyes. When her vision cleared, she found herself, not in a bed, but a small apple orchard, each tree loaded with smooth green apples ready for the picking. Standing before her were three small children; one of them, a sandy-haired boy, held the tree branch that must have been used to poke her. "Where am I?" The children only stared at her, and the boy with the stick held it before him as if to strike her. The black-haired boy on his right was a bit younger and somewhat afraid of her, and peeking around him was a little girl, younger than he and bearing an expression of awe on her soft features. All three were wearing weird, ragged clothing and they were all very dirty, as if they had been playing in the mud all day.

"In our apple orchard. Do demons not know what apple

orchards are?" the sandy-haired boy growled as he waved the gnarled stick.

Ralley forced herself to her feet, working out the kinks in her arms and legs from lying on the ground, and the children stumbled back a few steps. "I know it's an apple orchard, you little weasel. I meant that I'm not where I was a little while ago." She brushed the dirt from her pajamas, feeling quite annoyed at being poked at and a little confused. She realized as she scanned the area that she wasn't in her bedroom; she couldn't even remember an orchard being near their house. Trying to hold back the irrational panic that threatened to overcome her, she decided to find out just where she was.

The black-haired boy began to whimper. "Tolen, we should run. She might eat us or… or take us to the dark world!"

Sandy-haired Tolen lifted a protective arm in front of him. "You two run, I will take care of this demon myself!"

"Stop calling me a demon, you little brat!" Ralley snapped.

"See?" piped the little girl, "She's not a demon, she's one of the oracles of the goddesses!"

"Shani, you are such a fool! Oracles are supposed to have wings and silk gowns that glow." Tolen kept his eyes on Ralley.

"Those are angels, and besides, her clothes are strange, and she floated down from the sky with a man made of golden light," Shani protested.

In a flash of crazy images and feelings, Ralley recalled all the things that had happened to her before blacking out; her sister, the stranger, the mysterious black void and the comforting warm light that rescued her from that darkness. She realized something that made her quake with confusion. She still wore her pajamas! Patting her clothes to make sure they were made of flannel, she then reached up and pinched her cheek as hard as she could. "OW!!! Oh my gosh!! This is really happening! I'm in the middle of nowhere, wearing my pjs!" She stared in shock at her purple elephant lying only a few feet away in the grass; then she looked to Shani, realizing what she'd said. "Wait a minute, you saw it? The light I mean?" She took a step toward the children, but again they all stepped back in unison.

"Stay back!" Tolen shouted, "Or I shall poke this stick up your nose!"

"Say what? You watch your manners kid, or I'll take that stick and swat you with it!" Ralley snapped back in a voice she thought sounded too adult for her.

The shy little Shani stepped out from behind Tolen. Perhaps she found Ralley to be too much of a curiosity, or maybe it was the motherly tone that she'd just used. Whatever it was, she must have lost much of her fear at that moment. "Yes, I saw it. It was wrapped all around you and it put you down on the ground." She pointed in excitement, "Then it changed and ran away into the woods."

Ralley spun around to look in the direction Shani was pointing, hoping for some glimpse of light, a sign that he might still be lingering there, but there was nothing. She turned to face the small girl. "Changed? What do you mean by that?"

"I mean that he changed shape when he ran away. Was he your guardian angel?"

"I…I don't know…" Her mind felt ready to burst with all her questions, like, where was she? What was the strange light-man-creature and where had it gone? Why was she still in her pajamas? Where was Melanie? Who was the green haired guy? Was this all really happening? It had to be real; she could feel the pain of a headache, not to mention aches in her body from lying on the ground. As the children began to bicker about who she was, Ralley shut her eyes and took a deep breath, trying to clear her mind enough to work on one problem at a time. What was the priority? She must find out what had happened to her sister, but that could not be done until she found out where she was. She opened her eyes and looked down to the three children. "Alright, you are Shani and you are Tolen, and you are?" She questioned as she pointed to the black-haired boy.

Still somewhat frightened of her, he managed to stutter out, "A...Ayree."

"Hello, Ayree. Please don't be scared of me. I'm not going to hurt you or your friends. Tolen, I think you're very brave, and you had a right to be protective. Shani, I'm not an oracle or an angel, but I am kind of lost. I need to know where I am and how I can get back to my house."

No longer holding the stick as if he were going to beat her with it, Tolen shrugged. "You are on the west side of the village of Eagle Crest, in my family's apple orchard."

"Eagle Crest? I've never heard of a town called Eagle Crest, is it some kind of suburb?"

"What is a suburb?" Tolen asked, looking somewhat confused.

Sighing in frustration, Ralley shook her head. "Never mind. Do you think you could take me to your parents?"

Tolen shrugged and turned around. "If you want. I think Mom is in the kitchen."

"Alright, lead the way." Ralley scooped up her purple elephant before following after them and dusted it off. Shani eyed it with her ever-present curiosity.

The three children marched her through the orchard toward a small log home, resuming their earlier arguments. A gentle tendril of smoke rose from the chimney, and the smell of eggs and sausage drifted through the air, relaxing her and allowing her to forget about her problems and turn to curiosity. It must be someone's country home, but that was silly as she'd never heard of a country home in the suburbs. Then again, it struck her odd that no power lines reached the house, and she could see no other houses nearby. Shani bounded up to the wood door that stood wide open, motioning the others to follow. "Is Shani your sister, Tolen?" Ralley asked.

"Yeah, and Ayree is our friend; he lives closer to the village." Ayree nodded, his fear of her appeared to disappear now that they were closer to the protection of an adult.

"Mommy, Mommy, we found an oracle!" Shani squealed in excitement as she disappeared into the house. Before she could argue, Tolen raced up the steps and through the door shouting, "Nuh uh! She is a sorceress!" She sighed and slapped a hand to her forehead. Her eyes drifted down to Ayree.

At first he only looked up at her, but then a small grin played across his face, and a moment later, he too ran into the house. "No she is not, she is an elf princess!"

"Oracle, Sorceress, elf princess? What have these kids been reading?" she thought aloud as she stepped up to the door and politely knocked on the doorframe. Inside, she could hear the kids chattering in excitement and a woman's voice chuckling.

"Now, now, settle down kids," she was saying. "Tell her to come right in and we can offer her something to eat."

Ralley, hearing this, stepped into the house as the children ran back to her. It was a bit cooler inside, but the smell of breakfast warmed her. The furnishings were rather simple, almost homemade, but they had to be some kind of antiques. She noticed there were no photographs on the tabletops or walls, instead there were paintings that looked quite old. "Wow, so is your mom an antique collector?"

"Antiques? What do you mean by that?" Tolen raised a brow at her.

Rolling her eyes, she shook her head. What were they teaching these kids around here? The kids pulled her to a large, crude wood table and chairs. "I really can't stay long, I have to get back home, I...I'm wearing my pajamas for crying out loud!" The kids ignored her; Shani set the table with what looked to be wood plates and utensils while Tolen and Ayree pulled up extra chairs. Emerging from what had to be the kitchen was a tall and rugged woman; her dark brown hair was tied up in a bun and her rough sewn apron was covered with flour. She carried a large tray with bread, butter and a variety of vegetables.

"Well, well, what do we have here? I thought the kids brought over a new playmate, but instead they have brought a young lady!" The woman had a warm smile with crease lines around her mouth, indicating she must have smiled often. "Where do you hail from miss? I have never seen the like of your clothing in these parts."

"These parts?" Ralley wondered if this was some sort of country dialect.

"Aye, these parts, everything this side of Tradewood." The woman said, setting food on Ralley's plate.

"Tradewood?" This confused Ralley even more. She hadn't heard of that suburb either.

The husky woman raised an eyebrow. "Well, yes, dear one, Tradewood Village. If you be traveling from the north, you had to have passed through there."

Ralley looked at the woman, hoping she didn't look as stupid and confused as she felt. She had never even heard of such a place! Had she been kidnapped and dumped hundreds of miles from home? She needed a map. "Actually, I'm kind of lost. If you could maybe let me see a map for a minute, I might just be able to figure out where I am."

"Lost? Oh heavens, you must be from the city!" The woman said as understanding lighted her eyes.

"Yes, that's right! Do you have a phone? I could just call my parents if that's alright?" Ralley felt a bit relieved. Good, city, now that's something she definitely understood.

"Fone?" The woman asked, giving her an odd look.

She let out a sigh, trying not to get frustrated again. "If not, that's okay, if I could just borrow a map so I can figure out what's going on…"

"Sorry dearest, I do not have any maps, we have no need for something like that, and besides they are much too hard to get hold of." She said as she served the children.

"What?" Ralley glanced around the house, a bit confused. Was this stuff antique or was this a poor family that had to make their own things? What was the world coming to? She thought everybody at least had a phone, but these people didn't even have a TV.

Evidently reading the dismay on Ralley's face, the woman smiled and patted her shoulder. "Do not worry your lovely little head, dear, we will help you any way we can. If you just wait till my husband gets home, he can give you a ride to the market. You should be able to get a ride to the city from there."

Ralley nodded, still confused, but the thought of going to a public area was reassuring. She could look over a map at the local gas station and maybe use a payphone to call her parents and tell them where she was. "That sounds great. When does he get home?"

"He shant be too long. He was dropping off some apples to a good friend. You just eat up for now. You must be hungry."

"Now that you mention it...I guess I am a little hungry. I haven't had any breakfast."

"You poor dear."

As Ralley enjoyed the simple yet delicious homemade breakfast, she tried not to think about all the strange things that were happening, and all the questions she still had that none of these country folk could answer. Instead, she concentrated on the children's conversation that continued through breakfast between mouthfuls. Before finishing off her plate, she could hear the barking of a dog. Tolen and Shani jumped from their chairs and raced out the door, leaving Ayree to finish his breakfast.

Without looking out the window, the kind woman patted her hands on her apron and smiled, saying, "That must be him now."

~5~

CRASH MEETING

Melanie woke feeling dizzy. Her wrist throbbed. It felt like she was in bed, but there was something different about it. She rubbed at her eyes and rolled over, forcing them open to check the time on the sky blue fairy clock on her nightstand. Instead, she came face to face with a small stone statue of a gargoyle, its chiseled wings holding a lit candle. Melanie gasped and sat up with the rustling of lace.

"Where did you come from? And why am I sleeping in my prom dress?" Melanie's voice was hoarse as if she had been screaming. Had she? Then she remembered that she was supposed to be getting dressed for the prom! Had she been so tired that she dozed off? And what a crazy dream she had! But this wasn't her room, or any room that she recognized. The bed was enormous.

"What in the world…" She heard voices and tried to look around for someone, but the room was empty except for herself. It was much bigger than even her parent's bedroom; heck, you could fit a ten-person swimming pool in here and still have room enough for the spa and Jacuzzi. Two tall bookshelves filled with old volumes sat on either side of the room against the wall as well as three windows, though not tall, each as wide as her outstretched arms, two of them on opposite sides from one another. One was above the bed and the other above an old wooden desk and chair with piles of hand made paper and an inkwell with a feathered pen resting on its surface. Across from a stone stairwell leading downward was the third window, a cloth covered bench with pillows resting beneath it.

She heard the voices again; they were coming from downstairs. It sounded as if there were two of them, and one sounded familiar somehow. She held her still-throbbing wrist to her chest as the memory came to her. There had been a strange man who grabbed her arm and pulled her along into a dark room. Melanie had pulled as hard as she could to get away from him but his grip had been unbreakable. She realized she must have fainted, but now she could hear his voice down those stairs and knew she wanted nothing to do with him. Maybe there was a way to escape?

She slid off the bed onto the cool stone floor and stepped across to the third window staring in awe. The very building she stood in sat within the cone of a volcano, the molten rock far below churned within its base. Though she could see the warping waves of heat against the charred inner walls of the mountain, she only felt mild warmth within the room. The air was clear of any stench of the boiling crater. Stretched out beyond was a land like she had never seen. Sharp, rocky mountains hugged the outer walls of the volcano for a short distance until they smoothed out into grassy rolling hills; a small valley carved between them, a great tree rose up, its main bulk split into three large offshoots topped with bright green foliage. A forest of evergreens spread out beyond the hills, covering the land, and ending before a great expanse of water sparkling with the morning light. The sky itself was a brilliant blue as opposed to the hazy blue-gray smog of the city.

Melanie wanted to faint again. Maybe when she woke back up this would all have been a dream. "Don't panic, stay calm," She told herself. "Look on the bright side, the view is absolutely gorgeous! I don't get to see the beach much."

"Well, you can see the beach as much as you wish now." The strange male voice came from the stairwell, and she spun around. Standing there was a guy about Ralley's age, only an inch or so shorter than herself. His hair was short, thin, and brown. His baggy pants and simple shirt were totally out of fashion in boring brown and green earth tones. Melanie was already weirded out by him, but on his shoulder was an even odder sight; a grayish bird thing that reminded her of the gargoyle candleholder. She opened her mouth, ready to ask one of many questions she wished answered, but she forgot them all when she saw her kidnapper rising up from the stairwell to stand next to the first man. He was a good two heads taller than the first and better built, as well as having better fashion sense. He gave her a creepy smile that sent shivers up her spine. "My name is Brek and this is my demon servant Xenopus and the imp Ecnair," the shorter man said.

Melanie wasn't sure what to say next and tried to wrack her brain for the questions she was going to ask. "Um, I wanted to ask why you kidnapped me and...did you say imp Éclair?"

"I said Ecnair, and you were chosen to become a great Empress, my Empress." Brek glanced down at the floor. Was he blushing?

"Wait a minute, what are you talking about? What exactly do you mean by Empress?"

"Er, I had Xenopus bring you here to me, well not you specifically, but I asked him to provide me with a princess so that you will become my Empress."

"Are you trying to pick me up?" Great, she thought. She had not been here five minutes and already some guy was throwing lines at her. "I have honestly heard better pickup lines than 'Will you be my empress?'" Melanie said, mimicking Brek's voice, which wasn't hard since her throat was dry.

Brek frowned. "You should be honored! You will be the most powerful woman in this land!"

"Land? What are you talking about?" Melanie wondered if they were drunk or, "Wait a minute, are you guys on drugs?"

Brek blinked, appearing confused. This further convinced her that he was a user.

"Look, I don't go out with boozers or druggies, and besides, I have a boyfriend already, so why don't you guys just let me go?" She had a feeling that this wouldn't work, but she had to give it a shot anyway.

The guy stared at her a moment more and then looked up at Xenopus, shrugging as if to say 'duh, I don't get it.' Figures. Why did most of the guys that hit on her turn out to be such losers? Xenopus stepped forward and smiled his creepy smile. "I do not think you realize what is going on here; my master is offering you a position of great importance. Power beyond your imagination; you would be a fool to refuse such a great honor." His deep voice was somehow compelling, but that was because he was another good-looking creep like some of the guys she had dated. If it weren't for him calling her a fool, she might have decided to dump Eric. Melanie sighed; Ralley was probably right about him too. Ralley... Was she waiting for her at home or...?

Then she gasped in horror, bringing her hands up to her mouth. "You didn't hurt Ralley did you?"

Xenopus raised an eyebrow, his eyes lifting to the roof in thought and one finger tapping his chin. "Ralley? Oh yes, the other female." He shrugged, lifting his raised palms into the air. "Cannot say as I hurt her, but I doubt she will last long between dimensions."

Melanie blinked, not quite understanding the dimensions thing. "What are you people talking about? Where is my sister?"

"Floating about somewhere I suppose." Xenopus appeared bored with the entire conversation.

"You stupid jerk, that's my sister you're talking about! Is she alright or not?" Melanie had had just about enough of this guy and his uncaring mannerism. Ralley had to be in the building somewhere, and she had to find her and get the two of them out of here!

Brek stepped across the room and reached out for her hand. "I am sure your sister is fine, you need not worry about her anymore."

Melanie was not convinced, and she did not take his hand, but she did get a good look at the weird bird on his shoulder, which made her slide away from them. It wasn't a bird at all; it was some kind of gross looking bat with arms! It grinned at her, displaying a neat row of sharp teeth. "What the hell is that?" she sputtered, pointing at the disgusting thing.

Brek wrinkled his brow, turning his head to eye the creature. "Why, I told you, this is the imp Ecnair."

Having had just about enough, Melanie backed away. She was drugged, that had to be it; this was all some wacky hallucination! She had to get away before they shot her up with anything else. She bolted, shoving past the meeker Brek and racing down the spiral staircase into the room below. Only two windows at either side lighted this area, unlike the windows upstairs; however, they were not wide but tall. Across from the bottom of the steps was a wooden door, but she didn't want to take the chance that it was locked, so avoided it. Turning, she found tall, open archways on either side of the staircase. She heard Brek shouting in the room above. "What are you standing there for? Get her!"

Melanie hurried through one of the arches. Beyond was a short but wide hallway, lit only by two torches set in holders on the stone walls. It ended at a huge double door that looked far too heavy for her to open and was most likely locked as well. Feeling very much like she was in a horror movie, she spied another set of stairs heading downward in an alcove to the side of the doors. Hearing the deep, cruel laughter of the strange green haired guy, she rushed down the steps, these ones a bit colder against her bare feet as she wondered where her high heels had gone, or if she'd even put them on. This staircase descended along a curved wall, the other side open to an immense library. As she hurried down the steps, her eyes scanned the room for a possible hiding place or another way out. So intent was her search that she failed to notice the man at the bottom of the stairs until she blundered into him, toppling the both of them to the floor with a startled squeal.

-6-

THE BLADE BEAST

Drifting through the halls, Talon avoided any contact with the Empress, knowing that he would likely receive a disapproving glance and perhaps another lecture. As he entered the comforts of his own bedchamber, he waved away the waiting servants. They bowed and drifted off through the door, not to go far in the event that Talon changed his mind about being bathed or grew hungry. But neither appealed to him this evening, and so, with a heavy sigh, he shed his clothing and slid into bed. He was aware of each moment that slid by him, each one marking the time that the Blade Beast had yet to arrive. His dreams were a mix of unsettling pictures; the disapproving stare from his mother and the angry face of his father. The dream played with his desire that when he became Emperor, he would show the entire kingdom that action, not endless deliberation, was the easiest and most convincing way of running such a world as this. Citizens bowed their heads to him, hailing his wise decisions and what a great and strong kingdom it was that he had built upon his ideas. From a distance a band of horses raced towards him, their riders cheering and waving about the Kingdoms flags of red and gold colors emblazoned with his own family crest. As the horsemen drew nearer, the cheer of the crowd became louder as they chanted "Hail Prince Talon! Prince Talon! Majesty Talon!"

"But I am Emperor…" Talon mumbled. The cheering crowd vanished, and his eyes snapped opened, as he still heard the clatter of the horses' feet and the shouts from the people. Talon sat upright, aware of a banging on his door and the familiar voice of his sword master calling to him.

"Your Majesty Prince Talon, the Emperor sends for you! It is important."

Talon bolted from his bed and snatched up his trousers and shirt, pulling them on. Was the Blade Beast here searching for him? Was father alright? Making his way to the door he swung it wide. "Master Regence, what is going on? Is father well?"

"I am uncertain," spoke Master Regence "But you must come quickly." Without another word, Regence stepped aside, and Talon hurried past him through the maze of hallways and stairwells to his father's room, Regence keeping pace with him. Talon fretted over what his father wished to speak to him about. Had the Blade Beast returned to his father? A swift glance out a window as he passed told him it was close to dawn. Had he slept through the night? Moments later Talon was at the great doors of his father's bedchambers. His father's most trusted guards opened the doors for himself and Regence to pass. Standing at his father's bedside was his mother. Her eyes lit up as he entered, but after looking him over a moment, she turned them to the floor. His father sat up in his bed, waving away two healers who hurried out of the room before the doors were again closed. "Father what is wrong?"

"My son, as you know, the Blade Beast has left me." He spoke with a somber tone, his face showing no emotions. That bothered Talon more than the words he had just spoken. There was a long silence that followed in which Talon could no longer look to his fathers' disappointed gaze; neither did he look upon his mother, whose eyes were still downcast. Then his father took a deep breath and continued, "There is much to do, and we must make arrangements for the new Emperor, who is no doubt being led to the castle at this very moment by the Beast in its dragon form. Talon, I need you to lead the ceremonies, as I am unable."

Talons eyes snapped up to his father, who now looked down at his wife's delicate hands lain upon his own. "But father…" he began, except the words caught in his throat as his father's eyes lifted once again, eyes that now appeared old and frail; the eyes of a man who had lost something most dear to him. "Father… I…" and then Talon turned away, his back to his parents. "I will… do as you command." And without another word, the Prince hurried from the room and down the hallway, ignoring the guards, maids and other servants who made way for his passing.

So, the Blade Beast did not come after all. He entered his chambers and swept a single, frustrated tear from the corner of his eye, cursing it and the emotions that threatened to overcome him. In a flurry of cloth Talon dressed himself in his formal riding attire, mid-calf boots and a long hooded cape that, though well made, was a peasant brown. He could not get the image of his father's eyes out of his thoughts, but he had to cast it far from himself. He had to get away. Yes, he would ride out through the countryside, leaving all the problems that everything in the castle represented behind.

He burst through the doors of his chambers and made his way down the halls towards the north gates. He became aware of master Regence following behind him. Talon ignored his master until he came to the stables and commanded the stable hands to have his horse saddled and ready, hearing Regence echoing his words. "And where is it you think you are going Sword master?" Talon questioned, keeping his voice free of emotion, still facing forward.

"I am going wherever you are going my Prince." Regence replied in a casual manner.

"I do not need an escort." Talon said through gritted teeth.

"No, you need a friend," he said with a smooth tone.

Prince Talon turned to Regence, a small smile tugging at his lips. "Then, you are welcome to join me." The sword master smiled and gave a slight nod of his head. They stood in silence for a time until a stable hand rounded the corner leading a chestnut stallion and a white mare. The moment the chestnut spotted Talon it threw back its head, freeing its reins from the startled stable boy, and bolted with all speed straight for the two of them. The Prince felt his master's hand flick to his sword hilt as the stallion neared, though the chestnut skidded to a stop moments before bowling them over, kicking up dirt and pebbles.

"You should teach that one some manners," Regence grumbled as he brushed the dirt from his sleeves.

"That is simply part of Phoenix's charm." Talon patted the red mane as the stallion butted its head against his shoulder.

The stable boy apologized to him and handed the reins of the white mare to Regence, who smiled and gave him a gruff pat on the back to tell him he'd done nothing wrong. Talon swung himself onto Phoenix's back, the stallion snorting and shaking its head, eager to be off.

Regence too mounted up, the mare standing still and silent, awaiting the guidance of the rein. "Worry not, Crest, you too are charming, not to mention lady-like," he said, giving her a gentle pat on the neck.

Prince Talon and Swordmaster Regence rode side by side through the gates of the castle and down into the streets. All along the main road, merchants were emerging from their shops to set out their signs and display their wares. One merchant was hanging out colorful tapestries, another was arranging his stall with fresh fruits and vegetables; the smell of bread wafted out of the doorway of another shop, a rotund man stepping out of it, his arms full of pastries. The early morning customers, recognizing the prince and the master swordsmen, hurried aside, stopping to watch as they passed, many shouting out good mornings and hails to the prince. Talon nodded or waved back, feeling as if he was putting on a mask and pretending to be royalty. Though he would still be a prince when the new Emperor of Asatiria was found, he felt as though the title had lost its very purpose. He and his family would be granted land to rule over, though they would rule under the Emperor and his laws.

Regence nodded to the guards at the city gates, and they snapped to attention, saluting them as they passed. Beyond the gates, they rode through small crowds of farmers, wagons and travelers that were entering into the city to sell their wares, entertain, or tell stories of the mysterious lands far to the north. Phoenix pulled at the reins and quickened his step, eager to be free of the city walls and its people. Feeling the same way,

Talon guided him through the maze of wagons and people to the open road that ran west from the castle. Breaking free into open space, Phoenix put on a sudden burst of speed, racing down the road. Waiting only for Regence to prompt her, Crest too leapt forward to follow, keeping pace with the muscular stallion.

The pain, fear and anger of the morning was being left farther and farther behind him as Talon allowed Phoenix to race down the road, almost flying, passing the occasional farmer's wagon as if it had been stitched in a tapestry. This continued for a short time before Talons eyes were blurry from the wind, and he began to ease the reins back, slowing Phoenix to a walk. Regence did the same.

Breathing in deep, Talon caught the smell of fresh, cool air drifting down from the Eagle Mountains. He felt his troubles catch up to him; even Phoenix could never outrace them. Perhaps when the new Emperor arrived at the castle, things might not be so bad, or perhaps they would get worse? No, that was not the way of the Beast. It was to choose the most worthy of the land, and Talon was not chosen.

"Sire, I know you are troubled, and I am sorry for the sorrow you must feel. My duty and loyalty lie only with your family. I shall ride with you as far as you wish this day and for all days afterward, wherever the great winds of the Goddess Austia carry you," Regence said with a fist placed to his heart in a sign of loyalty.

A great sigh left Prince Talon's lips, and with it, many worries and aches in his heart, bringing about the urge to cry tears of relief and joy. His greatest friend and mentor would be with him whatever happened, and that was more precious to him than becoming a great Emperor. "Thank you, Master... I ..."

"Call me Regence for now sire. What is our destination to be on this fine day?"

"You will address me as Talon, and we are going to continue on to Eagle Crest Village, there is a quiet tavern where we can get a drink and good food." Still, Talon could not help but feel some sense that the events of the day were not going to vanish in his absence.

– 7 –

ESTAT'S PRIVATE STUDY

Estat remembered getting to the bottom of the steps before a wave of pain hit him and his white speckled vision went black. The next thing he knew, he was picking himself up off the floor, the white returning to his eyes. Had he passed out for longer than he thought? With his vision gone, there was no way to tell, and with his voice gone, he could not ask. Moments later he heard someone racing down the stairs towards him, and before he could decide what to do, the stranger had collided with him.

For a moment, his vision went black again. It took some time before he could see the white light, and that is when he heard a groan. The voice was female, and there was a strange lavender smell in the air. He realized it must be the woman that Xenopus had kidnapped.

There was a rustling of lace and a few moments of silence before she spoke. "Oh my gosh! Did they do this to you?" her concerned voice said. He put a hand to his chest where the blast had hit him. It was burning and aching like mad, but he resisted a grimace of pain. He nodded, knowing whom she meant by "they."

"Okay, we have to hide, I think they're after me." Estat heard the rustle of heavy clothing and heard her step closer to him. "You're blind!" she exclaimed after a long moment of silence. He could only guess that she must have held a hand to help him and he had only stared right through it. "Oh gosh, I'm sorry, I should have noticed!"

Estat shrugged; there was no way she could have known, as they had never met. He felt her grip his arm and help him to his feet. Estat decided that now was not the time to try and get acquainted. She had said herself that they may be after her; they had to get to his study and make sure Brek and Xenopus could not get into it. Estat nudged his foot around till he found the bottom stair. After getting his bearings, he faced what he knew to be the middle of the library. He then reached out a hand for the girl.

"What? Do you know someplace to hide?" her exotic voice asked, sounding hopeful. All Estat could do was nod, then point to the general area where he remembered the door to be located. He felt her delicate, soft-skinned hand on his. "Straight that way?" she asked. He nodded again. "Okay then, lets hurry." she said, sounding urgent, and then guided him forward through the library. Estat began to wonder where this princess had come from and how, if at all, he could get her home.

The girl stopped him, and there was the sound of a door handle being tested. "There's a door here with a weird lizard head on it, but it's locked."

Estat reached forward and found the golden, slender, serpent-like head that was embedded in the door. It was the head of Liquendia, the amarill that slept beneath this very tower.

Without his giving it any pressure the head bowed downward. There was the sound of large metal bars moving within the door.

"No keys? I hope we can lock it from the inside then." she said. He listened as the girl tried the handle again, this time he heard the door creak open. *Keys? Did this girl know nothing about magical locks?* He thought. Her warm hand clamped his wrist as she led him forward into the room that he had spent much time in. Though he could see nothing of it now, he recalled leaving it a bit of a mess. There were three long tables in the room, each pushed against a curved wall. The tables to either side of the entrance were filled with books, ink, figurines, empty bottles, papyrus, feather pens and candles. The third table held several more important items but was clear of clutter: three small crystal globes on stands, five tall red candles, a thick tome, a folded cloth map and a large clay bowl filled with water and a small water plant growing out of it.

"Wow, this room reminds me of one of those palm reader shops." He raised a brow and heard the groan of the door as she closed it. When the door slid back into the frame, the locking bars within snapped back into place. The girl squealed and grabbed his arm. He patted her shoulder, trying to reassure her and giving her an amused smile. "H…hey that wasn't funny at all!" She let go of him and stepped away. "Oh! There's a window in here! How can there be a window?"

Only momentarily confused, Estat remembered the enchanted mirror that hung just above the third table. It was not a window, but he could ask it to show him just about any place he had been before. He preferred to use it to brighten up the enclosed study. Estat listened to her feet pad across the room and he realized she was not wearing shoes.

"Oh my gosh! Is this a picture?" In the next moment she let out a frightened scream. "I can stick my hand right though it! How could there be a window? We came to the middle of the room!" She sounded as though she did not believe her own eyes.

Estat shook his head, not knowing if she was even looking at him. He had to find a way to communicate with her and find out where she came from. Reaching out, he sought a feathered pen from a nearby table, as well as a piece of parchment that should be free of writing. After finding the ink well he dipped the pen into it. Putting pen to paper he started giving her basic information like his name and asking her questions to find out where she came from and if she might be able to help him remove the spell. He heard her rustle towards him.

"What are you writing…I don't know that language." She said from over his shoulder. He dropped the pen half way through a sentence, frustrated. If she did not know this language, how could she speak it? Then he remembered reading of a spell that allowed a person to understand and unknowingly speak the language of the caster's choosing. If this was the case, she would only be able to understand him if he was able to speak to her.

"Are you okay? Was it something I said?" she asked, concern and worry in her voice. Estat sighed and tried to smile at her and shake his head to indicate it was not she that caused his anger. "This place is really strange, I wish you could talk and tell me where I am. I wish I knew your name and what we're supposed to do now that we're trapped in this room."

What indeed? Estat thought. He could not see to make summoning symbols, and he could not speak any spells either.

Above all, he could not communicate with the young woman, and that angered him more than anything.

"This is all so weird, are you like a fortune teller? You know, like reading palms and using crystal balls?"

Estat's thoughts snapped to attention. Of course! The Crystal Globes that revealed past, present and future! They sat on the table among the other more magical items in the room. Though their visions were limited and their magical charge was renewed only on a full moon, he knew he had not used them since the last one and their magical energies would be enough to show them what he needed to know, but he would need the girls' eyes. He sought out her hand and with the other he scanned the table, finding the stand that the middle globe rested upon.

"What is it? You want to tell my future or something? I hardly think now is the time…" He shook his head then decided to try using his hands to speak to her. He patted the globe that he had set her hand on, then pointed to his mouth, her and then his eye. "Charades? Well I'm not great at games but let's see… something about the globe and talking and what I see?"

Estat nodded and eased her hand to the middle globe, pressing her palm onto it. "Oh wow! There's smoke in it or something! It's swirling all around and…" Frowning, Estat waited a moment or two before squeezing her arm, tipping his head in a question. "It's Ralley! I see my sister! She's walking outside of some cabin… what's she doing in her nightclothes? Is this for real? Is this happening right now?" The young woman's voice was shaking, and she sounded as if she were panicking. Estat squeezed her arm again. This was not what he wanted her to concentrate on; the woman was thinking of her sister and he had to see what

Xenopus was up to. He nudged her arm and tapped his head, then pointed for the door.

"What? You want me to think of the guys chasing us? But what about my sister? Is this really happening? Where is she?" Estat clenched his fist. He could not answer her questions, and she knew that. He pointed for the door again and was sure there was anger on his face this time. She was silent for a long moment before she spoke again. "I see them, the guys that kidnapped me. They're standing in a big huge room with red fires burning and a big star inside a circle on the floor and the green haired one is looking at a page with weird symbols on it."

It was just as Estat had feared. Xenopus and Brek were going to use the summoning hall to bring more demons into this world. He had to stop them; the summoning hall would make it far too easy for them and the tower itself would protect them. He had to get them out of here, but how? If he could waken Liquendia, since she created the tower, she would have the power to force him out of it. He would have this princess be his eyes to get down to Liquendia's chamber, but first he must show her how. He moved her hand from the globe and placed his own palm upon it. Concentrating, he began to picture in his mind the winding stairwells and rooms below and the trap door at the towers bottom.

"What is this? What are you showing me? Oh I wish you could talk, all this stuff is starting to really confuse me! Do we have to get to that trap door? Is it a way out?"

Estat could only nod. Liquendia was a way out, but he did not intend to leave the tower. He withdrew his hand from the globe and stood. His head throbbed and he slumped back down in the chair. Estat began to wonder if he would have the strength to make it down all those steps.

"Are you okay? You're really in bad shape. What in the world did they do to you?" He heard her heavy sigh. "I'm sorry, I know you can't exactly answer me, but I have no idea what's going on. I was supposed to go to the prom, but I guess…I guess I missed it." There was regret in her saddened voice and Estat frowned. It was his fault she was here, his stupid mistakes led to her being kidnapped. He could do nothing for her now, but perhaps he could make it up to her after he got rid of Xenopus. "You need something on those wounds of yours. Do you have any medical supplies in this place?"

Frustrated at this delay, Estat gripped his aching head. They could not afford to waste time tending his wounds. He had to get Xenopus and Brek out of the tower before they could perform a summoning. Once again, he rose to his feet and began to stagger in the direction of the door. He felt the girl's gentle touch as she steadied him. "You're really going out there then? I guess I have no choice but to get you to wherever you're going. Besides, you're my only way out of here." He could only smile his thanks to her, and though his head pounded once again, and his chest ached with every breath, he was determined to set things right.

-8-

EAGLE CREST VILLAGE

Ralley could hear the clopping of hooves and the creaking of wooden wheels. Curious, she moved over to the door to peer out. Tolen and Shani had scrambled onto an old wagon pulled by a brown workhorse. The man at the reins was laughing at whatever they were telling him. She began to wonder if these people were Amish; it would explain a great deal, and was the only reason she found for them not having a car. Ralley continued to watch as the man, who must be their father, brought the cart to a stop and helped the children down. The children's father was well muscled, tall and with a rugged but handsome face. He also wore old, well-worn clothing that was covered in dirt.

Tolen rushed into the house, Shani at his heels, and the two of them ran to Ralley and shouted in excitement as their father entered. "See, Dad, see?"

"Well, hello there, young lady. The children tell me you are some kind of magical elfin oracle. I am honored you have blessed our house with your presence." For a moment Ralley found herself speechless, but she relaxed and even giggled a little as the children's father winked at her and chuckled.

"She says she is lost," his wife said as she brought her husband a plate of food. "I was thinking that perhaps you could take her to the village when you go today."

"Lost you say? Well, I do not mind helping the young lady out." He sat down at the table. "My name is Jerel, and this is my wife Nell. What might your name be? Or shall I call you Young Lady?"

"No, Ralley is fine. It's nice to meet you; I really appreciate you helping me."

As Jerel ate his breakfast and chatted with Nell about his visit to the neighbors, Ralley was tugged outside by the three children to meet Dancer, the family's brown workhorse, and Horace, a large hound dog. A short time later Jerel led Dancer around to a large barn where he began to load the wagon with sacks of apples, turnips, onions, potatoes, tomatoes and pumpkins. Tolen and Ayree stood in the cart, helping to stack everything as Shani held Dancers reins so he would not move about. Ralley, feeling that she should do something, entered the barn and picked up a sack of potatoes, marching it out to the cart.

"Lady Ralley, you do not need to do that, after all, you are a guest!" Jerel exclaimed as he turned from the cart.

"Don't worry about it. I feel silly just standing there doing nothing. Besides, you're taking me to town, and this is the only way I'll be able to repay you!" She said, hefting the sack into the wagon.

"It is nothing really, but I do appreciate the help," he said, adjusting the sack she'd brought.

After the wagon was loaded with as much as it could bear, Jerel drove it back around to the front of his house where he and

Ralley both gave Nell and the three children each a hug. "Thanks for breakfast, Nell. Tolen, Ayree, Shani, thanks for bringing me here. You are great kids."

"Take care of yourself dear, I hope you find your way," Nell gave her an encouraging smile.

Jerel climbed up into the cart and took up the reins. Ralley smiled and climbed up and sat next to him, waving to the children once more before turning to face the road. Jerel snapped the reins, and as the cart gave a little jolt Ralley yelped and clutched her seat. She had never been on a cart, she hadn't even ridden on a horse before, but she soon realized that it was a very relaxing and pleasant ride. The landscape was breathtaking, like something off of the Discovery Channel, and as Jerel began to lecture about how to grow the biggest and best pumpkins, Ralley took in the sights and sounds of the countryside. Babbling brooks, twittering birds, the mooing of cows in the nearby fields, even the smells of pine trees and flowers. Soon she began to see small homes similar to Jerel's spread out about the countryside. Each one had its own wheat field, cows grazing, or some kind of orchard. Occasionally they would pass someone walking along the road or another wagon, and Jerel would greet them in his cheerful manner and be greeted in return.

"There it is young lass, Eagle Crest. A fine and peaceful village, named after the mountains, of course." He spoke, nodding his head at the distant mountains to the north. Ralley glanced at them for only a moment before drawing her attention back to the village. It looked like someplace out of a storybook, but Ralley's hopes sank as they neared the buildings. They were no more than two stories and there were no street lamps anywhere, no roaring of engines, and no power lines! As the wagon rolled along through the small crowd of people moving to and from the village, Ralley groaned. Every single one of them looked like they had just walked out of a renaissance convention. "Is there something wrong?" Jerel frowned.

"Uh, no I just…bumped my elbow." She gave him a fake smile, trying to be polite. After all, it was their way to shun electricity right? She refused to be rude to them, even though she loved to laugh at Amish jokes. Besides, Jerel and Nell were actually rather nice and everyone here had smiles on their faces, were friendly, and very helpful. Now what was she going to do? There would surely be no phone here, perhaps not even a map! She watched the bustle of this little village as they went down the dusty road. Truly primitive, but it was somehow relaxing to see everyone so worry free.

"There we are, Ralley, you should be able to find something there at the market." Jerel said in triumph as he pointed at a cluster of small buildings ahead. On the outer side of these buildings were many small booths, most displaying food. A crowd of people moved from one covered display to the next, gazing at silvered trinkets, haggling over the price of apples, in some cases downright arguing as children dodged and weaved around them in a game of tag. A weird giddiness overtook her at the sight of it all. She felt Jerel's stare and looked up at him, finding his expression was a look of curiosity. "I would think this was nothing compared to the city."

"Ur…well, this is just so different from the city, I mean it's so much more peaceful here."

"I suppose you are right," he nodded and smiled, pulling the cart to a stop. "I guess you will be wanting to get off here. It was a real pleasure to meet you, Ralley, and I hope you find your way safely back to the city."

"Thanks Jerel. You and your family were so nice to me, I wish I could repay you somehow." She slid off the cart; her elephant tucked under an arm, and stepped back.

"Your company was payment enough." With a smile and a nod he flicked the reins and rode off through the crowd.

Watching him till he was out of sight, Ralley then turned her attention to the next task. She felt so stupid standing there in her pajamas, not to mention the slippers and her purple elephant. She walked up to the first stall she saw that wasn't food. It was some kind of clothing shop; the man behind the booth was trying to convince a woman to buy a scarf. Ralley waited for him to finish, looking over some of the clothing that was displayed along the counter and hanging from hooks. It all looked hand made and pretty much none of it was in fashion, not to mention all the girls things were plain dresses with boring colors.

She didn't notice the merchant till he was almost on top of her. "Milady! Can I interest you in anything? Are you looking for a work dress or maybe…" Ralley jumped a little and took a step back. The man was now studying her clothes, his sales pitch forgotten.

"Um, well, actually I wanted to know where I might get a map, do you happen to know?"

The man stared at her a moment longer before snapping out of it. "Huh? What? A map you say? Well…. you might be…able to…" His eyes wandered down to her bunny slippers, raising an eyebrow as his next words dropped into the abyss. This was getting embarrassing, and a bit annoying.

"Well?" Ralley said after a moment, impatience in her tone.

The man pointed down the street. "Maybe Rando has got one; his booth is just three down. Miss, could I inquire as to where you are from? Your clothes seem …."

"Yes, yes, very funny." Ralley intoned with annoyance. "I'm just trying to find a map and get back home, I …." She sighed. She really didn't know what had happened. Why she was dumped out here in her nightclothes far from home. "No, no, stop thinking about everything, just focus on one thing!" She told herself. "I really need to go, thanks for your help." And she turned, hurrying down the road, counting the stands. An odd sensation caught her and she looked back. She was leaving a trail of onlookers behind her, all staring at her clothes. Facing forward she quickened her pace and arrived at the third booth. The man behind this booth was straightening up a display of sculptures made of wood. "Um, excuse me, are you Rando?"

The man turned around and smiled a big smile. He was young, maybe around twenty and even kind of cute. Ralley blushed a little despite her anti-male attitude. "Well yes that is me. Are you interested in a figurine? Maybe some of the silver amulets? Let me think, I might have one that would look …" He paused as his eyes examined her further, his brows rising.

Oh, good grief! She shouted in her head; the blush was now one of embarrassment. "Do you have a map?" She asked before he could comment.

"Map?" Rando spoke, sounding distant.

"Yes," Ralley said with a menacing tone, and then louder, "A map!"

"Oh!" He blinked and turned away. "R…right, a map. I think I have one right here."

Sighing with relief, she relaxed a bit. Trying not to look around her, she felt more eyes upon her. After a moment of digging through some items behind the counter, Rando held out a rolled up bit of rough paper with a crude ribbon tied around it. "This is one of my best. I can give you a good price for it."

That was a map? "Well, I don't have any money on me obviously, I just need to take a look at it and find out where I am." She reached for the parchment but Rando snatched it away.

"No money? What are you doing in the market if you have no money?"

"Look, I'm just a little lost and I need to find out where I am so I can go home!" She held her hand out to him and he peered at it with doubt.

"You are in Eagle Crest, just West of…"

"I know! I don't know where Eagle Crest *IS* though, I need to look at the map if you don't mind!"

Now the man put the map back in the pile. "Look here now, you will not fool me, be off with you, before I swat that thieving rump of yours!"

She opened her mouth, about to give him a verbal thrashing when a roar of laughter erupted from behind her. She turned to see that she had indeed drawn quite a crowd that was growing by the minute. How embarrassing! She was being laughed at by a bunch of electronically challenged country bozos! Her anger bubbled to the top and exploded from her mouth. "SHUT UP!" She shouted then glared back at Rando. "Who needs your stupid map anyway?" And with that she stomped off, nudging her way out of the crowd. What was with them? It's not her fault she was stuck here! Hugging her elephant, she ignored the tear of frustration that slid down her cheek.

Someone reached over and put a hand on her shoulder. "Ralley?"

She looked up and sucked in a breath. "Jerel!" She flung her arms around him in a tight hug, squashing her elephant between them.

"It would seem you are still down on your luck, lass." He spoke in his fatherly tone, warm and soothing, as he put his arm around her and patted her on the shoulder. "There there, why not just come in the tavern, and I shall get you something to eat." Accepting the invitation with a nod, she allowed him to lead her towards a large building where voices spoke with spontaneous peals of laughter. Somehow, it didn't make her feel any better.

-9-

LIQUENDIA OF THE TOWER

"I must be crazy." Melanie mumbled. "It's like a maze in here!" She had led the handsome blind guy through the library and down another set of stairs. Below was a hallway that cut straight through the middle; along either side were evenly spaced doors. At the end of that hall was another set of stairs, which they descended before emerging into yet another room. This one was dark and filled with what looked to be crates and bales of hay, giving it an old barn smell. There was yet another staircase only a couple feet from the one they had just stepped from. "Down? We aren't going under the lava, are we?" He gave a soundless chuckle and shook his head. "Good...that would just be too creepy." The level below was huge and, except for the thick pillars spaced throughout the circular room, it was empty but for that ever-present staircase leading downward. "Just how far are we going...er...don't answer that...Well, I guess you can't answer it but, gosh I'm sorry, I must be annoying you."

He chuckled but of course there was no sound, then he squeezed her hand. She took this to mean that he thought she was no bother at all. How sweet of him! They continued through two more empty rooms. It occurred to her that they had not run into anyone else in this massive tower. "Where is everyone? Are they the only ones who live here?"

The blind mute shook his head and pointed to himself. "Well, I mean besides us..." He shook his head again and pointed to himself. "Wait, do you mean that only you live here?" He nodded. "That means they're trespassing, but, it also means you're all alone here." Again he nodded. "But...it would be so lonely!" And for a third time his bobbing head confirmed this. Melanie frowned, not sure what to make of that. How could someone live alone in such a huge place? She helped him down yet another staircase, becoming nervous about just how far they would go. At first it appeared to be as empty as the others, but she noticed as they walked into it that there was a large statue of a gargoyle, crouched on all fours, its thick neck supporting a pointed head with two horns cresting it. Wings decorated its back along with a ridge of spikes that went from neck to tail. It reminded her of something, but what? "Oh!" She exclaimed, remembering. "There's a statue here that looks just like the candle holder in that bedroom upstairs! But this one is really huge!"

The man nodded, a smile on his face. Was this what he brought her down here for? To see a statue? He ventured forward, his hands in front of him. She moved with him and guided him to the statue. He placed his hands on the head and felt along it until he came to the left horn and pulled it down and then back. For a moment she thought he had broken it, but it began to move, not just shake, or slide...but move! It lifted its head with a loud scraping noise, and then rose to more of a standing position, and she could have sworn the eyes blinked as well. It stepped back, revealing a trap door with a brass handle that it had been sitting on. It resumed its crouching position and became still. "Oh my gosh! It...it moved!" She stood frozen; her legs just didn't want to work. Had she just seen that stone creature come to life?

The mute bent down and ran his hands along the edge of the trap door before finding the ring, he then grunted, trying to pull it open. "Don't! That thing might hurt you or something!" But he did not listen. The trap door began to open an inch or so, but it dropped back into place as he let go, clutching his chest, his face contorted in pain. Concerned for him, she forgot about the now quiescent statue and went to his side, guiding him away from the door. "You're hurting yourself, you should sit." He shook his head and reached out as if trying to find the door again. "Look, promise me that statue won't jump up and eat me, and I'll open the door myself." He nodded, patting her on the shoulder, breathing heavy.

She hoped that was a promise as she turned and approached the trap door. She watched the statue a moment and then, satisfied; she grabbed hold of the brass ring and pulled as hard as she could. The door was not as heavy as she had feared, and she was able to haul it wide open with a heavy groan. As if opening the door to a boiler room, she felt heat pouring out from below. "Oh no! We *are* going too far, I knew it!"

Lurching to his feet, the blind mute shook his head and smiled, reaching out towards her. She left the trap door open and rushed over to take his hand so that he would not fall in the hole. He tugged on her and she realized he wanted her to continue. She looked to the trap door, feeling apprehensive, but there was a stairway leading ever downward, much to her dismay. With a nervous swallow, she led him down the stairwell. This one was different from the others, as it did not lead to another room, and the walls were rough as if it had been dug out to make room for the stairs. At the bottom was another trap door, a twin of the one above. "Another door…. should I, open this one too?" Oh, please say no, she thought. The image of hot molten lava spilling up out of the opened door filled her with dread. She batted his hand away in the next instant as he tried to reach out to find the ring in the door once again. "No, no, no, let me do it. Heaven's sake, I hope you know where we're going." She was beginning to doubt this man's sanity.

This door opened with ease, a red glow from below illuminating the room, and a blast of air, much hotter than the first, ruffled her dress. She latched onto him, expecting lava to bubble up out of the door any moment. She peeked into the open space, seeing a carved spiral staircase. "I don't think I can do this." He patted her arm and set it at her side smiling. He then got down and felt his way to the edge of the trap door, sliding his feet to the stairwell. "Wait! Don't you feel that heat? You're going to fry down there!" He continued to descend the steps backwards so he could keep his hands on the stairs as well. She got down on her knees and looked over the edge. The bottom step was not far, and it looked as though there was a small landing below. "Just so you know, this is against my better judgment." She wasn't sure he was listening to her, but she climbed down after him anyway in the same manner.

When she reached the bottom the mute found her hand once again. The heat was overwhelming and she turned to look at the small landing they stood on. It was only large enough for about four or five people, and a banister lined the opposite side. The rest of the room dropped away into a massive chamber, red light glowing from below. As he pulled her forward, his hand questing towards the banister, she gave a small whimper and tried to hold him back. "You might fall! There's lava down there. I don't see any way out at all!" She felt herself start to panic. Where now? There was no way out of the tower this way, and she did not recall seeing an exit in the other rooms, either. How could that be? How did people get out of the tower? "We're trapped," she whined.

He continued to tug her to the banister, his hand having located it. She whimpered again; the thought of falling into the lava below was just too much. The heat in the room was overwhelming, like the middle of a hot summer day. She inched to the edge and clamped her hands around the carved rail. She peeked over the edge, and gasped, her eyes felt as though they would pop from her head. Below her was not lava, but a massive creature; its skin was a patchy mixture of yellow, orange and red. Its entire body filled the bottom of the chamber; its incredibly long tail curled around it one way and its long neck the other. It reminded her of a Loch Ness monster or a type of plesiosaurus. "You have a...dinosaur? How is that possible?" The creature below stirred, its head lilting to the side and the tail loosening from around its body. "It's alive! It's moving!"

The mute smiled, and she decided he was definitely crazy, or maybe she was still drugged. "Oh, please, let it be the drugs." The heat began to make her sweat under her prom dress and she shifted, feeling uncomfortable. Below, the strange creature lifted its long head, its eyes opening and it tilted to gaze up at them. Its eyes were solid red with a twinkling fire inside them that made her cold despite the heat. "It's looking right at me!" She backed away from the banister but even as she did the creature below shifted and its head rose up from below; a frill rising along its neck and head gave the creature a frightening but beautiful sea serpent-like look. Fear gripping her, she reached over and grabbed hold of the blind man's robes to pull him away from the edge.

"Estat? What brings you down here?" The eloquent voice echoed in this room, but from where Melanie had no idea. The creature's large head eased towards the small landing.

She looked back at the stairwell but no one was there. "Who is that? Can you help us?" She tugged at his robes again, harder this time, but he held fast to the balcony. Was that a smile on his face?

The sparkling orbs of the creature focused on her now. "Who is your friend? It looks as though she will faint." The voice sounded female, but it was so elegant, beautiful and loud.

It couldn't be coming from the creature could it? It didn't even appear to have a mouth, or if it did, it was quite small and at the tip of its long but elegant head. "Who are you? What are you?" Melanie faced the creature, directing her questions towards it though it felt a little crazy, as everything had lately.

"I am Liquendia, an amarill. Might I have the pleasure of your name? It would seem Estat has forgotten his manners."

"Oh my gosh, you really are talking to me…" She stopped tugging on, "Estat? Is that his name?" She looked to him as he began to nod. "Wow…that's really exotic!" forgetting herself for the moment. She returned her attention to the creature.

"But he's mute, of course he can't tell you who I am. He's blind as well and wounded, please don't eat us!"

The creature's eyes closed and its head arched back. It made a rather strange gurgling noise. She had the feeling it was laughing at her. After a moment the amarill slid its head back down to the balcony its ruby eyes glittering. "I would not eat you. You are not hot enough, and I could never get you through my tiny mouth."

Sure enough, Melanie was able to note that at the tip of her quite elongated nose was a very tiny mouth opening. "W…well that's a relief!"

"But Estat!" Liquendia exclaimed turning her dazzling eyes to him. "I have many questions, perhaps…" The creature returned its attention back to Melanie. "You must explain what has happened."

"I can't even be sure myself! I was kidnapped by some green haired guy and his lackey, I think he's the one who did this to Estat." She couldn't believe she was talking to the creature, but it felt…natural.

"Intruders in the tower?" Liquendia asked, looking this time to Estat. As he nodded his head the creature gave a low rumbling growl. "Do not worry Estat, I promised you my services and you shall receive them! I will not allow the intruders to dwell here any longer."

Estat gave her a most graceful bow. He's so elegant and polite, Melanie thought. The chamber shuttered and another wave of heat swirled around the room. "What's happening? What are you going to do?" Liquendia was angry now and Melanie hoped that her movements didn't crack a hole in the very wall.

Once again her thoughts filled with images of lava pouring into the chamber.

"Stay here with Estat until I return; you should be safe." Liquendia dove down as if into a swimming pool. Melanie moved back to the ledge and looked over. Below, at the bottom of the chamber, the rock had turned to molten lava and the creature Liquendia had disappeared into it.

-10-

A New Ruler

Talon and Regence had wrapped their cloaks about them and hidden their royal emblems moments before entering Eagle Crest Village and now sat in a corner of the tavern enjoying their meals. Talon had decided it was best not to draw a crowd and alert the town to their presence. Regence had played along, and he appeared to be enjoying himself.

Talon thought the tavern a good place to distract himself, and he was not disappointed, for entering into the tavern was a strange looking young girl wearing the oddest clothing he had ever seen! The man leading her in was comforting her with soft words and a pat on the shoulder, and when Talon took a closer look, he noticed tears running down her cheeks. "Strange," he mumbled to Regence, "I have never seen that kind of clothing, and let me tell you, I have seen a lot of exotic clothing."

"As have I," Regence replied, before returning to his meal.

Talon continued to watch her, wondering at her plight. The man with her did not appear out of the ordinary as he ordered food from the serving wench then returned to the strange girl and sat at the table with her. For a time he could not tear his gaze away from them. He wondered from what kingdom she had come, or perhaps she was from Zeferia, a great continent across the sea to the southeast. But yet another distraction in the tavern made him jerk his eyes away. Several people near the entrance were shouting, women screaming and scrambling into the tavern. Talon and Regence stood as one, each with a hand to the hilts of their swords.

"Is that the Blade Beast?" Someone by a window shouted.

"Should it not be with the Emperor?" Shouted another.

"Is the Emperor dead? Has it come to find a new Emperor?"

The shouting grew along with the crowd. Some held their breath while others pushed and shoved to get to the windows for a glimpse of what was taking place just outside the doors. Talon stood frozen. Did he dare hope? Did the Creature come for him at last? "He's coming this way!" A boy hollered from somewhere near the doorway. All fell quiet as if they were candles and a great wind had blown them out all at once. The huddled bodies in the doorway drifted apart and formed a line through the middle of the room. Sliding his hand away from the hilt of his sword and leaning forward on his toes, Talon strained to see the entrance over the heads of the hushed villagers.

Gliding up the final step into the tavern like a nobleman was the creature, its elongated head tipping to the side, allowing a shining emerald eye to observe the crowd. A neat row of sharp teeth was visible as it parted its mouth long enough to let out a soft rumble like the purr of a cat. Two spiraled horns swept outward from either side of its head just above small feather tufts that were its ears. A magnificent feathered frill began at the top of its head and followed its long neck to its shoulders. Its body was covered with crimson scales, each one in the shape of a diamond. It moved much like a wild cat as it prowled forward, its tail swished about, the feathery tuft at its tip like strands of silk. Talon had never seen it in this form, though he knew it from his father's description. Its head swung to the right and Talon's heart skipped a beat as the creature's intense stare focused on him. This was it! Any moment he would feel the Creature open its mind to him. Any moment it would take its place at his side… any moment. Its head swung away from him and it moved in the opposite direction, its gaze intent upon someone else. His heart and hopes sank as the creature moved away, growling at the villagers, who shuffled aside.

Stricken and unable to speak, he only watched as the creature stopped before the table occupied by the oddly dressed young girl and the surprised farmer. He was ever the more stunned when it bowed low to her, the same young girl that had entered only a short time ago, wearing strange clothing and carrying an odd purple toy, a foreigner. A moment later the crowd began to sink to their knees in a bow honoring the new Empress. Talon hesitated a moment before feeling Regence's hand on his shoulder, then they too bowed before the foreigner. As he fought back the feelings of frustration and sorrow, he lifted his head enough to watch as the strange girl stared wide-eyed at the creature, frightened of it.

"What? You…you talk? What do you want? Empress? I… don't understand any of this! It's gotta be some dream!" The girl buried her face in her arms. The farmer reached out to pat her on the shoulder, trying to soothe her.

"My lord…." Regence prodded.

Taking a deep breath, Talon rose to his feet and slid the hood from his head. He then forced the emotions from his voice as he spoke in his commanding tone. "All hail the new Empress!" Talon's words echoed in the silent room.

Heads bobbed up long enough to see who spoke, and with their recognition of who he was, they bowed again and recited. "Hail the new Empress."

The girl lifted her head from her arms; tears were streaming down her cheeks, and she fought to wipe them away as she glanced around, bemused. Talon continued, "As the son of the former Emperor, I shall escort her majesty to the palace. Make way for the Empress!" He strode forward to stand before the foreigner and the creature; Regence joined him, standing at his right hand.

The girl rose from her seat, looking from Talon to Regence. She turned to the farmer and handed him the odd purple toy. "I .... would like you to give this to Shani ... I don't think I'll need it anymore."

The farmer, still on his knees, lifted his eyes to hers, and accepted the gift. "Thank you, your Majesty."

She shuddered at his words, then knelt down and hugged him. "No, thank you, for everything!"

The girl looked dazed, hypnotized. She acted as if she were a mechanical contraption as she turned away from the farmer to face her escort. Talon guessed she was in shock. Regence bowed low to the foreign girl. "Majesty, I am Sword master Regence De'Galen, and this is Prince Talon Endrayen of Degrail."

Talon bowed his head to her without a word, turned toward the tavern door and strode away. He did not look to see if she followed, but the creature slipped past him and bounded out the door. It paused, glancing back at him, then continued out.

It appeared to be very happy; it was as if the creature was laughing at him. As if all the gods were laughing at him.

Ralley had decided that this was no dream, nor was it an Amish village in the middle of the country. She also doubted it was a sort of theme park. What theme park could make large talking lizards? Had she imagined the lizard talking to her? She stood on the top stairs in the doorway of the tavern and watched as the one called Regence untied two horses from a hitching post just outside and led them to the young man named Talon. She pushed aside everything that had just happened as she stared at them. Sure, she had seen horses on T.V. and read about them in books, but living in the city, she never got to see one. Jerel's horse was kind of scraggly compared to these two beauties, and she was now eager to get close to them and touch their sleek coats.

She was once again aware of the crowd as she reached the bottom of the stairs. It was much bigger than the earlier crowd that was gathered to make fun of her, but this time there was no laughter, only low murmurs as they watched her with curious expressions. She tried to ignore them and strode up to the white mare next to Regence. "She's …. so beautiful, what's her name? May I pet her?"

Regence gave her a pleased smile. "Her name is Crest, and yes, of course you may."

Ralley placed her hand on Crest's shoulder and slid it along her side. She then smiled and turned to the chestnut near Talon. "And this one?"

Talon frowned. "His name is Phoenix, but I am afraid he does not like to be touched by strangers."

Ralley reached out to Phoenix and the stallion stretched its nose out to sniff her hand. She leaned forward to touch him, but Phoenix snorted at her, and turned away. "Ew! Horse snot!" She exclaimed and rubbed her hand on her flannel pants. Talon gave her an "I told you so" look that made her want to kick him in the shin. "So, uh…where are we going?"

"To the Palace… your Majesty." Talon spoke as if he was annoyed, which irritated her. Was she some sort of burden to him?

"Palace? And stop calling me 'Majesty'. My name is Ralley." She said with a slight glare. Was he making fun of her?

"As you please, Empress Ralley." He said with a nod of his head. Then he leapt onto the back of his horse, Regence doing the same. Talon reached a hand down to her.

"You…want me to ride him? But I've never ridden a horse in my life!" She exclaimed.

They appeared a bit surprised to hear this, but of course they owned these horses. Talon eyed her. "Well, yes, Empress Ralley, we would not make good time walking."

Ralley could have sworn he sounded sarcastic, but she ignored it. "Yeah okay, but stop calling me Empress, it's just Ralley." She took Talon's offered hand, and he pulled her up onto Phoenix's back to sit in front of him. As he put his arms around her to grab the reins she felt a warm and protective calm wash over her. This was all happening too fast; she felt she had no time to think about what she should be doing. But in that instant she felt security, the first real secure feeling since she had arrived here. She lifted her head to see the crowd of people, and recognized Rando, the one who embarrassed her. He looked at her with awe and she looked back at him with a smirk and made a slashing motion across her neck. His eyes went wide and he disappeared in the sea of faces. Ralley giggled to herself. Maybe this Empress stuff wasn't so bad after all, then again, the destination made her wonder. Her eyes caught sight of the strange dragon thing as it took the lead and she felt herself shudder but she refused to cry about her situation, besides…maybe these people could tell her where her sister was.

-11-

SCHEMING SETBACK

Xenopus smirked as he watched Brek scrambling to do his bidding. The insignificant speck of a human was so afraid of him; he had spilled the oil for the braziers several times as he filled them. He allowed this annoyance to continue out of the sheer elation he got from Brek quavering with fear, which gave him strength. Ecnair fluttered next to him, his grin telling him that the imp enjoyed this as much as he. Perhaps the greedy little bug would prove useful to him as well. Brek went through the motions of re-creating the previous portal, and it was close to completion. This time, though, Xenopus would control the destination of the portal. This would have been difficult had it not been for the excellent conditions that had been provided for him in this summoning hall. It would be most beneficial to make this place his own. He would have to finish exploring it as there was sure to be more secrets to it than he had thought.

Ecnair snickered as Brek fumbled with the chalk. Xenopus turned his attention to the creature. "Quite a fool, is he not? What do you intend to do with him?" He had decided to keep his pretend obedience to Brek even though he had been released into the world the moment Brek removed the symbols of his summoning to make way for the new ones.

"Whatever I please," The imp sneered. "I will use him, along with you, to do the bidding of the sorcerer, who will in turn reward me with riches."

What a cheeky little upstart, but his intentions were admirable. "I see, a sorcerer. I must meet this one sometime and thank him for sending you. What riches would one such as you desire?"

Ecnair wrung his tiny hands in thought. "He has promised me more treasure than a man can carry. Perhaps I shall even take this tower for myself or…"

Xenopus laughed, cutting him off. Brek, startled, dropped his chalk. When his amusement had subsided he eyed the man, who hastened back to work. "You are thinking too small, but I could still use you."

Ecnair glared at him. "Use me? It looks to me like you are the one who will do my bidding once I tell the human it is in his best interest to…."

With the snap of his fingers he caused the very air around him to swallow the sound around himself and the imp and with speed far beyond what the imp could ever hope to achieve, Xenopus plucked him from the air in a choking grip. "Dearest Ecnair," He began in a dangerous tone of which Brek was now oblivious. "I do not believe you understand the situation as well as you should. No one stands over me as master. You are either my slave or a nuisance, and if you are the latter, then you must be removed from my sight, permanently. The way I see things, you can be a useful tool, more useful than the human. Do not allow me to lower my opinion of you." He released his grip on the imp, and it fluttered awkwardly back from him; the fear in its eyes told Xenopus that it now knew its place.

It sputtered and gasped. "Y...yes my lord!"

Grinning, he decided to seal Ecnair's unwavering service with a most generous offer. "I have no need of riches or wealth, but if that is what you wish to have, I will give you all the riches of the kings of this land, once I have crushed them like the pests they are. Their screams of agony will please me far more than gold and jewels."

The imp's fear lessened and its greedy grin returned. "If that so pleases my master, then I will accept your generous offer!" As he had known, Ecnair's greedy nature had placed him in his lap.

"I...I am finished!" Brek exclaimed.

Xenopus grinned, and with a simple wave of his hand, the barrier ceased to be. "Excellent..." He moved closer to examine the symbols. However, Breks drawings were as clumsy, if not more so, than before. "Your work is ridiculous...perhaps I should not have been so quick to dispatch your previous master."

"Previous master?" He frowned and Xenopus could feel anger rising within him. "I am your master and I...I think its time you do what I summoned you for!"

Xenopus laughed, the sound echoing off the walls. Brek cowered back a step. "My, my you are getting bold are you not? I retrieved an exotic princess and this is the gratitude I receive?" He clicked his tongue.

"But...you are supposed to be my slave! Th...the symbols!"

Xenopus took a step towards him, Brek looking up to him, as all humanoids should. "You should have learned a bit more before summoning anything…perhaps you could have been more useful to me…" He grasped him by the shoulder, digging his nails into his flesh and forcing him to face the summoning circle. "Finish the spell."

Any protest Brek might have made came out in a cry of pain, much to Xenopus' glee. He released his grip to allow him to regain himself and read the incantation. Brek fumbled with the page and began to speak the words. Everything was going according to plan, and at any moment he would have new playthings to serve him. All would be destroyed in short order. A moment later, the room shuddered. Brek paused in his chanting, but Xenopus smacked the back of his head. "Continue!"

Ecnair landed on Xenopus' shoulder. "Master…is it the summoning?"

He did not answer; he felt another presence lurking behind the walls of this room. It was much too powerful to be the Grand Summoner, and he was certain there was no way for the man to use his summoning ever again, yet something was here. Perhaps he could use it as another of his tools. The circle began to glow, and in the next moment the far wall of the summoning hall melted like butter, and heat poured into the room as what remained of the wall spread across the floor, hot and red like the lava far below the tower. Brek yelled out in surprise and stumbled backwards. Incantations ruined, the growing brilliance of the red light of the star began to fade out. "FINISH!" Xenopus' voice boomed as he shoved Brek forward, sprawling him face first on the floor in front of the star.

He watched the intruder enter, large and serpentine; the tall frill cresting its head almost touched the ceiling. It crawled across the floor with its four large spiked fins. "I must say I do enjoy your entry, but you are disturbing my plans," Xenopus sneered.

"That is the point, Demon. I am no friend of yours, remove yourself immediately!" The elegant head breathed on a column and it began to melt to the floor, adding to the encroaching lava.

Did Brek's previous master summon this creature? That was impossible! If this creature destroyed this room, it would be much harder for him to open a portal for his minions. He stepped across the room to face the creature; he could feel Ecnair cowering down on his shoulder. "Who are you, and who brought you here?" Xenopus demanded. Brek had scrambled back to his feet and skittered back toward the summoning hall doors.

"I am Liquendia of the Tower of the Grand Summoner who brought me to this place that I may be comfortable within the volcano; in exchange I created this tower for him in its crater so he may practice his work in peace. You are disturbing that peace, and I hold it as my duty to cleanse the tower of you. Now, be off!" The molten rock spread farther, almost touching his feet. He was forced to step back.

In an instant he had become his terrible amphibian self, the tentacles on his back rising to touch the ceiling. Ecnair gave a startled noise and flew off to hide behind one of the pillars. She must be amarill, from one of the planes of power, but no matter; though this lava creature's size was much more intimidating, he would cut her down with his poisoned breath. Had she been more agreeable she could have been a wondrous tool. "It is a shame but I shall have to destroy you." The destruction and heat in the room was intoxicating. Yes, a shame. He opened his huge mouth and breathed out a cloud of greenish gasses.

Liquendia pulled back. "Poisons? You think that will stop me?" She sent a heat wave through the room that burned off the poisons as they drifted toward her. Xenopus stepped back farther as the liquid rock continued to spread. He flung his tentacles out at her head. To his interest, she did not flinch away but allowed them to hit her. A burning sensation gripped his feelers, and he snapped them back. She was almost as hot as hell itself; this would not be a pleasant battle.

Xenopus let out a great roar, backing up to the pillars. He let loose a stream of acids from the glands in his mouth that splattered across the creature's smooth neck. This too was ineffective as the acid boiled away. The molten rock began to disperse across one of the stars points, extinguishing the red flames and overturning the metal brazier, which began to melt into the lava. Xenopus roared in frustration. "You wretch! Look what you have done!"

"We are doomed!" cried Brek. "There is no bridge from the tower except the one that Estat summons!"

"Too bad for you, then." Xenopus croaked, but he would not allow this pathetic human to die yet, not while he was still useful. He did still clutch the page of summoning symbols and incantations in his hand, and that could still be needed. He backed farther away to the doors of the hall and swept Brek up with one of his tentacles, making him cry out. Ecnair fluttered toward the doors as well; Xenopus could feel the fear from both the imp and the human, and he fed from it. The lava now covered the entire floor, destroying the star and its symbols. "You win, for now…." He opened his wide mouth and gathered within it a great surge of crystalic power, energy used by many creatures from the planes of darkness. It shot from his mouth with greater force than when he had used it against the simple human summoner. It forced Liquendia back through the opening from where she had entered. Her angry howl told him she would not be held back for long.

Xenopus seized the human Brek and turned, exiting the room and forcing the two large doors aside with his bulk, the imp fluttering after them. He spotted a ledge to his left that was too high for a puny human to climb onto, much less see. He climbed up, his great bulk almost too much for it, but it was as if it was built for larger creatures and, he realized, it was a massive stairway that led to the upper level of the tower. It looked to be a wide hallway with large doors spaced evenly down the hall. He had no time for mazes; he hated them. The tower shook, and he could hear a long, high-pitched howl of anger followed by a wave of tremendous heat rising from the oversized stairway. Liquendia was pursuing him, and he had little doubt that she could melt this entire tower if she chose to; the very floor beneath him scorching his feet as if to validate this thought.

Once again, though it drained him to do so, he gathered together another crystalic beam that blasted through the wall of the tower. He escaped through this new exit and felt a searing heat as he did so. Only a few levels below them was a great pool of molten lava. No doubt Liquendia had caused it to rise up and it appeared as if it were swallowing the tower. Brek gave a wonderful, agonizing cry before passing out. Behind him, Xenopus could hear Liquendia crest the stairwell, and he looked out, spotting the lip of the volcanic crater. With a great leap from his powerful back legs, he escaped to the outer cone, Ecnair flapping after them.

Liquendia's head snaked out of the hole he had created. She had her victory and looked pleased with herself. The imp caught up to him and now fluttered next to his head. "What now? We had the advantage with this tower, what will we do now?"

Xenopus growled, "I assure you, it is only a minor setback."

-12-

A History

Ralley, Talon and Regence rode along the main dirt road heading out of the village. The crowd gathered along their path, watching in awe, some shouting hails to the Prince and to the new Empress. The strange lizard-like creature led the way, trotting along with its head held high. Ralley still wasn't sure what to make of it, so she tried not to think about it yet; perhaps she would work on that problem later. For now, she was actually enjoying riding Phoenix. It was nothing like riding in the bouncing cart behind Dancer. As the crowd thinned out, and the buildings ended to reveal endless grassy fields full of sunny yellow buttercups and black and brown spotted grazing cows. Talon nudged Phoenix into a gallop.

Ralley gave a surprised yelp and grabbed at fistfuls of Phoenix's flowing mane. For a time, all she could do was hold on and clench her legs tightly around the horse's sides to keep herself steady, her eyes tightly shut, hoping she wouldn't fall. She felt Talon lean forward, his head next to hers as he spoke into her ear. "You are too stiff; you will tire yourself out like that. Just loosen up and move along with Phoenix."

"No way! I'm gonna fall!"

"I have you," Talon spoke confidently and he gave her a gentle squeeze with his arms, reminding her of their protection. She slowly lifted her eyes to watch Phoenix's head bobbing in front of her. Studying the movements of the horse beneath her, she began to feel her body sliding into a comfortable rhythm, allowing her to relax her grip on Phoenix's mane. She was surprised at how easy it was to move with him; it almost felt as if he could leap into the air and fly.

After a moment, she smiled, "This is amazing!" she shouted. She stole a quick glance under Talon's left arm to see Crest pacing next to them; Regence moved so smoothly that it was almost like he was a part of his mount. He caught her stare and winked, smiling at her. Facing forward, she could see the strange lizard creature racing along like a cheetah. They continued along till the horses began to grow tired and their pace slowed. At that point, Talon pulled gently back on the reins and returned Phoenix to a walk, Regence doing the same. "That was so awesome, but now my legs feel like limp noodles, and I think my butt fell asleep." Ralley thought about stopping to rest. Her hands ached from holding on so tightly to the horse's mane.

"*Should not stop.*" said a voice in her head. It was the same voice that had spoken to her at the Tavern, the voice that came from the Creature.

"I was hoping I was imagining that," Ralley said aloud.

"Imagining what?" Talon sounded impatient and annoyed.

"That lizard. It's like it's talking to me, in my head."

"That is because it is, Empress," he replied, sounding unconcerned.

Ralley rolled her eyes and opened her mouth to give him a piece of her mind, but Regence cleared his throat. "He is a dragon and he speaks only to the Emperor, or in your case, Empress, of Asatiria."

Ralley turned her head to look at Regence. "Wait a minute! Did you say dragon?"

"That is correct Empress. He is a unique dragon. The only one of his kind, created by the seven," he replied calmly.

"The seven what? Dwarves? Thought they were miners, not biologists." Ralley giggled at her own joke, but neither Talon nor Regence appeared to get it.

Talon shook his head. "The seven Gods and Goddesses of course. Do you know nothing?"

"What is your problem?" She turned her head to see him out of the corner of her eye.

He frowned and would not look at her. "There is no problem."

Ralley turned her attention back to the dragon; it trotted along, head held high, tail swishing about. Maybe she was on a bloopers show? She sighed, realizing she was still trying to rationalize everything instead of focusing on finding her sister. It didn't matter what this place was, who these people where. What mattered now was finding out where her sister was. Going to this city of theirs was the best thing to do. There would be plenty of people there who might have some information. "So, how far is it to the city?"

"Only half a day's journey," Regence replied.

"Half a day? If you people had a car it would be so much faster, or maybe an ATV?"

Once again, they did not seem to understand. This was getting frustrating. "Okay, fine, so let me ask another question. Why do you guys believe the dragon when it says I'm the Empress? I mean, it sounds like a messed up system to me."

Regence smiled at her, answering her question. "As I said before, the dragon was created by the seven, more than a thousand years ago, to stop the war."

"What war? The Revolutionary War, or do you mean the World War? I got a D in history, so you're going to have to be more specific."

"I have not heard of that war," Regence said, watching her with a curious expression. "I speak of the war that lasted around four hundred years."

"Holey cow! Four hundred? I never heard of a war lasting that long!" Ralley wondered if she had missed that lesson in history class; she knew she played sick a few times, but there was never a pop quiz on any four hundred year war.

"It was a terribly long war," Regence continued, "The gods created the dragon and gave it to the peacemakers, who brought it to a great gathering of war leaders. They explained that it would choose the person best suited to be emperor of this land."

"And just like that, they believed them?"

"They did, since the elves and amarills could see the aura of the gods about them. But there were those who did not accept this, and to this day still do not," he said, sounding sad.

Ralley sighed. "The what and the what?"

"Elves and amarills. Do you not know of them either?" It was Talon who spoke, but this time he sounded genuinely surprised. "Not knowing any of these things can only mean you are not from Asatiria, but surely the mainland?"

"Mainland?" Was she on an island? Was this some kind of looney bin? An isolated island for crazy people? It would certainly explain a lot. Maybe she should humor them a little longer until they took her to the city center.

"The mainland is called Zefilliara. Does that sound familiar?" Regence asked.

Ralley rolled her eyes. "Not really, but your type may call it something other than what we call it."

"Then you *are* a Zefilliaran." Talon's tone had returned to 'grumpy' mode.

This gave a new twist on things, but Ralley was still at odds about the dragon. They rode on in silence. Ralley had to believe that the 'city' was really a facility. It was the only hope she had to cling to. But if that were the case, then why was she here? Was her sister here too? And who was that guy that had grabbed her? She wondered if her tactics should include finding the green haired creep who kidnapped Melanie. It would certainly be easy to point him out.

As the day wore on, the countryside became dotted with small farmhouses with fields surrounded by rickety wood fences. Cattle, sheep and horses grazed in the meadows along the roadside, occasionally lifting their heads to watch them pass. More than once Phoenix would neigh at a mare, inspiring her to nicker back.

As they crested the top of a small hill, Ralley could see many more houses below. The road split off, one fork meeting with a large stone archway set within a wall, the other continuing on and disappearing over another small hill. Far within the walls, nestled among smaller buildings that sat side by side, was a castle. Four square towers marked the corners, and one large circular one rose up out of the center, dotted with many small windows. Ralley could just make out the people, some on foot, others on horseback, those going in and several coming out, most of them following the road over the distant hill. She couldn't believe her own eyes. This was no facility for the mentally challenged! It wasn't even a prison!

"Is this it? This is the city?" Ralley stared in disbelief.

"It is, your Majesty. Is something wrong?" asked Regence.

"Yes! Everything is wrong! This is a movie set or a theme park, maybe a renaissance fair! I'm not supposed to be here! This is absolutely crazy!" Ralley stared at Regence, expecting him to laugh and say "Surprise! You're on Candid Camera!" Instead, he exchanged a glance with Talon before staring at her as if she were the crazy one. It was no use. She could not explain it, and she wasn't sure she wanted to try anymore. Her eyes began to water, and she bowed her head to hide it from them.

"Your Majes… Ralley, are you alright?" Talon's sympathetic voice surprised her.

She sniffed and rubbed her eyes with her sleeve, clearing her throat. "Yeah, sure… I'm fine. I'd be better if you told me this was Scotland…" she said, trying not to let her voice crack.

No one spoke for a time, and then Regence cleared his throat. "I am sure Talon's father will explain everything to you, and I am more than happy to answer your questions to the best of my ability."

Ralley nodded. "Thanks," was all she could manage to say.

They rode past two men standing like sentinels on either side of the open arch. They wore light armor that sounded like the banging of pots and pans when they moved to salute the royal party. Wooden buildings at either side of the main road sat so close together that there was only enough room for one person to squeeze through. The smell of food and flowers came to her, and she spotted many booths on either side of the road with bread, apples and other fruits she could not name. She even spotted the display where the flower smell had come from. It was beautifully arranged with flowers she had never seen before in an array of red, blue, white, purple and orange. The crowd parted as they spotted the dragon marching along, gasping and pointing. The multitude of people along the main road created a clear path to the open gates of the castle, where two more armored men stood holding long spears with double bladed ends. They too saluted them as they passed.

None of the people passed beyond these gates, but they crowded around just outside of them, the guards ceremoniously blocking the entrance with their crossed spears. Within these walls was a small courtyard, the path splitting to skirt around a water fountain with a stone dragon rising out of the middle of it, spouting water from its mouth. To either side were smaller buildings; women were busying themselves lifting bundles from a wagon and taking them inside. From the other emerged two young boys, laughing to one another as they raced towards them. Their light brown hair and clothes were covered in dirt as if the two had been rolling about on the ground. They stumbled to a halt when they saw the dragon as it paused to peer into the water of the fountain.

Regence dismounted. "Well, what are you two boys gaping

at? Get these horses to the stables and make sure they are cared for, and snap to it!"

Not taking their eyes from the dragon, one of the boys took hold of Crest's rein and began to inch his way back to the stables. The other boy stood, glancing quickly from Phoenix and back, waiting for them to dismount. Talon looped his arm around Ralley's and swung her to the ground. Her legs collapsed under her without warning, and Regence came to her aid, helping her back up with her unsteady and tired legs.

"You did that on purpose!" Ralley seethed, glaring at Talon.

"My apologies Empress, it must have slipped my mind that you are unaccustomed to riding." Ralley could have sworn she saw a pleased smirk on his face before he leapt off his horse. He patted Phoenix on the neck and handed the reins to the remaining stable boy who began to trek back to the stables.

"My butt is so sore I won't be able to sit for a week," Ralley grumbled, rubbing her backside. As the three of them headed to the huge doors, the guards there opening them with one hand while saluting with the other, Ralley couldn't help feeling like she was walking into a cage: a big, decorative, stone cage.

-13-

A LONG JOURNEY

The two of them sat waiting on the ledge in Liquendia's chamber. Estat could feel the heat all around him, but he ignored it to the extent that he could. He felt the great tower quake every now and then, and Melanie, clinging to his arm, gave a start each time. "Is she going to be alright?" she asked, her voice shaking. Estat nodded. Liquendia was strong, and in her element she was strongest. She had crafted the entire tower, and he had no doubts about her loyalty to him. Moments after another quake, Melanie shouted out. "She's back!" and she let go of his arm. Now he heard the movement of Liquendia in the room and felt her power radiating around them.

"The Demon has fled and I have repaired the damage done to the tower. He can no longer enter this place," she said with finality.

That was a great relief, and Estat offered her a smile and a polite nod of his head.

"So, what do we do now?" Melanie asked. "I should go find my sister…I saw her in the crystal ball thing upstairs, but I have no idea where she was."

Estat frowned. Her sister sounded as if she were in no

great danger, as she had found her way to civilization. But they themselves were far from the nearest village, and it would take them days to get there. And even if they did go, he would not be welcome there. They had other problems now. Even though Xenopus was no longer able to use the tower, it would not stop him from summoning others to him and wreaking havoc on the world. They had to concentrate on stopping him now before he did more. Without being able to summon, what could he possibly do to stop the demon? Estat realized he would have to travel to the home of Malstraun, an amarill able to summon great magical portals to other dimensions and worlds.

He placed his hands on his aching chest and then made a sign of going away. To his relief, Liquendia understood. "You wish to leave the tower. Very well, I will extend the bridge and return it again when you are gone. I shall protect the tower in your absence, but please be careful, small human," she said with genuine concern. Estat bowed low to her as the room rumbled, and he felt Liquendia sink back down to lay at the base of the tower. He took Melanie's hand and nodded to her.

"Great! So we're leaving, then?" Melanie asked eagerly as she led him back to the stairwell. "We should at least bandage you up before we go anywhere."

Estat slowly nodded. But there were things he wished to take with him. He counted the floors as they ascended, and when they came to the library floor he began coaxing her not to go up, but to go to the middle of the room, back into his study. Once there, he bungled about the room until he located three fair sized sacks. He held two of them out to Melanie, and she slowly took them. "What's this for?" she queried, but of course, he could not answer her. He turned and found his way to the crystal balls and took the middle one, placing it carefully at the bottom, then wrapping the sack around it to protect it. He then had Melanie hold open a second sack, and he placed the protected orb in the bottom of another. This should keep it safe; it would simply not do to have it break during travel. He then retrieved chalk, torches, two water skins, and two books, of which he showed the covers to Melanie that she might confirm what was on them. He then stuffed them into the sack and worked the crystal ball back to the top to keep it from being crushed. After all this, he sat for a time, his wounds still smarting. He would have to take care of this before he left, or he would never make it to the cave.

Leaving the study, Estat then allowed her to guide him up the flight of stairs to the doors of the summoning hall. But he passed these and took her to what would have been to her eyes a blank wall with a ledge high above their heads. He tapped three times on the wall, and it glided aside with little sound to reveal a hallway that led to a long stairway to the floor above.

Melanie gasped as they reached the next floor. "It's a hallway with huge doors! Like the one below the library, except this one looks like it's for giants!" Estat could only nod as they continued down the hallway to its end where they ascended another flight of stairs. This one, too, was long, and they were both out of breath when they reached the top.

"Why so many stairs in this place?" Melanie asked as soon as she caught her breath. Estat coaxed her on through this room, which was simply a very large kitchen along with crates of wheat, sacks of sugar and flour, pots of honey along with other simple provisions. "It hardly looks as if this kitchen has been used." Estat sighed heavily and nodded a bit. Only he had used it on occasion since Brek had little to no experience in baking. They came to the other end of the room, and he led her on through a hall barren of anything except the torches that lit as they passed. Melanie clutched him tighter. "I still can't believe this is all happening!" Estat led her to the hall's end where more stairs led upward to a circular storage room where many water barrels were stored. There was a rattle among a pile of boxes, and Melanie screamed and clung to him.

He patted her hand reassuringly. He could not explain to her about the black-skinned creature that lived within this room, that it would never harm them and most likely had now rushed to a dark corner to hide, being a very shy one. "There's something in here!" Melanie whispered harshly. Estat smiled at her and nodded, still patting her hand. "Hey! I'm serious! There is something in here!" Estat shrugged and felt around for the ladder. Ah, there it was! He began to climb. "Wait for me!" she pleaded as she scrambled after him.

Estat reached the trap door at the top of the ladder and pushed on it. It came open with a soft creak, and he climbed out, feeling the soft bed of grass on his hands. As Melanie climbed out behind him, she gasped. "A garden?" Estat came here often; it was a wonderful place to sit and think or read beneath the open sky. It was the top of a small tower that stuck out from the side of the main building, open to the sky and sun. A great apple tree rose from the middle of it, surrounded by lush green grass, red rose bushes, different flowers bursting with color, vines creeping along the circular wall, a small vegetable and herb garden off to one side, and a small vine covered fountain. Estat could see none of it, but the smells of the flowers, herbs and tomato plants were a familiar comfort to him. A few birds chirped and sang somewhere in the branches of the tree and he could hear Melanie walking all around the garden. "This is so beautiful! My gosh…those apples look so good!" This brought Estat back to his reasons for coming here. He opened the second sack and pointed in the general direction of the tree.

"Oh! You want to take some along? Great idea! There are probably no restaurants around here…." she said with nervous laughter, though he did not quite understand what she meant. He held the bag open as she began to fill it with apples. Then he led her over to the garden and began to feel for the correct healing herbs that grew there. There were not many of them, and he found it difficult to tell them apart from their mere feel and smell. Despite this he was finally able to choose the ones he needed. These he placed in his robe pocket. After filling the water skins at the fountain, they reluctantly left the garden. Estat led her back through the mysterious stairs and hallways, returning to his own room where Melanie told him she had first awakened and found herself. Estat rummaged through the desk drawers until he found a roll of bandaging and a very small mortar and pestle. He then removed the herbs from his robe. "Ah! Like healing herbs right?" she asked. He nodded quickly. "Excellent! Then we can get you fixed up! I'm so glad!" And to his surprise, she quickly took off his robe and got to work, grinding the herbs to a paste and applying them to his wounds; then, she wrapped his chest with the bandages as if she had done it all her life.

"Well, how does it feel now?" she asked when she was done.

Estat put a hand to the bandaging, giving her a satisfied smile and bowing his head to her. It felt as if a master healer had done it. Who was this girl? Was she truly a princess from another world? Or perhaps Xenopus had made a mistake and brought Brek a healer? "I've wanted to be a nurse ever since I was really little," she said as if she had heard his thoughts. "I don't know, it's like I just know what to do with injuries, and it makes me happy." Whatever it was, Estat knew she had a power, as he had felt it when she first arrived. However, thus far she had not performed anything more than what she had just done. He mentally cursed his inability to speak with her, there were so many things he wanted to know about her now. All this time he had been alone, he had never been able to speak with anyone but Brek, and even to him he spoke little, and now there was a wonderful woman whom he wanted to speak to now more than anything, and he could not.

"Are you sure it's okay?" Melanie put a hand on his. Estat realized he was frowning, and he recovered his smile and nodded. He then packed more of the bandaging and other healing supplies into the sack, using them as a cushion for the crystal ball. As he was doing this, he could hear Melanie fidgeting. "Um... Estat, this is kind of embarrassing but, I really have to use the bathroom..." He wrinkled his brow at her, not sure what she meant. She wished to take a bath? "You know... I really have to go!" Then he chuckled, realizing what she meant. He led her back downstairs into the side door in the lower hall. There was a small pantry here and on the other side another little door. He tapped the door and moved away to let her through. Estat was rather confused at her displeasure as she returned, but she washed her hands at a small water basin that was placed outside the door and began to help him fill the food sack with dried berries, raisins, nuts and seeds from the pantry.

He left her to do this while he took care of business himself, which was no easy task when blind. "Now what do we do?" Melanie asked after he made clear that he wished her to securely tie both sacks closed with a length of cord. Estat hefted the heavier sack over his shoulder, and before he could take the second, Melanie had snatched it away. "I should carry one, you're hurt. Now, where to?"

Estat smiled to her in thanks, and the two of them returned to the summoning hall, this time entering it. Melanie jumped a little in surprise. "The whole wall is gone on the back side of the room! It looks as if it's melted away, and there's a bridge leading outside!" Nodding to her, he nudged her to continue. "I can feel the heat of the volcano coming in . . . is it safe?" He could feel her nervously squeezing his arm, but together they moved forward and stepped onto the bridge that Liquendia had crafted for them. "I suppose it's plenty wide enough, and it will be a relief to be out of the volcano."

But Estat was not so relieved. They would be venturing northeast into the treacherous crags and mountains that surrounded the volcano. He remembered those mornings, when he would simply sit to watch drakes and other flying creatures play about the skies. Beyond that, they would travel through the northern forest where bears, mountain cats, and even monsters would be lurking among the thick growth of trees. As Melanie relaxed her grip, more at ease the further along the bridge they went, Estat became tenser. He felt so unprotected outside of the home he had known for so long, and to travel though the wilds of the north helpless and blind with only a princess who knew nothing of this world to guide him gave him pause.

-14-

CASTLE DEGRAIL

Upon entering the castle, Ralley was greeted by the smell of roses. The roof was twice as tall as the doors she had just entered through, supported by a row of pillars on either side of the room. Huge basins rested in the spaces between the pillars holding the red rose bushes, the roses in full bloom. As the small group trooped into the immense lobby, a tall, skinny man, wearing formal clothes, hurried up to them. He spotted the dragon as it prowled about and paused, his eyes wide. The man shook himself, blinked, turned his attention away and bowed before Talon.

"Inform my father that the Empress has arrived," Talon glanced back at her, eyeing her up and down. "And send hand-maids to attend to her." The man bowed again then scurried off the way he had come.

Ralley blinked and inspected her dusty flannel pajamas. "Will they get me something to wear?" She really did not feel like meeting a king in her nightclothes; of course, she wasn't sure she wanted to meet a king at all!

"They will do as you command, you are their Empress," he said with his familiar grumpy tone.

"You know, you're really starting to annoy me. Is that any way to talk to an Empress?" she challenged, her hands on her hips.

Talon grunted. "You know nothing of being an Empress. There is much for you to learn before I show you any respect at all!" Regence cleared his throat, and Talon ignored it, "You are probably the youngest ever to be chosen, a foreigner and a female," Regence stepped closer to him and spoke his name. Talon continued. "You show no respect for the rules and I do not see why the dragon chose you at all!" Regence elbowed him roughly in the side. Talon gave him an angry look.

Ralley glared at him. It wasn't her fault she got picked, or that she didn't know anything about this place, and she was downright proud to be a girl! "YEAH? Well, who wants your respect anyway?" Feeling like she properly deposited her two cents, she turned her back on him, crossing her arms, wondering if she should leave the room, or if ordering him to leave was well within her Empress rights. Before she could make up her mind, four servant girls hastened into the room. They said nothing as one of them, a short, black-haired girl who looked younger than Ralley, took her gently by the hand and led her to the other end of the room to a wooden door. She glanced over her shoulder to see Regence with his arms crossed, speaking to Talon. The dragon trotted after her, slipping into the room as one of the girls opened the door. The handmaid let out a squeak as it passed her but quickly composed herself and stepped aside to allow them in.

The door closed behind her and Ralley turned her attention to the room, which reminded her of an old bathroom. It had shiny white marbled floors and walls and there were several lit torches in holders giving it a warm glow. Dominating the middle of the room was a large marble tub; two more servant girls were filling it with buckets of hot water. She smiled, realizing she was finally going to get a bath. Two of the other girls, both with long brown hair and brown eyes, began to lift her arms and tug her nightshirt up.

"Whoa! Wait a minute!" Ralley struggled to pull her arms away and slip her shirt back down. "What are you doing? I'm perfectly capable of undressing myself!" But she was too late; the shirt slipped over her head and was tossed to the side as the girls both reached for her pajama bottoms. Ralley hopped back, covering her chest with one hand and stuck her other out to stop them. "No, no, no! I can do it myself!" The girls blinked at her but did not attempt it again. They stood by patiently while she removed her clothing and got into the tub. She suffered through the girls rinsing and scrubbing her until they finally stood back and left the room, leaving only two girls standing by the door and the dragon, who settled down next to the tub. She leaned on the side of the tub and stared down at it. A thought occurred to her: how had the dragon known exactly where to find her?

"So, you can talk to me right?" Ralley asked and the dragon nodded its head. "Okay, well, I have some questions to ask you, then. Can you find just anyone?"

"No," the dragon's chirping voice echoed in her thoughts.

"Well, how did you find me then?" She crossed her arms and settled her chin on them.

"Different. You have the aura of a true heart, strength and power of leadership and a great love for others."

"So, what you're saying exactly is that my aura sticks out?" she asked, raising a brow.

"Yes."

"Well, what about my sister? Does her aura stick out, too? Can you find her?" She lifted her head, staring at the dragon.

The creature cocked its head as if listening to something very far away. *"Not the same. She has a kind heart but not a good leader and still searching for love,"* it stated.

"Yeah, well I keep telling her that those guys she goes out with are…wait! You mean she's here? Where is she? Is she in this castle?" She wanted her clothes back and glanced up at the two girls standing by the door, but before she could ask them, the dragon shook its head.

"No."

"What? Where is she?" She hoped he would tell her she was safely back home.

"Far to the north, beyond the forest of demons," the dragon replied, stretching a bit.

"Forest of demons? She's here, as in on this island?" Ralley sat up in the tub and waved at the girls standing at the door. "My clothes! I want to get dressed!" They bowed to her, and one of them exited the room.

"Yes, she is in this world."

"What do you mean world? Are you trying to tell me I'm on another planet?" Ralley began to panic. "How far away from earth am I? Oh, my gosh! I'm gonna die from some alien disease or something!"

The dragon trilled happily as if it were laughing. *"No, not another planet. Just another world, not unlike your own. You traveled through dimensions, not space."*

Ralley sat back in the tub, considering the dragon's words. "So, you're saying more like another dimension?" She was not sure how this was different, but she guessed it meant she had not left earth.

"Yes, I suppose so."

At that moment three of the girls re-entered, one carrying a large towel, another holding what looked like clothes and the last carrying a bucket of warm water that she dumped over Ralley's head. Scrambling out of the tub, Ralley then suffered being dried by the towel girl while the others closed in to dress her. She allowed it to happen since it made things quicker and the clothes they put on her were complicated. It was a light purple dress made of silk that touched the floor along with a tight bodice. It left her shoulders and upper arms bare and the girls tied bands just above her elbow with see-through swaths of cloth that hung down to her knees. She was adorned with a jeweled necklace, earrings, two rings, and an elaborate tiara, each displaying an oval ruby.

"Wait a minute, what is all this about? Where are my clothes?" Ralley wasn't expecting to be dressed in something that looked like a ball gown.

The small black-haired girl stood back and bowed to her. "They will be cleaned and placed in your wardrobe if you wish. You must ready yourself for the ceremonies."

Ralley sighed, deciding this was better than wearing her pajamas. Well, almost. The outfit was tight and uncomfortable. "What ceremonies? I don't have time for that! My sister is somewhere on this island or world or wherever we are, and I have to go!"

The girl was too timid to argue with her. She stepped to her side and took her hand to guide her to a side door opposite the one she had first come through, the dragon following. The other girls busied themselves cleaning up the room as they vacated. "Where are we going?" Ralley said, hoping the girl was taking her to Talon or Regence and they could help her get out of here.

"To see their majesties, the King and Queen. You will be introduced to them so that you can be properly welcomed," she replied softly.

"What?" Ralley stopped in her tracks, forcing the girl to stop as well. "I don't want to see them!" The black-haired girl appeared quite surprised and tipped her head much like the dragon did in a questioning manner. "Look um … what was your name?"

The girl was yet more surprised, and her eyes snapped up then back down to the floor. "I … my … name is Firani," she stuttered.

"Wow, that's a really nice name." Firani's cheeks reddened. "Look Firani, I have a big sister somewhere in this world. I need to find her before something happens to her, so I don't have time to talk to a King. I want to talk to Talon and Regence."

"They will be in the throne hall."

"Good, take me there then." Ralley allowed Firani to take her hand again.

"B … but that is w … where the King and Queen are, too," she said, her eyes still on the floor as she stuttered, looking nervous.

Ralley gave an exasperated sigh. "Alright … just walk very slowly." She had to think this through and hoped it would take some time to get to the throne hall. She hadn't a clue how to act in front of royalty and wasn't eager to learn. Firani lead her down long side halls and through random doors. "I hope you're not taking a short cut."

"N...no your highness. We must avoid the main halls," Firani answered, taking her down a dimly lit walkway.

Ralley realized the girl was intimidated by her and tried to use a more calm and soothing tone. "Why is that?"

"The visiting dignitaries will be entering through the main hall, and you must not yet be seen. You must meet the King and Queen first."

"Visiting dignitaries? Who are they?"

"They are the local Lords, Barons and Dukes of Degrail. Those from Elstaff City and Eagle Crest Village will likely arrive in the morning."

"Morning?" This was becoming too much. She had no time to stay and wait for dignitaries to shake her hand; her sister was out there somewhere, possibly searching for her if not being held against her will. She had to escape from here somehow and get a ride north. Perhaps the dragon could lead her to her sister if she asked it to.

Firani paused before a great wooden door with decorative gold symbols on it. She knocked three times and a tall frail looking man answered the door. It was the same man that had first greeted them after entering the castle. "Ah, good! You are here, Empress. Please sit and make yourself comfortable. The ceremonies will be commencing soon." He stood back and allowed her to enter the large room. It was filled with comfortable chairs in shades of red and gold. Choosing a rather cushy looking one, she adjusted the heavily embroidered and tasseled pillows and sat down. The only other people in the room were two other handmaids she recognized from the bathing room. The dragon slid through the door and pounced onto a large crimson chair, knocking several pillows onto the floor as it stretched out. Ralley sat facing yet another decorated door, this one slightly larger than the last. The skinny man closed the side door and hurried over to stand before them, at attention like a soldier.

Before Firani could move away, Ralley grabbed her hand and whispered, "Stand here with me okay?" It was a desperate plea as Ralley grew steadily nervous, and she was determined to keep Firani at her side if only to offer some comfort.

"Yes, your Highness." Ralley looked up to see a tiny uncomfortable smile from Firani.

There was a knock at the door, and the tall man guarding it stepped toward her. "Your welcome is prepared Empress. This way, please." He moved to open the door for her.

Unwilling to move, she glanced to Firani. The girl helped her up, and as she faced the now widening maw of the door, she felt her heart threatening to beat its way out of her chest. She still held onto Firani's hand. "Stay with me?"

"Y...yes, your Highness." She stuttered.

Feeling far more nervous now that she was to see such important people, Ralley didn't want to be alone. If she screwed up, would she get beheaded? That thought didn't quite relieve the situation.

-15-

PERTURBING PROPOSALS

In his princely manor, Talon stood rigid next to the two highly decorated thrones. His fair-haired mother sat in the smaller seat; her hair had been tightly braided and wound about her head a time or two, the rest trailing down her shoulder to rest against her chest. She had been dressed in her finest, a dress made of crimson velvet, adorned in jewelry made of rubies and gold. Talon himself had gone through a rushed bath, a herd of servants fussing over his own blond hair and dressing him into an immaculate red velvet outfit that complemented his mother's to represent the Degrail royal colors. The great red and gold throne was vacant, and Talon sighed deeply. He had been informed that his father's leg had become infected and unusable, keeping him bedridden. There was no time to go and see his father, and he was unsure if he wanted to. The feelings of disappointment and anger from the morning would only be magnified by the performance of this very ceremony.

Messengers had been sent racing to every corner of the city to gather the various nobles who were now hurried into the great hall. Each noble of importance was being announced upon entering. Since Talon was at the other end of the hall and much talking was taking place, there was little chance to hear the introductions. Servants rushed to bring chairs to those who needed them, but most chose to stand as close to the long red carpet as possible so as to get a glimpse of the new Empress.

Regence emerged from the crowd to stand close to Talon. "Ah, it would seem Lady Tensia has brought all of her sons today. Do you think they will have a chance?"

Talon kept his gaze forward to await Ralley's entrance but acknowledged the question. "Chance? For what?" he asked.

"Why... with Lady Ralley of course, do you think they have a chance with her?" Talon followed Regence's gaze. He was eyeing the four young men, two standing on either side of a woman. She was weighed down with an abundance of silver jewelry and wearing a blinding yellow dress; the bottom of it was so full it looked as if it were swallowing up the legs of two of the sons closest to her.

"What in Asatiria are you talking about?"

Regence chuckled. "Do you not see? Tensia has four sons and two daughters, and neither of her fair daughters is standing with her. And look there, Baron Kelanz. He is looking mighty primped and polished is he not? Ah, and the three that just arrived, Lord and Lady Roan and their strapping young son, Byron."

Talon watched as the three newcomers filed into the room. He still did not understand what Regence was getting at; these were all nobles that the messengers had been sent to, inviting them to attend the rushed ascension ceremony for the new Empress. He was just about to remind Regence of this very detail when a servant entered the hall and spoke into the ear of the advisor announcing the arrivals. The advisor shooed the servant off and approached the middle of the hall where another red carpet had been placed, leading to a large side door where Ralley was to enter the room.

A sudden quiet swept through the room as the man cleared his throat and gestured to the side door. "All rise and behold the Blade Beast and his chosen, the new Empress, Ralley of Degrail."

All heads turned to the side door that now opened; out of it prowled the blade creature. It swiveled its head around, growling softly as if to warn those who were too close. The aisle widened slowly as nobles and dignitaries took several nervous steps back. As it approached the middle of the room where the advisor stood, it turned its head back to the door. Slow and hesitant, Ralley emerged into the crowded hall, a nervous handmaid at her side. Talon almost did not recognize her. It was as if she had gone through a complete transformation.

"She cleans up quite nicely don't you agree?" Regence whispered as he nudged him. "The men are going to be rather competitive."

Talon could not tear his eyes away from her, only nodding in response to Regence's question. He watched her walk down the isle towards the announcer, the handmaid following awkwardly behind her. The dragon creature continued past the advisor and faced the throne, continuing its warning growl as it made its way towards them, Ralley, the advisor, and the handmaid following. The things that his sword master had said began to sink in as he watched the lustful eyes of the men along the aisle. Ralley was an Empress, and eventually she would choose a companion. Though that man would not hold the power of the

Blade Beast, he would still be named Emperor. Anger bubbled up inside him as he watched Tensia's four sons smile and nod as Ralley turned her head their way. It grew ever more as she gave them a small smile back. The advisor stopped Ralley at the foot of the dais and stepped away, the handmaid following, the dragon creature standing at her side. She frowned as if upset to see the handmaid go. Talon met her eyes as she lifted them. She smiled at him, not the nervous smile she gave moments ago, but a genuine one. His anger softened, and he gave her a tiny nod in response. He glanced to Regence, who was positively beaming, which annoyed him.

His mother rose from her chair and stepped out in front of the vacant throne; her gentle voice was also commanding as she addressed Ralley, her voice loud enough for the crowd to hear. "We welcome you to Castle Degrail and pray your journey here was a good one. As the former Emperor is unable to conduct the ceremony, my son Prince Talon and myself will do so. Let all who stand before us witness this renewal of rule as we step down and give the throne over to Empress Ralley of Degrail, chosen of the Blade Beast." Talon stepped forward next to his mother and took her now outstretched hand. With all the control and dignity he could muster, he led his mother down the steps to where Ralley and the dragon creature stood. For a moment her face relaxed as he approached, but when he and his mother stepped to either side of her and turned to the throne, her face contorted in a confused and almost frightened look. The Blade Beast eased its way up the steps towards the throne, and for a moment, it looked as though Ralley would not follow. Talon spared a glance at her and found her looking right back at him, her brow wrinkled in worry. He nodded to her and gave her what he hoped was an encouraging smile before turning to face the throne again. Finally, he watched as she ascended the steps and reached the top turning to face the crowd. He felt a surge of envy of her and at the same time...something else. He shook the thought from his mind before it could be identified.

"All hail Empress Ralley!" came his mothers commanding voice. The entire room was filled with the hailing cry of the crowd as he and his mother knelt down before the dais. When the cries died down and the room again fell silent, the two of them rose to their feet and again his mother spoke. "We now take our leave, and may the gods bless your rule." His mother turned and glided down the hall away from the steps. Talon hesitated; something made him wish he could stay here. Was it because he was still holding onto some hope that the Blade Beast would realize it had made a mistake and swoop down to him? He forced himself to turn away and follow his mother towards the back doors of the hall. Or maybe it was because...

"Wait!!" Ralley's voice rang out across the room and Talon halted, turning back to face her. "I mean..." she glanced to Regence, who now stood next to the throne and straightened himself as if he had been speaking with her. She faced them once again. "I would be honored if you would join me for the remainder of the ceremony."

Talon opened his mouth but nothing came out; he was unsure whether to accept this or not. "Thank you, Empress," his mother replied. "My son and I are the ones who are honored to be your guests and to serve you in any way we can." Talon turned his head to watch his mother return to his side. He reflexively offered his elbow, and she took it with a warm smile, saying in a hushed tone, "She is quite exotic is she not?"

Talon blinked in surprise at his mother's question. "Uh…" he paused, "Yes, she is." he managed to say before they moved up the stairs.

As they reached the top, they remained standing as Ralley sat. She glanced down at the dragon beside her then back up to them. "Oh, please sit!" She offered.

His mother graciously accepted her previous seat, and Talon remained standing exactly where he had before. Regence stepped back around to his right hand side still retaining his ridiculous smug grin. "I suppose you are happy with yourself," Talon whispered through his teeth, keeping his eyes straight ahead as the advisor returned to the hall and stood at the bottom of the steps with his back to the dais.

"Of course, now you can make sure that no one steps out of line," he replied.

"What do you mean by that?" But Regence only gave a sly smile in answer.

The advisor began to read off names one at a time from a long list. As he spoke the names of dignitaries, they stepped forward and offered their allegiance to Ralley. When Tensia was named, she introduced her four sons and rambled on about their noble heritage and other nonsense. She must have hurried to rehearse this speech in order to make them sound desirable. Talon turned his head to watch Ralley, and much to his annoyance, she was leaning forward as if quite interested. Unable to say or do anything at the moment, he turned to glare at Regence, who must have found it all quite amusing as he pretended to clear his throat to poorly suppress a laugh. When Tensia and her sons finally filed back into the crowd, Talon leaned down to whisper to Ralley. "Do not be fooled; Tensia has been known to exaggerate."

Ralley did not seem to pay much attention to what he said. Instead, she scrunched up her lower lip. As the advisor announced a new name, she whispered back, "Do you have any maps I might be able to look at?"

The question caught him off guard. "Yes, of course we do…" he said, wondering what she wanted with a map at this moment. "…The cartography room is full of them."

Barron Kelanz bowed deeply before Ralley and recited the oath of allegiance. When he finished, he stood and spoke with what Talon deemed arrogance. "May I also add, most honorable Empress, that it would be a great honor if you would accept my services in familiarizing you with our fair city." Talon felt a great urge to pounce upon him for such a bold request. His eyes shot back to Ralley, hoping she would not accept it.

Again, Ralley's attention went briefly to the dragon before addressing him. "Thanks but…" She turned her head to face Talon. "Prince Talon has already offered to show me around."

Surprised again, he managed to regain himself for a slight bow. "Indeed, your majesty."

"Well, then, perhaps another time, your highness?" Instead of taking his leave, he waited there for her to answer.

"Cheeky little upstart," Regence mumbled, winking at Talon.

"Perhaps…" Ralley replied. When she offered nothing more, the Barron took his leave, and the official continued down the list of names.

The evening droned on as noble after noble stepped forward to pledge their loyalties. Ralley was interested for a while, but Talon could tell by her slackening posture and yawns hidden behind a casual raised hand that she was becoming bored by it all. "Welcome to my world." he thought, and for the first time, he felt a surge of pity for her. Yesterday she was a peasant, free of formalities, ceremonies and endless boredom. Now, she was just as trapped as he.

-16-

PROMISES

Scared and trapped in the coils of a demon, Brek had long since stopped trying to struggle after awakening to the world spinning about him. Xenopus was in his great demonic form and was leaping with incredible height along the mountaintops, his giant and powerful back legs carrying them far from the tower. His fear of what was to happen to him kept him awake, but they traveled west for a long time before he worked up enough courage to speak. "Wh...where are we going?"

"Someplace where we can work without being disturbed of course. Now hush and enjoy the ride, Master," Xenopus said in a deep croaking voice. Ecnair clung to Brek's clothing as the demon made another leap across a great canyon.

This was all too much for him. He had thought that he could get all he dreamed for with a simple summoning spell, but things had gone wrong, horribly wrong. The moment Xenopus had gripped him and commanded him to finish the spell was when he had realized that he was not completely in control. He should never have listened to that cursed imp! But what was the use of it now? He had betrayed Estat, the one man who had believed in him, the only one to take him in and teach him about the strange

-117-

powers that had once haunted him. There was no turning back now; he had realized that the very moment Estat had stepped through the doors of the summoning hall and cursed him for a fool but he had been too headstrong to listen. Tears welled up in his eyes and streamed along the sides of his head. He was not quite sure if it was the wind, his fear, or the realization that he had somehow lost something more than just a mentor.

Xenopus paused on the edge of a dizzying cliff side. If Brek were not so frightened for his life, he would have thought the view quite magnificent. He could see a small river trailing down from the craggy mountains into a woodland area.

"Hmmm...there is something interesting here," Xenopus mused. With another great leap, the demon carried them down to a bushy area beside the river. He began to move awkwardly through the brush toward the west.

"What is going on?" Brek whined, struggling against the demon's grip once more.

"Another tool, my Master, something I may be able to use... or rather, someone." His deep voice chuckled.

In the distance, Brek could have sworn he heard music. He dismissed it though, since he knew there were no human settlements beyond Sarr Village far to the south.

It was not long before they came to a great cave entrance covered in vines and an abundance of flowers. Similar flowers covered the ground around it and surrounded a large pond that was built with rough brick. The music was louder here, and was coming from inside the cave. Much to Brek's relief, he was lowered to the ground and released. He had to steady his urge to run, knowing his legs would not take him far. Moments later,

Xenopus had returned to his less intimidating human form. Ecnair climbed back to Brek's shoulder, muttering curses under his breath. Now that his feet were on the ground, he became curious about the music within the cave, and as Xenopus ventured forward into it, Brek followed quietly behind, fear still linking him to the demon and making the hairs on the back of his neck tingle.

At first Brek could hardly see in the dark cavern, and it was a struggle for him not to stumble or stub a toe. The dark had never worried him till now, as he had stumbled through dark rooms of the tower many times before. The imp left his shoulder with another curse after about the fifth or sixth time, but he did not hear Xenopus misstep even once. After a short time of going along in the dark, Brek could make out a faint light ahead. It grew along with the music, and in moments, they were standing in a large cavern. In its center was a small group of four minstrels, three of them playing simple instruments: a lute, a lap harp, a flute, and the fourth was singing. The light came from a few small globes that floated in place near the roof of the cave. Though the music was expertly done and the singing man's voice was perfectly on key, all of the players had a rather melancholy look to them.

A young woman sat on several cushions facing the musicians. She turned her head only slightly at their presence and spoke in a soft and elegant voice. "Who is it that disturbs my music?" When she spoke the four men ceased their song. The woman slowly rose to her feet and turned to face Xenopus. She wore a long peach colored dress with a lengthy train that she carefully picked up from the floor and draped over one arm. Her waist-length blond hair hung loose around her, and the only jewelry she wore was a silver band around her brow with four milk-white jewels dangling in front of her forehead.

Brek stared in awe at the beautiful young woman before him. He would gladly have had Xenopus procure this one for his bride since he had lost the other back in the tower. The demon stepped forward, giving her a wide smile. "I sense a great power coming from you, so I came to see if you might assist us in our…" He paused a moment in thought. "Quest. I promise to make it worth your time," he purred.

The woman's eyes looked Xenopus over thoughtfully, and she took a few steps towards him. "And who are you?" she asked with her silken voice.

"I am Xenopus, a powerful demon of the Under Dimensions," he said, his deep voice echoing in the cave.

"A demon? I had thought such beings could not enter this world freely," she tipped her head in a questioning manner.

"You are quite right. I could not, but this human has brought me here, and now I am…" he turned his deep green eyes to Brek, "in his service." He smirked, and Brek almost cringed at the look. He was relieved to see that the demon had turned away again, his attention returning to the woman. "I am in search of powerful allies. My master must have a great army at his side if he wishes to conquer this world."

Brek found himself being scrutinized by the beautiful lady, and he was caught up by her penetrating blue eyes. He felt held there, so drawn to her that he wanted to close the gap between them and take her in his arms, except that his legs would not respond. Then she smiled at him, and he wanted to melt. She turned her attention back to Xenopus and stepped closer to him. "I am Mioria, Sorceress of Souls, though my talents stretch father than simple manipulations." She smiled to the demon, and she lifted a finger to trace it across his chest. "Perhaps we can talk of what is worth my time." Mioria looked again at Brek, and her smile was intoxicating. She then turned and walked to a door set in the stone to the side of the cave. "Do enjoy some music while I speak with your servant, Brek."

"But should I not join you?" Brek protested, wanting very much to hear what it was that would make Mioria happy.

Xenopus turned to speak, but Mioria cut in. "Heavens no, dear one. You are his lord and master, and therefore you should not have to listen to such droll conversations. Worry not. We shall come to an agreement, and when we have, we shall be sure to relay it to you. I want you to enjoy your stay at my home. Please sit," she said, indicating the cushions. She looked to the four men standing quietly in the room. "Play for him, and do not speak with him." Her last words echoed in the room, a tingle of magic in the air. Then she turned and disappeared through the door, Xenopus following after. Ecnair had said nothing through this exchange, but now he flew off to join them. The door closed with a gentle sound behind them, and Brek was alone with the four musicians.

He sat down on the cushions, which were quite soft and indeed extremely comfortable. Brek's eyes turned to the musicians now, and they all exchanged glances. It appeared that they were agreeing upon what to play, but Brek noticed something now that he had not before. All these men did not quite seem to be here somehow. This startled him at first, as he had not realized before how they were almost transparent. It was as if you could almost see right through them. Perhaps the reason he had not noticed this before was that they were in a dark cave and the lights were not quite as bright. Each of them also had a silver band around their heads similar to that which Mioria wore, though their jewels were all solid black.

The first man cleared his throat and began to sing. There were no words, just the sound of his voice, but in this slightly echoing cave the sound was so magnificent that Brek forgot about their transparency. The second man next to him lifted the flute to his lips and began to play along with the song. This too sounded wonderful; the two complemented one another. The third man held the lute and began to strum his way into their song. Brek was amazed at how well he played. The notes were elegant, and his fingers moved so easily. As they continued their song, the last minstrel adjusted the small lap harp and began to play.

All four of them were in perfect sync, and the resulting music was like nothing he had ever heard before. These men were barely older he, and yet they played as though they had been doing it for an entire lifetime. It was as if the four of them had been destined to play together. "You are magnificent! How long have you been playing together?" he asked. The four men stared at him, their faces showing no sign of gratitude for his compliment, nor did they speak apart from the one who was singing. Then, almost as one, the eyes of the quartet drifted to the door behind which Xenopus and Mioria had gone. Again they exchanged glances, and the music began to gradually get louder.

The man playing the lute nodded to Brek and began to sing himself in a very quiet tone. Brek had to listen closely to hear what he was saying as the song grew. "The woman is a witch. You must escape, else she will rend your soul from your body and use it for her spells."

Brek's eyes widened. He did not want to believe this man, or rather, this ghost, this apparition. "W…what are you talking about?" he whispered back. "What are you?"

"What you see before you is only our souls, torn from our bodies. If you do not escape, you will end up as us, or perhaps worse if she sees no use for you," he sang, glancing towards the door and back again. Brek felt stunned. With his supposed control over Xenopus weakening, he began to fear what he and the young woman were talking over. The sensual looks she had given him took on a different meaning, and he scrambled to his feet. At that moment the door swung open, and Mioria glided out, glancing over at the musicians. "That will be quite enough," she said and lifted her hand. Brek watched as all four of them shimmered and dissipated before his eyes; all that remained was their instruments, which clattered to the floor. Stunned, Brek turned slowly to face Mioria. Xenopus had stepped around from behind her and was watching with mild interest.

Mioria glided toward him, her hand reaching out to take his. It was warm, and she was beautiful. "Brek, your servant tells me you have some talents that he requires." Her voice was soft and he refused to believe what the lute player had said about her. His thoughts wavered as he looked upon the four jewels on her headdress. They had changed, now half white, half black. "What is the matter, darling?" she asked in her silken voice. "You are master of a powerful demon, soon to control the greatest army ever seen and …" She placed her smooth, warm hands on either side of his face. "Be by the side of the most powerful woman in the world." Mioria pressed her lips to his, and all his doubts were instantly washed away. Yes, this is what he wanted, was it not?

-17-

WHAT MAKES AN EMPRESS?

Just when Ralley thought the boredom had ended, the former Empress stood and declared that a great feast would be held for the new Empress. Well, at least she would get something to eat; though she still wanted to get into that map room that Talon had talked about. She realized the last meal she ate was at the tavern and that was hours ago, or at least that's what her stomach was telling her. Still, she felt somewhat guilty that she would be eating while she had no idea if her sister was safe. There was a sudden flood of servants bringing tables, chairs and dishes into the great hall. One long table was placed right in front of her and chairs were brought to Talon and Regence. Two other slaves rushed over and spread a great cloth over the table, giving her a quick bow before rushing off again. A young girl hurried along the length of the table, placing an intricately painted clay plate before each of them. Following on her heels was an even younger girl, placing gold utensils beside each plate. Ralley watched the entire room of dignitaries and their families receive similar treatment, and in short order the room fell silent as the last of the scurrying servants disappeared into the side doors.

Her robes rustling loudly in the silent room, Talon's mother rose to her feet once again. With a unified rustling and rumbling of chairs, the entire room returned to their feet. Before Ralley could rise to join them, Talon put a restraining hand on her shoulder and shook his head. Not looking at her, he added in a whisper, "You must remain seated."

Ralley could not help but feel a bit annoyed at not knowing what she was supposed to do, but grateful that Talon was there to tell her. Remaining still, she stared out across the hall at the crisply dressed crowd.

"Long live Ralley, Empress of Asatiria, may she be loved by all her people!" The High Queen's words were echoed by all in the room. Moments after the queen retook her seat, the crowd in the great hall sank back into their own chairs. At that moment, the side doors of the hall burst open, and out of them flowed a multitude of servants, each carrying large platters. Some carried steaming soups, others held fresh bread and cheeses, vegetables, fruit, large fowl, and one burly fellow, perhaps one of the chefs, carried a huge plate with a cooked pig. Though the pig appeared unappetizing, the smell was mouth-watering. All this food reminded her of the fried chicken at the fast food place near her house, Thanksgiving dinner at her grandma's and her favorite restaurant all packed together in this one room.

Everything was as delicious as it had smelled, and as everyone ate, the servants continued to bring out more platters of food while taking away empty ones and refilling drained glasses. Ralley wasn't quite impressed with most of these "nobles" eating habits as they ate things mostly with their fingers. She soon pushed her plate away from her, feeling quite stuffed, and took small sips of her water, ignoring the wine glass. She had never gotten used to the taste of alcohol, her sister and herself having tried it when with a group of friends. This thought reminded her that she needed to get on with looking for her sister. She turned and waited for Talon to finish the mouthful he was working on before leaning over to him.

"Talon," she whispered, "how long will this meal take?"

Talon turned to her, looking a bit surprised. "Er, well, as long as you like I suppose…"

"What do you mean? I can tell everyone to stop eating and go home?" she asked hopefully.

He straightened in his chair. "That hardly seems appropriate for an Empress."

Ralley rolled her eyes. "Okay fine, I guess that sounds a little stuck up. What if I just left?"

"That could be considered quite rude as well," Talon said airily.

She spoke through gritted teeth. "What would be considered appropriate for me to do then?"

A smile crept across Talons face. "Patiently allow the royalty at your table to finish their meals."

"Stubborn jackass," Ralley mumbled as Talon returned to his meal. She decided to test the wine for the heck of it and found she still did not enjoy the taste. A short time later she noticed Talon was deliberately eating his meal as if every bite were sacred. She wanted to reach over and shove the rest of his plate down his throat, but of course that would be un-empress-like.

He caught her deadly stare and smiled cheerfully, nodding to her. Unable to contain herself, she kicked him. Thanks to that wonderfully long tablecloth, nobody saw it, though her effort only caused him to chuckle. This made him look very handsome, and she caught herself staring at him. She turned away to examine the former empress, Talon's mother. She appeared just as stiff as Ralley in the heavily beaded dress, but she held herself straight and regal. "Excuse me, but what happens now? What am I to do as Empress?"

The Queen turned to her and smiled. "Now we will leave the castle to you."

"To me? But what about you?" Ralley asked.

"That is up to the High King, but I cannot be sure," she replied patiently.

Ralley frowned. She felt now that she was kicking them out of a home that was once theirs. "Can't you stay?"

Her smile was soft. "Only if you wish it so, as you are Empress."

Ralley leaned forward, "Then I wish it! Please stay! Help me with all this Empress stuff! I want to know what is expected and what I can do and can't do." In the back of her mind, she told herself this was all temporary and if she up and disappeared, gone back to her own "dimension," as the creature called it, then they could go on ruling as if she had not been there.

The woman laughed, and it was a beautiful laugh. "As you command, Empress. When would you like to speak with me?"

"I would love to now, but... I don't want to be rude to the nobles," Ralley sighed and slumped back in her throne.

"Nonsense. If you wish to retire, then do so."

She leaned forward. "Really?"

"Certainly, simply stand, and Talon will escort you out, as is customary."

Ralley turned her head to gaze at Talon, a sly smile easing across her lips. "So that's it, is it?" With a ruffle of her dress fabric she rose to her feet. Talon, caught by surprise, dropped his utensils, almost choking down the last of his food. In an instant he had regained his regal composure and stood with her, offering his arm. He said nothing as she accepted it, and together, with the dragon creature taking the lead, they left the room, the Queen rising shortly after her and Regence offering his arm to lead her out. In moments they had left the main hall behind, and Ralley couldn't help but giggle.

"Something funny?" Talon said stiffly.

"Oh, just the look on your face." They moved through a great hallway, and at its end was a set of large, intricately carved doors. "So where are you taking me?"

Talon smiled a genuine smile. "You said you wanted to see maps of this world, so I am taking you to a room just off the library that holds every map we have of this land and its closer neighbors, including the land where you came from as well."

"Talon, I don't think I'm from that mainland you were talking about."

He quirked his brow at her. "Where else would you be from? The other continents are much farther but I suppose you could have…"

"Not exactly. I think… I think I'm from another world entirely. Or maybe I'm stuck in a dream? I don't know really, but I have to find my sister and we have to get out of here together."

Talon stepped ahead and opened the door for her and she swept into the room, the dragon at her heels. It was a giant library, and there were several servants dusting the shelved books or organizing small stacks to be placed back on the shelf. They bowed to them as Talon took her hand again and lead her across the room. "You spoke of your sister before. She is lost?"

"No, well, yes, I think so. She's in this world like me, but the dragon said she was far to the north, past some big forest."

"In this world? What do you mean by that?" Talon stepped forward to open another door on the other side of the library; this one was much smaller and only a single door, but there was a carving of an old medieval type of compass on the front.

"Weren't you listening to a word I said?" she asked hotly. She bunched her puffy dress and entered the small room; two servant boys had just lit the torches set in the walls. The room was half the size of the library, and the walls were filled with small to large scrolls that were tucked into specially made squares. There were two large, round tables in the room, and two chairs sat in one corner. The dragon climbed onto them and laid itself out as if lounging on a hot day. "I mean that I am not from your world at all. The dragon says that I passed through a dimension."

"Dimension? That is impossible! The only creatures who can pass through dimensions are demons!"

"Demons! That was it! The dragon said it was north beyond the demon forest!" Ralley looked to the servants standing quietly next to the torches they had lit. "I need a map of this country, please!" One of them, a black haired boy, turned and scanned the area quickly before drawing one out and moving to the table. The other boy dug into a small box on the floor that held large polished stones. He brought these to the table and placed them at the corners of the scroll as they unrolled it.

"Beyond? That cannot be. There are no kingdoms beyond the demon forest!"

Ralley leaned over the map and frowned. "I can't read the writing on this thing. Where is the demon forest?"

Talon raised a brow at her. "You cannot read?" He stepped forward and looked over the map. "Here," he said, pointing to a region at the top of the map.

Ralley ignored Talon's words and turned to the dragon. "Could you show me exactly where my sister is on the map?" Sliding off the chairs, the Blade creature approached the table and lifted its head to inspect the map. Rearing up, it put one leg on the table and stretched the other across the map, one claw pointing downward; it pressed it to a spot on the map that was blank.

Talons frown grew deeper. "She is in the depths of the forest, farther than anyone has gone; it is much too dangerous."

The Blade Beast shook its head and spoke to Ralley, its voice once again only heard in her mind. *"She is in the tower."*

She turned to Talon. "The dragon says she's in a tower."

"Tower? There is no tower on the map."

The dragon growled, *"Fetch me ink!"*

"He wants some ink," Ralley repeated, since it certainly seemed that no one else could hear him. One of the servants raced out the door and returned shortly with a bottle of ink, setting it nervously on the table next to the dragon. Ralley watched wide eyed as the dragon delicately dipped its claw tip into the ink, tapped the excess on the edge and began to draw a detailed tower within a volcano surrounded by craggy mountains and hills. He nodded his head, evidently satisfied with the art, and drawing his painted claw up to his mouth, he puffed a bit of flame to it, burning away the ink. "She's there then…" Ralley breathed. "Can you take me there?" She turned to Talon's stunned expression.

-18-

A Search Begins

Talon shook his head, amazed at what the Blade Beast had drawn. The creature was undoubtedly certain that Ralley's sister was in this tower. "This place is much too dangerous. They call it the demon forest for a reason, and it is not filled with little rabbits and quietly grazing does."

"Well, it's just a forest, so I don't see what the problem is. Besides, she's not in the forest, she's in a tower, as you can see," she said, gesturing to the drawing.

Talon crossed his arms. "You do not seem to understand, Empress. The Demon Forest is full of *demons*. It has been so for years; the Emperors before my father drove them out of our lands and into the north, and that is where they remain."

"Demons, huh? Yeah okay, then I guess that's more reason to get my sister out of there now, isn't it?" She marched towards the door, and one of the servants hastened to open it for her.

"Wait!" Talon called after her, "Where are you going?"

She stopped in the doorway. "To get my sister, what do you think?"

"You cannot! You are the Empress! Your duty is to your people, and you cannot just leave!" Was this girl truly crazy?

"I am taking care of Melanie. She's my sister, and besides, there are others who can take care of your people."

Talon frowned. "Like who?"

"You." Ralley smiled and stepped out the door. The Blade Beast slid to the door, and it paused. Its ruby eyes glittered as it stared at Talon for a time. It gave him a slight nod before it followed Ralley out the door.

Rule in her stead? What if she died out there in the forest of demons? Would the dragon then come to him? But what on earth was he thinking! He burst out of the door before the servant could think to close it and caught up to her. "Stop! I cannot allow you to go alone!"

She stopped in the middle of the library. "I guess you're right... I don't suppose you have a car or anything?"

He frowned. "What is a car?"

"Never mind. Yes, I would love to have a guide or maybe a couple of people to carry food."

"You have no idea what you are doing! I will escort you!" Talon could not believe what he had said, but he began to tell himself that it was the right thing to do. He could not let this foreigner empress wander into the forest where she would surely perish. As well, the thought of leaving the palace greatly appealed to him.

"You will?" She was quite surprised at this; her eyes stared into his as if trying to see if he were teasing her again.

"Yes... if you wish it." He frowned then, not wanting her to refuse.

Her eyes lit up. "Sure, alright, that sounds great. Does this mean I get to travel like royalty?"

"We will need to keep a low profile, and that means a smaller group." Talon's mind began to spin. He would be on an adventure and away from the castle; he felt like a small boy again, the yearning to leave the castle on far off diplomatic ventures bubbling up inside him. "I will begin preparations immediately. When would you like to leave?"

"Just after I talk with your mother?" She gave him a weak smile.

He blinked at her but smiled. "As you wish, Empress. It will give me time to prepare my men."

"Actually, I kinda want you to come with me...if that's not too much trouble?"

Talon frowned a bit. He did not think his mother and father would be very happy to hear of him leaving the palace with the Empress to find some girl in the Demon Forest. He cleared his throat. "As you desire."

She laughed. "Stop being so formal! Just say okay."

He raised a brow. "Okay?"

"That's better. Now where do we go?"

Talon turned to a nearby library servant. "Go and inform the King and Queen that the Empress and Prince will have audience with them shortly," he said in his commanding tone. The moment the boy hurried through the door Talon waved down another one. "Inform Regence to ready a small team of soldiers and horses with three turns worth of supplies."

"Three turns?" Ralley's brow wrinkled, "how long is that?"

"Around twenty one days," Talon replied, feeling suddenly eager to be off.

"Three weeks?" Ralley sounded crushed.

Talon shrugged. Obviously, she had no idea how far it was, but no matter. Talon waved down a third servant. "Retrieve the map that the Blade Beast has scrawled upon. Prepare it for travel and deliver it immediately to Master Regence." Talon then turned and offered Ralley his arm. "Let us consult with my father and mother before we set out, shall we?"

Talons father was still bedridden and did not look as well as he had only hours before. Despite this, he sat straight and addressed Ralley with his most eloquent voice. Talon listened quietly as Ralley insisted that his father and mother remain in the castle to rule the people as they would if she were not there so that she may set out to find her sister.

"This is highly irregular!" his father said, surprised. But his mother placed a hand on his arm.

"It is the wish of the Empress to do this, it is no longer our place to say what she should and should not do," she reminded him, her voice soothing. Talon had seen her do this many times when his father would otherwise have lost his temper.

Ralley frowned, her face becoming a mask of determination. "That's right, I want to do it. I can't just leave my sister out in this world all by herself."

The king sighed. "You have ceremonies to perform. Dignitaries will be arriving to meet you in the morning, countless treaties to sign…"

"They can wait till I get back," Ralley spoke, and Talon heard the anger in her voice.

"Why must it be you? Can you not send a troop of men to retrieve her?" the king continued.

"No, they wouldn't know what she looks like! I'm going, and that's final. You can handle things just as you did before." Ralley turned to Talon, looking as though she wanted him to say something in her defense.

Talon turned to his father. "I will escort her along with a small contingent of men; she will be well protected."

He was surprised to see his father nod in consent. "Yes, that shall be alright then. Please Empress, be safe on your journey and return swiftly. Your people need you."

Smiling, Ralley turned and lifted her hand. Talon took it in his arm, and the two of them retreated from his father's chambers. "That went well," she giggled.

"You have more authority than my father now, so of course it went well." Talon led her through the long hallways and up the winding stairs to a room where two young girls waited. "Her majesty would like informal riding wear." He turned to Ralley. "These girls will prepare you for the journey. Have them bring you to the stables when you are ready." She nodded, and he left her to the servants. She truly was a beautiful girl in formal dress, but there was simply no way she would be able to ride far in garments like that. Talon made his way to his own room, changing out of his formal clothing and into his informal riding gear. It felt good to wear them, and his excitement for the coming journey began to fill him with a joy he had always wished for.

Talon made his way down to the stables, eager to see Phoenix saddled and ready for him. What he did not expect was Crest, also saddled and ready. Regence appeared moments later, followed by seven skilled fighters and four archery masters. "Let me guess: you are going to come with me to keep me out of trouble?" He should have expected this, though he was far from upset.

"Of course! You think I'm going to let you have all the fun?" Regence laughed. "You cannot be rid of me so easily."

Glad to have him, Talon clasped his arm, and they smiled at one another. As acting general for the Empress, the men were now at his command. They bowed to him and stood awaiting orders. Regence had also ordered four strong male servants to assist them. Each of them would be driving a small one-mule cart that would carry their supplies.

Regence pulled a scroll case from one of his saddlebags and removed the map Talon had ordered sent to him. "So, am I to assume that we travel to the strange volcanic tower so lovingly drawn upon this map?" he questioned as he unrolled it.

"Yes, the Blade Beast himself has added it. I have never heard or known of it."

"Nor have I," Regence admitted. "I have not traveled to the northern kingdoms in years. I had hoped that I could go and visit them again … it has been so long since we have had any diplomatic ventures there."

"We may be able to find out more about the demon forest as we travel there." Talon had heard tales of the demon forest from his father, but he was only a boy then, and he began to wonder how many of those tales were true. "Regence, do you think the story of the wandering children is true?"

Regence replaced the map into the scroll case. "I suspect it has some truth to it, but whether it is due to a demon or if it is simply the mere carelessness of wayward children, one can never tell. Many a small child has been lost to a forest creature as simple as bears and wolfs."

Talon nodded. There were not only the stories of the demon forest, but also those of evil spirits, enchantresses and warlocks, things he had heard from peasants that passed through their castle. He knew there was truth to the black wolves that attacked his father, and he hoped that the warriors that remained here would take care of those.

Regence clapped him on the back. "You are not afraid to venture into such treacherous territory, are you?"

"Never! No demon will get the best of me." Talon eyed him, just waiting for his next jibe, but Regence had turned away and smiled at someone arriving at the stables. Talon turned to see Ralley, escorted by one of the young servants that had been in her quarters. Though the dress made her look like a shy princess, the riding attire transformed her into a commanding figure. She wore a simple shirt and a long dark red cape that matched his own, along with tight brown leggings and chaps. Her hair, tamed beneath the crown she had worn, was now loose and wild, framing her smooth face and rosy cheeks.

She smiled at them and Talon could not help but smile back. "So, are we ready to go?" she asked, eagerness in her voice.

Talon shook himself. Had he been staring? "Yes, we will travel as long as there is light. We should reach Elstaff by sunset and find a place to stay for the night there."

Regence ordered the servant girl to take Ralley to her horse. He turned to Talon and smiled. "Well then, Majesty, what do you think of her?"

"I think you should mind your own business," Talon smirked. "You are my teacher, not my father." He heard Regence chuckle as he mounted his steed. This would be a long journey indeed!

-19-

MOUNTAINS AND MONSTERS

The slow going down the side of the volcano made Melanie somewhat edgy. She had wanted to get out of there, but at the same time, this was nothing like leading Estat across the smooth floors or up the steps. Here the terrain was rocky and treacherous, and she had to lead a blind man through it. She had insisted they stop for a short time so she could tear part of the bottom of her prom dress to wrap around her feet, as the rocks here were sharp. It was a pity really, as she had liked this dress. It took forever to reach the bottom, and by the time they did, her feet were terribly bruised despite the cloth, and though Estat had shoes, they were not very useful for mountain climbing, and he was also favoring his tender soles.

"Maybe we should take a quick rest. My feet are killing me." Still she decided it was a good thing she didn't wear her heels since it would have been far more complicated to descend the mountain with them on. They sat down to rest; though their seats consisted of large boulders it was still nice to be able to get off her feet. Estat reached over and touched her knee, following it down to her foot where he frowned and his forehead pinched in concern.

"It's alright," Melanie assured him. "I'm sure none of your shoes would have fit me; it would have made it more difficult tripping around a rocky mountain with big shoes," she laughed. Estat began to rub her sore feet, and it felt good even though there were some overly tender spots. "So, where are we going anyway? Is there a town or something nearby?" Estat shook his head and felt around for the sack that Melanie had been carrying. He patted it, and she leaned over to open it for him. "I hope you brought a map, not that I could make much sense of it; I have no idea where we are, and I don't think I'm even in the same world." She watched as he pulled out the two books and felt the covers to decipher which one he needed. He chose the one that had a picture of what looked like three trees growing as one. It looked somehow familiar. She leaned forward as he opened the book and counted several pages in then turned it around for her to see.

"Ah! A map!" She studied it for a short time and found it to be a small map of the general area. "Here's the volcano with the tower in it. It's so beautifully detailed, and here! It's that tree on the cover! I've seen it before, outside the window of your bedroom in the tower." She pulled the book to herself as he nodded. She saw pictures of caves and rivers and to her delight, at the very bottom of the map was the picture of a man-made building. "Here, what about this place? I can't read this writing, but it's all the way down at the bottom of the map." She looked up to see Estat shaking his head. He reached over to feel the book and swirled his finger around the top area of the page and then put his fingers together in a peak. "You want to go to the northern tip?" He nodded again. Melanie looked over the northern tip of the map. "All that's on the map is a cave on this coastline."

Estat nodded again and smiled. He put a hand on her arm and then to his chest. Melanie sighed. "Yes, I will trust you, but after we go there to do whatever it is you have to do, then can we go to a village so I can find my sister?" Melanie asked, remembering the strange vision in the crystal that she'd seen of Ralley. Estat frowned, but he nodded. "Good, then let's get started." She had to get home somehow; she was sure her parents would be worried sick about them, but she found there was little she could do about it at the moment.

The trek through the craggy mountainous area was not an easy one. There were few grassy spots for her poor feet to walk on, and Estat too was upset; perhaps his feet were hurting him as well. A great shadow glided across the rocks ahead of them, and Melanie looked up to see a large bird silhouetted against the sky. After a few more steps, two more shadows glided across their path, and she looked up again to see at least three large birds. Were they circling? Perhaps they were vultures? A loud cry came from one of them, but it sounded nothing like the cry of a bird; it was almost like a human scream. She shuddered, and Estat came to an abrupt stop. He began to hide his face and then tug on her arm.

"W…what was that?" she asked, though he could not answer. He repeated the gesture again, but Melanie turned her attention to one of the "birds" as it swooped down and flew right at them. She squealed and threw them both to the ground moments before two great claws snapped at where their heads would have been. Sure, the claws were birdlike, but the rest of its body was not feathered, but scaled with webbed wings. "Those aren't birds! They're some type of flying lizards!" They scrambled to their feet, and she looked about the rocky area. "We have to hide!"

Estat threw up his arms in frustration, as if this was what he had been trying to tell her all along. Melanie shoved the bag he had been carrying back in his arms, still holding onto the one she had. "There are some rocks over there! We might be able to find a spot to hide. Hurry!" She took up his arm and led him in the direction of the rocks. It was difficult to keep her eyes on both the strange flying lizards and where she was guiding Estat. He ended up stumbling and tripping along, but he continued on without any angry looks, intent on wherever she was leading him. Another of the strange creatures dove at them, and again she was forced to pull Estat down. The lizard let out a cry of anger as it missed its target; this time Melanie spotted the long, thin, lizard-like tails. It began to circle around for another attempt.

Melanie pulled Estat back to his feet and led him forward again, spotting a great flat rock that leaned down atop a boulder, creating a small but sheltered area. She crammed him in and scooted herself next to him. "It's not much, but I think we will be safe in here."

She watched as he began to remove the torches, flint and steel from the sack and pressed them into her hands. "It's not that dark in here. What are these for?" He pointed up. "The bird lizards? But their not swooping down anymore. We're okay." At that moment, there was a loud thump over their heads, and she could hear the harsh scratching of claws against rock.

"Point taken." She began working the flint and steel in panic. She had never used these things before; all she could remember was her father starting campfires with them. Melanie had always thought him silly for doing it, telling him to use a match, but he had insisted on doing it the hard way. Now she wished she had paid more attention. Hearing a dull thud, she glanced up to see one of the things had landed a short distance from their little hideout. It was frightening, but beautiful, shining green scales with a long neck, a trail of spikes from its head to the tip of its long tail and a narrow head with rows of pointy white teeth. It only had two legs, and they ended in terribly long, horrifying claws. Its wings folded along its body smoothly as it turned and slowly made its way towards their little alcove, swiveling its neck, and its slitted yellow eyes zeroed in on her.

She began to bang the flint and steel together with all her might, a small cry escaping her lips. Estat worked his way to her and slid his hands around hers. With his guidance, Melanie saw sparks begin to fly. She moved it closer to the torch's tip, refusing to look up at the owner of those two great, clawed appendages as they came within several feet of them. Finally, a spark ignited the end of the torch, and she dropped the flint and steel, grabbing the torch and lifting it up. The blazing tip hit the snout of the creature that had landed above them and had peeked its head inside. Melanie screamed and swung the torch like a bat, smacking it square on the pointed nose of the second bird lizard. Both creatures screeched in surprise, and their heads disappeared from view. She held the torch out in front of her, watching the only one of them she could see. It used a strange little claw on its wing to brush at its burnt snout.

She almost felt sorry for it. For a few short, tense minutes the creatures paced about, both on the ground and atop the rock sheltering them. The third had joined the one on the ground but did not attempt to come close. She held the torch high and at times waved it at them when one ventured close or peeked down from above. A short time later, they must have decided to hunt elsewhere, and all three leaped up into the air and flapped their leathery wings, disappearing among the mountains. She didn't put the torch out immediately, and they sat there for a little longer. "Will they be back?" she asked finally. Estat shrugged. "Well, if they're anything like creatures in my world, they'll probably come back if they don't find anything else to eat. At least they circle about first; that will give us some warning." She was cautious as she left the protection of the stone. Melanie searched the skies for a long moment before helping Estat out.

He looked upset. "What's wrong? We're safe now. They're gone." He placed a hand on her arm and wrinkled his brow, still frowning. "Oh, I'm alright now… it's my fault, I should have gotten us under cover sooner." He shook his head and patted his own chest.

Was he saying it was his fault? But that was ridiculous; he was blind and could not have known what was going on. "It's fine, Estat. It's really not your fault." He was still frustrated, but she wasn't quite sure why, and there was no way for her to find out.

They continued their trek along the rocky passes between the mountains. The only way to tell if they were going the right direction was by following the sun, which had risen to the north according to the map in the book. They came upon a small creek and took a break, drinking some of the cool, clear water before washing the cuts and bruises on their feet. It was nice to drink water like this for a change. It tasted so clean, nothing like tap water or even bottled water. They each ate an apple before continuing on their way. The rest renewed her energy; Estat was also getting along a little better, though he still looked unhappy.

Time and again as they traveled, Melanie wished he could talk with her. She tried simply talking about her own world and what it was like, of her school, friends and even herself. By the end of the day her throat was dry, and she was happy to see another little stream trickling down from a cliff-side. Again they took a long break and re-filled the strange little animal skin pouches of water that Estat had brought. Melanie looked up to the sky. She had been walking away from the sun as it set to the south, but now it was sinking below the mountains, and she worried it would be more difficult to get their bearings.

"It's going to be dark soon. Should we keep going? Is there a small farm or maybe a few country homes out here?" Estat shook his head in response. "I suppose you didn't happen to bring a tent or a sleeping bag, did you?"

Again he shook his head no, and she frowned. "Did you expect me to find shelter out here or something? Why did we come out here anyway? Where are we headed?" She tried not to sound too frustrated, but she didn't relish the prospect of sleeping out in the open.

Estat frowned and turned his face to the ground. She immediately felt sorry for raising her voice in anger to him. "Look, I'm not used to camping out much. My parents did it when we were little and it was fun then, but I hated camping after I started high school, so we just stopped going." She sighed and sat down next to him. "I'm sorry, I guess I just have to accept the fact that we aren't in the city anymore, and I don't think we're even in Oregon. Heck, we just aren't in my world at all." For the first time since Melanie had arrived, she began to realize how far from home she really was. She couldn't stop the tears. Something in her voice must have alerted Estat, because he then put his arm around her and pulled her to him. She wrapped her arms around him and had a good long cry.

When she finally managed to stop, she pulled away and wiped her eyes. As she looked up into his face, she gasped. He had been crying, too. "How could I be so selfish? I'm so sorry. Here I am blubbering about that, and you're mute and blind! It must be awful." She hugged him tightly. Estat pulled her away and smiled to her, his gentle hands on her shoulders. He nodded once in thanks.

That night the two of them slept in a grassy patch under the stars. Melanie tried to start a fire again with the flint and steel, but after several failed attempts, she threw them down in disgust. Estat leaned over and his hand made strange flicks and waves over the fire pit and suddenly flames leapt up from it. "How did you do that?" she gasped in surprise. He only smiled and sat back. She stared at the flames in amazement, but of course, he could not tell her what he had done.

Melanie half expected to see three moons, but to her relief there was only one. She was thankful that it was also not as cold as she thought it would be; perhaps that was because this was a volcanic area, but this only made her more nervous about falling asleep. She heard the chirping of crickets and began to worry about spiders, mosquitoes and other insects as well as the lizard creatures, which only kept her awake longer. There were no constellations in the sky she recognized, but then again, she hadn't learned much about the stars. Melanie realized, too, how little she knew about surviving in the wild. Despite the new worries, she managed to slip into a fitful sleep.

-20-

ELSTAFF CITY

The journey to Elstaff was so much more relaxing than her crazy flight to the castle. The horse she had been given was white with solid black legs from its knees down and was called Swift. Regence had explained that he'd chosen her because she was gentle and safe for beginning riders. This proved useful since Ralley had to be taught how to hold the reins, steer, and make the mare speed up or slow down. Once she got the hang of it, things went smoothly, and Ralley found that Swift needed little guidance and simply followed the other horses in their little group. Talon rode at the front with Regence and herself riding just behind him. The supply wagons rumbled along behind them so the dust would not bother her, which she appreciated. The rest of the men, all of them riding warhorses, were positioned around the entire group with the exception of Talon, forming a sort of human/equine shield against any bandits. The Dragon had taken on its blade form, much to her utter surprise, a beautiful dagger with a large red ruby on the hilt that reminded her of its eyes. She carried it at her hip in a specially made leather belt and sheath, constantly reminding her of the strange world she had found herself in.

"Regence, can I ask you some questions about this place?" Ralley had gotten quite used to the slow plodding and felt comfortable enough in the saddle to start a conversation.

"Certainly, your Majesty, you may ask me anything you wish." His kind smile reminded Ralley of her father, and she wondered if that was why Talon liked him so much as well, since she could imagine that Talon's own father had little time to be with him.

"Dragons, castles, royalty and the bandits you guys keep talking about, they are all real. Does this mean that when you talk about the demon forest, there are big huge monsters with horns and stuff lurking around in there?" Regence laughed aloud, and it made her feel silly for asking such a question. "Well, that's good, I thought…"

"Of course there are frightening monsters in the demon forest. Otherwise it would not be called that," Regence continued to laugh.

Talon turned to look back at her. "Are there no monsters where you come from?"

"Of course there aren't!" Ralley frowned, feeling he was making fun of her again. "My world is monster free, and that's just the way I like it!"

Regence smiled. "It sounds like your world would be a good place to live. How is it you have no castles or monsters there?"

"Well, you could say our world has castles from older times, but now we build skyscrapers and sturdy houses and we just don't have monsters, just normal animals."

Regence raised an eyebrow, "Skyscrapers? What a strange name…"

"It's because they are so tall you can watch clouds go by right out the window." She giggled at his awed expression.

"Your world sounds truly incredible… and there are no bandits?"

"Unfortunately, there are, but we just call them thieves, serial killers and gangsters. I guess we have our own monsters… they're just in the shape of humans." She shrugged. "I suppose wherever you go there will always be good people and bad people." Regence gave a sad nod.

They rode on in silence as the sun began to set. Ralley stared at the fields and trees, the small farmers houses that they passed every so often. It was just like the ride with Jerel as they traveled to Eagle Crest. The scenery was beautiful, and instead of the sound of one wagon rumbling along behind a single horse, there were four clattering wagons, four mules and seventeen horses clopping out a beat on the dirt road. They passed many people heading for the castle, and Ralley wondered if any of them went there to see her. Most of them looked like simple farmers like Jerel, hauling their goods to a bigger market, but some appeared a bit sinister, hiding beneath heavy cloaks with large swords at their sides. She did feel much safer in this larger escort with the soldiers and their weapons. She was even a little eager to watch them in action, having thought all the movie sword fights she'd seen on TV were really cool.

Just as the sun was disappearing and more people on the road were coming their way, she could make out many dim lights of the city ahead. Talon slowed their party with a raised hand. A man from the small crowd heading their way shouted, "Welcome to Elstaff City, Majesty! Have you news of the new

Empress?" This caused several more shouts from the gathering of people, hailing the prince and asking questions about the new Empress.

Ralley leaned over to speak with Regence. "How do they know about that? I thought you people had no way to communicate so quickly."

"We have sent messengers to ride out all over the country and inform villages, cities and kingdoms of any news from Castle DeGrail. They are swift riders; I am sure the messenger sent here has already gone, as well as the two others that passed through here."

"Where are they all going?" Ralley remembered the map she had seen in the room off the library and tried to recall how large the continent had been.

"The first is bound for Castle Ravens keep to the South, another is riding east to Castle Foresta, and the final one will travel the longest to the village of Tradewood, where he will give his message to another, who will in turn spread the word to the north."

Ralley brightened. "Tradewood! I've heard of that one from Jerel."

Regence nodded and smiled to her. "Yes, it is a prosperous town, sitting at the very center of our country. Trade is best there since goods from both the northern and the southern countries are traded there. It is a good place to send messengers for news from the north as well."

It sounded like an interesting place to Ralley, and she decided she definitely wanted to see it. For now, the sights and sounds of Elstaff pulled her eyes this way and that. Talon pressed on through the crowd, nodding politely to the din of questions assaulting him. He paid them little mind and did not, in any way, indicate that Ralley was the very Empress they asked about. This did not surprise her so much. It wasn't like the messengers had a picture of her to post up in shop windows, and she wasn't dressed in any extravagant or flashy clothing. Still, she felt like a celebrity with the crowds pressing in to get a look at the royal procession. Talon brought them to a two-story building with a large stable attached to it. Ralley realized, by the simple picture of a bed engraved on a wooden sign in the front, that this was an inn.

The innkeeper hurried out, followed by two small boys. He bowed low as Talon dismounted. "Welcome your Majesty, welcome to Elstaff! My wife will prepare you and your men a feast!"

Talon smiled and nodded. "I thank you. We are on a diplomatic mission for the Empress; give us four of your best rooms."

The innkeeper bowed deeply and instructed his two boys to take their horses to the stable and care for them, the cart servants doing the same. He then led them all into the main part of the inn that had several tables, which they filled. The meal was not as extravagant as the one she had before leaving the castle but it was just as good, prepared with care and served by the man's wife and his daughter, who was not much older than herself. The girl smiled at Ralley with a look of envy, then served Talon, blushing brightly as he smiled back and took the plate. Ralley rolled her eyes, annoyed, but realized that Talon too had celebrity status and was probably well known as the richest available bachelor in the entire country.

For the first time, she saw him in a new light, the handsome and strong young prince out to fetch his princess. She giggled out loud, Talon and Regence lifting their eyes from their meals to rest on her. "Sorry, just a funny thought." She went back to her meal with a vengeance. They must think her very strange, she thought, trying to put herself in their shoes. A girl from another world where there are no unicorns and dragons, showing up in her night clothes talking of cars and telephones.

After the meal, they left for their rooms. Five of the warriors were chosen to take shifts throughout the night to guard their wagons and supplies from thieves. The warriors, archers and cart drivers were split among three of the bedrooms, which left Talon, Regence and herself a room of their own. With only two beds, Regence insisted he would be the one to sleep on an unrolled mat on the floor that had been included in their supplies. There was a small partition in the room where one could privately dress, and she used this to get into her sheep pajamas that had been cleaned and returned to her. She would have felt rather silly wearing such a thing in front of Talon and Regence, but they had already seen her wearing it out in public, so it no longer mattered; besides, it was the only thing from her world that she had with her now, and the riding clothes would have been uncomfortable.

Long after Talon and Regence had fallen asleep, she found herself lying awake, staring at the only window in the room. Unlike the city back home, this one was so much quieter at night. She climbed back out of bed and pulled open the window and shutters. She stood at the window, gazing down at the road below, watching, as an occasional horse and buggy would pass and perhaps a person or two. The roof creaked and she jerked in surprise, the adrenaline tickling her toes. She rolled her eyes and shook her head, thinking it must have been the sounds of the old roof settling. Again the roof creaked right over her head, and she jumped back from the window. The next moment a dark figure swung into the opening and she wheeled back in surprise, letting out a short scream as she tripped over one of her boots and landed on her back.

The dark figure pressed forward, raising its arm. She caught the glint of a short blade as it descended upon her. Something came to her hand, and just as she grabbed hold of it, Talon's sword swung over her from her left and met the attackers' blade with a loud clash of metal. He leaned forward and forced the intruder back. Ralley scrambled backwards until she met the wall, not yet looking to the object in her hand. Talon and the stranger began to exchange blows, and she watched as Regence joined the fight. She scrambled to her feet, but remained standing against the wall, as far away from the swinging swords as possible. The dark one was holding the two of them off, and she gasped in horror as Talon took a sword blow to the shoulder.

"I am with you," came the dragon's voice in her head. Her eyes darted wildly around the room and spotted the sheath that held the Blade Beast, but it was no longer there. She now lifted the object in her hand to find she already held the jeweled dagger. Not knowing how best to use it, she flung it toward the intruder.

Ralley had always been horrible at softball, and throwing blades was definitely not her thing, yet when she hurled the blade, it flew like a bullet from a gun and embedded itself into the leg of the stranger. Yelling out, the intruder fell to one knee, and together, Talon and Regence drove their blades into his chest. Ralley clamped her hands over her mouth, horrified at what had just taken place in only a matter of seconds.

The door burst open and several of the warriors from the next room hurried in. "Search the area around the inn and stables!" Talon shouted to them. "There may be more!" The warriors bowed and hurried out of the room.

Regence rushed over to her. "Are you alright, milady?"

Ralley's eyes darted from the prone body to Regence. "Who is that? Is he dead? Was he trying to kill me?" Regence did not answer her questions; he only put a comforting hand on her shoulder.

Talon kneeled down and pulled away the cloth that covered the face. "He is no one I would recognize ... Regence?"

Patting her shoulder a final time, Regence straightened and moved back over to the body, looking him over a moment before fishing out a strange emblem that hung around his neck. "An assassin by the look of it."

"Assassin?" Ralley could feel her whole body shaking. "H ... how do you know?"

"The symbol is from an assassin's guild. The question is," Regence said frowning. "Was he after you, or Talon?"

Talon shook his head as his eyes met hers. "I do not know, but this means we have a problem."

~ 21 ~

THE ROAD TO TRADEWOOD

For the remainder of the night, Talon had decided that he and Regence would keep watch in two shifts. The warriors had returned with nothing to report, and the time had gone by without further interruption. Talon surmised that the assassin had been alone, but his target was a mystery; Ralley could simply have been in the way when he burst through the window. Regence bandaged Talon's shoulder where the intruder had caught him with his sword and after some time of tossing about, Ralley had finally gone to sleep. The next morning, Talon had refused the innkeeper's offer of a meal and bade his men to eat from their own supplies. Ralley had been severely shaken and remained quiet for most of the morning until they sat down to eat their rations at the inn.

"Talon? Is your arm okay?" She was not quite looking at him and fingered the coarse bread in her hands.

"It is...fine..." He watched her a moment, somehow glad that she had asked. "What about you?"

"I nearly got skewered then watched a guy die right in front of me. How do you think I feel?" she snapped.

Talon frowned and leaned back in his chair, sparing a glance to Regence and giving him a confused shrug. But Regence merely shook his head and continued to eat. "Ralley, such things can happen often when you are… er… in the company of royalty, but we are here to protect you," Talon tried to explain in hushed tones.

"What?" Ralley said with surprise, dropping the bread back to the table. "What do you mean they happen often?" she shouted.

"Keep your voice down," Talon warned her through gritted teeth, glancing at the innkeeper, who was talking with several guests who had come down from their rooms.

Ralley eyed them and then returned her gaze to Talon. She must have realized that all the shouting would be rather dangerous. "I see… that's why we aren't traveling in style. So, how many people are out to kill me?" she asked, keeping her voice low.

Talon frowned at her. "You should not be talking about that here. Someone could hear you."

"Like the people trying to kill me?" Her eyes swept the room. "It looks to me like the innkeeper is having them eat far away from us. Besides, all these warriors around us doesn't exactly hide us now does it?"

"That is not the point," Talon growled. "They know who I am, and the assassin could very well have been after me. You were just in the way."

Regence put a hand on both of their arms. "Talon is right, this is not the place to talk about this. Best we hurry and finish our breakfast. The sooner we leave for Tradewood, the better. We can talk on the road."

The three of them remained quiet for the rest of their meal. Talon apologized to the innkeeper for what had happened that night and the body he must tend to. He then thanked him for the good night's rest and yesterday's meal. The innkeeper's sons and their own servants had the wagons and horses ready to go when they stepped out of the inn. They resumed their protective formation and proceeded through the streets of the city as its occupants were readying for the new day. Talon kept a sharp eye out for anything out of the ordinary as they paraded through the center of Elstaff, leading their party at a quick pace, wanting to get through the city as quickly as possible. Glancing back every so often, he could see Ralley looking around her. She appeared nervous now, maybe even vulnerable. Feeling somewhat responsible, he tried to offer her a smile when she met his eyes. Instead of smiling back, she sneered at him and turned her head away. Talon grunted and turned back around in his saddle. Some Empress, he thought. She is nothing like Mother at all, nor any other Empress who has ever sat on the throne. And yet… this appealed to him, even though he did not want to admit it. The remainder of the ride through Elstaff went smooth and quiet. Some people cheered his passing; others stared on in quiet wonder, and most bowed or curtsied.

As the houses along the roadside thinned, he slowed the party to a more comfortable pace and spared another glance back at Ralley. Her attention was on the homes they were passing, and she had loosened her hold on the reins of her horse; her body moved more freely with the equines movements. She became progressively more relaxed as they traveled farther away from the city. Talon too became more lighthearted as they went. He had never been past Elstaff City. His father had rarely allowed him to travel far, and Talon had never truly understood this. He felt his father was constantly holding him back, and perhaps that was the reason he wished to go on this trek. Now that he was past Elstaff, his spirit was lifting into the air like a caged bird set free.

"It looks like we have a little company, your Majesty," Regence called out.

Talon turned in the saddle to see a small group of riders some distance behind them on the road. He counted five of them, and all of them wore hoods over their heads; the gleam of long swords could be seen at their hips. He waved to catch the attention of the men surrounding the carts. "Keep on alert, men, and keep an eye on the riders at our backs." The swordsmen and archers nodded, not saying a word.

"Wait a minute! What's going on?" Ralley called out, her voice telling Talon that she was growing nervouse again. "Are they after us?"

"It is alright, milady, there are but five of them and twelve of us, excluding those of you who need not fight of course," he heard Regence say. It was true; those men were few, and his warriors were expertly trained. Still, he felt uneasy about them and decided to play it safe.

They continued on at a fair pace, and the small group behind them kept the same distance. They traveled this way for half the day, constantly keeping their eyes on the mysterious riders behind them, though they continued to keep their distance. Having enough of it, Talon called a halt. He turned Phoenix about. "Regence, stay with her, I want to know what these people are up to."

"Nonsense, Majesty, I am coming with you, I cannot let you meet them on your own."

"Do not argue with me, I am still a prince. You must stay here and protect our Empress. I will not go alone." He motioned to the warriors. "You four, come with me." He nudged Phoenix forward, not wanting to give Regence any time to argue with him. He led the warriors back down the road towards the group, who had stopped as well. He halted his horse several lengths away. "You there, what is your business?" Talon called.

One of them rode forward and stopped. Talon assumed that he must be the leader. "You are Prince Talon Endrayen from Castle DeGrail?" the man questioned.

Narrowing his eyes, Talon put a hand to his sword hilt. "I am. Who are you and why do you trail us?"

"We are only curious your Majesty, who is the woman who rides with you? She has a foreign look about her."

"That is none of your concern," Talon replied.

"I assure you Majesty, we are simply interested if she is a prisoner?" the man said, leaning forward. "We can certainly take her off your hands."

This took Talon by surprise. He had not realized that it might look as though they were transporting a foreign prisoner. His mother had once told him that not so long ago many kings of other kingdoms would transport prisoners in such a way and refer to it as a "diplomatic mission," but that was so long ago, and the first great Emperor had abolished much of the slavery and imprisoning of foreigners. He eyed these men more carefully. Something was familiar about them, their hooded cloaks. In moments he realized what it was and drew his sword, his men immediately doing the same. "You wear the same garb as the assassin who came after us at the inn!" Talon shouted. His men needed no encouragement; they rushed forward, and Talon swung his sword at the leader, who had drawn his blade in time to block his attack.

"What is wrong, your Majesty? We only want the girl; she would fetch a mighty fine price." The man chuckled as he viciously attacked Talon.

The leader's swordplay was good, but Talon had trained under the best swordsmen in the land; he easily blocked his attacks and struck a blow on the dark one's thigh. "So you are slavers then!" Talon shouted between thrusts, "Your man nearly killed her!"

"Then we would have sold you; a prince with such lovely hair could make good money in foreign lands," the man said smirking.

Talon's angry blows forced the man to take a more defensive stance with his sword, and he struggled with his horse as Phoenix pressed in upon it and began to bite at its legs. How could such a thing as slavery still exist hundreds of years after it was banished, and how dare he insult the prince of DeGrail? The man's horse danced back, and he took this opportunity to turn it sharply about, his heels goading it forward as he charged through his small cluster of men, still fighting with Talon's own warriors. Talon realized that the man was shouting a retreat as he slapped the rump of his steed with the flat of his blade, commanding it forward at full speed. The two able to disengage did so and hastily followed their retreating leader. One of the cloaked men lay dead on the dirt road, his horse trotting into the fields; the other had lost the reins of his mount to one of the warriors, and apparently his sword as well, for he sat hunched over the saddle in pain, clutching his injured arm.

"Shall we follow them my lord?" one of the warriors asked.

"No, leave them. Recover the horse of the dead one and secure the injured one." Talon watched as the three disappeared down the road. He wanted badly to go after them, to make sure they were unable to come back and try their luck again, but he felt certain that his warriors had far superior swordsmanship than that group of pathetic louts. He turned Phoenix back towards the others. Regence had a proud smile upon his face as Talon pulled up to them.

"Looks like you did splendidly, Talon. I had the archers ready, but it seems you did not need them."

Talon frowned. "Three of them escaped. What if they return?" He had not felt that things had gone well. He would have preferred if all the riders were either dead or their prisoners.

Regence smiled. "Then we will be ready for them."

Talon chuckled. It was true; if they returned, Talon would finish them off. He spared a glance at Ralley, and she nodded to him, not quite smiling, but seemingly satisfied that she was still well protected. Once again, Talon returned to the front of the group, his warriors returning to their original positions, with the exception of one, who rode next to their prisoner to keep him boxed in. They continued on in silence, the prisoner resigned to his fate, traveling eastward until the road began to curve to the north through a forest. Talon was going through some questions in his head, considering what he wanted to ask the prisoner once they stopped.

"Look at that fog!" Regence exclaimed as they entered the wooded area.

At first, Talon ignored him, but when Regence repeated himself, Talon took note of the fast rolling fog that blew in through the trees around them. There was something strange about this haze, something unnatural, something… was coming.

-22-

IGNITING A FLAME

Estat woke and rubbed his eyes; they were a bit fuzzy. He tried to look about him, but he still saw only a dull yellow color. He panicked only a moment before remembering that he had lost his sight. He cursed himself, but no sound came from his throat, and he sighed, remembering also that he could not speak. There was movement near him, and he remembered Melanie. He put a hand out and came in contact with her shoulder. He gently shook her until she groaned. They had to get moving before the mountain drakes found them here.

"Huh? What ... ?" He heard her sit up and gasp. "Oh, I forgot where I was!" she exclaimed after a moment.

Estat gave a soundless chuckle, as this was how he himself had felt. He got to his feet and began to stretch his sore muscles. His chest still ached, but it was far better than it had been. She had done such great work, he wondered if it was the magic he saw in her, but he had not heard her chanting any spell. They made a small breakfast of the food they brought and drank from their water skins, re-filling them with fresh mountain water before moving on. His feet felt cracked, and he stumbled over almost everything they encountered, slowing their progress immensely. Melanie kept apologizing each time and he guessed she felt it was her fault. Finally, he pulled on her to stop and sat down.

"What's wrong? Are you alright?" she asked, her gentle voice filled with concern.

Estat pulled off his lightly made, and now quite tattered, shoes. He heard her gasp and realized it must be as bad as he thought.

"How awful! I'm so sorry! No wonder you were stumbling about like a blind man … er … no offence."

Estat chuckled, and though no sound came, she must have seen him for she laughed as well. "Here, let me get some more of those herbs." He could hear her rummaging through the bag again, and after a moment, he felt her warm hands and the tickle of herbs as she treated and wrapped his feet with immense care. "What are we going to do? I can't carry you very far, and you're not going to be able to walk much on this."

If only he had his eyes and voice back, he could summon Malstraun to him, and this long trek would not have been necessary. He reached out to find her hand and instead found her cloth-covered foot. She too had been walking all this time without any shoes at all! Curse this blindness! And curse him for a fool for bringing her on this trek of hardship! She must have seen the pain in his face, for she took his hand in hers. "Estat, don't worry, I'm fine, not as bad as you are at this point. As a matter of fact, I can wrap my feet in these bandages; it will help protect them. According to the map you showed me, we should be out of these mountains and into a forest before too long."

He nodded, glad that she knew how to get her bearings and follow the map even though this world was foreign to her.

"I was wondering, Estat, you made a fire last night with your hands, why didn't you do it on the torch when the lizards attacked us? Wouldn't it have been easier?"

Estat pointed to his eyes then went to clap his hands together, purposefully missing. With such a small target as a torch head he would have needed to use his eyes to concentrate on one spot; without doing so, he could have missed and set fire to something else, even her. It was difficult to get the point across to her, but after a time she finally guessed it.

"Well, thanks just the same then, but is that magic something anyone can do?" This confirmed what he had been guessing, that Melanie had no idea of the power that she carried within her. He shook his head, but pointed at himself and to her. She laughed. "You're saying that not everyone has the power, but we do? I haven't done anything like that in my whole life."

Estat pulled a book from the sack and ran his hand along the cover, making sure it was the one with the hand symbol on the front. He placed his hand on the book, then pointed to his chest, then pointed at her.

"You're going to teach me?" She sounded excited, but a little doubtful.

He nodded and smiled, passing the book to her. The first thing he had to do was get her to be able to read the book, and that took a simple few hand gestures that he knew he could easily teach her; it would be a reasonably safe thing to teach. After showing her the hand movements with his own, he pointed to her and bade her to try it over the book. She did so several times, insisting that she had done exactly what he had but nothing had changed at all, but he was a patient teacher, and he felt her soft hands as she went through the motions, correcting tiny mistakes of the positions of her fingers. When he was satisfied that she had it correct, he signaled her to try again. It took several more attempts till he heard her gasp.

"I think something happened! I saw, a flicker of light around the book!" Estat nodded happily and reached over, finding the book in her lap and opening it. "Oh!" She exclaimed, her voice filled with wonder and excitement. "I can read it!" She began to read the first page. "Hand Magic takes time and patience to learn. One must practice each hand position many times before trying the more difficult magic. It is important to have a quiet room with little to no distractions so that one may practice without interruption since this often leads to broken learning." She paused and he could hear her flipping through the pages. "It's readable now, and so beautifully hand written!" Estat gave her a proud smile and a nod. "Wait a minute … it says here that it was written by Estat Valoren. Isn't that you?"

He chuckled and nodded, feeling prouder still. "That's great! I've never met an author, and the book is huge. Your handwriting is wonderful!" Estat could not have felt more pleased at that moment. Only his mother had ever given him such loving praise. Estat could feel his face growing hot and turned his head down, not wanting her to notice. She must not have since he could still hear her flipping through the pages. "Even the pictures are so well drawn; you are absolutely amazing!" He heard the book close at that moment. "Estat? What's wrong?"

Estat had not thought of his family in many years. He felt a tear trickle down his cheek. They were tears of joy, and he smiled happily at her and took her hand, kissing it softly. She had stirred memories and feelings within him that he had abandoned long ago, but it felt wonderful, and he wanted to take her into his arms and kiss her but settled with placing the back of her hand to his forehead, feeling its warmth. Moments later it was she who slid closer to him and held his face in her hands; pulling him close and kissing him with her full, smooth lips. She then hugged him against her. "I don't care where we're going, I just want to spend more time with you, and I want to find out more about you." Estat smiled, sliding his own arms around her; he wanted the same, to know more about this young woman who, though he could not see her, was more beautiful that he could ever imagine. He wished to do something special for her, but what?

An idea came to him, and he pulled away from her, pulling the sack close to him and fishing out the cloth wrapped orb. He uncovered it and placed it in her hand. "Can I check on my sister?" she asked eagerly. He nodded, his smile brightening. After a few moments she began to tell him what she saw. "She's riding a horse through a countryside. There's a man riding ahead of her with really long blond hair and another man with a fancy hat. It looks like they're being escorted somewhere with four big carts pulled by horses and armored men with swords."

Estat listened, but there was no way to tell where her sister was, or where she was going. The crystal ball only showed images of things that were happening at the current moment and it did not let you hear what was being said. After a short time, she thanked him and handed the orb back. When she did, he thought about Malstraun and waited for Melanie to tell him what she saw. "I can't see much; it's a cave I think, really dark with huge stalactites and stalagmites. Wait a second; I think I see something moving just a bit. Yes it... oh... it's huge and long! Like a giant anaconda, but I've never seen one that big before! Is that its head? It has got horns on its head like a bull but they're longer and come closer together..."

Satisfied that Malstraun was still resting in his cave, he nodded. Taking the orb back, he re-wrapped it in the cloth and placed it back into the bag. "Wait a minute! You mean we are going to see that thing? What if it eats us?" Estat laughed hard at this, though all she would have seen was the shaking of his shoulders, and heard his breath as he let it out and gasped for more.

"What's so funny?" He could hear the annoyance in her voice, and he put his hand to his lips and made a soured face. Malstraun had never been much for eating animals, much less people. He then tried to wiggle his hand like a fish. "Oh... he eats fish? Well that's a relief. He looks like he could eat a dolphin!"

Soon they stood and trudged on, their feet still sore. The short break and wrapping had helped his feet tremendously, and again he marveled at her skill. Oh, to speak to her would have been such a joy. To learn her otherworldly ways and to see it through her eyes in the crystal ball. Curse his foolishness for allowing Xenopus to catch him off guard! Their continued trek went on mostly in silence accept for an "oops sorry!" Or "watch out, there's a ledge here" from Melanie. As the yellow light in his eyes began to fade, he realized it must have been approaching evening, but to his delight, Melanie paused saying, "We've come out of the mountains into a forest!" Estat let out a great sigh as if he had been holding his breath all this time. The walking would be far easier from here on. He nudged her onward. It would be best to sleep under the cover of the trees and find wood for a fire, since they would need it now that they were out of the heated land of the volcano.

They found another stream coming out of the mountains and into the wood, and here they took another break. Melanie re-wrapped his feet with the same great care as before, and she commented that they had looked far better even though they had trekked across the rest of the mountainous countryside. They refreshed themselves and moved on, heading north following the sweep of the mountains. This would help them keep their bearings easily since the mountain range ended a short distance from the sea, and Malstraun's cave would be there at the northernmost tip of the land.

They stopped in a reasonably open area with a nice patch of grass underfoot. Estat waited there while Melanie gathered wood from the nearby trees and brought it back to make a fire. Estat showed her the hand signs to make the fire, but in the end he lit the fire himself. He could not explain it to her, but firemaking was a bit more advanced, and he did not want to push her into such things. As the two settled down for the night, a distant howl could be heard. "What was that?" she asked with tinge of fear in her voice. If he could have said anything, he would have told her not to worry; then again, the forest of demons was not just home to demons, but all manner of monsters. He tugged gently on her arm and patted the grass, bidding her to relax and get some rest. But when next the howl was heard far closer than the first, he too sat upright.

-23-

BLACK WOLF ATTACK

The fog thickened around them, making it impossible for Ralley to see five feet in front of her. Talon raised his hand, bringing the soldiers and their horses to a halt.

Ralley brought her horse to a stop just to the right of Talon. "What's wrong?"

"I do not like this fog; there is something strange about it." Talon peered ahead.

The fog appeared normal to her, other than the fact that it had spread around them so fast. "Scary woods, scary fog… seems appropriate to me." She was still a little shaken from all that had happened to them since they left the castle, but fog didn't scare her in the least.

Moments later a metallic howl vibrated the air around them, sending a shiver up Ralley's spine. Horses shuffled, stamping the ground, and she found herself fighting to control her own mount as she shifted underneath her. "What in the heck was that?" It had sounded like the howling of a wolf through an old loudspeaker.

"Could it be the black wolves?" one of the soldiers asked Talon.

"Black wolves?" Ralley glanced up at Talon, raising a brow.

"Black wolves attacked my father the morning before I left for Eagle Crest…" Talon began, but three black wolf-like creatures racing towards them from the fog ahead interrupted him. They came at them so fast that there was little time to react. The one in the middle was closest, and it bounded off the ground and into the air straight at Talon, fangs bared, its eyes glowing red.

"Talon, look out!" Ralley screamed as she swung her hand up as if to stop the beast. Before Talon could draw his sword, the Blade Beast had wrenched free of its sheath and shot at the black wolf, lodging itself into its neck, hurtling it off course to crash to the ground between Phoenix and Crest. Another wolf leapt on the guard to her left, knocking him from his mount, the guard screaming as the two of them wrestled with each other, threatening to get tangled underfoot of her mare. Her mount reared up with a piercing squeal, and she gripped the front rim of the saddle and hung on as tightly as she could. Her horse spun around and bolted away from the others into the fog. Ralley freed one hand to fumble with the reins; she had to stop the horse before they got lost. "C'mon!" she whimpered, reaching just a little farther to take hold of the thin strap bouncing against the frightened horse's neck. Then she saw the low tree branch materialize just ahead of her. She swung her free hand up in time to block her face as she collided with it. There was a loud crack and a flash of white light, a moment of weightlessness, then a sickening thud.

Talon struggled to keep Phoenix under control as several more of the black creatures raced towards them through the fog. Regence jammed his sword into the head of one that had bitten down into Crest's foreleg. Though the horse squealed from the pain, she still remained under Regence's complete control. Phoenix, however, fought Talon's attempts to steer him, wanting to stomp on the nearest of the beasts. Talon decided this would be best and gave him free rein as still another black wolf bolted from the trees and leaped at him. This time he was ready for it. He tucked his sword's hilt in the crook of his arm, and much as he expected, the creature impaled itself upon it. Talon was nearly unseated by the sheer weight of the creature, but Phoenix danced to the side to avoid a bite from the black beast in front of him, giving Talon a chance to regain his balance. He dumped the impaled monster off his sword and used this moment to make sure Ralley was all right. To his horror he did not see her anywhere.

"Regence, the Empress!" Talon shouted. But there was not a moment to spare. Regence had his hands full keeping two more of the black creatures off his mount while the rest of his men defended the servants and their supply wagons. The creatures were everywhere, and their prisoner took this moment to turn his horse, attempting to escape. A black wolf rose up near the prisoner's mount and caught the man in the arm with its jaws. Seconds later, it had pulled him free of the saddle and was dragging him into the thick fog as he shouted in fear. Talon held on as Phoenix pounded his hooves into the beast near its feet. It did not take long before it was no longer moving. Talon spun Phoenix around and nudged him forward to aid another of his warriors struggling to defend his mount from yet another beast. Again Talon allowed Phoenix free rein as the horse pressed forward to assault the creature with another of his mad kicks. Talon spotted still another beast racing at him from the fog, with another seconds behind it, but much to his surprise, the second beast leapt upon the first and began fighting with it. The former was swiftly dispatched and lay dead at the feet of the latter. In the moment that the creature stood there and looked at Talon with shining blue eyes instead of red, he was able to discern that this one was quite different from the others. Its fur was sleek and shone like metal. It was also far thinner, with longer legs than the large bulky beasts, and it appeared more similar to a wolf. Talon moved his sword to point towards the beast. Instead of coming after him, it growled with that same metallic sound as the howl he had heard before, showing its fierce white fangs, and dashed away into the fog.

Phoenix and the warrior he had come to help, dispatched the beast they had first fought, though the solider had a severe wound on his arm. "Where is the Empress?" Talon shouted.

"Her horse bolted into the fog with her, that way my lord." The wounded soldier pointed the way with his working arm.

Talon urged Phoenix forward into the fog. He heard Regence shout out for three men to follow with him and moments later they had all caught up to him. "We must find her as quickly as possible and get back to the wagons," Regence said. Talon nodded; they had to hurry, else the other warriors and the wagons were lost.

The next thing Ralley knew, she was on her back gasping for breath. She sat up groaning and had lost feeling in her left arm; she examined it as it lay limp at her side and knew it must be broken. What now? She was still surrounded by thick fog, and her horse was nowhere in sight. Behind her she could hear the distant shouts of men and neighing of frightened horses.

"Talon!" Ralley shouted, not sure if he could hear her at all. Should she try and make her way back to them? Was it safe enough? She struggled to a sitting position, wincing from a tingling pain in her shoulder and arm. Then she spotted a white form emerge from the fog in front of her. It was definitely not her horse, but it was the size of a Great Dane, its long legs supported a sleek, furry body. Ralley tensed as she gazed at the almost wolf-like creature; it was far larger than a real wolf, and it trotted forward until it was only three feet away before stopping and cocking its narrow head at her. The white wolfish creature appeared curious, which made her relax some, and its eyes were a bright green instead of the frightening red glow of the black ones.

"Nice wolfie, good boy, want to chase a stick?" Ralley quested about with her right hand for a stick, her eyes on the wolf thing; maybe she could get it to leave quietly? Feeling stupid for offering it a stick as if it were a dog, she gave a nervous laugh, all the while thinking about those shows on TV telling you not to show fear to wild animals.

The white wolf gave a soft growl and turned its head to stare intently behind it, a great black form hurtled out of the fog from that direction, and its red eyes flashing as it spotted the wolf before it. The black creature was far bulkier than the white wolf she had just met; its fur was ragged and its claws were huge, reminding her of prehistoric raptor talons. The dark one growled, its canine teeth like vampire fangs, and it dodged to the side of the sleek white creature, intent upon Ralley. Her good hand reached for the Blade Beast but it was no longer there. The white wolf was not to be ignored; it intercepted the black creature easily, halting its progress. Was the white wolf protecting her, Ralley wondered? Or was it simply unhappy with the intrusion? Either way, the two of them engaged in a brawl of teeth and claws, the black monster roaring like a lion. It was hard to tell who was doing better; their movements were much too fast for Ralley to figure out. She scooted away from them, not wanting to catch their attention. Maybe she could slip away while they fought and get back to Talon and the others. She spotted another black figure bursting from the fog. Panic gripped her as the new red-eyed creature leapt high into the air and descended upon her. She wished Talon were here.

Its fangs were only a foot away when another creature bowled into it, knocking it to the ground. It was the Blade Beast in its dragon form, rolling back to its feet and leaping forward to wrestle with her attacker, its long tail wrapped about its bulk as the two rolled about. Ralley heard the pounding of hooves and turned her head in time to see Phoenix gallop into view, Talon on his back, sword in hand. Ralley smiled, relieved to see him. In moments, Regence and the rest of her escort surrounded the white wolf, which stood next to the now prone creature it had fought. Several crossbows were cocked and pointed at it, but the wolf simply perked its ears and crouched down, ready to bolt.

"Wait!" Ralley shouted, getting up on her knees, "Don't hurt him! That one helped me!"

"What are you saying?" Talon dismounted, sword in hand and stood next to her.

"He killed that black thing with the glowing eyes! It was after me, and he stopped it." She then glanced over her shoulder at the blade creature, which was also now standing over its unmoving victim. It trotted between the horses and examined the white wolf. For a moment it appeared as though they spoke to one another, the dragon making low rumbling noises from its throat as the wolf creature relaxed and sat on its haunches, ears perked, its green eyes intent upon the dragon. Satisfied, the Blade Beast turned and slipped passed the horses to circle Ralley, reverting to its blade form and replacing itself into the sheath at her hip.

Talon bent to help Ralley to her feet. She winced, her arm dangling uselessly at her side. "Are you alright?" Talon spoke to her in a gentle tone.

"I think I broke my arm," she said, a little flustered. Ralley glanced up into his eyes. Those blue eyes framed by his long blond hair that reminded her of when she was rescued from the blackness. Realizing that she was staring, Ralley turned away, feeling her face grow hot.

"What shall we do with the wolf, Sire?" asked one of the guards.

Talon regarded the white wolf for a moment. "Restrain it. Perhaps it will still be of some use."

"Hey! Wait a minute!" Ralley grabbed hold of Talon's cloak with the hand of her good arm.

"We cannot be sure this wolf is not just as dangerous as the others." Talon insisted.

"Well, I'm the Empress, and I order you to let him go!" Ralley retorted.

Talon stiffened. "You cannot simply go about waving your authority around that way!"

"Of course I can! I'm the Empress, and I can do whatever I want to!" Ralley shot back.

"That's ridiculous! There are rules to being Empress!"

"If I'm Empress, then I make the rules," she said putting her hand on her hip.

"You cannot change the rules as you please!" Talon crossed his arms.

There was a soft chuckle. "Well, actually she can."

Talon spun around to eye Regence, but he shrugged his shoulders as if to say, "Wasn't me." Ralley glanced around at the guards who had all been staring at her and Talon while they spoke, but now they all stared down where the white wolf had sat. In its place was a man; though he appeared to be around Talon's age, there was something odd about him that she couldn't quite pinpoint. He had pale skin, the same glittering green eyes as the wolf, and his loose shirt, pants and ankle boots were all as white as his shoulder length hair. He sat there, legs crossed, hands resting on his knees, watching the two of them with a merry smile.

-24-

THE SYMBOL

B rek had been exhausted from his ordeal and spent the
night curled up on the pillows in the main cavern. Mioria
had requested more time to speak with Xenopus and Ecnair
remained with the demon now. Later that morning, Brek was
instructed to continue the work he had begun in the tower, but
to do so he needed a summoning circle. He had never drawn
a summoning circle himself since it was permanently embedded on the floor of the summoning hall. Mioria removed one of
many bottles from a shelf that glowed with a bluish substance.
She spoke the magic tongue as she intoned a spell, opening the
bottle as she did so and allowing its blue glowing contents to
drift out like a ghost. It surrounded Brek, and he cringed as its
cold tendrils brushed against him.

"Be still," Mioria whispered to him. "Think of the summoning circle, create a clear picture in your mind." Her voice was
soothing, and he closed his eyes, the image of the star within a
circle forming in his thoughts. He winced as a tendril of chill air
brushed his forehead, but he kept his eyes shut tightly. "Good,
very good," she said, her smooth voice returning to the spell.
Moments later she bid him to open his eyes. The spectral blue

light had drifted away from him and was now expanding into a large star and circle that settled to the cave floor.

"Yes, that is correct," came Xenopus' deep voice. "Now, begin your work. Create the portal that will bring forth my minions into your service."

"But... I do not know how to summon anything else but Malstraun. Those are the only symbols I know," Brek protested.

"It makes no difference. Make them as you did before, and I shall instruct you on the changes when you come to the proper symbol," he said, sounding agitated.

He wondered why it was that he was required to do all the work, but was this not what he wanted as well? To be the Grand Summoner himself? He spared a glance at Mioria, and she smiled encouragingly to him. Buoyed by her confidence in him, he stepped forward to examine the star and circle. "I need braziers at each of the points, and a red burning candle as well," he said, trying his best to sound more important than he felt.

Mioria disappeared into the second room and returned moments later, the four musicians from before were carrying the braziers and she herself was holding a red candle. "I have everything you require," she whispered as she handed him the candle, her hands lingering a moment as they touched his.

Brek felt his pulse race and he straightened, trying his best to look as though he knew exactly what he was doing. The four musicians put the braziers in place and stepped back, their faces as forlorn as ever. The lute player was staring at him intently, but Brek turned away, digging in his pocket for the chalk and parchment. He repeated the gestures he had done when he summoned Xenopus. He was aware of Mioria's gaze as she watched his every move. This made him slow his progress, wanting to get everything right and taking great pains to make the symbols correctly.

It was late in the day when he began to work on the symbol representing Malstraun, but Xenopus' deep voice halted him. "Enough, I shall instruct you on the next symbol." He had already procured a delicate piece of parchment from Mioria's stores and let it go to drift to the floor next to him. Brek took it and examined the symbol drawn there. For some reason it made him rather sick to look upon it. It was extremely detailed and reminded him of many a nightmare he'd had. The longer he stared at it, the more nauseated he felt. The symbol was alive somehow, trying to reach out of the page with open fanged mouths, frighteningly curved claws and horribly disfigured bodies, all of them tangled together.

When he heard a moaning sound in the back of his mind, he tore his eyes from the page. "What is this?" He said, not liking the sound of fear in his voice. "I've never seen a symbol like this… it moves… I could hear it…" He was at a loss for words. This was too much. "I cannot draw this!" he moaned. "I can hardly look upon it!"

Xenopus and Mioria exchanged glances. When Mioria turned to face him again, she gave him a warm smile. "Do not worry, Brek. I am certain you can do it." She walked back to him and placed a hand on his arm. "There is nothing you cannot do. If you need time to study the symbol, then take all the time you require. You must remember, you must have the strongest army possible, and that requires your expertise."

Brek faltered. "Why must I do it? Should I not have my

servant do it for me?" he said, his hopeful eyes reluctantly turning to Xenopus.

Xenopus grinned in a way that Brek found to be far too amused. "I am afraid I cannot. I am from the nether realms, and I do not have that kind of power here. Dimensions are fickle that way. I can cross into those realms that occupy the same space as this one, but those such as the nether require far more power from the home realm, which I do not possess. It must be done by your own hand."

Brek shook his head. "But it moves! How can I draw this if it changes?"

Xenopus gave him a chilling grin. "Oh, you can draw it. It is possible, and you will draw it. If you want your army, you must." All the while, Ecnair hovered nearby, snickering.

"I do not want that kind of army! I… I want an army of men not monsters…" Brek protested, his eyes darting from Xenopus to the chiding imp. "There has to be another option."

Xenopus looked at Mioria, and she turned to Brek, taking him into her arms. "Shush now, do not worry darling. Let us be logical about this, hmm? A human army could easily be defeated, and one cannot simply summon humans. They can think for themselves and decide to go with you or against you. An army of nether monsters is mindless and must do exactly as you command. We would have thousands of them, and they would not be easily defeated. Humans would cower from them, and even run. They would devastate any army that the people here placed against you. Does that not sound wonderful?"

Brek hesitated. "But… the symbol, it sickens me… how can I…"

"Worry not about the symbol, my love, it is only a drawing. Perhaps if you simply study it long enough, you will be able to draw it." Mioria gave him a gentle kiss and caressed the hand that held the chalk. "Come, try it again," she coaxed.

Brek, feeling a little dazed, returned to the star, Mioria just behind him. He knelt down and placed his chalk just above the stone floor. With a swallow, he gazed upon the symbol again. He tried staring at a single line, though it quivered a bit, he drew it on the floor. The moment his eye drifted elsewhere on the page, the line he'd drawn moved significantly. "It has moved again. What should I do?"

Mioria smiled at him. "But you did draw a line, how did you do it?" she asked.

"I…" Brek hesitated. "I just stared at one line and it held itself until I looked away…." Brek glanced at another line, concentrating on it, and there it remained as if pinned down by his gaze. He quickly drew this line as well then looked away. It moved once again. "I think I understand now," he said, a bit unsure.

"Good," soothed Mioria as she stood and backed away. Brek returned to the drawing, concentrating on another line. He was able to draw several lines on the floor, but after a while, he became too ill to continue.

"I cannot finish this now…. my eyes…" he scooted away from the drawing, leaving the paper lying next to it. "I feel sick… I keep seeing things…" he mumbled. Brek realized it was getting late, and he had barely just begun to draw the complicated image. Mioria soothed him and helped him to his feet, taking him into the other room where there was a soft, inviting bed and the lights were dim, floating about the roof of the cave like little fireflies.

"Here now, lie down and relax a while; you can finish after you have had rest." Mioria said in her sweet voice. It soothed him and Brek sank into the bed to relax. She caressed his cheek before straightening and moving out of the room as if she were floating. Her touch was enchanting, and her movements made him sigh, relaxing further.

Brek lay there for some time after the door closed behind her, staring up at the dark ceiling of the cave. Surprisingly it was not damp here, and he was thankful for that. The room even had a few home-like touches. He could make out the image of a woman on a tapestry that covered the far wall of the room. He thought it looked vaguely like Mioria, though something like that could never match her actual beauty. There was a small round table next to the bed that was rather intricately carved with birds and flowers. Atop the table were three small jars with glowing blue lights in them. They gave off a strange, almost cold, feeling and he scooted to the far side of the bed away from them.

As he stared into the darkness of a blank wall, he thought he saw something moving. The longer he stared into the darkness, the more it moved. An image took form in the etchings on the wall. It was frightening, and familiar, reminding him of the twisted image of the symbol. Brek struggled to pull the silken blankets over his body in an attempt to protect himself. He closed his eyes a moment, and then opened them again. It was gone. Brek breathed a sigh of relief. Turning over, he now faced the jars, which did not help to comfort him. The little globes of cold blue essence swirled with images of their own. He was quite certain that a man's face peered out at him with frightened and pleading eyes through that blue light, and he turned over to face the blank wall once again. The sudden outline of a monstrous shape made him gasp in fright and bring the blankets over his head.

Brek curled up underneath the flimsy protection the sheets had to offer. He shut his eyes tightly and whispered out a prayer to any of the seven gods or goddesses that would listen. He had never been much for religious prayers, nor had he ever gone into a temple or any other place of worship. The only thing he could remember now was the name of the Goddess of mercy, love and affection. "Austia," he whimpered, "Help me!"

He heard the sound of glass tinkling close to him. Sitting up in a swift motion, he eyed the room. The tapestry on the far wall quivered with the passing of a cold breeze. The jars on the bedside table clinked together, producing the chilling sound he had heard. Was it Austia speaking to him? Was she trying to reach him? To help him? He cried out, the sound was almost a mixture of joy and fear. He leapt out of the bed and ran for the door, yanking on it with all his might. He staggered back as the door blasted open, throwing him to the floor. What he saw sent him into a panic. Expecting to see the other room behind the door, he was not prepared for the black flames of hellfire that crawled into the room along the floor and walls. Standing in the doorway was a great fanged beast, its jaws wide open, screaming with the sounds of thousands of tortured souls. Its body was twisted around another beast that was broken and beaten, its body covered in burnt fur. Four pairs of claws came towards him, the tips dripping with blood. "NO! I will not finish it!" Brek screamed.

~25~

VERU THE WOLF

Talon was aghast at the white haired man sitting where the wolf-like creature had been. A shape shifter? He recovered from his surprise and swung his sword around to point at him. "What are you?" he commanded, stepping forward to get within striking distance.

"But I have not introduced myself yet!" he said cheerfully as he stood up. "I am called Veru…"

"I asked what you were, not who!" Talon snapped. "Are you the leader of these black beasts?"

"Leader?" He began to laugh, which agitated Talon all the more. "Of course not. We have been hunting these cursed beasts for quite some time."

"We?" Talon pressed his sword closer.

"My brother and I, of course," he grinned. "I shall assume that you must be Prince Talon Endrayen of DeGrail, correct? And she is the Empress; what might your name be?" He turned to gaze at Ralley.

"How do you know who I am?" now Talon's sword point was against the man's chest, but he took little notice of it; instead he watched Ralley, awaiting her answer.

"It's Ralley, from Portland," she said awkwardly.

"Port land? Is this a coastal village?" he asked, his head tipping to one side like a curious canine.

"Enough!" Talon shouted, pressing the point of his sword into Veru's chest. "I will not be ignored! I demand to know what you are and why you are following the beasts who attacked my father!"

Veru looked down at his chest. "I get the point," he said, taking the point of the sword between his two fingers and pushing it away from himself. "I am of the amarill, and my good brother and I are simply out to destroy the black beasts that began hunting in our forest but a few nights ago."

Talon wrenched his sword from Veru's grip and returned it to where it had been. "A demon, are you?" That was reason to trust him far less.

Regence dismounted from his horse and stepped over to them. "Amarill are not demons, though over time, everyone has forgotten that. Can we trust you, Veru?"

Veru dipped his head in a half nod. "Yes, it is true that men have forgotten us, and yes, I am quite trustworthy."

Shaking his head, Talon lowered his sword. "Amarill? I thought they had all left this world, allowing demons to appear in their place."

"That, my oddly educated friend, is simply a fairy tale," Veru chuckled. "There are good and bad amarill same as there are good and bad humans. When humans began to unknowingly stumble upon those cruel amarill who wished to be left alone, it is no wonder that they were obliterated, giving life to the tales of demons and monsters in the northernmost forest."

"…And thus giving it such a cruel name." Regence added with a nod.

"So there are no demons in the demon forest?" Ralley questioned.

"None that I have seen in my many hunts," Veru shrugged. "Though, if there were one, we would surely have seen its handi-work. They are rather notorious for causing destruction and grief wherever they go."

"We are getting off track," Talon said, refusing to sheath his sword just yet. "Where did the black beasts come from?"

Here Veru frowned. "We are unsure who brought them here, but they are beasts summoned from another world through strong magic. These brutes began roaming the forest; tearing apart anything they came across to soothe their lust to kill. We grew tired of them pillaging our forest, so we decided to hunt and destroy them."

"Who is this other one you speak of?" Talon asked, still suspicious.

"My brother Axle? Oh, he is a wonderful chap. I do hope he comes to meet you; he is such a joy to have around." Veru laughed aloud as if someone had told him a most clever joke.

"Is he a white wolf too?" Ralley asked. Talon could hear the eagerness in her voice.

"Oh no, he is quite the opposite of myself, a shining black with the deepest blue eyes you will ever see!"

He spoke of him with such a fondness, yet Talon recalled well the wild look of the metallic wolf he had locked eyes with. "Bind him by the wrists and bring him with us," he said stiffly.

"Wait a minute!" Ralley turned to Talon, narrowing her eyes. "What do you think you're doing? He saved my life!"

"We still cannot be sure of his motives. I saw the creature that he calls his brother, and I am taking all the precautions I can to make sure you are safe." He sheathed his sword as one of the warriors cautiously bound the man's arms.

Regence slowly shook his head but made no comment. "We must return to the wagons," he said. "They may still be in danger. I am sorry you are inconvenienced, Veru, but would you mind coming along all the same?"

The white haired wolf man chuckled softly. "Why, I would be honored to travel with the Empress and Prince of DeGrail, and I thank you for such a gracious invite." He grinned from ear to ear.

Talon gently helped Ralley to his saddle and mounted up behind her. Though Phoenix turned his head to eye her dubiously, he relaxed his ears and appeared satisfied. "So damned hard to see through this thick fog, I am not sure of our bearings."

"Oh!" Veru exclaimed with what Talon thought was fake surprise. "I do apologize, I forget that you humans do not have as sharp of senses as we." He made a wave with his bound hands and the fog instantly began to lift.

This made Talon all the more uncomfortable with this new prisoner. Amarill, Demon, it did not matter what he was; he had a magic about him and could very well have summoned the black monsters himself. They found the wagons in short order as the fog lifted and dissipated, allowing the sun to send shafts of light through the trees. The black beasts had gone, and only those beasts that had been touched by either the strange wolf brothers or the Blade Beast had been killed. The rest, much to the surprise of all, had staggered to their feet and fled, arrows still in their sides, and in one case a sword. Talon was even more grieved to find that one of his warriors had perished along with one of the servants who had been driving the foremost cart. He ordered them wrapped and placed on one of the carts so that when they got to Tradewood he could send them back to Castle DeGrail for proper burials. The previous prisoner was not found but after what viciousness they had seen of these black beasts, Talon was certain that justice had been served.

As they prepared to move northward once again, they heard the great metallic howl echo through the trees. All eyes turned to Veru, who now sat atop the foremost cart, his feet bound now as well and his hands tied to the reins. "He has picked off the injured and tells me there are only four left," Veru chuckled. "And he wishes to know if I will stop playing about and join him."

"You are coming with us to Tradewood as a prisoner. From there I will find out more information on who has brought these beasts here. I believe them to be the same black beasts that attacked my father and his hunting party."

"Very well." Veru did not seem upset about this in the least. He tilted back his head and gave a loud, long howl. It was not as strange sounding as the black ones howl; it was somehow softer and more graceful, but it still echoed around them. There was an answering howl with several short, sharp barks and then the woods were silent. "He says he will finish them off himself." Veru smiled.

Talon had a feeling that was not all he said, but that was no matter. If this Axle came among them, he would take him as a prisoner as well. Ralley fidgeted and moaned. "What is it?" he asked, concerned.

"My arm ... it hurts ...." She did not look him in the face, but he had a feeling there were tears of pain in her eyes.

"Then we must hurry on to Tradewood. You will need to see a skilled healer as will the injured warriors."

Talon led them northward once again. They passed by the road that led southeast toward the village of Kuriot, a place Talon had seen on the maps along with Castle Foresta. Veru was silent, not saying a word as he stared out across the countryside with a smile on his face. They traveled as far as they could, but the day was coming to an end, and Tradewood was still a good half day's journey ahead of them. Talon was forced to halt the expedition as they came to a break from the forest. He could just make out a small home lit up with lamps. There was a great barn a few yards away and a large field of wheat. Talon motioned for Regence to follow him and the three of them, Ralley still sitting in front of him looking pained, ventured forward to the little house. Talon and Regence dismounted and stepped up to knock gently on the door.

The door creaked open, and a hunched, gray haired old man stood in the little doorway. A warm heat and the smell of corn rolls from within the home rushed out to meet them. "Who is it that knocks at my door this late at night? Another traveler heading to Tradewood?"

"It is as you say. I am Prince Talon Endrayen of Degrail and this is Sword master Regence De'Galen. We ask for shelter from the cold night in your barn."

The old man stepped out of his doorway and looked over

their party. He then concentrated on Ralley a moment before looking back to Talon and bowing as low as his old bones allowed. "My wife and I are honored to have your royal highness and his little army stay at such a tiny barn as we have, but you are always most welcome to it. But if I may make a suggestion my lord, we have two rooms that are reserved for travelers such as you since we get so many along this stretch of road. Please, for you and your sword master and those who look to my old eyes to be injured, take these rooms for yourselves as well as accept my wife's hospitality of warm mash with late winter berries and corn rolls."

"You are most gracious, kind sir, and of course we accept!" Regence said. Talon bowed his head in thanks and turned away. He ordered all but the injured to set a camp within the barn and keep Veru under constant watch throughout the night, then returned to the old man's home and helped Ralley from his horse and into a warm room. After they all had a share of the simple but delicious meal, Talon made sure that Ralley was comfortable.

"Regence and myself will keep watch over you tonight. Be sure and get plenty of rest, and we will see about getting you to a healer at midday tomorrow." Talon offered her a gentle smile, and this time she gave him a smile of her own.

"Thanks, Talon... I'm sorry if I'm putting you all in danger. You should all be back at Castle DeGrail eating and sleeping like the royalty you are."

It surprised him to hear her talk like this; it was not something he had expected her to say. "Do not be silly, Ralley. I wanted to come. Being royalty is not all as wonderful as most think, and it is good to get away from it for a while."

"What about the others?" she asked, genuine concern on her face. "And those who… gave their lives?"

"They are warriors of DeGrail, and it is their duty to be here with us and an honor for them to die protecting us," he said softly.

"And Regence?"

"He is my sword master, but he is also a great friend to me and he would sooner beat me senseless than be left behind," Talon said, chuckling. He then rose to his feet. "Rest for now Empress Ralley. We will leave at first light."

"Oh stop calling me that," she groaned.

Talon laughed and stepped out. The old woman living there went inside to re-wrap Ralley's arm. Moments later she emerged and without a word went into the second room to tend to the other wounded warriors. Talon turned to the old man. "Thank you sir; you and your wife do us a great service. Have you any desire that I might repay you with?"

The man smiled and waved a hand. "There is no need Lord, we serve you without needing payment."

Regence walked up to the man and placed a hand on his back. "Now then, I am sure you could use a goodly sized inn with several bedrooms that you could rent out to those many travelers that pass through. It would be a mighty nice little business, and you would have plenty of rooms for all those who came past, and your good wife would have a large kitchen enough to feed an army. What say you?"

"I must say that would be a wonderful business to turn over to my strapping son when he returns from his vending in Tradewood." The old man pinched his chin in thought.

"It is done, then," Talon said in a most authoritative tone. "I trust you will see to it Regence?" The sword master winked at him and walked off in deep conversation with the new innkeeper. He marveled at how he could come up with such suggestions and hoped that he, too, could do so someday, but then again, would he ever be in the position to be such an authority? It was a silly thought since even though he may be removed from Castle DeGrail, he would always be a prince and highly eligible to marry any princess of any of the kingdoms he chose. He shook his head, not wanting to think of such a thing, and yet, it gave him hope that though he would not be Emperor, he would still be a King and heir to some sonless kingdom. Talon could not sleep easily after his watch that night. He thought of the hooded strangers, the one who had been dragged away by the black beasts and where they were from…and where the black beasts were from as well. Veru had said they originated to the north by some magic. These thoughts wandered through his mind along with his worry for Ralley, the events that had taken place and his excitement for the journey ahead.

-26-

Night of the Screamers

Melanie pulled more wood onto the fire from the small pile she had made, hoping that whatever it was that was getting closer to them would be afraid of it. Estat scooted closer to her and began going through the hand motions for fire. "Now is not the time," she whispered harshly, but he gave her hand a quick slap and did it again. She felt like she had been scolded and began obediently doing the hand motions with him. As before, he would make her pause between signs as he felt her hands, making sure she was doing it properly. His hands were nothing like a football jock's. He had long, elegant fingers, well trimmed fingernails, and the only callous was on the left hand finger where a pencil might touch. He had her go through the hand motions once more, and this time she didn't watch her hands; she was staring at his face. She realized she had done this only once, the moment they met, and she also found that she could do this without his really knowing it. He was concentrating hard on the position of her hands, and though his face was smudged with dirt from traveling, he was as handsome as ever.

A screech echoed through the trees, and Melanie jerked in surprise, snapping her gaze away to face the wood. The sound was close now. Too close. She forgot about the hand signs and sidled up to Estat, clutching hold of his arm. There was a rustle in the brush just out of the firelight, and Melanie had to clamp a hand over her mouth so she would not scream. There were strange snuffling sounds, but she could not pinpoint where they came from. Then she heard an awful growl that made her shudder. She clung to Estat's arm so tight that he began to pry her hands away. Something stepped gingerly into the firelight. It was far bigger than a dog or even a wolf, and its fur was a faded gray that stood out from its body, making it look bigger and unnatural. Its yellow eyes flashed with an eerie glow from the light, and it hissed, lashing its tail, which looked nothing like a wolf's at all, but long, whip-like and pointed at the tip. It paced back and forth, never quite getting much closer. Its great paws were tipped in catlike claws, and it opened its maw, revealing a vicious set of fangs and sharp teeth.

It let out another scream, shorter than the last, but it frightened Melanie so badly that even though she had covered her mouth, she still gave a short cry of fear and felt frightened tears forming at the corners of her eyes. Estat yanked his arm from her and lifted his hands towards the beast as it hissed. He made quick symbols with his hands, and she recognized they were the hand motions to make fire. Instantly a flame sprung up about a foot before the beast, and it gave a shriek of surprise and anger. It leapt back from the small blaze just out of the firelight and hissed angrily. Similar hissing came from all around them, followed by short squeals and rustling in the bushes.

They both scrambled to their feet now, and Estat nudged her to lift her hands as he made the first symbol of the fire-starting spell, holding it in the air. Melanie felt the tears wetting her cheeks, and she hastily wiped her eyes. She was not sure she could make the symbols under such stress, but she realized that if she did not at least try, she would surely die. They would both die. The woods around them went silent again, and for a moment, Melanie's hopes lifted. Perhaps the creatures had been too afraid of the fire and decided to give up on their prey just as the flying lizards had done. That hope was dashed the moment she heard a slight rustle behind them; when she turned, she could see the creature suddenly bolting towards them. There was no time to make a symbol, and though she could dodge, Estat could not see them, so she did the only thing she could and leapt at him, shoving him hard. The two of them tumbled out of the way as the great beast lunged. She heard the loud snap of its jaws as it missed the back of her head.

Estat lost his footing and fell to the ground, but Melanie managed to keep her feet. She spun around to face the monster, lifting her hands and making the symbols as swiftly as she could manage. The beast opened its great jaws and hissed. It crouched on its hind legs as it prepared to lunge at her again, but she had finished the last symbol. A bright red flare burst around its muzzle and it screamed so loud that Melanie had to cover her ears. The beast backed away, shaking its head as fast as it could, pawing its nose to rid itself of the flames. Its squeals of pain lasted even after the flames had gone out, and it retreated back to the safety of the trees. She helped Estat back to his feet in time to hear another creature burst from the trees, charging their way. She spun Estat to face it. "Now!" she cried. Estat went through the motions, and a blaze ignited the fur on its neck.

The monster veered away, and she moved Estat again, and

once more he made the symbols, another flame appearing at the monster's flank. It hissed and spat angrily and shook itself like a dog to rid itself of the flames. Two more of the creatures emerged from the trees to both their left and right. Melanie turned to face one of them and locked eyes with it. The monster opened its jaws and let out a piercing scream that made her cry out and cower at Estat's feet, covering her ears. She felt her whole body shaking and she couldn't stop. It charged forward, and she flung her hands before her to make the fire symbols, but she was shaking so uncontrollably that nothing happened. It was as if all time was frozen for an instant, and she saw the great-toothed jaws of the screaming beast opened wide and coming for her.

Then something large and red burst from the trees like an arrow and struck the side of the attacking monster with such force that it easily carried it along through the air and over the fire. For that one moment, the red creature was lit up and it appeared much like a very small and thin horse with folded red wings at its sides and a small figure sitting upon its back.

Clambering to her feet, Melanie watched as the winged animal dropped the now dead screamer to the ground, revealing a great-spiraled horn, red with blood, atop its head. The person on its back turned and faced her; the glow from the fire lit up his boyish but beautiful face, and she thought he appeared a bit younger than Ralley. "Behind you!" his voice rang out young and clear, but before she could pull her eyes from him, he had drawn a bow, knocked an arrow to it and let it fly. It zipped in a line past her head and struck something behind her. When she turned to see, she found one of the screamers laying two feet from her, an arrow between its eyes. She gripped Estat's arm;

his look told her that he was confused, but as relieved as her. In the next instant the boy had struck the third beast in view with an arrow to its chest. There was a moment of complete silence, and the boy turned his head slowly in one direction, then the other. Melanie covered her mouth to hide a gasp as she realized the boy had long pointed ears. His mount perked its ears and turned its head this way and that, also listening intently.

Melanie watched amazed as the boy drew another arrow from the quiver on his back, knocked it, and let it fly into the brush. There was a scream and a burst of sound as the bushes all around them snapped and rustled.

The sounds died out into the night and the boy relaxed, replacing the bow to a holding strap on his back and dismounted. He was still fairly tall despite looking young, and he had short red hair. "Are you two alright?" he asked in a soft, calm voice.

She nodded, still shaking. "I… I think so."

Without another word, the boy threw more wood upon the fire, causing it to blaze brighter. "You should keep your fire large when you stay out like this, or not have one at all. The Mortix are attracted to the sounds and have strength in their numbers." His eyes wandered back to them. "Who are you that you would risk coming this far into the wood with no weapons?"

Melanie tried to control her body's quivering. "Mortix?" she managed to ask.

"Yes, the screaming beasts that roam this section of forest," he replied.

Estat had stepped forward and bowed low to the man. Melanie wondered if he knew this person. "This is Estat; he lives in the tower in the volcano, and I'm Melanie, I used to…"

"The tower?" The boy looked surprised but not angry.

"Yes, do you know him?" Melanie asked, canting her head to the side a bit.

"I know *of* him, but I had heard he lived there alone, practicing his magic. I am Weiland Skyseeker, and this is Immuraudi," he said, pointing to himself and the winged and horned equine.

"It's so beautiful. Can I pet it?" Melanie asked.

Weiland chuckled, and the equine stomped its hoof and even looked annoyed. "I am not an It! I am female and a coramira as well, not some common horse!" The sound came from the shining red creature, but its mouth didn't move at all.

"It talked!" Melanie gasped.

Immuraudi's ears flattened, and she stomped her hoof again. "What did I tell you Weiland? Humans have no manners!" She shook her head; her red silken mane bounced like the hair of a supermodel.

Weiland smiled, his gaze returning to Melanie. "Do not mind her, she is just in a mood this evening. Why is your friend there so quiet?" he asked, stepping toward Estat.

Melanie felt as though everything was happening too quickly. First it was a talking bat, now a talking unicorn! She tore her gaze from Immuraudi, trying to focus on Weiland's question. "I'm afraid he's blind and mute. It's a bit of a long story." Estat frowned and nodded.

"I would dearly love to hear it; please, let us sit by the fire and have it told." He took Estat's hand and touched his forehead to it in some sort of greeting. Then he led Estat to the fire and bade him to sit. Melanie followed and marveled at this boy's wonderful manners. She sat down next to Estat and began to tell their tale and all about the Demon Xenopus. During her tale, she noticed that Estat was listening carefully; though his eyes could see nothing, he faced her the whole time. Weiland too was far less like a fidgety boy and more like an old man listening without interruption, not even asking questions till the tale was finished. Immuraudi had stood silent a few feet away from the fire, though she did have an ear turned in their direction.

"So then, where is it that you are going Estat?" he asked, turning to him.

Estat had been rummaging in the bag and had removed the orb again, unwrapping it and holding it up for them to see. Again the image of the great sleeping serpent within the darkness of a cave appeared. "Ah," Weiland nodded, "You seek Malstraun the amarill, the Great Black Serpent, Destroyer of Ships and Master of the Void."

Melanie's eyes widened and her eyes snapped back to Estat. He was nodding his head with a generous smile. "Destroyer?" She wasn't sure she liked the sound of that.

"Indeed. They say he sunk a fleet of royal sea vessels during the Great War over a thousand years ago, which earned him such a title."

"Royal sea vessels? Why are we asking for help from a creature with such a scary name who destroys ships? Wait a minute; did you say a thousand years? Wouldn't it be dead by now?" She frowned, feeling a bit confused and nervous now.

"Well, of course not!" Immuraudi snorted. "Weiland is almost a thousand years himself and in the prime of his life! Amarill can live several times that, maybe even longer. Of course, no one has dared ask the age of one."

"What?!" Melanie gaped. This boy with the pointy ears was a thousand years old? "That's crazy! You look younger than my sister!"

"Elves can live long if they keep themselves out of trouble." Immuraudi gave Weiland a sidelong glare.

"Elves, amarill and coramira?" she sighed. "I guess I have a lot to learn about your world, Estat."

He reached over and laid a hand on her back. She looked up to see his smile.

"That will have to wait," Weiland said as he rose to his feet. "We should move on. The Mortix will be back to try us again if they find no other prey tonight, and the blood of the dead ones here will lure them back."

As tired as Melanie was, she nodded. She wanted nothing to do with the Mortix, or whatever they were. She was also eager to learn more about this place now that she had someone who could answer her questions.

-27-

BANDITS

Ralley's arm still hurt, but the sling was helping to ease the pain. Talon was trying hard to hold Phoenix at a fast walk instead of the jarring trot the stallion was trying for. She faced forward most of the time, and occasionally he would ask her if she was all right. She figured this was because he was afraid she would pass out. This was a silly thought to her since the pain was enough to keep her awake, though she sure wished she wasn't. The road along which they now traveled was not as wide as the ones closer to DeGrail, but it did have a fair amount of room on either side of the road for camping and an occasional little house. In those homes they passed, she could see curious little faces peeking out the windows or from behind a tree or barn. The trees beyond were thick on either side, and every now and again she would see a deer or rabbit bound back into the safety of those woods as they passed. Traffic along this road was very thin, but they did see a messenger from DeGrail riding back in their direction from Tradewood; he came to a stop when he spotted Talon raising a hand to him.

"Ho there! You are leaving for Castle DeGrail?" Talon asked him.

The dark haired man astride the light saddle horse nodded. "That I am, your Majesty; is there a message you wish me to convey?"

After a moment's pause Talon replied, "There is. Tell my father that we are soon to pass through Tradewood. The black wolves that have injured him attacked our party and only a few of the beasts remain. We have lost two of our men; tell him that all else is well, and those men injured are to see a healer."

The messenger repeated everything Talon had said, and he nodded his satisfaction. "Ride swiftly, and tell no one but the king this information, or your head will be forfeit!"

"I understand and obey my lord!" the messenger said with a great air of importance. The threat appeared not to bother him, but then again, he probably sent such secret messages for the royal family often enough that this threat was simply a reminder of the consequences of not keeping the secrets entrusted to him. In the next moment he was off down the road they had come from, his horse at a full gallop.

They resumed their northward journey at a steady pace. The sun had almost reached its highest point, and Ralley became more eager to get to this healer as her arm began to really pain her. "Will we be there soon?" she moaned.

"Yes, very soon…" Talon said, but at that moment Phoenix began to chomp at the bit, his ears flattening.

"What is it? Is he tired?" Ralley asked.

"That cannot be; he has ridden harder than this before," Talon said though he looked a bit worried.

Then, bursting from the trees on either side of the road came a large group of men. Ralley panicked all over again as there were at least five on either side of them. They shouted angrily and charged them with glittering curved swords. Why was this happening again? Talon drew his sword and began to shout orders, and just like when the monsters had attacked them, things became so loud and confusing that it was hard for her to focus on any one thing. Phoenix danced about underneath them, and she struggled to hold onto the saddle with her working arm. As Talon turned him to face the others, Ralley could make out the nervous stamping horses that pulled the cart behind them. She also caught a glance of Veru, still bound by the wrists and ankles sitting in the wagon seat. He didn't look as frightened as she felt; she even thought he looked a bit amused.

"They are after the wagons!" Regence shouted above the din of sword clanging and random yelling.

As Talon moved Phoenix to a position where he could see, Ralley caught a glimpse of one of the attackers attempting to climb up to a cart driver, but before he could succeed, an arrow struck him in the gut, and he went tumbling to the ground, disappearing in the dust stirred up by the nervous horses.

"Keep your eyes on the wagons!" Talon shouted back to the archers. But Ralley could see that they too were busy fending off several men on foot who had run up to them from behind.

Another man rose up from the dust onto the left wagon and yanked the cart driver from his seat and down to the dirt. "Talon, over there!" Ralley called before she could think.

Talon nudged Phoenix forward, and Ralley found herself struggling to stay in the saddle and hold on with only one arm. "Talon no! Not with her!" Regence shouted after them, also struggling to keep the two men attacking him from pulling him off his horse.

The thief had spotted him coming and whipped the horses, turning them as sharply as he could. Talon rode right up to the side of the wagon and swung at him. The man ducked as the sword whizzed just inches past his head. He kicked out at Phoenix and scored a hit right on his nose. Phoenix reared up with a scream and kicked out at the wagon. Ralley couldn't hold on and felt herself flying through the air. She heard Talon shout her name. Then something white streaked through the air towards her, and in the next moment she was in Veru's arms as he landed gently on the ground. "Where did… weren't you…" Ralley began.

"Tied up? Of course, but would you rather I let you fall?" he asked, raising a white eyebrow. "I do not think you want another broken limb," he said with a quick smile.

As Veru stood up, she could see Talon. He was struggling to his feet, sword still in hand. Phoenix was bucking and twisting in a blind fury not far from him. "Talon!" she shouted.

Finally on his feet, Talon staggered towards them. "Ralley, are you alright? I am…"

"Now is not the time for apologies your headstrongness, the thieves will get away with their prize," Veru spoke casually as he stepped towards him and pushed Ralley into his arms.

Talon took hold of her, and the two of them watched as Veru shifted into his white wolf-like form and bolted towards the wagon. He bounded up and knocked the thief from the seat. He did not stop there; he leaped off and raced ahead of the frightened horses, then rounded on them and let loose a strange howl. At first the equines looked frightened and screeched to a halt, but after a bit of nervous shuffling and snorting, they calmed down. Veru's speed was incredible as he bolted off and tackled several of the bandits that still fought with Talon's men.

In no time at all, what was left of the bandits ran back to the cover of the trees, Veru prancing after them, snapping at their heels as if it were all a game. Ralley looked up at Talon and felt herself flush. He had been holding her the entire time. "You… can put me down… I can walk, y'know…" she stammered, her face hot with embarrassment.

"Oh… sorry." He gently let her back to her feet, but his eyes did not leave hers. Ralley suddenly found herself wishing she'd have kept her big mouth shut.

Talon frowned and went down on one knee, his gaze shifting to the ground. "Forgive me Empress, I put you in danger."

"What?" Ralley blinked at him. "What do you mean? It was an accident!"

"No, Empress." he continued, still bowing his head low and not lifting his eyes. "I rode into danger with you upon my horse and injured. I was not thinking, forgive me."

His sudden chivalry surprised her, but she offered him a smile. "Hey, it's alright. I'm just fine thanks to Veru. Maybe you'll listen to me the next time I tell you to be nice to someone."

"Yes… Empress." Talon said, his tone still serious.

Ralley giggled. "Hey c'mon, you said you were sorry, and I forgive you, so don't worry about it, and stop calling me Empress. We're supposed to be under cover, remember?"

"That is right milady, we are; however the people who see you will suspect something," Regence said as he rode to them. "The bandits will speak of their discovery to others. Talon, I suggest to you that we go with all speed to Tradewood; it should not be far now, and we should not waste any time. We must do what we can there and continue on before news of the empress spreads."

Out of the frying pan and into the fire, Ralley thought. Talon agreed, and they took the next few minutes to re-organize their wagons. Phoenix still bucked wildly when anyone approached him, and Talon was nearly kicked a time or two before he was able to calm him, rubbing his nose gently. The servants had not been injured and were able to continue driving the carts. Though Veru volunteered to continue to be a cart driver, Talon insisted that he be given one of the horses that had belonged to a fallen warrior and ride just behind him next to Regence in the party. Ralley rode with Talon once again, but this time he swore to her that he would not put her in danger. She couldn't believe how kind he was being to her.

They rode as swiftly as they could, and in a very short time from when the bandit battle had taken place, they found themselves among more and more homes and pasturelands, wheat fields and orchards. Ahead was Tradewood, not as large as Elstaff city had been, but not small either. In comparison, it was far busier, more people heading in and out of this town than truly living within it. Such a cacophony of smells came to her that she felt like a mall saleswoman was squirting a hundred different perfumes up her nose, and not all of them pleasant. The people of Elstaff were far more cheerful than these folk, though, and Ralley could feel the very air heavy with tension. Talon must have felt it too, for he ordered his men in tighter formation about the wagons.

People stared here, but not like those in the city. They did not shout out Talon's name or even bother to hail him. At first

Ralley wondered if it was simply because they all looked quite a lot less like a royal party than when they passed the city, but this idea disappeared as they progressed through the main road and people continued to stare, some looking quite angry with them and others simply curious.

"It is not like the Tradewood I remember," she heard Regence say. This only made her nervous, and she refused to meet the eyes of anyone else.

"The north is troubled, Swordmaster. Much has happened in the last few years of the Endrayen family's reign," Veru replied while waving cheerfully to the people, though none of them waved back.

They found a healer's signpost, the symbol of a glowing hand on it, and Talon dismounted and helped Ralley down. Talon led the way through the door, closely trailed by Ralley and Regence. Though none said a word to him, Veru too dismounted and followed them inside.

Talon nodded to a man that sat in the most comfortable looking chair in the room. He wore a full white robe with a symbol on it much like the one on the signpost. "Are you the master healer of Tradewood?" Talon asked, once again in his more princely tone.

"I am," said the man as he looked up at Talon, his face a bit wrinkled; but there was a kindness there, unlike some of the faces she had seen as they came here. "Who might you be? A baron or duke, perhaps?"

"Prince Talon Endrayen. I need you to tend to this lady; her arm is possibly broken, and we still have a long way to travel. I would pay you handsomely, of course. I ask that you attend to my injured men as well; though they are minor wounds, I would rather they be in top condition."

The healer rose to his feet and nodded politely. "Certainly, but I will not serve that one."

All eyes turned to whom the healer was now pointing. Veru simply beamed a smile at them all, his canines particularly visible. "Very well, I shall simply wait outside," he said smoothly. He regarded the healer with his lupine green eyes, and for that moment his face lost its smile. "But I expect you to do your best." He then gave a courteous nod of his head to Ralley before exiting.

-28-

WEILAND'S JOURNEY

When the morning came, Estat found himself waking to the smell of meat being cooked slowly over a warm fire. He had slept far better that night, his mind at ease that they had found Weiland and Immuraudi.

"Ah, you are awake," Weiland's voice said softly. "Breakfast will be finished shortly, hope rabbit is to your liking."

Estat smiled in his direction and moved a bit closer to the source of the heat. He reached around where he had last heard Melanie and touched the edge of a thick blanket.

"Worry not; she is quite warm and sleeping soundly. I would ask of your story, but due to your condition, I suppose you will have to settle for mine."

A water skin was pressed into his hands, and he nodded his thanks. He took a drink of it, but found it not to be water, but a honeyed Elvin wine. It was a welcome change. Weiland shifted, and he could hear him stirring the fire. "I come from a long for-gotten tribe of wood elves that live deep in what the humans call the Forest of Demons. Unlike the known tribes in the far south, we are highly attuned to the spirits of the woodlands, so much so that in the beginning our tribes had bond animals. They were simple ones at first: wolves, bears, birds of prey and other large woodland creatures that you would normally find. Over the long years, we began to feel a more mystical attachment with our magical neighbors. Our connection with unicorns, griffons, drakes, wyrms and other such beings that we now call bond brothers and sisters, became strong enough that those who have great hearts are lucky enough to become linked with them. I myself was fortunate to have Immuraudi, herself coming from a rare herd of winged unicorns."

"That's right, and I am just as fortunate to have you Weiland, though you can be troublesome," the equine cut in. Yet her tone betrayed a sisterly love for the elf.

He heard Weiland chuckle melodically. There was a stirring of cloth, and Melanie could be heard sitting up. "Smells good..." she said sleepily.

"Perfect. It is ready; let us have breakfast and I will tell the tale of how I came to be here in the northern forest." It was a pleasant breakfast of rabbit, red wine and a strange bread that Weiland had with him. It was quite soft, though he said it was made some time ago. It was a welcome change from the water, apples and stale bread they had been eating since leaving the tower.

"My journey began shortly after I left my dwelling one morning. I sensed, as did many others, a change in the spirits." At this point Melanie must have been quite confused, for Weiland felt he must elaborate. "Spirits are what we call the tiny beings that inhabit places all over this world. Most humans cannot see them, but they dwell everywhere: in the water, the earth and floating in the sky. In places where they are plentiful, you will find that the plants are healthy and the water clean. But on that morning, they were agitated. I left the village and went to a quiet place where I could speak to them, but it was not easy to understand them. They were upset, almost fearful, and they gathered about me as if for comfort, or perhaps to protect me from harm. I realize now what I did not at that moment: that a demon had been brought into this world. I returned to the village and spoke with our elders. They all agreed to send those of us with strong Bond brothers and sisters to seek out knowledge of the source of the spirits' disconsolate behavior."

Estat wanted to ask Weiland exactly how he had discovered the release of a demon into the world. Perhaps, being a magical being himself, he discovered it by the feeling he had gotten when approaching the tower, just as Estat himself had felt Xenopus' presence the moment he had awakened that fateful morning.

"Immuraudi and I set out the next day, flying high and to the west," Weildand continued. "I was curious to see the volcanic tower and wondered if Estat here would have some insight to the problem. We came to a small hill and landed for a rest; the mountains were still quite far off. Then something caught my eye. It was a little red spirit… this fellow."

Weiland must have brought out the spirit, for Melanie gasped. At the same time, Estat realized it must be the same spirit that he released from the small glass marble when he had first encountered Xenopus. He had given up hope that it had found anyone to help them and had forgotten it, thinking perhaps it was happy to be free and had fled to live among the other little spirits, but it had remained loyal after all.

"Oh my! It's just a tiny red light floating in the air!" Melanie said in awe. "Can I... hold it?"

Weiland chuckled. "Certainly, you see, it seems to like you. You must have good magic in your veins to allow you to see them; most humans cannot."

"It feels so warm," she said softly.

"Yes, it is a fire spirit. I am quite sure there are many of them living in and around the volcano. This little spirit acted so strangely; it would fly out to the west and then come back to me again. It repeated this several times before we decided to follow it. We spent the first night in the shadow of the mountains and were off again the next day. But the spirit changed its direction and began northward, and the evening of the next day it had led me to you just in time to stop the Mortix," Weiland finished.

"And a good thing too!" Melanie agreed. This made Estat feel horrid for bringing her into such danger and also being so useless to stop the Mortix. Had he his sight, he could have drawn a summoning circle and retrieved a small being to protect them, or perhaps if he had his speech, he could have been able to cast more fierce fire spells or wards.

"What's wrong with it?" Melanie asked after a moment.

"As I said before, the spirits are unhappy, and this one's light is dim as all the others now that its mission is finished," Weiland replied sadly. "The demon will destroy this world, and the spirits can sense the destruction. Even now, he must be causing great damage as he searches for a place to begin summoning lesser demons to help him."

"I'm just starting to like this place, too. What are we going to do? Are we going to ask this Malstraun to defeat Xenopus for us?"

Weiland chuckled. "It would be ideal, but I am not so sure even the Great Black Serpent could defeat Xenopus alone. He may have been driven from the tower, but he is not as weak and feeble as you might think. He is likely still bound by some of the laws of summoning that perhaps this Brek fellow is not yet aware of. Am I right, Estat?" he asked.

Estat gave a grim nod of confirmation. Once Xenopus was finished with Brek, there would be no reason to keep him alive, and it would be far more beneficial for the demon to kill him.

"By the time we get to Malstraun, we may be too late," Weiland said as if reading his thoughts.

"Too late?" Melanie sounded quite confused. "Too late for what?"

"Too late to stop Xenopus from killing the one that summoned him," Immuraudi cut in with a stomp of her cloven hoof. "That will release him completely, and then he will be far too powerful for a single amarill to defeat."

Estat gave a few slow nods. He despised his former apprentice for doing something so outlandish, but he was still just a young stupid fool who was being led on by a golden-tongued demon. He did not wish for his death, and certainly did not wish for Xenopus to be fully released. If they could stop that from happening, they had an opportunity to send the cursed demon back where he came from.

"So why are we trying to get to Malstraun again?" Melanie said still sounding rather confused and annoyed.

"Were you not paying attention?" Immuraudi snorted. "We must get to Brek before Xenopus kills him. Malstraun is the Master of Portals; he can get us to Brek with a single blink of his eye without our having to spend precious time searching for him."

"Which reminds me, we must get moving if we are to make the beach by sundown," Weiland said. Estat could hear him get to his feet and the hiss of the fire as he put it out. "You two will ride Immuraudi; we will make better time this way."

"What about you?" Melanie asked.

"I can keep up."

Estat was certain he could. He had heard of the elves and their tireless endurance. Melanie helped him to his feet, and together with Weiland, managed to get him onto the winged unicorns back. Moments later he felt her light frame settle in front of him, and he automatically wrapped his arms around her to hold onto Immuraudi's mane. "This is the first time I've ridden a horse. What do I hold onto?"

"Worry not. Estat has you; just hold on with your legs and move with Immuraudi," Weiland offered, his tone patient.

As Immuraudi began to move, Estat felt Melanie nestle down into his arms. He smiled as her soft hair tickled his nose, smelling of rose oil. Slow at first, Immuraudi began to pick up speed until she settled on a light gallop. "It's like we're flying along the ground, but your wings aren't moving, and Weiland is keeping pace with us!"

"Silly Human," Immuraudi replied.

"Whatever," Melanie grumbled.

The air grew colder as they went along at a steady speed, and though Estat had not ridden a horse in years, he found it far easier on a coramira, with her fluid movements and the feeling of almost floating just a few inches over the ground. They traveled in silence, and Estat could only tell the passing of time by the slow change in light. It was turning late in the afternoon, and just when Estat was getting hungry, he heard the twang of a bowstring. Immuraudi slowed to a stop.

"That was amazing, Weiland!" Melanie exclaimed. "You got it with one shot, and you were running and everything!"

Weiland chuckled from somewhere a short distance off, and then Estat heard him approach. "Thank you, I have had much time to practice. It looks as though we will eat well again tonight."

"When will we reach the coast?" Melanie asked.

"We should reach it by sun down, but the sky is darkening to the north; a storm is coming in, and it will be treacherous to climb the cliffs in the rain, for the rocks will be slippery and the wind is picking up. Immuraudi will not be able to fly us to the cave mouth if it gets worse."

Estat frowned. He had hoped that they would make it to Malstraun by the end of this day with their current speed, but now it sounded as though they would be delayed. Indeed, the wind worsened as they traveled on. There was a short lunch break during which they ate dried fruit, bread and apples and stretched their legs. Melanie complained of being sore, but this was normal for someone who did not often ride horses. Estat himself could not complain; then again, he was mute. They continued on, and Estat could sense the overcast sky with its chilling wind. Weiland passed his cloak to Melanie, and she insisted on wrapping it about Estat as well. She huddled into Estat's arms for warmth, and he welcomed her embrace. He felt a light rain begin to fall, hitting him in the face. Immuraudi slowed, and Weiland told them that he would scout ahead for shelter. After only a short time, he returned with news of a promising place for them all underneath an overhanging cliff. It sheltered them from the wind and rain, and they built a large fire to ward off the cold. "We are near the coast," Weiland said quietly after Melanie had fallen asleep, her head on Estat's lap. "Get some rest; we shall be in Malstraun's cave tomorrow."

Estat nodded, this news giving him cause to relax. He just hoped they were not already too late.

-29-

TROUBLE IN THE NORTH

Talon watched as Veru made his way out of the healer's home and closed the door. Talon turned to the healer. "Tend to the lady, but I would dearly like to hear why you sent that man out."

"Then come back here where I may talk with you three more privately." The old healer led them back to a smaller room where a cushioned table sat in its center. He helped Ralley to sit upon it, and he began to undress her arm. Talon and Regence sat down on a bench near the wall. There was a small window in the back, but a heavy cloth was drawn over it to darken the room. There were candles all around, emitting a fresh scent of beeswax. Opposite from where they sat was a table filled with canisters of different oils and ointments, bags of herbs, and a basket full of clean bandages.

"That one you travel with is a demon," the old man said, drawing Talons attention back to him.

"We know what he is; he was our prisoner until he saved this lady's life," Talon said in a stiff but authoritative manner.

"Demons are masters of deception. They will pretend to be your ally and then betray you at a critical moment." The old healer began to put a salve on Ralley's arm. "The people of this town will be angry with you for bringing him here."

Talon frowned and looked to Regence. He had been suspicious of Veru from the beginning, and a part of him still distrusted him, but he had saved Ralley and could have abandoned them at the time the bandits attacked and allowed them to take the supply wagon.

Regence nodded his head. "Perhaps he might be a demon, but what if you are wrong? If we cast him from our group, he may then become like the demons you say. What if he is amarill?"

"That race left hundreds of years ago, leaving behind the demons we know today, demons that ravage the northern countries, set kingdom upon kingdom. You will see the damage that has been done if you continue north. The Myriad City Ruins, Freewind, Nourin, Ogto, Sarr, all these places have stories that you would not believe."

"Castle Nourin. I have been there, the northernmost kingdom." Regence said, smiling. "How does it fare?"

As the healer began to re-dress the wound, he shook his head. "King Darman and Lord Gelon have both had their daughters taken by a demon of the woods; they are at war with it."

"War?" Talon and Regence intoned together. Talon had heard nothing of war to the north; there would have been messengers sent.

The old healer nodded quietly as he finished the dressing. "Hush now, I must perform the healing."

"I thought that's what you just got done doing..." Ralley began, but the healer hushed her.

He began to speak in an arcane tongue, and Talon could feel

the tingle of magic about them. Ralley appeared uncomfortable, glancing towards the door, but the healer had hold of her injured arm. Talon had seen this done before and was quite used to it, but it looked as though Ralley had never known it. When the healer finished, he released her arm, and she pulled it too her, giving the man a suspicious glare.

"What was that all about?" she asked, holding her arm close to her.

"That was a healing, milady," Regence said chuckling. "Have you never been to a healer? Surely you have?"

"Well, in my world, they call them doctors, and they don't mumble over your arm in weird languages, and that feeling was just really weird… Hey!" Ralley said as she moved her arm. "It feels lots better! Ouch!" She had extended her arm and now pulled it back. "Still sore, but way better!"

"Of course it is." The old healer said. "Nothing matches a healer's spell."

Talon stood. "Tell me about this war you speak of!"

The man began to clean up his little table, replacing lids and folding unused bandages. "It is nothing to concern yourself with. They venture into the forest to destroy its denizens and reclaim their daughters. I have heard many strange things, that it is a ghost or spirit that stole them away, or that it is a possessed monk that once lived within the castle walls itself. Others say it is simply a demon that has taken up residence in the woodlands to the east of the castle. Whatever it is, it strikes only at night under cover of darkness so as to take the men by surprise."

Talon and Regence exchanged glances. It sounded more to him like a silly rivalry than a war, but putting such a word to it meant so much more and always involved other kingdoms, towns, and innocent people. He should tend to this … but wait, why him? It was Ralley's duty now to take care of such things. As he looked to her, she smiled, more interested that her arm had now mended before her eyes. No, he would deal with this; she had no idea how to solve it and knew nothing of their current laws.

Ralley slid off the table. "So, how did you know that Veru wasn't a normal person?" she asked as casually as if she were talking of the weather.

"His eyes are full of mischief, and his white hair is not normal. I can feel his power; he is not to be trusted. You must rid yourself of him as quickly as you can. But do not allow him to bear any malice for this town. Take him beyond our borders swiftly; we do not want trouble."

"But you're the one who has insulted him already by kicking him out. Are you saying also that anyone different from you is some evil demon?" Ralley asked, putting her hands on her hips. "What about a normal child born with white hair? If it were your own child, would you disown him?"

"That would not happen." The man spoke calmly.

"Why not?" Ralley snapped, "Are you so perfect that you will always have perfect children?"

The man wavered under her anger. "I am a healer, of course I would have perfectly healthy…"

"How can you be so sure? Accidents happen all the time. You above all people should know that!" Ralley was so irritated her face had begun to turn red.

Regence stepped to her and put a hand on her shoulder to calm her. "Milady…"

She seethed, but attempted to calm herself. "You medieval people and your ridiculous superstitions!" And she turned about and stomped to the door. She glanced back long enough to say. "Now that I'm the empress, all that will change!" Ralley stepped out and slammed the door behind herself.

"Empress?" The healer whispered with wide-eyed astonishment.

Both Talon and Regence pulled their swords as one and pointed them at the healer. Talon narrowed his eyes. "Say not a word about what you have heard here, or your tongue shall be removed and your honorable status as a great healer will be no more." It would never do to have this man helping spread rumors that the empress herself was traveling northward; they would have more trouble with assassins, bandits and rival kingdoms, not to mention how it would slow their northward progress.

"Y… yes your Majesties!" the healer spluttered.

Talon and Regence sheathed their swords, but their stern expressions did not change. They left the hut to find Ralley pacing about outside. "Allow the rest of the injured men inside, and let us retrieve our backup supplies as fast as we can. I want to leave this place immediately." Talon's voice was commanding, and his men hurried to their tasks. He watched Ralley a moment and stepped over to her. "Ralley."

She turned to him, her face still angry for a moment, but she relaxed her features when she looked into his eyes. "Sorry, I just get so mad at people like that."

"Do not worry yourself, we will leave this place and continue north as planned; do not forget what you have come this far for."

Her face brightened. "I won't forget; I came to find my sister," she said with renewed determination.

Talon nodded and led her to her horse. "I trust you can ride now?" She nodded, and he helped her to the saddle. There was something different about her now. She sat straight in the saddle and turned her head this way and that to look at those villagers who had gathered round the armored party. Only moments before she sat huddled in the safety of his arms, her eyes downcast. Talon had no time to think this over. Regence placed a hand on his shoulder. "Majesty, where do we go from here?"

"Ever northward my friend, to Lacavi. But I do not trust the people of Tradewood. I would rather we leave immediately and travel till dusk." Talon spoke this as his eyes wandered to angry faces in the growing crowd.

"I agree," the sword master said without looking.

In what felt like hours to Talon, the men were healed and in tip-top shape, and the water barrels on the wagons were refilled from the city well by the wagon drivers. No sooner had this been completed than a few teenage boys began jeering at them. "Demon lovers!" one shouted. "Get out!" yelled another. Ralley's face was set in anger, but she said nothing, nor did she look at them. Talon's eyes drifted to Veru, who sat atop the horse he was given. He had a pleasant smile on his face that seemed permanently fixed. For some reason it still irritated him, but he motioned the party to move out. Regence rode next to him as they went as swiftly as the traffic would allow. Most of the villagers got out of their way, more than happy to let them leave. Several more teenagers had congregated with the previous ones and continued their jeering as they followed to the right of their party.

Matters became worse when they began to target Veru himself, calling him such things as "Demon Spawn" and "Son of the Under Demon." At first, none of what they said changed his features. Veru held his head high and proud, smiling all the time, nodding to an occasional villager that met his eye. Talon was not sure it was possible, but his smile grew. As they approached the north end of the town market, a tall, brave boy in the crowd stepped out and threw an apple with impeccable aim at Veru's head, shouting "Get out, Devourer of maidens!" Veru caught the apple in a single, swift motion. Several people in the crowd gasped as if ready for him to leap out and tear out their throats. Even the other jeering boys grew quiet and slowed their pace.

Veru lost his smile for only a moment. His eyes narrowed, and the boy could not turn his eyes away from him. When Veru turned away to look at Talon, his smile had returned in full bloom, and he held the apple to his mouth. "Kids these days." He gave a little chuckle and bit into the apple.

The boy stood stunned for a moment more, then stumbled back and disappeared into the crowd, a look of horror on his face, once again, the healer's words of warning edged into Talon's thoughts.

-30-

FOREST OF LOST CHILDREN

Once out of Tradewood, Ralley could tell everyone was more relaxed. They had to have one of the flanking soldiers drive the buggy, and he was the only one who looked a bit out of sorts. The sun was casting its light over the taller trees, and she began to wonder when Talon would set camp. There were many farmhouses along the road, and all he kept saying was that he wished to get beyond them. He said that he didn't want any trouble with the town, and Ralley didn't blame him, but still, a soft bed and warm fire would have been nice. Though her arm wasn't broken anymore, it was still hurting, and her shoulder began to ache. The entire party trudged on. She felt a moment of hope when Talon called a halt, but he simply requested that the torches be brought out and lit, and afterward they continued on. They traveled by torchlight for what she thought was way too long, until at last they came to a wide grassy area next to the road, and to her relief, Talon called a halt.

"We set camp here for the night. Prepare a fire and set up a double watch." Few tents were constructed as most of the soldiers slept around the fire for the double watch. Ralley was given her own tent for privacy and because she was the empress.

She lay in her heavy but soft blankets, wearing her cleaned sheep pajamas and stared at the roof of the tent. There was always something relaxing about listening to a crackling fire, the chirruping of insects and frogs as well as the low murmur of talk. She began to drift off to sleep, but something kept her awake. It was a soft sound at first; one could barely hear it over the cacophony of sounds already in the night air. Just when she thought it was nothing and began to relax, she heard it again. It sounded like a whimper, or a puppy or a small child. She sat up, fully awake and strained again for the sound. There it was. It certainly sounded like a kid.

Ralley got to her feet in the tall tent, picked up the leather pouch that held the Blade Beast, and went to the tent flap, parting it far enough to see the men around the fire. Most of them had gone to sleep by now, but there were two of them up, talking in low whispers, their backs facing her tent. They didn't seem to hear what she heard, and she didn't want to bug them if it was nothing, so she snuck out and tiptoed to the edge of the camp. Hearing the sound again, she began to slowly make her way in the direction of the whimper. It was quite dark, but once her eyes adjusted, she could see the dark tree trunks and low bushes. She was careful to keep quiet as she waded into the dark woods and glanced over her shoulder several times, keeping the campfire in view so she could get back. Now she could hear crying. "Hello?" she spoke into the darkness, though she still couldn't see anything.

There was no reply, but she could still hear the crying. "Hey, there's nothing to worry about. I won't hurt you, and I want to help." Again she glanced over her shoulder, just making out a slight glow where the camp should be. A bit nervous now, Ralley ventured forward into the thick trees. "Hello? Where are you?" The crying was just ahead of her, was the kid running away from her? "Wait! Please wait, I'm not gonna hurt you!"

Again she glanced back, but this time she couldn't see any light at all. This made her stop dead. She strained to listen, trying to make out how far ahead the kid was. "I will wait here, you can come back to me okay? I just want to help." Then she heard something a bit unexpected; a giggle. It sounded as if it came from her left side. She looked in that direction but couldn't see anything but dark tree trunks. There was a whisper behind her, and she jumped, spinning around and looking, but again, there was nothing there but dark bushes and fallen branches. Another giggle, then a laugh, and the crying stopped quite suddenly. She turned and looked all around her but still could see nothing. A trick? Was it someone luring her away from camp? She turned in the direction she had come from and began to make her way back. This was just too creepy, and now she felt a prickle of fear that made her rush through the bushes as fast as she could. This proved disastrous as she tripped over a log and landed on her face. Scrambling back to her feet, she looked frantically around her but still did not see the glow of the fire. There was more giggling, and it sounded as if there were many voices surrounding her.

"Hello?" she called out, her voice shaking with fear. "What do you want?" As she said this, Ralley pulled the blade from its pouch. It was the only weapon she had and maybe she could get the dragon to help her get back to camp. What she really needed was light so she could see where she was going. As if it heard her unspoken thought, the blade began to glow. Now Ralley could see her immediate area and could continue on safely. The giggling stopped, and she heard whispering among the trees.

Ralley decided to ignore it and moved on. "Where is that campfire?" She glanced to her left and there she saw a white glow. "Ah!" She turned and quickened her pace. After a short time of following this light though, she realized that it was moving. It kept dodging to the left or right. This wasn't the campfire! How could she be so stupid! It wasn't even a yellow glow! She halted in her place, and a great uproar of childish laughter came from all around her. "STOP IT!" She shouted. "It's not funny! If you're not in trouble, I want to get back to camp and sleep!"

She began to wonder if they were fairies. There were countless bedtime stories that her father used to tell her about mischievous fairies and pixies. "Are you fairies playing tricks on me?" Ralley called out. There was plenty more giggling at this, and she lost any fear she had left and became angry. "I have heard plenty of stories about you fairies! Always playing tricks and thinking it's harmless!" There came a sudden hush over the area, and for a moment Ralley thought she had figured them out. They must have scattered into the forest. That was good because now she could get back to camp without them bothering her.

"Stories?" Came a tiny girl's voice from behind her.

This time, when Ralley turned around, there before her was a little girl. She was glowing with a white light, and Ralley could see right through her. Ralley took a step back. "Are… you a ghost?" she stuttered.

The little girl nodded. She had beautiful curly hair and wide eyes, but there was no color to any of her; even her adorable little dress with its wide ribbon around her waist and in her hair had no colors. She was white with gentle blue hues where there might have been a dark color. "Can we hear the story about the fairies?" she asked innocently.

"We?" She glanced around and sure enough, sitting on tree branches, bushes and boulders were a dozen or more of the ghostly children. They were all different, little boys and little girls, some dressed beautifully in little dresses like the first and the boys in wonderfully made pants and puffy sleeved shirts like princes with handmade shoes; some of them were a bit shabby with holes in their pants or dresses, dirty looking faces, unkempt hair, worn out shoes, and even a few with no shoes at all. Ralley gasped as she looked around at them all. Had all these children died at the same time? "Where did all of you come from?"

"Seselna," one boy in a tree shouted out. Several others shouted the same.

"Crysna," shouted others.

"You all have come from only two different places? Is this some sort of gathering place for child ghosts?" It was horrid to think that all these children had died so young.

The children all giggled. "No, it is not like that," one smartly dressed boy said as he came towards her from the bushes. "It is just where we came because we did not want to be around the grownups." All the other children nodded agreement.

"Grownups? You mean you were haunting your parents?" Ralley asked doubtfully.

The boy that had spoken shook his head. "No, they were just very unhappy and none of them wanted to play with us any-more, so we came here so we could play together."

"Your parents, they're ghosts too?"

All of the children nodded. How dreadful! How could so many people have died and become ghosts? Why didn't they, well, move on? She decided not to ask what it was they died from, since it was probably horrible, and these children may not even remember it. "Why are you still ghosts? Aren't you supposed to go into the light or something?"

The children began to laugh and giggle again, and when they finally stopped, the well dressed boy said. "No, we cannot go right now. There is something that has to be done first, but we do not know what."

"Oh, I wish I knew what it was. I would help you all to go wherever it is you're supposed to go when you ... well, when you go." Ralley struggled with her words, not wanting to frighten or upset the children.

"What about the story?" asked the first little girl. All the others echoed her words, waving their arms, jumping and floating around her in excitement.

Ralley felt sorry for all these children; they must be bored, well, to death. She cringed at her own pun. "Uh ... sure I guess I could tell you one of the stories my dad told me." Ralley found herself a boulder and sat down. "Once there was a man lost in an enchanted wood. He came across a small group of fairies. They were so beautiful and their voices were soft, soothing whispers. He just knew they would help him, and so he asked them to lead him back to the road of men. They agreed to help, but he would have to give them something in return. He told them that he had nothing to give them but the clothing he wore, and of course the fairies had no need of that. Then he had an idea. He asked the fairies if there was anything he could do for them instead. They all glowed brightly and flew around him, telling him in their excited voices that he could rid them of a horrible oversized toad that thought them a better meal than bugs.

"This sounded like an easy task, and he agreed, having them take him to the place where the toad would be. Two of the bravest fairies led him to a large pond in the wood where the toad lived, and when the man spotted him, he was amazed to see that the toad was indeed as large as a dog. He had no weapons to kill the great toad, so he would have to use what he could find around him. He spotted an old haggard tree with its empty branches that leaned from weakened roots. The man told the fairies what his plan would be and that he would need them to lure the great toad out to the tree. The braver of the two ventured out and dropped pebbles upon the sleeping toad, then flew to the leaning side of the old tree, taunting it.

"With a great leap, the large toad followed the fairie, snapping out its tongue to catch the it, but the clever fairy dodged away from him and flew high into the air, leaving the toad in the shadow of the tree. The man jumped upon the tree, his weight too much for the weakened roots to hold, and the tree came down upon the toad, pinning it. He then broke off a branch of the tree and plunged it into the helpless toad, ending the threat to the fairies. They were so grateful for this, they brought him to the road of men, picking berries for him and singing to him all the way," she finished.

The children were so happy with her story that she decided to tell them a few more. They became intent upon the stories and leaned forward, never interrupting her as one would imagine small kids might. Sometimes they even nodded, as if they had been told such stories before. She felt as though she sat there only a short time, telling them story after story until at last she thought she could no longer stay awake. "… And that's how the knight won the joust and the hand of the princess. That's all the stories I have tonight. I really have to get back to camp for some rest." She stood up, and all the children groaned at once.

"Do not go! We love your stories!" they begged.

"I thank you all for listening to them, but I really must go. I'm so tired. Maybe I could tell you some more stories another time?" She wasn't sure she would ever come back this way, but she certainly didn't want to see these ghostly children angry.

"Please, oh please just one more!" begged two girls who appeared to be twins.

"Uh… well… only if you help me back to camp when I'm finished." She smiled, glad to tell them another story and to possibly get some help back to camp, too.

"No," one boy with patches in his pants said, jumping down from a tree. He looked a bit older than the others and had messy hair, making him appear like a hard working country boy. "You have to promise to find a way to help our parents too." The boy crossed his arms.

This took her a bit by surprise. How would she be able to help them? She didn't know the first thing about ghosts in this world, much less how to make them cross over. She thought a moment, and then smiled. "I promise to try and help you all to move on, and if I don't, you can come find me and haunt my dreams or something. Will that be enough?"

The children all agreed to this and listened to another of her stories. When she was finished, they kept their word by leading her back to camp. None of her party seemed to have noticed she had been gone, but she was unable to sneak back into camp without the soldiers jumping up and pointing their swords to her. They relaxed and bowed to her when they saw who she was. She insisted that she simply had to take care of bodily needs and didn't need an audience for that. Before she slept, Ralley thought for a long time about how she would help the ghosts and decided to tell Talon and Regence about her encounter in the morning, wondering if they would be angry.

~ 31 ~

A Maddening State

When Brek woke, he found himself curled up on the floor in front of the door leading out of the bedroom. Was last night just a dream? Had he been sleepwalking? Everything he had seen had been so vivid. It stuck in his thoughts even now, and he could recall every detail of it, much to his dismay. He picked himself up from the floor and inspected the room. It was the same as it had been last night when he was cowering in the bed. It had been too real and frightening, but then again, dreams were always like that, were they not? Brek put his hand on the door and hesitated, dreading the vision he had seen behind it. Slowly, he pulled it open. There was a light behind it, but not like the hellfire, so he stepped into the next room and searched for any sign of Mioria, Xenopus or Ecnair. On the floor, just as it was yesterday, was the incomplete summoning circle. The items still sat about just as he had left them the previous day. Was it morning? There was little way to tell here in the cave, so he headed for the entrance, walking cautiously out to what he hoped was sunlight. He could hear a moaning, and for a moment, he was not sure he wanted to continue.

When he did get to the cave mouth, he discovered that the

sky was darkening and the wind was blowing through the trees. There, standing next to the fountain a few feet from the cave entrance, was Mioria, her long golden hair blowing gracefully around her in the wind. She appeared to be talking to herself as she stared down into the fountain's water.

"Lady Mioria?" Brek said, taking a few steps towards her.

She turned slowly to observe him. "Ah, Brek, I have been waiting for you to wake. Did you have any trouble sleeping?" she asked sweetly.

Had she known that he was sleepwalking? Brek glanced away. "Er…yes, I was having a nightmare," he said, feeling a bit cowardly.

"What was it about?" she asked with her voice of silk.

Brek shook his head. "N…nothing. Where have Xenopus and Ecnair gone?"

"He has gone to find other powerful beings to join us. He seems certain that there are other creatures here that would be helpful to the cause. So then, are you ready to finish what you have started?" Mioria asked, walking past him now toward the cave entrance.

"W… well actually I…" Brek began. But Mioria cut him off with a wave of her hand.

"Xenopus said the symbol has much power in it. To merely gaze upon it is to look into the nether realm itself." Mioria said this as if it were a mere legend.

Brek, reluctant, followed her to the cave. He did not want anything more to do with the symbol, but how could he tell Mioria? He would feel like a coward, and she had such confidence in him. "I did have a strange dream last night," he said, not sure if he should quite reveal its nature to her. "But it was just a dream, I suppose," he added, hoping she would not discover how fearful he was of that dream.

"Oh yes, just a dream, I am sure. Come, I shall stay with you while you work on the symbol and make you more comfortable," she said in her soothing, honeyed voice. She glanced at him over her shoulder and gave a playful wink.

He felt a light blush on his cheeks, and though he felt sick just thinking about the symbol he would have to finish, Mioria's presence eased his thoughts. Brek followed her back into the room where the symbol sat waiting for him. He found the chalk and then hesitated at the paper with the symbol. He picked it up off the floor as if it were going to bite him. Swallowing, he spared a glance at the symbol as a whole. It moved, twisted, growled… he flinched away, his eyes settling on Mioria. She gave him another encouraging wink and then spoke a few words in the magical language. The jewels on her silver headdress turned white, and the four musicians materialized in the room, taking up their instruments that had been placed on a shelf. For a moment he watched as they tuned them up, and then began to play a soothing melody. He wanted only to listen to the music, but Mioria nodded to the summoning star and waited.

Focusing on one line in particular, he began as he had the evening before. At first, he tried to listen to the music, but it was soon drowned out by a strange thrumming noise that came from the symbol. Mioria hovered about at the edges of the star, always encouraging him and providing him with an occasional drink and at times something to eat. Brek began to see things when he was not working on the symbol. Twice he could have sworn that the water in his glass contained images of horrific demons, and there were several spilled drinks. Mioria would speak with him soothingly and refill his cups, easing his fears.

As the morning turned to evening, the symbol truly began to take shape on the floor. Now Brek had to make sure he was not looking at either of the symbols as a whole, for now the one on the cold cave floor began to twist and move as well. This made it far more difficult to keep the images out of his head, for now they magnified with the creation of the larger drawing. The world around him became foggy as the world within the symbols became sharper, more real to his eyes. Mioria was like a ghost now, drifting about the circle at the edge of his vision. When Xenopus returned from his exploration, Brek paused to gaze at him wide eyed. His truer form hung about him like a cloak, though he was in his human guise. On his shoulder was Ecnair, his eyes darting over the summoning circle greedily.

"Is he not yet finished?" Xenopus grunted.

Mioria floated to the demon's side. "He sees things, monsters, coming at him from the water he drinks," she offered.

Waving a hand absently, Xenopus turned to Brek, who had stopped to watch them. "The symbol is a doorway to the nether world; it is expected that you cannot handle the view. People like you would not last even a moment in a world like mine." Xenopus gave him a cruel smirk. "Just finish the symbol. I promise you that everything will work out just as planned."

Somehow Brek did not believe those words, but he returned to his work. He had to. Not because Xenopus wished it, but because the symbol was calling to him now. He could hear the thrumming of it in his ears. It wanted to be finished; it even stopped moving at times so that he could better draw it. Brek tossed aside another piece of chalk and reached for those that Mioria provided. Time flew by as he scribbled on; at one point, he looked up to see the musicians still playing, though he did not hear the music. One of them, the lute player, frowned at him and shook his head.

Before he knew it, the room had grown darker, and outside the cave a storm raged. He could just hear the howling wind through the noise of the symbol. Mioria had made the musicians disappear again and was now lying down in the pillows. Xenopus leaned against a wall, watching as he continued his work. Ecnair flitted in and out among the jars on the shelf, amusing himself by tapping the glass and watching the blue glowing lights flicker in response.

Brek worked on into the night as the storm stirred the floating lights in the room and Mioria fell asleep on her pillows. He was always aware of Xenopus' eyes on him, the haunting noises of the symbol and the sound of crackling fire. He could feel heat too, a black heat unlike anything he could describe in his own world. It crawled up his arms like a living thing and into the shirt he wore. It crept along his skin, making it prickle with feverish heat, but it did not make him sweat as he thought he might.

He was almost finished, only a few more strokes to go.

The darkness rose around him like a heavy black fog, but did not obscure his vision. The symbol was even more visible to him than it ever was before. His eyes felt as though he had not blinked for hours, and his mouth was dry, tongue leathery. The black flames of the nether world crept through his skin; his breathing became rapid and his lungs began to ache.

One stroke left.

Brek's entire body felt heavy with the black fire that penetrated into every fiber of his being. He could hear his heart beat in his ears, or was that the loud thrumming of the symbol? Yes, the symbol was alive, complete. The chalk fell from his hand, and he rose to his feet. The ferocity of the storm outside seemed to be celebrating. He stared at the creatures within the drawing as they tore at each other in their attempts to free themselves. They clawed at the very stone floor as if they could travel away from where they were drawn. Brek noticed Mioria stirring from the corner of his eye, and somehow he was able to lift his vision away from his work to watch her as she gaped at the scene.

Xenopus wandered around the circle; his eyes were glowing eerily, and he looked pleased. "It is ready."

"What is wrong with him?" Mioria demanded.

"He is bathed in the hell fire of the netherworld. It will more than likely consume his body in time," Xenopus replied absently.

Mioria spun on him with anger. "You have compromised his soul! We agreed...."

"His soul is intact, I assure you. There will be plenty of time to do as you wish. For now, he still has a task to complete."

Brek stared at them through the thick black fog that radiated from his body. "What are you talking about? What will happen to me?" he asked, panic surging back to his muddled thoughts, but the rest of his body was relaxed.

Mioria eyed Xenopus before turning back to Brek again. Her posture and soft expression returned, as did her silky voice. "Do not worry, my love, everything shall turn out fine. You must finish what you have started. I promise to protect you with my power. You have nothing to fear."

The thrumming in his ears eased, and the fog lightened. Yes, she was protecting him even now. She loved him, and she would be his queen. Yes, there was much to do. He must get to work, but his body was sluggish and his vision blurred. The black fire was weighing on his body like lead. He felt as though he carried two soldiers on his back. He heard Xenopus speaking to him, but he paid no attention to it as he walked towards Mioria. She was a vision that was pleasing to his eyes, the only one here that loved him. She was all he needed.

"He must rest. That thing has taken the strength from him," he heard her say through the low throb of noise in his ears.

"There is not much time," Xenopus growled, his tone dangerous.

"I will make time," she said evenly. Brek then heard her speak the archaic language. A tingling feeling swept through his body, and he could no longer feel it; even the thrumming had gone. The silence was wonderful, but also strange. He had heard those sounds all day long, and now to be without them was almost uncomfortable.

For a moment all was blackness, and then, a light. It came at him like a wild fire of black, red and orange flames. He screamed as monsters rose up out of the inferno, their claws and fangs flashing in the light. The black tendrils of fire wrapped around his arms and legs, holding him there while grotesque beasts of all kinds hovered around him, ready to do unspeakable things. As they reached for him with massive clawed appendages, he screamed for the Goddess Austia to save him.

Somehow he opened his eyes, though he had thought them already open. There she was, the goddess herself, clad in silken garments, her long golden hair surrounding him and her sparkling eyes gazing down into his. The most beautiful smile came upon her lips, and he was smitten with her. He opened his mouth to speak her name, but she hushed him before he could.

"It is time to finish your task, my love. You have rested enough," her familiar silky voice intoned.

-32-

Selfish Decisions

While Ralley slept in that morning, Talon questioned his men. He had not expected one of them to inform him that her Majesty had wandered back into camp rather late that night, the guard having been unaware how long she was away from her bed since they insisted that they had not seen her go. Talon admonished them in their laziness, warning them about keeping more alert and sent them off to finish their morning meal. When Ralley finally emerged from her tent, she was neither groggy nor bedraggled. Talon found her to be quite excited, and she wished everyone to join her around the campfire. She related to them a story of how she had gone out that night after the cry of a child and found a band of ghost children that bade her to tell them stories.

"And I promised them I would at least try to help them. If any of you know anything about this, I want you to tell me. I want to help them."

Regence stood. "I might have some information about where they came from Majesty. Sit down and have something to eat, and I shall tell you what I know."

Talon had heard stories of ghosts as children's tales, but

never imagined them to be true. Though he was not happy with Ralley having gone off alone, he was very interested to hear what she had seen. He joined them in a breakfast of bread, cheese, potatoes and fresh pheasant caught by the archers. The morning light was just beginning to lance through the trees, illuminating the once dark forest around them.

"Almost a thousand years after the Great War and only two hundred years ago, The Kings of Castle Nourin and Castle Aurora came to a disagreement. King Seidric of Nourin was a young king, having come to power early through his father's untimely demise. He became a tight fisted ruler, a tyrant, and when the beautiful princess of Aurora caught his eye, he pressed her father, King Venure, to arrange for them to be joined. But King Venure was a good man, and he refused to wed his daughter to him. Seidric was overcome with anger and declared war against the kingdom of Aurora. The hatred passed on to Seidric's son, Deidrec, and through him the war between the kingdoms continued. King Venure lived to see his daughter wed to Arion, a duke's son who continued to rightly defend the kingdom against Deidrec. The war plagued those villages between the kingdoms of Nanya, Seselna and Crysna. Deidrec's men constantly occupied the city of Nanya, and it was said that his soldiers did as they wished. Deidrec trampled Seselna and Crysna, for they claimed loyalty to Aurora. Arion's forces fought bravely to save all they could from the massacre. This caught the attention of the current Emperor, Creig Dayel, who took a mighty army and fell upon Nourin, destroying Deidrec's army and dethroning him. I would like to say that all the hate between the kingdoms stopped that day, but unfortunately, it was not the case. Emperor

Creig appointed Duke Erland to rule in Deidrec's place; unfortunately, this did not completely stop the rivalry between kingdoms, but it did lessen it considerably. The current King of Aurora is a young man named Saruda; it is said that he ended the war between the kingdoms shortly after his father's death."

Regence slowly sat back down and began to help himself to a flask of red wine.

"So all those children were killed by Deidrec and his army, and their parents too?" Ralley asked. Her face was a mixture of sadness and anger.

"I am afraid so," Regence said in a quiet voice.

Talon remembered being told this story when he was quite young, though he had forgotten all about it till now. "Then their ghosts have been wandering in unrest for almost two hundred years."

Regence nodded; his expression was thoughtful.

Ralley finished her breakfast and stood. "I want to visit Seselna and Crysna. It's on our way, isn't it?"

"It would mean a four day delay," Talon said, also standing. He removed the map and took it to the back end of one of the wagons, spreading it out. Ralley hurried over to him and leaned over to inspect the map. As she did so, Talon found himself staring at her, examining the way she put a finger to her chin as she thought, the way her brow wrinkled as her eyebrows lifted.

She must have felt him staring, and she turned to meet his eyes. "Yes?" Her voice was soft.

"Uh… nothing…" he said hesitantly turning to the map. "You see? If we cut back to the crossroad we passed, we head this way towards Layahal. It is a two day travel there and then another two days trekking back around through Aurora and the Ghost Lands." Talon tried his best to hide his excitement. He wanted to move through the countryside and avoid all the castles he possibly could. This way would provide that, and they would only have to pass through Aurora.

Ralley undid the clasp on the pouch with the blade and pulled it out. "I need to talk to you. I need to know where Melanie is and if she's doing alright." The blade quivered in her hands, and she let go. It changed shape and stretched until it grew a neck, head, legs, tail and wings. The transformation was too quick for Talon to see much. He watched and waited as the Blade Beast appeared to be speaking with Ralley, though Talon heard nothing. "He says that she is surrounded by three other bright lights. They are farther to the north as well." Ralley frowned.

"Then she is safe for now; we have time to go the alternate route," he said, smiling. This was good; Ralley would not have to worry about her sister now and would decide to go to the Ghost Lands.

Ralley wrinkled her brow. "Well… I guess…."

"The Blade Beast says she is protected; there is nothing to worry about," he said, seeing her indecision.

"But she's gone farther north. She's getting farther away from us, and if we travel four days out of our way, then there's no telling where she will end up."

Talon could see her decision wavering. "She can go no further than the northern coast. She will have to stop, and we can catch up with her then. She has others with her who will protect her, just like the Blade Beast has said. Perhaps she will even head south again after she reaches the coast."

"But how can I know that for sure?" Ralley asked with her eyes to the ground in thought.

"Do not forget, Ralley, you made a promise to the ghost children, did you not?" Talon reminded her as he began to roll up the map.

"I guess you're right," Ralley said, though she did not sound fully convinced. "I did make a promise to check things out for them… I guess we can head to the Ghost Lands and at least take a look, it's just…"

"Good," Talon said smoothly, tucking the map away. "I will make the preparations." Talon turned and marched off, leaving her little choice but to nod after him. He gave his orders to prepare for the journey. Already the men had begun packing up tents and putting out the fire.

"Talon, what is the plan?" Regence asked. "You seem eager to leave."

"We are heading to the Ghost Lands at Ralley's request," he said in a most authoritative voice.

"Four days out of our way? She agreed to this?" Regence asked, his brow furrowing.

"Of course. She consulted with the Blade Beast; her sister is currently safe, so we will take a bit of a detour and help her keep her promise to the Ghost Children." Talon could see his sword master's doubt. "She has made her decision. We go back to the crossroads and take the Road to Layahal."

"Her decision, or yours?" the man replied in a low tone.

"I appreciate your council, swordmaster, but it is not needed at this time," he said stiffly, not looking at him and striding toward Phoenix, who had been saddled moments ago. He easily swung himself onto the stallions back, and his eyes drifted to Regence, who had already turned away and was taking the reins of his own mount. He felt a twinge of regret and watched his good friend swing into the saddle and ride off to the road, calling orders to a servant who had fallen behind in his task. Talon sighed heavily and surveyed the four wagons as the servants hurried to hitch the horses and pull the wagons to the road facing to the South.

Then something nagged at him, something that had been slightly tickling at his thoughts that morning, but that he had never quite taken notice until now. At that moment, one of his men ran to him "Sire, the Demon man is not within his tent!"

"What! Where has he gone? Was there not a guard posted at his tent?" Talon had insisted that Veru use a tent so they could keep watch on him that night despite the demon's protests at wanting to sleep under the stars. His trust in this so-called amarill was taking a turn once again. "Check the immediate area! I want that demon found! I want…" But he was interrupted by the sight of the white wolf marching as cheerful as a chipmunk into the camp and right up to Ralley, who stood by her own saddled horse.

Talon nudged Phoenix and rode over to them, glaring down at Veru. "Where have you been? You were told to remain in your tent! I do not fully trust you to go wandering about, and again you have betrayed my trust in you! Must I put a collar on you and tie you to the wagons?"

The shift from wolf to man was as mind blowing to watch as the Blade Beast's. It was quite fast, and a strange misty fog surrounded him for a brief moment during the process.

"I apologize, your Majesty, I was simply getting myself a fresh rabbit for breakfast and happened to run into my good brother. He is quite displeased with me, I am afraid, but I talked things out. He is such a loyal brother, so concerned for me, but a bit overprotective." All this was said with an air of such cheerfulness that Talon questioned his sincerity.

The Demon's childlike nature was annoying, but in a way there was a strange charming manner to him. "Your brother, you say? I should like to be sure this brother of yours will not hamper our progress … it seems there is little I can do to restrain you, much less both of you."

"Axle is of a mind to stay clear of you, Lord. He would no doubt be a bit unhappy at being restrained, but I assure you, he will do nothing to you or your little band of men as long as I am unharmed."

"You will not be harmed as long as you follow orders," Talon growled.

"Of course, my lord, I shall behave myself." His strange lupine green eyes met Talon's with an innocent twinkle in them. Talon did not believe it for a second.

He turned away without even looking to Ralley. Talon did not want her to change her mind, and he would give her no chance to speak with him long enough to do it. After the wagons were pulled back to the road and pointing south, he made his way to the lead position. Regence joined him moments later. "I am against this detour my lord," he said evenly.

"I know," Talon said with a dismissive tone.

-33-

A Hidden Power

As the sun slowly rose over the countryside, Ralley became more restless. The constant creaking of the wagons and plodding of hooves marked each minute that they traveled in the wrong direction. There was plenty of time for her to wonder why she even decided to do this. There was no guarantee that her sister would remain safe. Hadn't she gone between safety and danger several times already? Ralley sighed and suffered a light shiver, pulling her cloak around herself a bit more. It had gotten colder since leaving Tradewood.

"You look troubled, Empress," Veru said softly as he rode next to her.

Ralley lifted her gaze from the passing road to stare into the gentle green eyes of Veru, who still smiled, though his voice was filled with concern. "I just... don't know if I should be going so far out of my way when my sister could get into trouble. I don't know how we both ended up in this world, but we are here, and there are man-eating monsters and ghosts and all kinds of things I don't know about lurking out there. She's traveling like I am, to the north, but if that's true, she could run into danger at any time." She turned away for a moment, her eyes scanning the trees of the forest. It looked so peaceful and beautiful, but out of the woods had come the black monsters and the bandits. "Will she be safe?" She turned back to Veru and searched his elegant features. His white hair, the way he held himself, the way he spoke, the very air about him only magnified the fact that he was not human.

"There is no way to tell; it all depends on who she is traveling with," he said in his soft tones.

"The Blade Beast said she was in a tower, and he drew it on the map. It looked like a tall building inside a volcano."

"Ah yes, The Grand Summoner Estat. I am sure he will take quite good care of her." He chuckled happily and turned his face forward as if everything were solved.

"Estat? He is good?" Ralley asked, still not convinced of her sister's safety.

"Oh, I am quite sure he is good; however, the village that turned him away thought he was quite bad," Veru said, tapping his finger to his chin and appearing thoughtful.

This didn't help much. "You *were* starting to help make me feel better. Why did they think he was bad?"

"Because he is a summoner of many things, monsters, demons, even amarill like myself, though I have not had the pleasure of meeting him yet."

"Maybe he's the one who kidnapped her! He had green clothes and green hair!"

"The one who took your sister did?" Veru ticked his head like a curious dog.

"Yes, and he went though a dark portal, and I followed them into blackness."

"Hmm, that does not sound like something a summoner does. He would not have come through the portal himself; he would have one of the creatures he summoned do it for him, but you do have a good point. It could have been the Grand Summoner himself who wished to kidnap her." Veru still smiled, as if this new news was quite exciting. "Very interesting, a mystery."

Ralley frowned, wrinkling her nose. "This isn't a game! She could be in big trouble! And here you are smiling and laughing. Do you even care?" She was angry, but how could she expect someone else to feel concern for someone they didn't even know?

"Oh my, I do apologize, but I find it far easier to look on the bright side than try to dwell on the depressing facts. As it is, you have no current means to reach her quickly unless you wish to face possible dangers on your own, so there is very little you could do for her if she were currently in danger. You do have one good thing going for you." Veru's smile was less irritating; it was now almost warm and encouraging.

"Yeah? What's that?"

"You are in a position of great authority, Empress Ralley." He winked at her.

Ralley blinked and faced forward, her eyes falling on the back of Talon's head. Veru was right! She was the Empress wasn't she? If she wanted to turn back, then he had to do what she wanted. She gave her horse a soft nudge, something that Regence had shown her how to do, and it patiently trotted up next to Phoenix and Talon. "Talon, I think I've changed my mind, I… I want to go back, to head north and save my sister."

Talon slowly glanced over at her. "What do you mean? I thought we discussed this already. You should not just change your mind on a whim like that."

"Well, I was talking with Veru, and he says…"

"Ah, I see," Talon interrupted, shaking his head. "Look, Ralley, Veru is not to be trusted, especially with matters of such importance. I have done my best to take the burden off your shoulders and give you strong and solid advice. You would take his words over my own?"

Talon looked genuinely hurt, and Ralley was immediately sorry she had said anything at all. The wind had leaked out from the tear in her sails, but what Veru told her was beginning to make her worry. "Please, Talon; I really think we ought to go back. The thing is, what if she gets into trouble while we are off wandering around other places? Who knows how long it will take to fix the problem with the ghost children? Besides, they are ghosts. I am certain they won't mind waiting a little longer for their freedom. Just long enough for me to get my sister. And who knows, maybe she can help." Ralley smiled at him encouragingly.

"Ralley, we are already on our way, why not just finish what we have started?" Talon faced forward once again.

Why was he so determined to go this way? She understood they would be backtracking, but it was only the beginning of the day. If they quickened their pace, they could make it back to the crossroads and begin their northward travel in half the time. Talon did not look at her and even nudged Phoenix a bit to pull ahead of her. This annoyed her; he had closed the door of discussion. Her father had done this to her many times with the same air of infuriating arrogance. In moments, both Regence and Veru had pulled up on either side of her as Talon slipped further ahead. "Why is it he reminds me of my dad at times? What a royal snob!" She spared a glance at Veru and then Regence. They both gazed back at her, and though Veru had a smile on his face, they both had the raised brows as if they expected more of her. "What?" she grumped, eyeing each of them in turn.

"Would her Majesty also wish to hear a third opinion?" Regence offered gently.

She blinked. "Er… yea sure." Ralley replied with slight hesitation.

"I think you should listen to your heart. There are many things in this world that can dissuade you from your goal, but if something is genuinely important to you, you should do your best not to allow anything to get in your way."

Regence reminded her of her grandpa. She didn't get to see him much since he was always away on some business venture that took him out of the state, occasionally taking her father as well when he needed a younger opinion. Why was she thinking of home so much? She supposed it was because she had genuinely begun to miss it now. "Thanks, Regence… and you too, Veru…" She paused as she turned to him. Veru was still giving her 'the look.' "What is it?"

"Come now, you will not let a little thing like a prince stand in the way of finding your sister, will you, *Empress*?" He said, putting special emphasis on her title.

"Right," Ralley said with finality. Talon was not her father, and he was no longer the son of the Emperor. How dare she allow him to push her around like that! If she was Empress over him, she had to step up to the role and stop being such a little girl. She gave her mount a sharp nudge, and it readily jumped forward, catching back up to Talon. "We are turning back," she announced with an air of authority that would make her father proud.

Talon raised a brow and looked at her. "I thought we were done with this…"

Ralley almost lost her composure a second time. She spared a quick glance back at Veru, and he lifted a triumphant fist to her in encouragement. She straightened her back and looked back to Talon. "I am Empress, and I order you to turn these men around!"

This must have struck a chord, and Talon frowned at her. "Ralley, I will be happy to explain…"

Ralley had had enough. She tugged on the reins and brought her horse to a halt and lifted her hand in the same manner that Talon did to halt the men. This worked as efficiently as it would have if Talon had done it. She turned her horse to face the traveling group to find that they had all stopped and their eyes were on her. Veru was smiling brightly at her as if he were quite proud of her, and Regence too seemed quite pleased at her for making a decision. She cleared her throat, straightened further in her saddle, and spoke as loudly and authoritatively as she could. "I have spoken with the Prince and his advisors and have decided that this detour is unnecessary. I order this expedition to be turned about at once and return to the crossroads where we shall continue north!"

She felt quite proud of herself for coming up with such elegant wording on the spot. It was greeted with several positive sounding shouts of "Yes, Empress!" Regence himself bowed formally to her. "I shall see to it, your Majesty." He turned Crest around to face the men. "You heard the Empress. Get these wagons turned immediately!"

Talon was beside her before she realized it. "What are you doing?" he asked, his voice cracking with anger.

She eyed him. "I did what I had to do to save my sister."

"She is not in any danger, and you have a promise to keep. What does your sister matter next to thousands of others?"

"What does she matter?" Ralley shouted, her anger taking a dangerous leap. "She's my sister! The ghost children and their families are already dead! I don't want my sister to join them. You don't even care about her, do you? You're just out here for your own selfish reasons!" As she spoke, her horse's ears laid flat against its head, and it gave a nervous snort.

Talon's eyes grew wide, and he appeared to want to say something, but Ralley was not interested in what he had to say anymore. "Don't even think about talking down to me anymore just because I'm female, and younger than you! I'm the EMPRESS!" With that last word, she slammed her fist on the saddle, and it was like a shock wave burst out around her. She figured it was just her anger; she was so mad, she was seeing red. Her horse reacted, tossing her head and shuffling. Phoenix also became agitated and reared, tossing the surprised Prince from the saddle.

She heard Regence shouting, but she couldn't make out what he was saying. She felt a strange sensation of floating, and she watched through a red haze as her horse bolted out from underneath her. The last thing she saw was a giant star within a circle outlined on the ground in a glowing, almost flaming red color with unrecognizable symbols in each of its points. Then she felt her anger drain away along with the red light, Talon, Regence, Veru and the burning red star.

-34-

CAVE OF THE VOID MASTER

The night had gone by surprisingly well for sitting in the midst of a coastal storm, and Melanie had little trouble falling asleep. Weiland had cast his own magical shield over them to protect them from much of the wind and rain for the night. The storm didn't let up till some time later that morning, but the wind had slowly died down, and the sun's rays began to dry the rocks on the cliff. They settled for a breakfast of apples, berries and the rest of Weiland's bread. Their water supply was still holding up quite well, and Melanie was certain there would be plenty of fresh water after such a storm.

They made their way to the cliff, Estat once again riding Immuraudi and Weiland moving ahead. He jumped easily along the rocks and peered over the edge to get a good look at the strip of beach below. "Looks like it will be just fine for Immuraudi to land. So then, Melanie, are you ready to fly?"

"W… what me?" She had an idea that they would be flying to the beach, but she hadn't taken the time to think about what that meant. She had never ridden a horse before Immuraudi, and she certainly didn't know how to ride one when it was flying. The mere thought of it made her queasy. "Why don't you go first?"

"I will ride with Estat since he cannot see. "Weiland winked at her and swung himself up behind Estat. "Immuraudi will be back for you; do not worry, it is little more difficult than simply riding, and she will take it easy and tell you what to do."

This didn't comfort her much, and she watched as Immuraudi ran a short way along the cliff and leapt into the air, her red feathered wings spreading out on either side of her. She flapped several times, and then began to gently glide downward. Melanie stepped forward, carefully navigating the rocky area so she could get a good look at their landing. The beach below appeared far narrower than she had expected. Immuraudi and the others grew smaller as they approached it, giving Melanie a sense of how far it was. She shivered a bit, not just from the cold, but also from the sheer height of her position. She found herself on her hands and knees, peering over the rock like a frightened baby bird.

She watched as Weiland hopped off and helped Estat down. Immuraudi easily bolted back into the air with a few quick bounds and flapping of wings. She swept back and forth, ascending the cliff until she rose a short way above Melanie and landed in a level patch between the rocks behind her. "Well? What are you waiting for?" Immuraudi said, stomping a hoof impatiently.

Melanie slid back away from the edge and hurried back to the coramira. "So, uh…"

"Just get on as you normally would."

Melanie slid onto her back and grabbed fistfuls of the red silken mane, tightening her legs, hooking them around the spot where the equine's wings met her body. "Please don't go fast!" Melanie begged.

"Stop being such a foal!" Immuraudi gave a musical laugh and straightened, starting forward at a normal pace, heading right for the cliff's edge. She bounded once or twice to a few large, flat-topped rocks and spread her wings. Melanie cried out as she watched the cliff disappear beneath the equine's legs, and then there was nothing between them and the sandy beach far below. For a few moments they seemed to float in the air, gliding out toward the ocean. If Melanie had felt safer, she would have enjoyed looking out at the deep blue sea, but Immuraudi's wings pulled closer to her body. Melanie's stomach did a flip-flop as they dropped through the air before Immuraudi's wings flicked back out again and they returned to a glide.

"What was that all about?" Melanie cried, fear and anger mingled in her tone.

"Sorry," Immuraudi replied, though it didn't sound very sincere. "You are heavy."

"I most certainly am not!!" Melanie yelled back. For a moment her anger made her forget about her fear, and for a short time she was able to scan the sparkling ocean. She'd never seen it bluer in her life. Then again ... she had to face the fact that this wasn't her world. She squeezed her eyes shut as Immuraudi made a few more short dives before leveling off again, and then she glided down to the sand. The landing was smoother than she thought it would be as the equine flapped several times to slow them and made a short glide, her legs galloping before she touched the sand. Weiland was there to help her slide off, and she stumbled a bit, trying to get used to being stationary again.

"See, not so bad now was it?" Weiland asked, smiling at her.

"Yeah well... let's not do that again anytime soon..." She eyed Immuraudi, but the coramira took no notice.

Melanie turned to face the cliff and discovered a great gaping hole in its side about two stories high and almost the same width. The entrance was brightly lit and covered with moss and small flowers, giving it an almost inviting look, but when she peered deeper into it, she could make out stalactites and stalagmites galore, reminding Melanie of teeth. Estat sat on a boulder near the cave, and though she'd thought he was quite tall, he looked terribly small next to the cavern. "So...how big is Malstraun, anyway?"

"Not sure. I have never seen him myself, but I am eager to meet him." Weiland said as he helped Estat return to Immuraudi's back. "Shall we take a look?" He turned, and as agile as a cat, he leapt onto the rocky cave entrance. She thought she could hear Immuraudi giggle as she moved forward, a little more attentive to the rocky steps than Weiland, but doing so far more easily than Melanie, who found herself stumbling over them. Rock climbing was definitely Ralley's thing, not hers. Ralley. She wondered where she was now, and if she was still safe.

The inside of the cave was damp, but strangely humid, which she was glad for since she had been a bit cold. She could hear the dripping of water all around her, and even running water from time to time. There were patches of moss here and there near the entrance, but as they began to move deeper, she could no longer see them. She started to trip more often in the growing darkness and began to lag behind. "Weiland, I can't see!"

"My apologies, Melanie, I forget that humans do not have the sight that we elves do." She heard him make his way back to her, and he reached down, picking something up from the floor and whispering in a language she didn't understand. Before she could ask what he was doing, a tiny light appeared in his hand. It wasn't bright, but she could see quite well by it.

"What's that?" she asked curiously.

"A simple pebble that I put a spell on to make it glow. Take it; it will help light the way. I will slow down a bit so you can keep up as well." She could see Weiland's smile in the light.

"Thanks!" Melanie held it as if it were a ruby. "What a useful spell!" As Weiland headed forward, she held it out in front of her and hurried after the group. Its light reflected off the water dripping from the stalactites and even made Immuraudi's horn sparkle. She could make out the shape of Estat on her back. He sat straight, but his head did not skim any of the upper rocks, as Immuraudi was carefully avoiding the stalactites that extended down too far. She made her way to the equine's flank and glanced up at him, putting a hand on his leg. Estat smiled down in her direction; he seemed far more relaxed now that they were reaching their destination.

After a short time, Weiland came to a stop, and when Melanie and Immuraudi caught up, they fell silent. Something was out there; she could hear its heavy breathing. The cavern here was thick with humidity, making it harder to breath, and she thought she heard more water. Weiland stood atop a high boulder, his concentration forward, presumably on whatever was making the breathing noise. Melanie timidly climbed up next to him and held out her glowing stone. For a moment she saw nothing, but as she peered into the darkness, she made out something moving up and down along with the sleepy breath.

"Oh, my gosh…" she whispered ever so quietly. The thing was huge! Its body width was similar to her neighbor's truck, but there was no telling how long it was since it appeared to be curled up like a rattlesnake. "Is… is that?"

"Yes." Weiland's voice was soft as ever. "It is Malstraun, master of the void."

"Maybe… we shouldn't wake him…" Melanie wanted to say that perhaps they shouldn't talk to him at all, considering that he looked as though he could crush them all in his dark coils.

Weiland chuckled. "I am sure he has already heard us; besides, you would not want to insult him by running away, would you?"

Indeed, as he spoke, the great black body began to stir; its breathing changed, and a great head began to rise up into the darkness. She thought she could make out two slits that must have been eyes as they opened, casting a slight yellow glint before that too disappeared into the darkness of the cave. There was a rumbling within its bulk, and she heard a booming voice that echoed through the cave. "Estat? Zaioma shianme."

At the mention of his name, Estat lifted his hand in greeting, but there was a rumbling far greater than that of the voice she had heard that shook the cave walls. A sudden gust of wind blew out from around the monster before them, nearly blowing her backwards off her feet. A red light burst into the room at the base of the great black creature that was Malstraun. "En ro ina idenia'et…" spoke the booming voice again. Melanie didn't recognize whatever language it spoke, and she was far too distracted by the constant wind that blasted them. Its source came from the glowing red light that formed into a giant star within a circle. The monster gave an ear-shattering roar that boomed like thunder over their heads as the red light engulfed it. "En namo naia vako, umate en teru verun," it roared as the glowing red star and circle rose up along its body. The light was so bright that Melanie had difficulty seeing the event. What she could see was that as the star passed up along its body it disappeared into it, the bottom half of its body completely gone. It continued up along its neck until it reached the horned head and many-toothed maw of the great serpent Malstraun. In moments, that too had gone, and the entire symbol vanished, leaving a crimson haze behind that swirled about in the dying wind.

"What in the world just happened? Did we make it mad or did we scare it off?" Melanie climbed back up to Weiland who stood peering into the darkness where Malstraun once was.

"No, he was summoned... this is unexpected," he whispered almost to himself.

Melanie turned to see Estat hunched over, an expression of anger on his face, his fists clenched. She hurried to him and put a reassuring hand on his leg. "Estat? What's wrong?"

Immuraudi turned her head to Weiland. "What if the demon has summoned him?"

"It is not certain. Have patience, Estat. Malstraun said he would return. It will be best to wait here for him since there is no telling where he has gone." Together Weiland and Melanie, setting the glow stone atop a nearby boulder, helped Estat down from the coramira's back.

Once he was on his feet, he took Melanie in his arms and hugged her tightly. "Estat!" He seemed so upset. It was so unfair! The one guy she really liked and he didn't even have a voice to tell her a thing about himself, his life, his likes and dislikes. It just wasn't fair! "Oh, I wish you could just talk to me!" She cried desperately. Melanie wrapped her arms tightly around him too and at that moment something strange happened between them. A tingle ran through her and along her arms like the feeling one got from a leg falling asleep. She told herself it was just her anger and exhaustion from the trek.

"Me...too..." his unfamiliar voice wheezed into her ear.

-35-

THE GREAT BLACK SERPENT

Talon recovered from falling off Phoenix and turned to see Ralley floating off the back of her own mount, which startled out from under her. A red glow had engulfed her entire body, and the ground beneath their feet began to quiver. Regence and the others struggled to keep their horses from panicking. A short distance from him a star within a circle swirled into existence, glowing as red as Ralley, its circumference spanning the field next to the road. Crimson flames flickered about the strange symbols within, and a gust of wind blasted out in every direction. It rose up into the air, and as it did, it left behind a giant, black, coiled body. The wind spread an angry red haze that hung like fog around them all, as if Ralley's anger had now become a visible substance. The huge red symbol dissipated two levels above them, leaving behind the gigantic neck and head of a black serpent. Two, ebony, bull-like horns ran parallel to one another and ended at sharp points half a pace from its face. Its huge yellow eyes examined them all as the vertical pupil adjusted to become as narrow as a cat's in bright light.

What had happened? He thought. *Had Ralley summoned this beast? Was she a sorceress? And if so, why did she not tell us?* He glanced back at her, but she had fallen to the ground and lay unmoving; the red light had left her. Talon spun back around to face the oversized serpent and drew his sword. Whatever it was, it did not look friendly. Indeed, it appeared quite annoyed, and it opened its huge jaws, letting out an angry, thunderous roar, its mouth full of gleaming sharp teeth. "Regence! Get the Empress!" he shouted, not taking his eyes off the monster as he began to back up. *Where is that damned horse of mine?*

With surprising speed, the serpent's head lunged forward, its horns diving down at Talon. He threw himself to one side in time to avoid them. The horns of the monster slammed into the earth where he had been standing. Talon picked himself up as fast as he could, stumbling back a few paces. For a moment he thought the serpent had gotten stuck, its horns embedded in the soil. Its pupil shifted to settle on him, and the thick skin around its mouth curled back in what appeared to be a sinister grin. Its head tilted to the side and came toward him, the horns cutting through the dirt like a ship through water.

Again Talon lunged back out of its way, but this time he swung at the beast with his sword, though it only glanced harmlessly off one of the projections that crowned its head. The serpent drew its head back up into the air, dirt and grass flying. From behind he heard the twang of many bows and a volley of arrows streaked overhead, bouncing off the thick hide that covered the beast. It took no notice of them, and its coils shifted along the ground as it slid forward. He could hear Regence shouting orders, but he was too distracted to understand what he said. The gigantic creature chuckled as it reared its head back for another strike. "You are rather light on your feet." said a deep booming voice.

Was that the monster speaking? Talon readied himself, and as the head came down at him, he ran forward toward the main bulk of the serpent's body. Behind him, he could hear the horns slam into the earth once again, but he continued on, holding his sword like a lance and ramming it into the thick skin. It penetrated a hand span into the hide, and it took a considerable amount of strength on his part to wrench the blade free, but he had at least done some damage. Thick, deep red blood oozed out of the wound, and he felt a surge of hope that this beast could be defeated.

"Happy over a little scratch?" said the voice again. Talon whirled around to see the head of the beast turned to the side so that one yellow orb stared back at him.

"I shall scratch you a thousand times if that is what it takes!" Talon shouted back, again lifting his sword and racing at the head in an attempt to stab it through the eye.

The giant beast lifted his head away from Talon's attack, dirt clods and grass raining down on him. Another volley of arrows shot up toward the serpent, and it closed its massive eyes to protect them against the missiles. Regence and the other warriors used that moment to charge in, their own swords held in the lance position. They swept past Talon towards the monster, their six swords plunging into the body of the beast.

The great serpent roared, "You will have to do better than that!" and its body began to uncoil.

"Away!" Talon shouted to them. As one, Regence and the

others pulled their swords from the thick hide and retreated back as the beast's tail appeared on their right side. With the sound of rolling thunder, the appendage swept towards them along the ground. "Jump!" Talon yelled. The tail came to a thin point, and as it swept at them, Talon leaped over it and sent himself into a roll on the other side. When he got to his feet, there was a cloud of dust around him, but there were also the shapes of his men rising to their feet. It looked as though they were all able to make the jump, including Regence.

"Talon above you!" the sword master shouted.

The prince's gaze snapped up to see a large black head coming at him. As he turned and tried to throw himself out of harm's way, there was a heavy thud on either side of him, and something hard rammed his hip. His body hit the ground, and the wind was knocked out of him. At the same time, he heard someone scream. For a terrifying moment he found his lungs refused to breath the air, and he wondered if the scream had come from his own lips. When he finally gasped and took a breath, it was filled with dust, and he began coughing. He turned on his side and found he was pinned between the monster's ebony horns, its razor sharp teeth inches away from his hip. Regence and the other warriors tried to charge in at its exposed head, but one of the serpents' coils slammed down in front of them and threatened to sweep them away, forcing them to retreat.

The one who had screamed called out his name. It was Ralley; he could see her standing next to Veru some distance away, and the demon made no move to halt her as she came running towards him. Talon tried to tell her to stop, but he only sucked in more dirt and coughed harder. The great black beast's jaws opened, and a thick red tongue snaked out to wrap around one of Talons legs, intent upon drawing him into the vicious maw.

"NO! Stop!" Ralley screamed at it. To Talon's amazement, the serpents tongue released his leg and disappeared back into its mouth, and its head pulled away from him, leaving two large holes in the earth where its horns had been.

"Go away!" Ralley shouted as she rounded Talon and stopped between him and the black serpent, her arms outspread. "I... I un-summon you!" she said somewhat awkwardly.

The monster paused to examine her, and then gave her a wide toothy grin. "As you please, Mistress Summoner. I have other things to attend to, but perhaps we shall meet again." As it spoke, the summoning symbol that brought him here appeared over its head with a swirl of red flames and gusting wind. The beast even nodded to her just before the symbol descended over its entire length till it reached the ground and vanished along with the black serpent.

Talon's coughing calmed some and he struggled to his feet. "You... you did that?" he wheezed.

"Well... Veru said I did... and... he said I could get rid of it..." Ralley stammered. She appeared to be amazed at what she had done and maybe a little frightened.

Regence rushed to his side to help him up. "Are you alright Prince Tal..."

"Men! Bring Veru to me immediately!" Talon shouted as he was pulled to his feet. He could not believe that Ralley had done it; it had to be something done by the powers of a demon, or amarill, whatever he chose to call himself. Talon slapped the dust from his clothes, coughing a few more times to clear his lungs. "I am fine, Regence." he said, sounding a bit on edge.

"What's going on?" Ralley asked, concerned, her eyes following the warriors as two of them took Veru by his arms and brought him their way.

"It was you!" Talon shouted as Veru was brought in front of him. He drew his sword and held it to Veru's chest. "What are you planning? That thing almost killed us all!"

Before Veru could answer, a black shape bolted towards them from the nearby brush and caught Talon's sword in its mouth. He stood stunned for a moment, examining the wolf-like creature that stood before him. Its eyes were a clear blue, and its ebony fur shone like steel. Its growl had a strange metallic ring to it like the sound of two swords clashing.

"Oh, dear... I did tell you that my brother was quite protective," Veru said without alarm.

Talon attempted to pull his sword free, but the jaws of the black wolf held it tightly. "Men..." But as his men lifted their swords Ralley spoke up.

"No!" She said as she stepped up to Talon. "It's my fault. I summoned it, Veru told me I was bathed in red light. I was, wasn't I?"

She was right, Talon had seen her, and he was loath to admit it. "Very well, now tell this... *thing* to let go of my sword." He hated being wrong, feeling so powerless.

"You're Axle, right?" Ralley asked, stepping close to him. "Your brother told us about you. Please let go of Talon's sword. I promise he won't hurt your brother; Veru is my friend."

Axle narrowed his eyes, but he let go of the sword and watched Talon as he sheathed it. Then he turned his head to eye the men holding Veru's arms.

"Release him," Ralley said, and they obeyed.

Axle growled with that strange reverberation, showing his mouthful of sharp teeth. Veru chuckled. "It is alright, it was just a misunderstanding. Yes, I intend to stick around for a while. I am enjoying myself, are you not?" Axle snarled in response. "Now, now, do not be that way."

"You understand all that noise?" Talon said a bit surprised.

In moments Axle had shifted from the wolfish shape to a human one. He appeared opposite to Veru in color and style, though his face was very similar. His clothes were roughly made and as black as his fur, though the style was like Veru's. His hair was also the same length as his twin's but once again ink in color. Even Axle's skin was a few shades darker. "You had better watch your step, Prince!" he spat, one finger jabbing at Talon's chest.

Talon returned his hand to his sword hilt. He could take the demon's head off in seconds if he wanted, but Ralley had put a soft hand on his. "Wait," she said, and turned to the brothers. "What was that thing, and how did I summon it?"

Before Veru could open his mouth, Axle cut in. "Hah! That 'thing' you summoned was Malstraun, the Great Black Serpent, sorceress, and he will not take kindly to you if he ever sees you again."

"What?" Talon said with great awe. He remembered the tales he had heard, legends of many demons and monsters that had kept him dreaming of epic battles since he was young. It was as if his dream had come alive. He had fought against, and survived, a great legendary demon!

"I'm not a sorceress!" Ralley insisted. "I don't know how I did it, or why, I'm just an ordinary girl! I was just angry, that's all!"

"An ordinary girl, from another world, who is now an Empress," Veru corrected gently.

"And you have a power that you did not expect," Regence put in.

"And you are very brave," Talon admitted, recalling the image of Ralley standing, arms spread, between himself and the legendary Black Serpent. She had protected him at risk of her own death, and he had done nothing but put her sister at greater risk by sidetracking their rescue mission. "I am sorry Ralley, this is my fault. I was the one who angered you, and your anger must have been the catalyst for summoning Malstraun," he said, his eyes turning to the ground with the guilt he felt before gazing back at her.

"Yes, well, I was pretty mad wasn't I?" Ralley smiled, forgiveness in her eyes.

Axle smirked and crossed his arms. "I would say so. Passing annoyance would have summoned a common snake."

Talon ignored him and turned to Regence. "We return to the crossroads immediately!"

"As you command," the sword master replied with a fist to his heart. He then turned and ordered the men to their mounts.

"We're going to get my sister, then?" Ralley asked, stepping forward and gazing up at him.

"With all speed, Empress Ralley," Prince Talon replied with a deep bow.

As he straightened, Ralley threw her arms around him and hugged him tightly. He vowed at that moment that he would protect her to the greatest of his ability and vowed too that he would never again act so selfish or doubt the wisdom of the Blade Beast's choice.

-36-

ESTAT SPEAKS

Estat pulled away from Melanie. He was shocked to find that he had spoken. Over these long days, he had been unable to utter a sound. He had almost grown accustomed to his own silence.

"Estat! You spoke!" Melanie squealed in excitement. "I was just wishing that very thing! I wanted you to be able to speak with me, and you spoke!"

There had been magic involved; Estat felt it, but he could not tell how, though he did know that it was Melanie, and she appeared to be oblivious to it. "Melanie…" he said, his voice hoarse. He found himself coughing, and Melanie patted him on the shoulder.

"Take it easy. I'll get you some water and you can try again more slowly. If you try it in a whisper, it might lead to less coughing," she said, still sounding quite excited.

He listened as she rummaged through one of the bags and brought him a water skin. He took slow gulps to wet his rough throat, and then took her hand. "Melanie," he said in a whisper. "I am sorry I got you involved in this." He paused to clear the tickle in his throat. "I should have had you stay in the tower where it was safe."

"No, it's good that I came. You never would have made it on your own anyway, and you know that," Melanie insisted.

"That is no excuse. I put your life in danger…"

"You have to stop Xenopus so he doesn't destroy your world; it was the right thing to do," she countered.

"Not if it means your life," Estat wheezed. There was another fit of coughing, and Melanie bade him to drink more of the water and soothe his rough throat.

When he had calmed, she wrapped her arms around him. "You just got your voice back. You shouldn't try to talk too much at first. I'm just thankful that you 'can' talk. And don't say another word about bringing me out here; I accept your apology, and I'm glad I came, even if we are too late."

Estat hugged her in return. "Thank you, Melanie," he whispered into her ear. If they were too late to save Brek, if they were too late to save this world, at that moment he did not care; he had come to know this otherworldly princess, and he felt as though he could reverse time itself.

"Alright, so what do we do now?" the coramira asked, breaking the silence.

"We wait," Weiland said gently.

"If Malstraun does not return soon, I am afraid to linger would be a waste, but there is not much else we can do," Estat whispered as he let go of Melanie. The three of them sat down together to wait. Estat could hear Immuraudi pacing about, her cloven hooves making a distinct clicking noise on the stone floor of the cave. Melanie had retrieved the glowing stone and was asking Weiland what else he could make glow like that.

They did not have to wait long. There was a sudden gust of

wind, and Estat could feel the energy in the room increase as the power of a reverse summons swept through the cavern.

"Tuenta en'ro ushente." Boomed the voice of Malstraun. He spoke in the language of the amarill, one Estat could speak just as well as common. "Estat, zem kula shianme'ro nen tai'ze?"

"Niz," Estat said as he got to his feet. "They are good friends of mine; you can speak freely around them." He spoke aloud so Malstraun could hear him, but this only sent him into another fit of coughing. Melanie clutched his arm, pressing the water skin into his hand.

"My apologies for the wait," Malstraun boomed, "It would seem you are not the only one who enjoys my company. Though the one that took me away seems to have done so by accident. What has become of you Estat? Why have you traveled here to my cave and not simply summoned me to you?" His voice was closer now, and Estat could feel the hot breath of the amarill as he spoke. He wondered briefly at whom it was that had the powers to summon him away, even if by accident, but there were other matters that were more important right now.

"Brek betrayed me," Estat whispered. "He has summoned a demon into this world, and if we do not stop him from killing Brek and gaining back his power, he will summon lesser demons to destroy us all." He paused, taking another drink of the water until it was empty. "I tried to stop him, but the demon Xenopus took my sight and my voice. The latter of which I have only recently recovered." He felt Melanie squeeze his arm.

"I see..." Malstraun rumbled. "Then we must rescue the betrayer? I would sooner swallow him than save him, but for you, friend, I will restrain myself."

"Thank you," Estat said, a small smile coming to his lips. It was good to have Malstraun's humor again; it had been some time since he had spoken to him last.

"I will guess you wish to begin as soon as possible… and I shall assume a more compact form so as not to continue to frighten this maiden of yours," he chuckled, the sound of which was like rolling thunder.

Estat wrinkled his brow and turned his head in Melanie's general direction. "Is that why you are squeezing the life out of my arm?" he asked in a joking but gentle tone.

"Oh… I… I'm sorry…" Melanie stuttered. She loosened her grip, but Estat chuckled.

"Not to worry, I was only teasing. Malstraun can be a bit intimidating in his true form…" He began to cough again. This time Weiland handed him his own water skin and took the other.

There was a roaring sound that Estat remembered well. The first time he had heard it was ages ago when he had first summoned the Great Black Serpent Malstraun to him. His massive form had diminished with a swirl of silver and gray haze. What had been left in its place was a tall man with short, wild black hair, dressed in comfortable silver and black clothing that, to the eye, appeared much like leather and matched the hide of Malstraun in his former guise. The disturbance of the air around him brought him back to the current moment. He could hear the footsteps of Malstraun as he came towards them.

Melanie gasped. "You're… a human? How did you do that?"

Malstraun chuckled; though his voice was not the thunderous one of moments ago, it still had a deep, dramatic tone. "All amarill have two forms, but the truer form is the one you saw moments ago. This one is simply a far easier frame for coupling among our kind."

"Coupling, you mean… oh… well… okay. That makes sense…" Melanie loosened her grip farther. "It's certainly a little less intimidating."

"I shall begin searching for Brek. I will need some time," Malstraun said. Estat could hear him walk away.

"What does he mean?" Melanie asked. "Isn't he going to take us to the demon?"

"Yes, but first he must find Brek. He has met him before, so it will be far easier for him to open a portal to wherever he is than to try and find Xenopus," Estat explained, coughing slightly.

"If Malstraun were to try and seek Xenopus himself…" Weiland began, "Then the demon would feel his mental presence and know that we are coming, yes?"

Estat nodded in reply.

"And there would go our surprise rescue," Immuraudi added.

Again Estat bobbed his head.

They all stood waiting in silence; whether it was fear of the impending meeting with Xenopus or perhaps to keep Estat from talking too much, he was not quite sure, but he hoped it was the latter. He did not want anyone getting hurt, and fear was no great help in staying safe. He could hear Malstraun approach them a short time later.

"Well then, if you are all ready, I shall begin," he said with his smooth, deep voice.

"I don't know how much help I'll be, but I will come too… I can't leave Estat without a pair of eyes," Melanie said, reclaiming his arm.

"I have already put your lives in danger. I cannot ask you all to go with me." Estat put a hand to one of Melanie's.

"No need to ask, we come of our own will," Weiland said decisively. "We must stop Xenopus, or none of us will have a home to go back to. It is the responsibility of us all."

Malstraun cleared his throat. "If that is all settled…" There was a great rush of power and a chilling breeze that stirred the air.

"Oh, no…not another one of those!" Melanie moaned, squeezing his arm, and Estat realized she spoke of the portal. Of course, the first time she had seen one would have been the moment when Xenopus had kidnapped her.

"You could always stay behind," Immuraudi snorted.

With a firm hold, Melanie led Estat forward. He could feel the portal looming over him. The cold wind surrounded it, and it was like a solid wall of power to his magic sense. Since the taking of his sight and voice, he had grown more in tune with that mystical awareness than ever before. Melanie hung back hesitantly. He frowned and took her hand as if to gently remove it. "You do not have to go," he said softly.

"I want to," she whispered back.

Together they strode through the great portal. The temperature dropped dramatically, chilling his throat. This did not help much, and he coughed several more times. They became weightless, and he felt the ground disappear beneath him. Melanie threw her arms around him and drew him in tight. "Is this supposed to happen?" she whispered. It was a natural reaction not to shout here, for there was no sound in the void.

"Yes," Estat replied, also whispering. "This is the world between all worlds."

"It is empty as Melanie's head," came Immuraudi's voice a short distance behind them. Weiland's chuckle was heard somewhere just above it.

"Oh? You're lucky I like this glowing stone, or I'd throw it at your head," Melanie hissed.

"Everyone present and accounted for, I see." Malstraun gave a deep chuckle. "Do not make me leave any of you behind."

"Malstraun, be sure to leave the portal up once you have opened it. We must have our escape route ready," Estat whispered.

"As you request," Malstraun replied.

"Wouldn't Xenopus come after us? He came through a portal and got me… would he be able to do that again?" There was fear in Melanie's question.

Weiland spoke first. "You are with us now. There are several spells that can prevent him from finding us. I am sure he figured Estat would never come to find Brek, so he had no need to place wards on him."

"His mistake," Immuraudi retorted.

"Then let us not waste the opportunity," said Malstraun as another rush of cool wind swirled about them and that familiar magic tingle signaled to Estat that a new portal had opened up in the emptiness. Estat could feel the strong hand of the Void Master as he pushed him through the portal. Melanie hugged him tight, and moments later, their feet touched ground, and it was all he could do to keep from tumbling face first into it.

Estat's magic sight burst with activity, and wherever his head turned, there was a multitude of magical presence. *Oh no….* He thought. *Are we already too late?*

-37-

A Bigger Problem

The trip through the strange black portal had been frightening, reminding Melanie of the time she had been kidnapped by the green haired Xenopus. However, their destination was even more unnerving. They had arrived in a small clearing before the mouth of a cave. There was a stone fountain in the middle of the grassy area that was big enough to swim in. Melanie didn't really mind all that; what she did mind was the fact that they were completely surrounded by the most grotesque monsters she had ever seen. There were beasts with multiple tentacles that had come straight from her nightmares, crawling about in the grass, which withered away at their touch. Clawed beasts that looked similar to apes except for their long gangly hair and bulbous noses hung from the trees, destroying the branches and stuffing leaves into their tusked jaws. Slimy green blobs hovered around the fountain as if they wished to meld with its water, but none of them attempted to touch it. Yet more beasts clung to the sides of the cave, their multiple eyes twisting in their sockets to gaze at everything at once. Melanie cried out and clung ever tighter to Estat. She didn't want to see them anymore, and out of the corner of her eye, could see yet more beasts emerging from the caves entrance.

"They're horrible! Let's go back!" she cried, forgetting why they had even come.

At the same moment, the gruesome creatures around them took better notice of their entrance and began to move towards them. Weiland and Immuraudi came through the portal, and the elf immediately drew his rapier from its sheath at his side, his other hand snatching something out of his pouch and lifting it, a green glow emanating from the tiny object. Immuraudi reared, kicking her hooves and swinging her horned head.

Estat put his free hand on her arm. "Stay close."

Malstraun had come through moments after, his dark eyebrows lifting at the sight. "It would seem we are a bit late. It has begun." He strode casually into the clearing. Behind her, Melanie could hear the portal they had stepped through collapse, and with it, their escape out of this madness.

"Do you see Brek?" Estat asked.

Melanie shook her head. "No, no I don't," she said quickly. "What do we do?" Melanie just wanted to leave, but it looked like they were stuck for now until they could locate Brek. "Maybe he's in the cave …." she said doubtfully.

She should not have mentioned this as Estat began to nod. "Let us go, and hurry," he said, loud enough for the others to hear.

At first, Melanie didn't move a muscle. She watched in horror as one of the green slime balls sloshed forward and strange globby protrusions shot out the top of it at Malstraun. He lifted his hand as if to block it, but the effect was more than she'd expected. The appendage disappeared just in front of his hand through a small portal that had appeared and it pulled back in surprise moments after, covered in hundreds of little white specks that were drying it out. Malstraun glanced back at her. "Salt; gets them every time... you coming?" She hurried forward with Estat in tow, deciding that next to Malstraun would be the safest place.

Weiland and Immuraudi covered their backs as they all hurried forward to the cave. When a many tentacled creature threatened, Immuraudi lashed out with her horn, severing three of the limbs with one swipe. It appeared rather bewildered as it backed off and kept staring at its stubs as if hoping they would grow back. Weiland threw his strange green ball of light at the feet of a small group of monsters that were also getting much too close. It burst into many small lights that began to dissipate and Melanie wondered if the spell was a dud, but then the ground erupted with vines that quested for limbs and loops in the monsters that it could wrap around, efficiently tangling them in a mass of greenery that continued to grow despite the creatures biting and tearing at them.

When they came to the entrance of the cave, a figure sauntered towards them, and then stopped just before the entry. All the demons approaching them backed away. Melanie recognized him; it was Xenopus, the man who had kidnapped her. "Ah, Estat, what brings you stumbling back to me?" His voice was oozing with cruelty. "You do realize that you are too late, I take it? The portal is open, there are already demons flooding out of it." Even as he said this, creatures were gathering in the shadows just behind him.

"Yes, you are right," Estat said rather calm. "But it is not too late to do something. Malstraun, I need to get in there."

Nodding, Malstraun lifted his hands toward Estat, and the air around them shimmered and blurred. Melanie wasn't sure what had happened, but now there was a thin membrane of clear jelly-like liquid surrounding Estat and herself. "You have ten minutes," Malstraun warned, his last word deepening further as his body began to change. In moments, he was once again in his former, serpentine shape. Rising to meet the challenger, Xenopus swelled into a monster himself, a great green toad-like creature with undulating tentacles upon its back, tipped with barbs.

Melanie hesitated as she examined the course around Xenopus to the cave, but he didn't appear concerned over guarding its entrance as he made a lunge for the Great Black Serpent. "Hurry, this way!" Weiland shouted as he and Immuraudi charged forward into the mouth of the cave.

Estat gripped her hand tight as they ran for the entrance. She wasn't sure if he was nervous himself or if he was simply making sure that she didn't run in fear. Just inside the cave, Weiland and his equine companion began to clear a path for them, lashing out at yet more demons that tried to block their path. One managed to reach a long, claw-tipped arm at them, but it sank into the strange shimmer surrounding them. Seconds later it had emerged; most of it was gone, and what was left of it was melting. The demon howled in pain, then was lost in the tide of other demons vying for a chance at fresh meat. Melanie realized this shimmering shield around them was another portal to someplace rather unpleasant. It moved easily with them, but she became aware that whatever they happened to brush against would suffer the same fate as the previous demon.

A shrill cry came from Immuraudi as a monster scored on her flank. Weiland was struggling to hold back the monsters that were crowding into the small cave tunnel. "We have to hurry!" Estat urged.

Yes, he was right; they only had ten minutes. Ten minutes of what? The shield? Melanie gripped Estat's arm. They had to hurry through so that Weiland and Immuraudi didn't have to protect them. "Fall back to Malstraun, we will be alright!" Melanie shouted to them and hastened forward. She came to a halt and cringed as she spotted a demon lunging straight at them. It disappeared into the portal shield, causing those behind it to reconsider their attack. When the demon did not re-emerge, Melanie resumed her forward momentum. The other creatures in the cave did not jump at them, but they were each keen on testing this phenomenon out themselves. Claws, arms, tendrils and even an occasional head came into contact with the barrier, but each one came out in various stages of disintegration. One particularly large demon with three heads and two pointed tails hunched down in front of them. Melanie paused for only a moment, then pursed her lips, glared at the demon, and walked forward. It was much taller than Estat and herself, and as the shimmering portal brushed against its belly, it blinked in surprise. Melanie continued on, her eyes widening as they passed through him like passing through a tunnel. Once they were through him, Melanie glanced back. She realized she should have expected the gruesome scene behind her as there was now a hole in the demon. Thick blood stained the area as the demon screamed, wavered and fell over.

When Melanie snapped her gaze back around, the demons were rushing to make way for them. Now none of them challenged their passing, and she was able to run along the cave, coming upon a large room filled with red light. Upon the floor was a glowing star within a circle with various symbols in its points. Hovering just above it was a great swirling red portal where all these monstrous things must have come from, for others were still spilling from its opening. Black flames flickered about at its edges, and the room was thick with an overpowering burnt smell. It also gave off a feeling of despair, loss and devestation. It was the gate to a world of evil, and she could feel it in every part of her body, like a devil whispering in her ear, wanting her to do the most horrible things. She shivered violently at the visions she had.

"The portal… it is strong," Estat said as if he could sense it himself.

"How do we stop it?" Melanie wasn't sure she wanted to try. It looked as if the slightest upset of this strange magical disturbance would make it explode.

"Where is Brek?" he asked.

Her eyes scanned the room. It was filled with monsters, and the two humans in the room weren't too hard to spot. They stood next to a wall in the cave with shelving crowded with bottles of blue glowing things. She even recognized the strange little Éclair creature from before hovering over them. "I think I see him… he's with some woman…" A blond haired woman in a prom style dress; damn… she hated missing the prom. They didn't notice Estat and herself yet.

"We have to close the portal and get him out of here alive," Estat insisted.

"How, exactly, do you close down a portal?" she asked, staring at the mass of symbols and red flames. She began to worry at the time. Had it already been five minutes?

"Just push over the braziers, it will stop the fires from burning, and then you must quickly erase the symbols, starting with the one in the south west leg of the star."

Melanie's eyes scanned over the symbol that he spoke of and gasped. It was a sickly thing that was moving all by itself. She had to turn away after a moment. "S… so just knock these down?" she asked, feeling a bit hesitant.

"Yes, hurry! We only have a few minutes left until the shield breaks."

Melanie shuddered at the idea of the shield dropping with the demons pouring into the room but hurried forward, pulling him along, and began to allow the braziers to be swallowed up through the portal shield. This alerted the strange woman sitting with Brek, and she shouted something to them that sounded rather unpleasant. The shield did not extend through the floor, so when Melanie came to the symbols, she had to erase them with the hem of her dress.

"STOP!" The blond woman shouted, running toward them as the portal overhead wavered and the stream of monsters coming out began to thin. Brek trailed after the furious woman, a mixture of concern and fear on his face. "Stop them, fools!" she screamed at the monsters around them. They all growled, hissed and screeched, but after having reached out at them a few times and lost limbs, they glared at the woman as if to say, "YOU go fetch them."

"Hurry!" Estat hissed urgently. Was he keeping track of the time? How much did they have left? Melanie rushed to the next symbol. It was the one that was squirming and clawing about. She hesitated, scuffing at the tail in the drawing with her foot. When it easily disappeared, she crouched down and began erasing the rest. The moving symbol was quite angry with this, but in only a moment or two it had been completely erased. The great red portal shifted, wobbled, and then collapsed, leaving behind an acrid smell and thick black smoke. The shield around them shimmered, and there was a rippling effect all around them. Then it was gone, and they stood completely exposed to the last of the demons in the room. The blond woman gave them a cruel smile and began to chant in an odd language.

-38-

Wayward Hope

Melanie clutched to him now, and Estat knew what it meant. Malstraun's protective shield had collapsed, and now he could hear the ancient magic language being spoken into a spell close by. He turned to face the direction of the voice, also speaking several words in the mystical tongue as he lifted his hand into the air. He felt the blast of power and a scream from Melanie as the woman's spell flew through the air towards them and hit the deflective barrier he had just thrown up, redirecting the blow somewhere over their heads. The walls shook and sent a shower of rocks to the cave floor. He could hear the howl of a demon behind them just after a heavy thud.

"Melanie, we must take Brek and go!" Estat urged.

"But he's with that blond chick, and there are demons all over the place; they're coming toward us. What do you expect me to do? I only know one spell!" she cried, still clinging to him.

"Then use it," he said. "I have not the eyes to see, so you must counter attack, quickly, before she begins another spell," Estat could do little else than block spells, if he were to cast blindly he may well hit Breck or even bring more rocks down upon them.

He felt the burst of magic moments later as it erupted from somewhere to his left and shot across the room. The sorceress was already chanting the deflective spell and sent the fireball off in another random direction, the ground shuddering as the fireball impacted the cavern. Estat had to do something, or else she would easily overtake them with a more destructive spell. "Again," he said, tapping Melanie's arm.

"But the demons!" she protested.

"Again!" Estat corrected sternly.

He felt the magic gather to her once again, and again the sorceress began to chant, but this time, Estat tore away from Melanie's grip and ran straight for the chanting voice. Behind him, Melanie abandoned her spell with a cry of alarm, and the enemy stopped chanting as well, but he could still feel the tingling in the air of the magic on her fingertips even as she stepped aside to avoid his charge. He turned sharply and bowled into her. She cried out, and he also heard a surprised grunt from Brek. Estat put a hand to what he was certain was the woman's midriff and chanted a quick spell while fending off her flailing arms with his free hand. In moments, his spell had been completed and the woman lay prone underneath him.

"Austia! Austia!" Brek's voice whimpered next to him. "How could you? How could you?" He gripped Estat's arm and tugged at him. "What have you done to her? You cannot do that to her! She is Austia, do you not see?"

"Thanks to you, I do not." Estat growled, attempting to pull his arm from Brek's tight grip. Behind him, he could feel and hear another blast of flame from Melanie and the howl of a demon. In the next instant she was next to him.

"You're crazy, you know that?" she hissed, pulling him to his feet. "We're surrounded, and the cave is coming down around us. What do I do?" she pleaded frantically.

Her words alerted him to the sound of stones hitting the floor around them. "We use it to our advantage. We have to find an exit, even if we must blast our way out," he said. Brek had let go of his arm, but Estat reached out and managed to take hold of Brek's wrist. "You are coming with us," he said with finality.

The cave shuddered again, and he felt pebbles hitting him on the head and heard them landing all around them. "This way, quick!" Melanie said, pulling Estat along. "I see light!" He felt the blast of her fire and heard the scream of a demon as they went, Melanie dragging him and he dragging Brek, who was still mumbling about his goddess. Something grabbed at his leg, but he tore it away, feeling its claws rake the ankle, but he pressed on. If he stopped, there would be worse. "There's a cave-in; we'll have to climb," she said, turning and sending another blast at a creature that screamed like a mountain cat.

Indeed, Estat stumbled onto the rocks as she spoke, and he could feel the sun on his face and the blackness in his eyes lightened. The cave quaked again, and he could hear large boulders crashing around him and demons screaming and howling. He began to climb, feeling his way as quickly as he could, scraping his hands. It was dangerous doing this without eyes as well as dragging someone along who was quite reluctant to leave. "But the Goddess!" Brek shouted in dismay.

"Blast you, she was no goddess!" Estat shouted above the noise of the crashing rocks. He slipped a bit as he tried to climb while holding onto Brek, but a hand caught his arm and returned it to its previous position.

"You alright?" came Melanie's concerned voice.

"Yes, but let us get out of here quickly. I can feel the aura of spirits fleeing from this cave." Though these strange auras were many, they did not seem malicious and seemed intent on simply escaping toward the light.

"I can see them too," Melanie huffed as she assisted him in climbing along the rockslide. "They're bright blue; I saw them in jars in the cave after you knocked over the sorceress."

After a most painful climb, Melanie assured them that they had reached the top of the slide and were now standing upon a great mound. "Do you see Malstraun and the others?" Estat asked, hearing the worry in his own voice. He was not sure how Malstraun would hold up against a demon like that.

"I… I don't see them, just demons. They're coming this way! Flying ones!"

"We cannot fight them all; we must escape!" Estat could feel Brek tugging at his grip, but he refused to let go.

"Where? We have no place to go! There's nothing but shrubbery around here!" Melanie panicked, holding to his other arm.

Estat could hear the monsters approaching; the flapping of their wings and the sickly auras that they generated grew stronger. Another aura was approaching from a different direction, but this aura was not like the first ones. He turned to face it, and moments later, Melanie called out. "Immuraudi, over here!"

He was relieved when he heard the equine land next to them. "I cannot carry the three of you!" she protested. "Two perhaps, but three is far too much weight to lift off!"

"Then we shall have to ride. Brek, get on." But Brek struggled against Estat's hold and screamed out for Austia.

"If we did not need the fool, I would suggest leaving him behind," Immuraudi snorted. "We do not have the time for this!" Estat could hear her make a swift movement, and a demon cried out in pain. "They are upon us, defend yourself!"

Again Melanie began to use the fire magic that Estat had taught her. It had gained potency with her repeated use as the magic aura felt far stronger now than when she had first used it. She let loose several blasts that sent the demons squealing. Estat again struggled to allow Brek to mount the coramira. "Get on; your life is in danger, do you not realize that?" he snapped.

Brek continued to struggle. "No! I cannot leave her I…"

There was a loud thump, and the earth beneath them shook. He heard Melanie gasp somewhere to his right and he stopped wrestling with Brek. "What is it?" He asked.

"Xenopus!" Melanie cried.

"Curse that serpent! He was supposed to keep that sickening green toad busy!" Immuraudi intoned.

This worried Estat, since Malstraun was his most trusted friend. He knew he could take care of himself, but the thought of his friend being torn asunder by this beast was devastating. He shook his head as he could now feel a familiar aura moving towards them in a snakelike zigzaging motion.

"And where do you think you are going with my master?" Xenopus spoke, his voice dripping with sarcasm.

"Back off, toad boy!" Melanie shouted, though Estat could hear the fear behind her voice. "Estat, can't Brek control this guy?"

"Not anymore, and I honestly do not believe he had complete control over him from the very beginning. Besides that, I do not think Brek understands what is going on anymore," he said, frowning.

"NO!" Brek shouted. "It is the Demon God Kain! Brother, help me!" Brek ceased his struggle from Estat and instead clung to his arm.

"What on earth is he talking about?" Melanie said. "I thought his name was Xenopus."

"He is pathetic, is he not?" Xenopus drawled. "He thinks the very gods are toying with him, but that does not bother me; I do not mind being referred to as a god." His harsh laughter cut through the air.

"Austia is a goddess of mercy, while Kain is a god of pain and darkness," Estat explained. "So it is no surprise that he refers to Xenopus this way. However, I had no idea he could have thought of me as a brother instead of a teacher," Estat said frowning. *He was just as secluded and lonely as I was,* he thought.

"Now is not the time to be regretting things; we should be escaping." Immuraudi urged.

"Melanie, Brek, get on!" he said, trying once again to get Brek to climb onto the equine's back, this time meeting with some success as he seemed eager to leave now.

"What about you?" Melanie asked after getting on. She grabbed hold of his arm as if to make sure he was coming with them.

"She cannot escape with the three of us. Go!" He pulled his arm from her grip and slapped Immuraudi on the haunches.

He was almost knocked over as the coramira leapt into

the air and flapped her wings. Xenopus gave a deep, loud and sinister laugh. "You think I will let you escape me that easily?" Something whistled overhead, and there was a sound like the cracking of a whip. Estat heard Immuraudi squeal and Melanie scream. Moments later something made a heavy landing several feet away.

"Melanie!?" Estat shouted urgently. He began to make his way toward the thud, trying to feel for auras and praying to Austia that none had been harmed. He tripped over something and landed with a grunt. "Melanie? Immuraudi? Brek?" But the only response was more sickening laughter from Xenopus.

-39-

MAKING TRACKS

The back tracking was not as long as Ralley had expected, and she was happy that Talon had been right. Before she knew it they had passed the camping spot they used last night and were traveling through new country. Clouds drifted overhead, lazy white ones at first, and then the wind picked up and brought in darker ones. These only dropped a few occasional showers that they escaped by resting under large trees. The supplies were well covered and suffered little damage. Though this slowed their progress some, Talon assured her that they would reach the small town of Lacavi before it got too dark. Ralley began to wonder if the people of Lacavi would treat them similarly as those at Tradewood. Veru still traveled with them in his human form. His brother Axle had disappeared into the trees in his wolf form with an angry growl that Veru translated as his displeasure at traveling with them. Of all the polite things that Veru had said about Axle, she felt that in reality he was a sort of evil twin.

Ralley nudged her mount in the flanks to catch up with Talon. Regence had been a terrific riding teacher, and she felt confident in the saddle now. "Talon, will we stay the night in Lacavi?" she asked, concerned.

Talon was thoughtful for a moment before answering. "I think we should since the weather looks uncertain… but we will have to conceal Veru if we expect to be treated well. Because of my own selfishness, word of our approach may already have reached the townspeople and they will be unhappy to see the tale is true."

Ralley put a finger to her mouth and bit at her nail. "We could always put a cape and hood over him, but I suppose that would just make it more suspicious."

"Or I could simply go around Lacavi altogether as my brother will do. I do not want to cause you any turmoil," Veru called. Apparently his wolfish ears worked just as well even in human form.

"I think that would be best," Talon said nodding, not bothering to look back at him. Then he turned to Ralley. "If that is alright with you, of course, Empress."

He looked so serious that Ralley had to giggle. It was all so strange to her to be the one whom everyone felt was the final judge on what happened. "Yes, it sounds like a good idea to me too." She turned in her saddle to face Veru. "As long as you're not offended or anything… but you are pretty cute in your wolf form," she called.

Veru gave her a rather polite half bow. "Not at all. I am happy to think that my most comfortable form is pleasant to your eyes. I shall see you on the north side then." And without even dismounting first, he shifted into his white wolf shape. For a moment he was perched atop the equine with a lupine smile, and in the next he had leapt over Regence's head and landed with a soft thump on the ground. He gave them one last glance with his gentle green eyes before bolting off the road and disappearing into the trees.

Ralley smiled after him. "There, that is solved. Are there any other concerns?" she asked with a somewhat smug tone as her eyes came back to Talon.

"Certainly, your Highness," Talon said with equal smugness, even giving her a light bow of his head. "Shall we choose an Inn at Lacavi, or would you prefer the tents again on the outskirts?"

Ralley turned her head away to the trees in thought. She certainly liked the idea of a soft bed to sleep in, enclosed in a warm room. A cheerful fireplace, bath water, fresh meals; but when she thought of the experiences she'd had in previous towns, those things seemed trivial. The attack on Talon and herself at Elstaff, the horrid glares and terrible treatment of Veru in Tradewood; there was no telling what troubles awaited them in Lacavi. She also had to take into consideration the dark attackers, the black wolfish creatures in the forest, bandits and the ghost children, all having taken place outside the towns. Finally, she had to take into account Talon's concern about the weather. The sky was only darkening further and the wind had grown chill.

"I think we should just see how things go while we ride through town. If they don't take to us, then we can always continue on and camp on the other side," Ralley finally suggested. Talon agreed, and they continued on to Lacavi. As they passed through the streets, the people of Lacavi stopped to look. Again there was a mixture of emotions, and though they did not have Veru with them, there were still angry glares and contempt on their faces. Ralley tried to follow their gazes, but she couldn't quite tell who they were angry at. Many of them targeted Talon, and others simply eyed the soldiers around them.

Ralley also noticed some of them smiling at Talon, or simply looking on in curiosity. She frowned at a group of younger girls that were eyeing Talon in a way that made her want to run her horse over them. They soon approached a small inn toward the north end of the village

Talon called a halt and rode back to Ralley and Regence. "What have you two to say?" he asked as the inn's proprietor, a tall, strong looking man, emerged from the building.

Regence stared at the innkeeper for a short time before answering. "It appears as though we are welcome, for the most part. What we would have to worry about is the various thieves and potential brigands who would wait for us in the dark of the wood."

Ralley blinked at him, a bit surprised. "What do you mean? How can you tell that?"

"Many of the shadier people here look poor and frightened. The kind to attack in the night, but this village does not look large enough for an organized guild of assassins or thieves. Most of these will likely go after our supplies than risk a direct attack for our lives," Regence finished.

Nodding, Talon then turned to Ralley. "And you?"

"Uh… well, what he said makes sense," Ralley shrugged.

The two of them chuckled at her, but they settled on staying at the inn. The innkeeper was polite to them and made sure they had good rooms and stable stalls for their horses. They split the guards and archers so that half would be with their horses and supplies while the others had the next room. They rotated watches through their room to be sure they were safe, making Ralley feel much better. As she settled down into the comfortable cotton bed, she put her hand over the Blade Beast's dagger form. It was warm and made her feel that much safer. She slept well that night without interruption.

After a fresh meal that morning and a small amount of whispered conversation, they were off again to leave the waking village of Lacavi in a low dust cloud. It was quite some time after they had left the last farmhouses at the north end of the village that a white blur came streaking across a wheat field towards them. It dodged around one of the guardsmen and bounded to the empty saddle of a very surprised horse. Ralley giggled at the white wolf as it gave the soldier holding the reins of the mount a rather sloppy looking lick on the cheek. The soldier expressed his displeasure by issuing a curse and tossing the reins at the wolf as it shifted its shape into a human, catching up the reins in a hand and straightening himself in the saddle as though nothing untoward had taken place.

"Welcome back, furry friend!" Regence called, not even glancing around to him.

"Thank you, sword master, and greetings to you both your Majesties. I would have been here sooner, but my brother and I were having a bit of fun with the brigands that we spotted awaiting your passing along those farmhouses," he said merrily.

"Oh?" Regence said curiously, now turning in his saddle to look back at him.

"Are you both alright?" Ralley asked with genuine concern.

Veru laughed. "Of course, but I cannot say the same for the thieves. My dear brother plays a bit too rough sometimes."

Ralley had to hide her smile. In a way she felt bad for the men, but what she had to realize was if they had not had Axle and Veru with them, the bandits could have taken their wagons, or worse. She began to think of them as muggers and druggies in her own world. This made things a bit easier to understand. "So where are we heading now?" she called out to Talon.

Talon reined in Phoenix so that they could catch up. "If we travel quickly, we can make it to Pheren before sundown. Unless…" he hesitated. "Unless you wish to speak to someone at Castle Silverwind?"

She thought he looked rather upset at the thought of stopping at a castle. "Well, who lives there?" She asked curiously.

Regence was the first to speak up. "A king named Othniel. My last visit was long ago, and things may have changed, but he seemed hospitable enough."

"I don't see any reason to speak to him, I mean, my sister is farther north, so he probably doesn't know a thing of her." she said with a shrug.

Talon smirked. "Good, then let us continue past them as soon as we can; the faster we travel, the better." Everyone agreed with passing Silverwind, but Ralley couldn't help but wonder how bad being a king could be. Surely her job as Empress thus far wasn't terrible, but then again, she had insisted on traveling instead of staying behind for elegant dinners and ceremonies.

She pondered on the life of royalty for the first half of the day and all the things that had happened to her so far. The weather had cleared during the night, and the clouds overhead were white and fluffy. When Castle Silverwind came into view at around high noon, she couldn't help thinking about what it would be like to live there. It was built atop a gently sloping hill, and the city surrounded the bottom of it, clustered against a wall that kept the encroaching city from crowding the actual castle walls. This allowed a thick ring of green grass to grow unhindered between the city and the castle. It was a most beautiful effect. The castle itself had tall towers, all of which were built at different heights. Each cone-like tower top had a flag waving in the breeze. She couldn't quite make out any real details from this distance, but there was a backdrop of forest beyond it that was similar to the one behind Castle Degrail.

"Wow! It's beautiful!" Ralley said happily. Moments after she said this a large, dark object could be seen in the sky some distance beyond the castle. At first Ralley thought it to be a large bird, but as it continued to come toward the castle, she realized it was far bigger than any bird she had ever seen. "What's that?" Ralley asked, pointing.

Regence squinted against the bright sun. "Not sure… it is big though. A roc, perhaps?"

She wrinkled her brow and gave him a look. "You mean you have flying rocks in your world?" she said sarcastically.

"He means a giant eagle," Veru clarified, "but that particular creature is not a roc."

"Then what is it?" Ralley asked, her eyes still on the thing that continued to get bigger the longer she kept her eyes on it.

"That happens to be Kurnok, the great swamp dragon of Deadwater Bog, and he looks unusually unhappy today," Veru said in his usual way of understating everything.

-40-

GODDESS' MERCY

Melanie felt pain when she moved. When she opened her eyes and blinked to rid herself of the blur, it registered to her that she had blacked out. What had happened? It took a moment to remember. They were flying away, leaving Estat behind, and then a crack like that of thunder. She heard Estat calling for her, and when she turned, she saw him crawling her way. "I'm here," she said, a bit breathlessly. "What happened?" Melanie could hear a ringing sound in her ears, but there was something else too.

"You alright? Where is Brek?" Estat asked, taking hold of her hand.

She got to a sitting position, pain in her hip and right leg making her groan. "I see him, I think he's okay." Several yards away, Xenopus stood in his hulking frog-like form, his mouth wide open as he issued his deep croaking laughter.

"And you?" he asked again, his hands questing for her face.

"I...I'm just fine, really," she said, gritting her teeth against the pain. Her face grew hot as his hands rested on her cheeks.

"Immuraudi?" he asked. But before Melanie could answer, the coramira nickered angrily.

"Damn fool got my wing! Curse it, I will never be able to fly out of here now!" The equine struggled to get to her feet.

Brek whimpered as he lifted himself to look in Xenopus' direction. "We are doomed. I never should have trusted him."

"He's got us right where he wants us." Melanie spoke with a quaking voice. "What are we going to do?" she added, trying not to panic. She took Estat's hands, and the two of them got to their feet. Xenopus was still laughing, and it began to irritate her. She let loose another blast of flame from her hand almost without thinking.

Xenopus merely snapped it up into his mouth like a tossed piece of popcorn. He then resumed his bellowing laugh as smoke curled out from his maw. "You think you can stop me? You are all pathetic." He took a small leap that brought him down just in front of them all. Melanie and Estat were nearly knocked to the ground again. "It has been a pleasure, but now I must stop playing with my toys so I can get back to bigger and far more entertaining carnage." With that the two large tentacles came down towards them. Melanie wanted to run, but she felt frozen to the spot, and she couldn't leave the blind Estat to fend for himself. He was already beginning to chant a spell, and she felt a confidence in him that he would get them out of this... at least she hoped he would.

One of the tentacles wrapped around her waist, the other around Estat's neck, cutting off his chant, doing the same to any hope Melanie had that a random spell could get them out of their predicament. The two were lifted high off the ground. "Ah ah ah," Xenopus scolded as if they were pre-school children. "No spells from you. Your time has come."

Melanie struggled with all her meager strength. If she did not do something, Xenopus would choke Estat to death. "Stop it! Why don't you just eat me instead? Leave him alone!" she screamed. She knew he would kill them both anyway; he seemed like the type to do so. But perhaps if she could stall him long enough, she might be able to think of something.

"My tastes run more toward equine," Xenopus laughed, but continued to keep hold of Estat, who was gasping for a breath and clawing at the tentacles.

All appeared hopeless as Xenopus made her watch as Estat begin to lose consciousness. Then she felt something; it was coming up fast. She turned her head in time to see the Great Black Serpent charge forward, his great bull-like horns stabbing into Xenopus's back, cutting his evil laughter short.

Xenopus gave a loud angry croak and tipped forward onto his smaller front legs and using his larger back legs, delivered a blow to Malstraun that shoved him back several feet, his ebon horns covered in bright green blood. Malstraun didn't seem too shaken by this blow, and he roared, showing his large jaws with rows of razor sharp teeth. He looked a bit roughed up though, with several gashes along his black body, some of them deep.

Xenopus turned to face Malstraun, still holding onto Estat and Melanie. "Back again? I must say, you are a tougher beast than I thought. Is there no way I can convince you to join me? Perhaps if I spare your friend?" he said, loosening his grip on Estat, who was too weak to take in a good breath.

"Tai krint en zem zu noka?" Malstraun replied, again using the strange language. Melanie did not understand the words, but she could hear his questioning tone and the edge of sarcasm.

Again he dodged in for an attack; his aim was high, toward the head, but when Xenopus went to duck the blow, Malstraun snapped his head to the side, his great mouth full of teeth clamping down on the undulating tentacle that held Estat in its grip.

A very un-toad-like screech escaped from Xenopus as he attempted to yank the appendage from Malstraun's grip, but he only succeeded in coming back with a green bleeding stump. His angry croak bellowed out like thunder, and suddenly Melanie was flying through the air, spinning end over end for a few moments before feeling herself falling toward the ground. It all happened so fast, that she didn't scream until she felt herself stop. Her landing was rough, but it wasn't quite the heavy thud she feared. Realizing her eyes were closed, she popped them open to discover herself lying atop Weiland. "OH! I'm so sorry!" She exclaimed as she slipped off of him, feeling new aches and sore spots as she did so. "Are you alright, Weiland?"

The elf groaned and sat up. "My, you are a bit heavier than I anticipated," he said, rubbing his backside.

Melanie was still a bit too shocked to give him a harsh reply. She turned to see the battle between Malstraun and Xenopus continue. The two of them dodging blows and making the ground feel as though there were a constant earthquake going on. She couldn't see the tentacle that held Estat dangling in Malstraun's mouth and realized he must have dropped him. "We have to save Estat!" she cried and headed back toward the two gargantuan combatants.

"No! You may be crushed!" Weiland shouted, running after her. "Let Immuraudi take you!"

Melanie stopped and turned to him. As if on cue, Immuraudi

galloped towards them, the whimpering Brek on her back. "You called? I thought you wanted me to get this pathetic lump to safety?"

"No time!" Melanie said, racing to her side and helping Brek down. "Weiland, take care of him!" she said, climbing onto the coramira's back. "Hurry, let's go!"

Weiland lifted his hand to her as if to argue, but she had made up her mind, and Immuraudi raced back toward the battle. "You are absolutely nuts, you know that? But I like your spunk; let us save that crazy blind love of yours."

"Love?" she spurted as they passed several grotesque demons that had gathered to watch their leader in battle. "But we aren't… I mean he isn't…" Melanie protested as she clung to the coramira, her eyes scanning about for Estat. The ride was smooth as glass despite Immuraudi racing along at incredible speed.

"Oh, stop your stuttering; I could see it even if I myself were blind!" she snorted, then angled to the left as she skirted around Malstraun's coiled black body as the serpent prepared for another strike at the demon. "You are risking your neck for the man! Admit it, you stubborn human!"

"Fine!" Melanie shouted, though her voice came out sounding almost joyous. Was that because she finally admitted she loved him, or because she now saw Estat lying close by? Perhaps both? Immuraudi must have spotted him too, as she poured on an extra burst of speed straight for him and skidded to a stop two feet away. Melanie swung down, stumbling from the momentum and her own inability to dismount properly. She tumbled to the ground next to him and pulled the remnants of Xenopus's former appendage from his neck. "Estat! Estat!" she shouted urgently. "Breathe!" She turned him over on his back and put her ear to his chest. She couldn't hear his heart! "Oh my gosh! What should I do? I don't know CPR!" She looked up to Immuraudi desperately. "Do you know CPR?" she asked without thinking.

The equine's ears and head lowered in dismay. "Melanie, we should get out of here. We could get caught in the battle; there are demons everywhere," she reminded her in a controlled tone, though most of them seemed content to simply watch the ongoing battle.

Desperate, Melanie turned back to Estat, suddenly angry that Immuraudi sounded as if she had given up. "Damn it! Wake up! I can't carry you!" she shouted at him, though his face was growing pale and he did not respond. "Breathe!" she yelled, gripping him by the shoulders. "BREATHE!"

Something happened at that moment. It felt like a shock wave that traveled from her own body, through her arms and hands into Estat, and his body convulsed. Shocked, she jerked her arms away from him, her eyes wide. For a moment, she sat there stunned. Estat began to breathe, though it was shallow. Melanie reached out and placed her hand on his chest to feel it as it rose and fell. Immuraudi's ears flicked forward, and her crimson eyes went from Estat to Melanie. "Why did you not tell me you could do that? Things would have gone far smoother. Now hurry, let us get him on and get out of here before Xenopus steps on us!"

Indeed, the two combatants were still lunging at one another, and the earth continued to quiver. Melanie would have protested that she didn't know she could do it either, but she would have to settle that later. Whatever had happened, Estat was breathing, and that's what mattered. Together with Immuraudi's help, they managed to pull Estat across her back. Melanie climbed up behind him to secure him as the coramira took off again, skirting back behind Malstraun's attacks.

"You will not escape so easily!" Xenopus shouted, drawing Melanie's attention. The demon had wrestled Malstraun's head to the ground, one of his large back feet raised to crush it. Malstraun's body had curled up in reaction and began to wrap itself around the demon like a snake coiling around a mouse. Xenopus abandoned his attempt as his larger legs became entangled. When Malstraun tried to lift his head away, Xenopus reached out with his front legs, gripping the ebony horns on either side of the Serpent's head and trying to pull them apart.

Immuraudi caught up to Weiland and Brek. They had been cut off by several demons, but Weiland was handling them without too much trouble. "We should go, now!" Weiland shouted when they had gotten to them.

"What about Malstraun!" Melanie said, still watching the struggle. There was a sickening crack that echoed off the distant mountains as one of Malstraun's horns had given way under the tremendous strength of the demon, and now Xenopus held it in his bulky fingers like a weapon. With the sudden release of pressure, Malstraun pulled his remaining horn free of the demons possession and thrust its tip into Xenopus' thick throat, tightening his coils at the same time.

Xenopus choked and desperately thrust his new weapon down on Malstraun's thick coil, penetrating it and causing him to loosen his hold. In that moment, the demon positioned his legs and uncoiled them to leap out of Malstraun's hold. He landed several yards away, gurgling out what Melanie believed were curses. Malstraun took this moment to create a gateway beneath him.

"Hurry, to the Portal!" Weiland shouted, gripping Brek's arm and pulling him along. Immuraudi moved just ahead of them, and in moments they were at Malstraun's side. With this up close view of the massive serpent, Melanie was aghast at his injuries: deep wounds bleeding thick red blood down his black body.

Xenopus croaked angrily, leaping towards them once again as Weiland pulled Brek towards the portal. "NO!" Xenopus bellowed, lobbing Malstraun's broken horn towards them.

"Look out!" Melanie screamed. But the aim was dead on, the chipped ebon horn plunged through Brek's torso and into the soft earth, pinning him to the spot. Weiland held onto the man's arm for a moment more, listening as Brek spoke to him in a voice far too soft for Melanie to hear. She gasped in alarm and disbelief as blood trickled from Brek's mouth moments before the man shuddered and fell limp, his eyes still open though they could no longer see.

-41-

Sky Fright

Talon wanted to shake that ridiculous smile off Veru's face. His giddiness was not infectious. Ralley's previous carefree manner had vanished, replaced with awe and fear.

"A dragon?" She asked.

"No no, a Swamp Dragon, each dragon is quite different you see…" Veru began, but Talon cut him off.

"We do not want a lesson in dragons Veru, we need to get out of sight." But as Talon swept his gaze around the field, he realized that they had very little cover in this area. "What in the nine hells is a swamp dragon doing this far south anyway?" he growled under his breath.

Veru smirked. "Getting away from all the trouble stirring in the north, of course."

Talon turned Phoenix so he could face Veru without twisting in his saddle. "What trouble in the north?"

"Oh, my apologies. I forget that humans cannot hear nor see the little spirits that reside all around us," he chuckled.

Ralley tore her gaze from the dragon and turned to face him as well, rather curious. "Spirits?"

There was a thunderous roar from the sky, and the horses

snorted and began to struggle against the control of their riders. "Enough talk!" Talon shouted. "Head for the brush to our right, quickly!" There was little cover there, but it was better than sitting about on the road in plain sight.

The great dragon wheeled in the sky, and Talon suspected that their movement was already catching its eye. Regence took the left flank of their wagons and Talon led the way, Ralley and Veru just behind him. When they got to the brush, Regence ordered the wagons to be abandoned and for everyone to dismount and tie the horses underneath any of the sparse trees they could find. Talon dismounted and did the same, though reluctantly. A great shadow passed over them, and when Talon glanced up, he could see the great underbelly of the dragon. It was so close to the ground now that he could make out the black scales. As it passed, its tail whipped the top of the tree they were under, tearing the top off and scattering twigs and leaves everywhere.

Talon drew his sword and glanced to Ralley. "I hope you know how to use the blade."

Her eyes went wide and she fumbled with the strap, pulling the Blade Beast out of its sheath. "Please tell me you're kidding…."

Frowning, Talon turned away from her to watch the dragon as it turned in the air and came back their way.

"How interesting that he is so intent upon us, do you agree?" Veru asked. He had dismounted and tied his horse like the others, but he had stepped back out from under the tree to watch the dragon.

"Curse it, Veru, get back, he is heading right for us!" Talon hissed.

Veru shrugged and turned to face the group huddled underneath the bushes and trees. "Do you think all that will protect you from its poisonous breath?"

Talon swept the group with his gaze. Could this little group of men defeat a dragon? He did not want to lose anyone else, and they were all depending on him. Ralley had summoned the serpent that attacked them, but she had no idea how she had done it, and this was not something she could get rid of in the same way. He gripped his sword and glanced to the archers. "Aim for its eyes and mouth," he called, and then turned to Regence and the footmen. "Find its weak spots." His eyes fell on Ralley, and she cringed. "Stay down," he ordered. She nodded, but it did not appear as though she truly approved of the command. The dragon was nearly upon them, and he lifted his arm to signal the archers.

"What about me? Am I part of your team now, or do you still not trust me?" Veru asked, his lip stuck out in an over exaggerated pout and his eyes as forlorn as a pup begging for a morsel.

For a moment he considered ignoring him, but decided better of it. "As long as you are going to help us, then yes. If it lands, do not let it use its poison."

Looking rather satisfied with his orders, Veru nodded. In moments, he had transformed into the white wolf-creature, crouching down and staring intently at the incoming dragon.

Talon dropped his arm, and four well aimed arrows shot over his head. The dragon flared its wings as the arrows glanced off its cheek, chin and forehead. One of them lodged itself between the scales in his neck and though it had not done much damage, all the arrows did their job. Kurnok had reared its head back to protect itself and instead of flying off, he landed several feet from them, crushing the brush underneath him and shaking the earth. Talon led the charge as they raced forward, swords ready. He thrust his sword between the larger scales on its belly and it roared angrily, twisting its head back down towards them. Damn it, he knew Veru was not to be….

But even as the thoughts went through his head, a white furry streak leapt atop the dragon's head and latched its jaws onto one of the horns crowning it. A gentle white haze began to drift around the dragon's head, expanding as it did so. The dragon began to thrash its head about, attempting to dislodge Veru.

Talon yanked his sword from the body of the giant lizard and moved to the base of the neck. This would be a far more lethal hit, he decided. And as he wedged his sword between the scales, the dragon roared, and a clawed leg reached out, swiping at him. Talon was knocked to the ground, but the adrenaline was keeping him going. He returned to his feet and came back to do the same once again. Kurnok spread his wings and with one great flap sent a blast of wind out, knocking most of the guards off their feet. More arrows whistled through the air, striking the thin membrane of the wing.

Rising up behind the dragon was its barbed tail, and it struck towards its own head. Veru let go and dodged, leaping down to its back. Its head free of Veru, it twisted it around and opened its maw at Talon. Something whizzed through the air at that moment and struck Kurnok in the jaw, twisting its head away from them, causing its poisonous breath to spout out over its back.

"Veru!" Talon shouted. But the white wolf was no longer there. He had already raced back up the dragon's neck and perched once again on its head. This time, Veru clawed at its black eyes, but Kurnok thrashed his head, throwing Veru off.

Talon lost sight of the white wolf as he landed some distance away in the brush. Hoping his archers could handle it, he went in for another stab at the thing, staying away from the cloud of poison drifting down. He could see Regence shouting more orders to those around him as he found weak spots in its scales.

The dragon roared angrily as the blade pulled out from its cheek and glided through the air back to Ralley's hand. "I did it!" she shouted.

Talon had no time to cheer for her. Kurnok was furious now, and his tail lashed about in a wild arc, sending two soldiers flying through the air; they too disappeared into the brush. The dragon continued to thrash, not quite looking where it was stomping its massive claws; its head swiveled down and its jaws opened and shut with a great snap. Talon's sword had missed its mark, glancing off a scale, and the dragon turned its head in his direction. As it came at him, he leapt to the side just as the jaws re-opened and issued a blast of toxic air where Talon had stood moments before. The wind was in their favor and blew the poisonous breath away from them, but this would not help for long if the dragon continued to have its way. Talon readied his sword: this time he would be ready for the open jaws, but the dragon swiveled his head to focus on Ralley. Then Talon noticed the dragon's eye that Veru had clawed. It appeared to be filled with a strange fogginess that leaked out of the eye through the claw marks. Veru had successfully blinded Kurnoks right eye.

"The beast is half blind!" he shouted to Regence and the others.

"Fools! Idiots!" roared a voice from high above. Was it the dragon that spoke? Talon peered up to see Kurnok glaring down at him with his good eye. "I know you, Talon, Prince of the Emperor! Die quietly!" the dragon hissed, lashing his front claws out at him.

This took Talon by surprise. How did this Kurnok know of him? He was sure that all kingdoms might know, but why a dragon of the swamp lands? And why would he care? "Then you have come after me purposefully?" Talon shouted.

Kurnok shifted his bulk away from them, making a sound that Talon took to be sarcastic laughter. "My purpose is to destroy both you and your father the Emperor; once that is done and the Blade Beast is destroyed, chaos will rule among human kind, and I will be rewarded." The swamp dragon roared, and Talon hurried out from under a plume of poisonous breath.

"Then I end your quest here!" Talon shouted back, racing forward to stab once again at the creature.

The dragon suddenly dipped to its side and began to roll. Regence shouted a hasty retreat, and he and the soldiers scattered through the brush as the dragon turned its head, snapping at Talon. He was able to swing his sword at Kurnok, lashing at its open maw with his sword and feeling it come in contact with the rows of teeth.

"His father is no longer the Emperor! I am!" Ralley's voice shouted above the monstrous dragon's growling.

Kurnok snapped his jaw shut and turned his head towards Ralley in time to catch her thrown blade right in the snout. For a moment it was lodged there, and he shook his head violently. When it dislodged, it flew straight back to Ralley and returned to her open hand. "Is that so? Then this will be easier than I thought," Kurnok hissed and began to move toward her, now ignoring Talon.

"Ralley! Run!" Talon shouted. Panic welled up inside him as he stabbed at the monster, trying to stop him, but there was no way to halt a swamp dragon of his size. Why had she said such a thing? Now she was in danger, and there was little he could do to help her. "RALLY!"

The Blade Beast had slipped from Ralley's hand and reverted to its draconic form, but Talon saw no way it could overpower Kurnok, as the Blade Beast was smaller than a horse. Ralley had backed against the little tree where they had tied their horses. Next to her, Phoenix pulled at his reins, desperately thrashing about to free himself.

"You fool headed woman! RUN!" Talon yelled. Regence and the other soldiers were rushing towards the dragon, but they were much too late. Kurnok had already made it to the tree and his head lowered towards Ralley, its maw wide open.

-42-

KURNOK THE SWAMP DRAGON

Ralley could see every single one of Kurnok's sharp teeth as his great big jaw opened wide. At that moment, the Blade Beast snapped its tail on Phoenix's rump. The already enraged equine dipped his head low and his back legs swung out, delivering a double kick to the lower jaw of the dragon. There was a loud crack, and the force threw Kurnok's head back into the air. The hulking beast gave a strange squealing moan like that of a wounded dog trying to howl.

"That ought to teach you!" Ralley shouted triumphantly. Talon and the others caught up to it and began lashing out at him once again. Kurnok roared in frustration, spreading his wings wide and turning away from them. He had enough, but Talon and Regence continued to try and stop him. They had little success, and as Kurnok began to lift off, the wind that his wings created knocked Talon and Regence back. "He's getting away!" Ralley shouted.

An echoing bark of challenge came from somewhere in the brush near her. She turned to see a black creature bolt off toward the fleeing dragon. It jumped out of the brush and onto Kurnok's back. Ralley recognized Axle, Veru's twin, as he raced along the neck of the dragon to its head. Everyone watched as the dragon began to lift away into the sky, but a deafening metallic bark vibrated the air. The effect was astonishing. Kurnok's head dipped down so sharply that the dragon was sent into a mid air summersault. In moments the huge beast had toppled to the ground with a heavy thud, shaking the earth.

Ralley followed Talon and the other men as they all ran to the crash sight. She stopped several feet short from the others, not feeling quite brave enough to come face to face with the dragon a second time. The Blade Beast followed and stood beside her, watching the dragon. For a moment nothing moved, though she could still tell the dragon was breathing. Then Axle climbed out from under a wing to leap atop the dragon's rump and stand on it, his chest thrust out with pride. She couldn't help but laugh aloud, all the pressure and fear escaping in one big burst with the proud look on Axle's muzzle. "That, was so, so awesome!" Ralley blurted between bouts of laughter. She had never felt so excited and relieved in her life, but she had also never had such an adventure as this one either.

Axle growled and jumped down off the dragon, shifting into his humanoid form. "I suppose I shall take that as a compliment," he said in a rather grumpy way.

"And I'll take that as a thank you," Ralley said with a smile.

He crossed his arms, but Ralley could tell he looked pleased. "You can thank me better by coming with me and helping Veru," he said, taking hold of her arm now and pulling her along, the Blade Beast following.

Ralley glanced back at Talon and the others, but they were intent on inspecting the dragon, so she hurried along through the brush with Axle, some of her giddiness disappearing. "Is he alright?" she asked, now concerned, as she hadn't seen Veru since the dragon threw him.

"If he is not, it will be his own fool neck!" Axle spat. "I told him to stop playing around with you humans, but he never listens to me." She could tell he was angry, but Ralley got angry at Melanie loads of times, but it was usually due to the fact that she was worried about her hanging out with all her weird guy friends. Axle loved his brother as much as Ralley loved her sister. She smiled at this despite her worry. Axle didn't bring that dragon down for them; he did it because the dragon had hurt Veru. Ralley was in this strange world, facing dragons and monsters because Melanie was here somewhere and maybe in trouble. It was time to stop fooling around. She had to find her sister as soon as possible.

The two came upon Veru, curled up in the brush, his white fur full of burrs. Ralley knelt down beside him and began to run her fingers through his soft fur to check for anything that might be bleeding or broken. "Veru? You alright?" she asked in a calm voice.

Axle stood by, watching in silence. A few minutes passed as she tried to check for a possible head injury and she even listened to his heart. He was still breathing, just unresponsive. "I... don't know, maybe he just bumped his head or fainted." Ralley was no doctor or nurse, and she never paid much attention in health class.

Frowning, Axle knelt down next to him. "Wake up, curse it! Stop fooling about! I cannot hunt without a pack!" he shouted at him.

"Do you truly mean it?" Veru's voice said, surprising Ralley as she didn't realize they could talk without changing their forms. "Why, brother! That is the nicest thing you have ever said to me!" Veru lifted his head and gave Axle a mischievous wolf smile.

"Tai noka!" he exclaimed in surprise and anger. "I shall tear you limb from limb!" Axle lunged for him and Veru bolted. "Katar!" This last word came out as a half bark as Axle shifted to wolf form and took off after Veru.

Ralley laughed as she watched them race off through the brush. She stood up and decided she should return to Talon and the others, but before she turned to go, she noticed the Blade Beast. It was watching the twin brothers as she was. *"You are well protected,"* came its strange but soothing mental voice.

"Yeah, I guess I am. What about my sister? Is she still alright?"

The Blade Beast closed its eyes for a moment or two, then shook its head and re-opened them. *"She is in great danger, but she too has worthy companions."*

"She's in danger? We should get going then!" she said, heading off toward where she had left Talon, the Blade Beast trotting alongside her.

"We are still many days away," the Beast said in a strange but gentle tone.

"She has to hold on; I'll get there… somehow," she said, coming upon the huge dragon. "We need to get there fast," she said to herself. What she wouldn't give for a jeep, not that the horses were too slow, but she honestly didn't like the sluggish nature of their journey. They were wasting precious time, and her sister was out there somewhere getting into trouble. She was betting it involved guys. If only she could simply teleport there just like… Then it struck her. The Black Serpent had teleported to and away from them. "Talon, I have a question!" she shouted to him as she ran up toward the small group crowded around the dragon's head.

Talon held up a hand. "You should stay back, it's still alive."

"Oh." She frowned. "Are you… going to kill it?" she asked tentatively. Talon's men were looping ropes to its horns and spikes, holding it down. As she stood there staring at the beast, she couldn't help but feel bad that they had done this to such a magnificent looking thing. She'd seen many versions of dragons in art, on fantasy book covers and wall paintings, but seeing one in real life was no comparison. Ralley began to feel a bit bad for it. After all, how many dragons like this could there be in this world? Then again, who would want a gigantic man killing evil beast like this around?

"We shall glean some information from it first," Regence said with a smile. Ralley was uneasy with this, but she watched and waited until the dragon slowly stirred and opened its eyes. The scarred eye was no better than it was before, but it didn't have fog roiling out of it anymore. A low, angry growl escaped from the dragon as he tried to move his head up and found he could not.

Talon crossed his arms. "Alright then Kurnok, who is it that sent you after the Empress?"

Kurnok gave a dark chuckle. "If you live to see him, you will regret it; best to allow me to eat you all and spare you that fate."

"I am not amused." Talon spoke dryly. "Who is the one you

speak of?" Kurnok growled and attempted to lift his head again, but with his current weakened state and the weight holding his head down, he could not lift it. Talon stepped closer to the monster and drew his sword, aiming it at his good eye. "It is your choice, Kurnok. Tell us what we wish to know, or you loose your other eye."

Kurnok issued a muffled roar and shifted his body, but Talon's sword came closer to his eye and he ceased his activity. "He calls himself Largus, a warlock from the southeast."

"A warlock wants us dead? Does this have anything to do with the Summoner and the woman he kidnapped?" Ralley was surprised he asked this, but was anxious to hear the reply.

"Summoner? Woman? I know nothing of them. The warlock was alone when he came to me."

Ralley's heart sank. She had hoped to hear something more of her sister, her location, or her condition. She supposed it was a good sign that she wasn't running about with a warlock, though. But a thought occurred to her, and she moved down closer to the dragon despite their warning. "Kurnok, what did the warlock look like?" she asked.

Kurnok glared at the sword that sat near his eye before answering. "He was tall for a human I imagine, but dark of hair and not much to look at with his ragged robes." He grumbled.

The man that had kidnapped Melanie was indeed tall, but he'd had green hair and green clothing. This didn't seem like the same man at all. "Are you sure he wasn't wearing a disguise?"

"Do I look like the kind of dragon that could be fooled by appearances? Humans are all the same." He sneered. "They all annoy me," he added, glaring at Talon.

"Then why do as he says?" Ralley asked.

"Because when you are at war with one another, there is more meat for me," he snorted.

"Sick." Ralley wrinkled her nose, utterly repulsed. "Whatever, he doesn't know about Melanie. I want to know about teleportation," she said, looking to Talon now.

Talon raised a brow at her, still holding the sword point in place. "What do you want to know about that for?"

Before she could answer Kurnok hauled his head away from Talon's sword. The surprised soldiers stumbled and were dragged along as they struggled desperately to hold onto the ropes. The dragon brought around one foreleg, his claws slashing through the air towards Talon. With amazing speed, Regence leapt forward, planting a rough shove to Talon's back, sending him sprawling to the ground. It was Regence who received the damage meant for Talon as the claws contacted and ripped great gashes in his side, the force of which threw him several feet to land on the ground unmoving.

Kurnok turned to Ralley now, his terrible grin exposing all of his teeth. It disappeared as a metallic howl rang loud and clear just behind her. An equally loud but melodic one followed it as Axle and Veru charged forward toward the balked dragon. With a growl of annoyance, he turned and took to the air, his great wings thrusting out and knocking the soldiers holding him aside, the ropes slipping from their grasp. His wings began to pump furiously, blasting dust into their faces as he rose into the sky in a hasty retreat.

-43-

THE HEALER

M elanie found herself riding through the dark void, holding Estat's body with one hand while gripping Immuraudi's mane with the other. Tears floated from her eyes in this weightless environment. How could everything have gone so wrong? She felt Weiland's hand on her lower leg, and moments later, a gigantic shape loomed over her. The light of a portal swelled into existence before them, and Immuraudi floated on through.

They were back in the humid cave that Malstraun called home. Weiland helped her down from the coramira's back, and then together they lowered Estat to the ground. She began to check him over again. "I think he's okay..." she said, trying to hold back her tears.

"It is because of you that he still breathes. Did you not know you had the power to do such things?" Immuraudi replied, though her tone was no longer annoyed or mocking. She even lowered her horn to shed more light over them all.

"No! I, I don't know what happened," Melanie protested. "I just couldn't let him die! I couldn't leave him behind."

Malstraun slid along the smooth rocks of the cave and curled himself around a boulder. "You have a power that is similar to my own. Yours is a healing ability, and though it is not as strong, I think you will be able to help him."

"But how? I have no idea what I did to make it work," she said, looking down at Estat. Even though he was unconscious, his face was set in a grimace of pain.

Weiland put his hand on hers. "I will help you." He then moved her hand to Estat's chest. Melanie could feel a strange tingling sensation as he did this. "Just concentrate on Estat. What did you think and feel while you were there with him the moment you touched him?"

She closed her eyes, trying to recall that moment. "I thought he was dead; he wasn't breathing and he had no heartbeat." She felt more tears slip down her cheeks. "I didn't want him to die. He was so brave going after Brek even though he was blind. He thought I was beautiful even if he couldn't even see my face. I couldn't leave a man like that… like him. I won't let him die." Her words poured from her mouth straight from her heart. Then she felt it: a power that crept along her arms. That's what she had felt that moment! It was fast and sudden then, but this time it was slow and relaxed. It traveled through her fingers; she could sense as well as feel it spreading through Estat's chest, finding bruises, scratches, punctures, repairing fibers, muscles, nerves and bones. Once she had found it, she refused to let it go, allowing that power to spread through him from head to toe.

A groan escaped from Estat's lips, and Melanie opened her eyes. The healing contact broke away and together, she and Weiland lifted their hands from him. Estat stirred, and his own hands made their way to his head and face, rubbing at his eyes. When he opened them, they were no longer a pale gray, but now a shade of amber. He stared directly at her face, no longer staring as if seeing right through her. "Melanie?" he inquired, his voice far clearer than before.

"You...can see me?" she said, a bit stunned at what she was witnessing. Had she really repaired him so completely?

Estat sat up, his eyes never leaving hers. "You are more beautiful than I could ever have pictured," he whispered. Her face growing hot, Melanie lifted her hands to hide the blush, but Estat took them into his, lowering them back down again. "I have waited so long to see you, and you would hide your face from me?" A bright smile swept across his features.

With his eyes and voice fully restored, he almost seemed a stranger. She felt too flustered to say so, but Immuraudi cleared her throat, bringing them both back to their current situation.

Estat's eyes swept the cave. "Brek?" he asked.

Melanie frowned. All the awful things that had happened came back to her, and she shook her head. "He... didn't make it," she said softly, trying to control her quavering voice.

Closing his eyes, Estat squeezed her hand. "The portal is down, and now they have nobody to draw the symbols," he said. He opened his eyes again, and Melanie thought they appeared a bit distant and sad. "I have my sight and my voice. We have to get back to the tower and gather an army of our own."

"I am not sure Malstraun will be up to it..." Weiland said, gazing after the large serpent.

Melanie squinted in the dark to look, bringing out her glowing stone. By its light she could see blood smeared along the cave floor and the boulder that Malstraun had curled around. His yellow eyes peered out at them.

"Do not worry about me, I shall pull myself back together," Malstraun's deep voice responded.

"Malstraun! I'm so sorry!" Melanie jumped up and hurried over to him. "If I can heal Estat, then I can heal you too!"

"I am very large and you have already used your powers to heal Estat. There is more than likely not quite enough left for me. There are consequences for overusing your abilities, Melanie. You must learn this," he replied.

"Weiland, can you help me again? Like you did before?" she asked, not willing to give up on helping the black Serpent.

"We can try. But as he said, we are limited." Weiland stood, walking over next to her as she stood within reach of the thick black hide.

Together they placed their hands to the cold black skin. It was harder this time to send the tingle down her arm. She now felt that limit they spoke of, as if her tank were mostly empty. She concentrated on the deeper injuries she sensed, ignoring the minor cuts and bruises, even the broken horn. There were several that were crucial to heal, but she went after them one by one, her eyes closed though she could see every little tiny scratch in his enormous body. Then she felt herself sag, and someone put their arms around her and lowered her to the ground. "Melanie? Are you alright?" Estat spoke somewhere over her.

When she opened her eyes, she could see him by the light of a new glowing stone, his long white hair framing his amber eyes. "Yeah, I think my tank ran dry," she said. Estat's brow rose, appearing confused and concerned. Melanie giggled at him, and his face relaxed, now appearing amused. "Just an expression… is Malstraun…"

"He is going to be just fine." Weiland said, "I think we should all rest a bit. It has been a rather eventful day," He gave a soft chuckle. "I think Immuraudi and I shall go and find something for us all to eat," he said, winking at her. He stood and headed off along the cave with the coramira at his side.

Estat smiled down at her. "I will never forget what you have done for me, Melanie. There are so many things I wish to ask you. But Weiland is right; you should get your rest."

"No, I'm okay. I have questions too," she said. Having waited so long to speak with him, she would not go to sleep until they had a proper boy/girl conversation. She made herself a bit more comfortable, finding a spot that was relatively smooth. "I'm not sure where to begin. Maybe you could tell me something about how you came to live in the tower?"

Estat nodded. "That is certainly quite a story. It was my first real adventure." He smiled down at her. "There is a village some distance from here called Ogto. It is where I grew up, and when I was fourteen, I discovered I had a power unlike any other. I could summon creatures to me using simple runes that I had been studying. These symbols came to me in dreams and visions, and I even traveled to Castle Nourin to gather information on such things. I found very little, however, and returned to Ogto. I planned on leaving for other larger cities and kingdoms to learn what I could, but my parents forbade it. They became upset about the things I saw and wrote of…they were… fearful," he added, his eyes drifting around the cave now. "They took away my inks and books, hiding them, and refused to allow me to venture further into this phenomenon." He paused for a time.

"Your parents rejected you for being magic?" Melanie asked, sitting up now.

"Yes. They were afraid of what I would do with my power. I had summoned several small magical beings, and they were afraid of them as well. I began to dream of leaving Ogto village, and dreamt of more symbols. I decided these symbols would help me leave, to travel to new places and find out more about my power. So late one night, I snuck into my parents' room and discovered the hiding place of all the things they had kept from me. I stuffed them into my traveler's pouch and returned to my room. I hid it under my bed until my parents had gone to sleep, and I began work on a symbol in my own room, moving everything I could, as I somehow knew it had to be large. Early that morning, I had finished all preparations and began to summon the being whose symbol I had dreams of. His summoning shook the foundations of my home, and as he rose up from the floor, destroyed the roof with his huge ebon horns." Here Estat smiled, as if recalling a rather humorous memory.

Melanie was sitting up now. She giggled. "So he destroyed your room. What was his name?"

"He went by many names. But he told me he preferred to be called Malstraun," Estat said, glancing over at the resting Serpent.

She could make out a large toothy grin on the dark figure by the light of her stone. She laughed and turned back to Estat. "And then he took you here?"

"It was strange," Estat replied, "but when I realized I had the power to summon the amarill, I was not so sure that other kingdoms would have what I sought. Malstraun agreed, but thought it would be best that if I wished to know more, I would have to find whatever I could. Together, we went to several kingdoms and gathered material. I was able to work here and there for my money, and Malstraun was more than willing to do whatever I asked of him. Villagers looked at him with suspicion though he traveled in his human form, so I had to cloak him to keep his true identity a secret. When I had gathered all I could carry, I asked him to take me somewhere where I could study without ridicule. He brought me far north towards the volcano and found a large cave that would do wonderfully for a time. However the cave soon became too cold when winter set in. I began to wish for something far more practical and protected. That is when I had the dream of Liquendia's symbol. I summoned, and asked her to build me a fortress within the volcano. She was more than accommodating and even wanted to sleep in the towers base."

"And you have been there ever since?" Melanie asked.

"Yes. I gathered more information and items to stock the tower and then became involved in my studies. I had not time for anything else. Some time after that, Brek discovered my home. He begged me to teach him what I knew, telling me that he had powers as well and had heard of me from those in Ogto Village." Estat sighed, lowering his eyes.

"I'm sorry about Brek," Melanie said softly, putting a hand on his shoulder.

"Thank you, Melanie, I think … it is best for him now. He was … troubled." Estat frowned, his eyes meeting hers. "But … now I have you to keep me company. While you are here, that is," he added with a troubled expression.

The thought of going home was no longer a happy one despite the fact that she missed her parents. Melanie found herself wanting to stay with Estat, but what about her sister? She would return home, and she'd never get to see her again. Then there was her parents, friends and boy... no... Estat was far more than the boys she had ever known. He was a man, and she loved him. "For as long as I can... I want to be with you, Estat."

His expression brightened, and he lifted his eyes to gaze into hers. Slow and deliberate, he closed the gap between them, and their lips touched. At first it was gentle, as if he was testing to see if she wanted to kiss him back. Melanie threw her arms around him and pulled him to her, and her return kiss was deeper.

-44-

Castle Silverwind

Talon picked himself up off the ground just as Axle and Veru shot past him in their wolf forms. The dragon was already high in the air, but the pair was not attempting to jump at it; they only paced along the ground as he flew north. It took a few more moments to remember what had happened, and then he turned and ran to Regence who lay a short distance away, unmoving. Blood covered his side where the claws of the dragon had struck him. Talon knelt beside him, knots building in his stomach and throat with worry. "Regence?" he called, touching the man's arm. When he did not stir, Talon's fears grew. "Sword master, have you not been through worse scrapes? What of my training? I still have need of your skills…of your friendship…"

"I am not dead yet, you fool," Regence groaned. "I will be if you keep rambling on instead of stopping this cursed bleeding."

Letting out a relieved breath, Talon waved over two of the soldiers who had medical experience. "Get to work on him right away. The rest of you, check the others." He turned to Ralley, who stood behind him. "Are you well?"

"Yeah, I'm okay. Will he be fine too?" she asked, her forehead wrinkled in worry.

"I think so…" Talon said, with a bit more confidence than he felt.

Regence did not respond, and Talon found he had lapsed back into unconsciousness. He stood up and glanced to Castle Silverwind. "We need to get him to the castle quickly." he turned to face the remaining six men of their escort. "The others?" He asked. But one of the men shook his head. They were so few now, what should he do? "Soldiers, get the wagons on the road. You…" he said, pointing to one of the archers. "Bandages and salve, now," he commanded. He turned to Ralley. "Mount up. We are leaving the moment I can get Regence onto a wagon." She nodded without a word and turned, running to the tied horses.

It took some time and great care, but Talon made sure that Regence was bandaged and carefully lifted to the back of the lead cart. Moments later, Veru had returned, though his brother Axle was not with him, as expected. After the white wolf had returned to a human form, Talon tossed him a hooded cloak. "Put that on if you are to go with us into the castle. I do not want you saying a word to anyone, much less look at them."

"As you please, your Majesty," he said with a slight tilt of his head. He offered a smile, but Talon did not return it. He had much on his mind, and smiling was not going to help any of it.

It was not long before the entire party moved out and headed for Silverwind. As they approached, it was apparent that this kingdom was not open to visitors. Those working in the fields or herding sheep had simply stopped to watch them pass, but upon entering the small village in front of the castle, all had grown quiet. Even the people in the streets had retreated to side alleyways or through doors. Shutters swung closed on most houses, but the curious left them open just enough to get a good look at the small group of soldiers moving through their village. Talon could not stop and ask about all of this, as time was important to Regence. Perhaps he would speak with the King about this the moment he knew his sword master was safe.

When they arrived at the drawbridge to the castle, however, the portcullis was down, and two soldiers stood unmoving just behind the bars. A quick glance to the top of the outer wall revealed eight archers, their arrows aimed at them. Talon was bothered by the delay, but he held up his hand to halt his party and rode forward alone. He decided he would speak with those soldiers poised at the entrance. "Hail Castle Silverwind. I am Prince Talon Degrail of Endrayen. I have an injured man here that needs immediate attention. I ask that you open your doors to us in the name of the late Emperor." He waited while the two men exchanged glances.

One of them nodded and turned back to him. "I shall inform our King," he said stiffly. He then turned and marched back.

It was a painfully long wait. Every moment that inched by made Talon far more worried and agitated. He remained where he was, but kept glancing back to the cart that held Regence. Finally, the soldier returned. Talon straightened in his saddle, ready to motion his men onward, but the soldier was shaking his head. "Sorry, your Majesty, but we are unable to open our gates to you," he said diplomatically.

Talon frowned. He had tried to keep his head during the long wait, but this was straining his last nerve. "Allow me to elaborate on my situation. I have a man who will die if he does not get the immediate attention he needs. I DEMAND that you open these gates in the name of the Emperor!" he said, trying to calm himself.

"The King has considered your plight and has already heard of the fall of the late Emperor and the choosing of the new. In light of the conflict between Castle Nourin and ourselves, he has decided to remain cautious," the soldier replied.

That last nerve snapped, and Talon's sword arm twitched. As he opened his mouth to utter a threat, Ralley's voice cut into the open air. "Then tell your King that Empress Ralley herself demands that you open your gates!"

Nearly snapping his neck, Talon turned to watch as Ralley rode forward, coming up next to him. He wanted to argue with her about revealing her true identity, but she looked so confident. That, and Regence was losing precious moments. This statement threw the soldier off his guard. He stared at her incredulously. "M ... my King would require proof of your identity."

Ralley gave him a haughty and insulted look. Talon figured she was acting, but the soldier was riveted. Ralley removed the blade from its sheath and held it up for all to see. She then tossed it toward the front of the gates and before it could clatter on the stonework, it shifted to the form of the Blade Beast, who gave a low rumble, its emerald eyes watching the soldiers. Talon turned his attention back to the soldiers at the gate and regained his calm composure, even managing a haughty look himself. The soldier's eyes widened and he spun about and ran back into the castle. The second soldier tried to do his best to stay stoic through all this, but his eyes flicked nervously from the Blade Beast to Ralley.

The first soldier returned far sooner than even Talon had expected, shouting for the men within the walls to open the portcullis. Ralley and Talon exchanged glances. She winked at him, a beautiful smile on her face. Talon's eyes lingered on her features for a moment. She was far more grown up than he had thought when he first met her in that little Tavern; her travel roughed hair and her strange clothing. He watched her face turn pink, and he realized he was staring. He smiled and turned his head, clearing his throat, as the portcullis was now fully open.

"This way, your Majesties," the soldier said, giving them a formal bow and turning to march ceremoniously through the archway.

This was more like it! Talon lifted his hand and motioned his men forward. Ralley and himself led the way, side by side, through the castle's courtyard and to the steps that led to the doors of the castle keep, the Blade Beast trotting just behind them. Here they dismounted, and servants raced up, taking the reins. Talon had to give Phoenix a few pats on the neck, hoping to calm him enough that the stable boy could handle him, but the stallion was too tired and hungry to be a nuisance and gladly followed the boy.

They prepared Regence to be moved, and a small group of servants hurried out with a pallet for him. After he was safely loaded onto the carrier, the castle's men carried him inside. Talon attempted to follow, but the soldier from the gate stopped him. "You must come to see our King first. Do not worry, your friend will recieve the greatest of care from our healers."

Reluctantly, Talon, Ralley, Veru, The Blade Beast and his two remaining soldiers followed the guard into the entrance of the keep. The four archers and three servants were left behind to secure the supplies. The inner keep was lavishly decorated with deep blue tapestries and silver columns, which were Silverwinds flag colors. The tapestries were hung all down the main hallway, alternating between those that were blank and ones with images of serpents and aquatic equines, each one with a symbol over it. Talon recognized the jagged shape with a left side curl and the circle nesting on top as the symbol of the Goddess Lcre. Though he was not yet fully versed in the beliefs of the seven Gods and Goddesses, he recalled Lcre being a Goddess ruling over the soul.

Ralley stepped closer to him, drawing his attention. "Talon, what do you know about the King here?"

"Not much. Like I told you, I have not traveled this far north. Regence would know far more than I, but …." He cut himself off here, wishing Regence were here to shed some light on the situation they were now in.

"Don't worry about him," Ralley said, smiling as if trying to cheer him up, and doing a good job of it. "They said they would take care of him, and besides, they wouldn't try anything with the Empress around right?"

He was doubtful that all Kings would be perfect saints in the face of an Empress, but Talon would have to judge for himself when he spoke to him. They were soon led through another set of large doors into a large council room headed by the King's throne. The guard leading them halted them a short distance from the dais. A long table sat between themselves and the throne along with several chairs lining one side. The guard bowed low before the throne. "My liege, the Empress, Prince Talon Endrayen and escort have arrived."

At first appearance Talon thought the King looked rather short and spindly. Quite young as well, but as he rose to his feet, Talon's eyes widened. This King was only a child, younger than himself! This boy could be no more than 14, though he was decked out in kingly robes. His hair was a sandy blond and almost as long as Talon's, though it hung loose along his back. For a moment, he was too stunned to remember formality, but after a moment he cleared his throat and gave the "King" a polite bow. "I thank you for allowing us into your kingdom. I am deeply honored that…"

"Silence," the boy snapped. "I wish to know why the Empress has come to Silverwind," he demanded.

Talon frowned. He had not expected to be outranked by this child, much less to be talked down to. He glanced at Ralley and thought she appeared ready to turn this boy over her knee. Returning his gaze to the young king, Talon replied, "She is traveling north on a very important mission. We were attacked by a swamp dragon and…"

"Then it sounds like she will have to delay her journey," the King said with curt force. "I cannot allow any of you to leave here."

This was not what Talon had expected to hear.

-45-

PRISONERS

Ralley couldn't believe her ears. This little brat was telling them that they were prisoners? "You can't do that!" she shouted, losing that superior look she was using. "I'm the Empress!"

"You are in MY domain!" the boy shouted. It was hard for her to believe that this skinny punk was a king. He crossed his arms and shot her with a smug, snobbish countenance. "While you are here, you will obey my laws. There is little you can do to resist me with such a small force."

"You are making a big mistake," Talon growled. "Are you willing to risk war with Degrail, home of the Empress?" His hand went to his sword hilt, but there were guards standing all around the room, and they all drew their swords.

"Ah ah ah," the young king said, uncrossing his arms and waggling a finger at Talon. "One false step and you all die. I am a busy man right now and cannot be bothered with…."

Ralley had not attempted to suppress her laughter. It had come bursting out like the explosion of a volcano. "You? A man?" she managed after a moment before bursting into more peals of laughter.

"Silence!" the boy shouted angrily. His face was turning red, which didn't help to calm Ralley's laughter. Even Talon appeared to be holding back his own chuckle as he turned to watch her, his hand now off his sword. "Silence I say! Guards!"

Ralley's laughter died off as the men moved forward, their swords pointed at them. Great, she ticked off the Napoleon wannabe. The Blade Beast moved in front of Ralley and hissed at the soldiers who pointed weapons at her. They halted their forward progress, not sure of the power of the Blade Beast. "You want a fight, do you?" she said and glanced back at Veru. He knew exactly what she wanted and pulled his hood down to reveal his strange features.

She returned her gaze to the prince, but he appeared unconcerned. Just as it appeared as though they would have to fight back, a woman's voice echoed through the room. "Enough!" All turned to see an elegant figure walking down the great hall towards them. Her hair was a long strawberry blond that was tied up into a simple headdress with deep blue sapphires. The dress she wore was a deep blue with more sapphires decorated into the bodice. It took two handmaidens to carry the train that flowed behind her. A tall man was with her; his hair was long, just past his shoulders, and an earthy brown to match his dark skin. He didn't appear to be dressed as royalty, but wore a plain pair of brown pants and a sleeveless shirt. Ralley would have considered him quite plain upon first seeing him, but she realized he was sporting a set of wings the same shade as his skin. She couldn't help but stare at them, wondering if this was real or just a fancy cape. "I will not have you deceiving the Empress. She must hear the truth if she is to help us resolve our current situation," the woman continued as she approached them. The guards moved out of the way, sheathing their swords.

The boy sneered, but sat back down in the throne. The woman and winged man walked around them and stood on either side of the throne, turning to face them. "Please forgive my son. Falkon has lost his father in this war and is now forced to rule as its King."

"Forgive me, Majesty," Talon said, regaining his royal composure. "But would your high Duke not take up the King's place until the Prince had come of age?"

The boy scoffed but the queen spoke first. "The kingdom's only Duke was slain in battle, and we dare not choose any other for fear that the enemy is already here. We carry ourselves as though our King has never gone to keep the enemy at bay. I dare say we cannot keep up this ruse for long, but as long as it continues to be believed, we can have a hope in winning the battle between our enemies. Empress, I must ask you to remain here. Your knowledge of our kingdom can change this battle's outcome."

"So you would keep me as a prisoner?" Ralley demanded, not liking the way things were going.

"To save our kingdom, we must have you become our guest," the queen replied gently. "I am sorry, but we did try to turn you away."

"We had a wounded man!" Talon shouted.

"And he will be well cared for, I assure you," the woman said, slightly bowing her head.

"You are making a big mistake," Prince Talon warned, his hand lying on the hilt again. "You would be making another enemy by doing this." He stepped forward, ready to dispatch any guard that came for him.

It was then that the winged man stepped easily in front of the throne, spreading his wings protectively and lifting his hands that were tipped with cruel claws. Veru stepped forward and nudged Ralley gently. "Looks like things are somewhat even here."

This caused Ralley to think a moment about battling their way out, but she dismissed that thought quickly. Regence was still wounded; their horses were in the stables. There would be no way to get out of here even if they could fight their way out of the room. Ralley refused to let anyone get hurt on her account. She stepped forward, her eyes on the queen. "I would keep your secret. Please, I have to go north to find my sister. She is in danger, and I can't stay here. Perhaps when I have finished that, we could help you by settling your feud."

"I am sorry," the queen said, waving to those men lining the room. They stepped forward, swords drawn. "I must insist that you remain here. You will be well taken care of, but you must not leave this castle. I have lost my husband... I will not lose my son, at any cost."

Talon made to draw his sword, his own few men preparing for the same move. "No!" Ralley shouted before things got out of control. Veru had said things were even here, but Ralley wasn't so convinced. They were outnumbered, and though Veru was an amarill, these people appeared to have a man capable of holding his own against him. As well, she wasn't sure what the Blade Beast would do to defend her, and she wasn't so sure she was ready for more death. "Talon, please don't fight them. It won't help Regence, and we can't leave without him."

This quelled Talons anger, and he lifted his hands in surrender, his men doing the same.

The castle guards began to remove their weapons, but none of them made a move to approach the Blade Beast, who curled its tail around Ralley, glaring at anyone who dared come near her. One of them stepped up to Veru, though he was hesitant to search him for weapons. "Majesty, this one is not human…"

"He travels with the Empress; he will be treated no differently," she commanded.

In short order, they were all ushered to rooms. Thankfully, they allowed Talon and Ralley the same room, as she certainly didn't want to be alone, and of course the Blade Beast would not leave her side. Unfortunately, Veru and the others were taken to separate quarters, effectively splitting up their party.

After the door was closed and guards posted just outside, the Blade Beast reverted back to weapon form and Ralley placed him back in the holster. At least she had a weapon, but what about an escape rout? Ralley headed to the window, but it turned out to be no good as the wall was far too high for a jump. It faced northward, the way they wished to go. The view was wonderful, but she was far too angry to enjoy it. "How am I supposed to help Melanie now?" she said, throwing up her arms. "Maybe we should have fought our way out, this is hopeless! She will never listen!"

"No, Ralley, you were right." Talon's voice was gentle. "We do not know where Regence was taken. We would have to battle our way through the entire castle with the few men at our sides. We would have lost. I was allowing my anger to get the best of me."

"Well, what am I supposed to do now? Isn't there some kind of Empress' handbook for diplomacy? I can't stay here!" Ralley cried, her voice faltering as her anger turned to hopelessness. "Just because mommy wants to spoil that little brat!" she spat, her eyes beginning to blur though she continued to pace about the room. She thought she heard Talon say her name, but she ignored him. "And here I am, stuck here in a world with no video games, no T.V, no freaking hamburgers." She could feel the tears sliding down her cheeks, her voice cracking, and the knot in her throat threatening to cut her ranting off completely. Talon called to her again, but she wasn't finished. "She can't do this! I'm the Empress, damn it!" She turned to continue pacing but Talon had stepped in her path and the moment after her head met his chest, she felt his arms around her. Unable to hold back her frustration any longer, she clutched the sides of his cape as sobs racked her body. The weight of everything that happened hit her and her knees gave out, but Talon's strong arms kept her from falling. Together, they both sank to the floor. She couldn't quite believe that she was breaking down like this. Ralley had to get to her sister; she needed help.

"Ralley… you are doing it again," he said. His voice was comforting, but his words didn't make much sense.

She hadn't recalled crying in front of him before. She attempted to calm herself, enough to speak between sobs. "Doing what?" she managed.

"You are glowing," he said, his voice still gentle.

This took a second to register in her mixed up thoughts, but she managed to stifle some of her sobs and lift her head up to look at him. "Is … is that bad?" she asked, a slight nervous laugh breaking through.

Talon smiled and brought a hand around to wipe the tears from her cheeks. "I do not know. You are still a bit of a mystery to me." he said, his eyes locked on hers. "With your…. 'tee vee' and your 'freaking hamburgers.'"

Hearing Talon say those words made a laugh work its way through her emotions. "You're so cute!" she said, wrapping her arms around him before she realized what she'd said. He was chuckling though. She wanted to stay like this for a while, feeling his arms around her, again feeling that safety she'd felt when she had first ridden to castle Degrail with him.

The moment didn't last as long as she'd hoped as Talon suddenly pulled them both to their feet. "What is that?" he said, his voice alert.

Ralley released her hold on him reluctantly and followed his gaze out the window. A brilliant yellow light could be seen, and it was growing with every moment. She took a second to examine herself, but she didn't appear to be glowing anymore. When she returned to observe the light, it was closer. "It's coming this way… but somehow… it's kinda familiar." This light reminded her of the one she'd seen in that strange dark void, and even as she thought this, she could see the thing taking on the same equine shape as it had before. Together, Ralley and Talon backed away from the window as the light filled up their view. In a stroke of good luck, or perhaps bad for them, the window happened to be plenty wide enough to allow this horse-like creature into the room. There was a definite clicking noise as the hooves hit the stone floor and the light faded from the creature; as it did, it took on a human shape. It was now a young man clad in well-kept and colorful clothes. Though he was only a few inches taller than the boy Falkon, he looked as though he had lived far longer; there was something in his sparkling blue eyes that made him seem wiser and also familiar.

"You... you're the one that rescued me from that dark place," she said, recalling the only things she could remember of that moment when she saw the blue eyes staring down at her and the bright golden light. To see that he had short black hair was intriguing, as well as the two streaks of white hair that dangled playfully at his forehead where a gold star-like tattoo rested.

"I am," he replied; his voice was young, but he spoke without slurring. "My name is Kiran," he said with a small bow of his head. This caused his hair to shift, revealing pointed ears.

"Are you an amarill too?" Ralley asked, wondering if perhaps he was an elf like in all those fairy stories.

Kiran chuckled; it was somewhat musical, reminding her of a wind chime. "No, I am a unicorn," he stated.

This was unexpected, though she should have known. She turned to Talon. "I didn't know you had those here!"

"They are... just stories," he mumbled, his eyes still on Kiran.

"True stories, at least some of them," the unicorn said with a shrug.

"Did you come here to help me?" Ralley asked hopefully.

"I came here because you summoned me, just as you did the first time," he said.

Ralley felt like she was starting to put two and two together, but before she could ask him any more questions, there was a noise outside the door, and Talon took her arm and pulled her away from it. Muffled voices could be heard, and then two heavy thuds. There was the sound of a key in the lock, a click and the door opened.

-46-

PARTING

As the door swung wide, Talon readied himself to pounce. Hand to hand combat was not something he used often, although it was one of the first things he had learned, but without his sword he had little choice. He realized he had nothing to worry about when Veru's furry form, Talon's sword in his mouth, came trotting into the room, looking rather like a satisfied cat that just brought their master a mouse. Both guards lay unconscious on the other side of the door.

"It is about time," Talon said with a smirk.

Veru flicked his head up, tossing the sword to Talon. "Well, I had to stop by and check on your sword master. Unfortunately, he cannot join us."

Talon placed his sword back in its sheath frowning. "Is he alright?" he asked anxiously.

"He is alive, and it is true they are taking good care of him." He cocked his head at the elfish man standing by the window. "A unicorn? My my, you certainly like making new friends," he said, turning to trot over to Ralley.

She smiled at him, reaching down to scratch Veru behind the ears. "I guess I do." She giggled and her eyes returned to

Talon. Her expression became serious. "I have to go find my sister," she said. "I can't stay here when she's in danger. I understand if you can't go with me. You need to stay here and make sure Regence will be okay."

Talon suddenly found himself caught with a difficult choice. He did not want to leave Regence here, but what about Ralley? She knew nothing of traveling in this world, and she traveled with strange company. It was true she had the Blade Beast, but she was not sure how to use it, or of the depth of its power. "Well… I…." he began, wishing he did not have to make such a decision.

"You will take me north to the demon summoner's tower, won't you?" Ralley asked Kiran.

"Certainly; you have summoned me, so I am at your command… as long as it does not go against my well being or beyond my power's limits," he said. And in moments, the light returned and he shifted to his equine form. The light faded, revealing a great horned beast, though Talon hesitated to call it a unicorn. His vision of such creatures was of a white horse, a long flowing white mane, cloven hooves and a great golden horn. Kiran, however, was smaller than Regences' mount, Crest, and far more delicate. His hide was not pure white; instead, it had black stripes along its legs, flank and neck. Its mane, though silken, was short and in some places was black instead of white. His long spiraling horn was not gold, but silver, along with his solid hooves. Kiran swished the whip like tail that ended in a soft plume of black and white strands. "Ready?" The unicorn did not move its mouth, yet it spoke aloud.

Ralley too was frozen, her mouth hanging open in awe.

"That... is so... cool!!" she breathed. "You're like a zebra unicorn! So, so cool!" Like a giddy child, she rushed over to Kiran and reached out, touching his flank. "Yeah, I'm ready," she said.

Kiran lowered his body, allowing Ralley to climb on. He glanced at Talon. "You are a virgin; you may still come if you wish."

"What?" Talon blurted. "That is ridiculous!! Of course I am not…"

"Hum, perhaps I am mistaken," he said, turning back and stepping to the window.

Veru trotted after him. "Do not worry about Regence. They would not dare to hurt him, not when there are three people running about free who could reveal their secrets." Veru gave a wolfish shrug. "And there is nothing wrong with being a virgin," he added, turning and bounding out the window past the unicorn.

Talon seethed, refusing to meet Ralley's gaze. "Fine! I am a virgin, now wait for me, curse you!" He could hear Ralley giggling, but he chose to ignore it, and with as much dignity as he could muster, he strode over and climbed onto the unicorn behind her.

"Why do unicorns want virgins anyway? And how are we going to get out of here?" Ralley asked.

Kiran turned his head slightly. "Well…. who would not want one?" He nickered almost as if he was laughing and faced the window. "Why, the conventional way of course." Before either of them could protest, he leapt from the window.

Talon suddenly flung his arms around Ralley and gripped the short mane for his life. Ralley was screaming as Kiran dropped through the air for a short distance. "Watch your legs." He commented over the whistle of the wind around them. Sprouting from his sides was a pair of white-feathered wings with black tips that fanned out and turned their drop into forward speed; Ralley's screams subsided, and after a short distance, she began to watch the world below pass by. Talon realized he was holding his breath and finally let it out. He chose not to comment on what Kiran had said; it seemed that he had Veru's mischievous nature. He turned slightly to gaze back at Castle Silverwind as it shrank away. "I will be back for you, Regence," he vowed.

Over the course of that day they passed over a river, fields, and the road that led between the kingdoms of Nourin and Aurora; below them was a barren stretch and a ruined city. All the while Veru raced along below them, joined by Axle, a white and black pair that streaked along the landscape, chasing Kiran's shadow.

"This is so amazing!" Ralley cried. "What are those ruins down there?" She asked curiously.

Talon's eyes drifted back to the abandoned city. "That must be Seselna. Crysna should be half a day's ride east of here. The land between them is called the Ghost Lands."

"Crysna and Seselna!" Ralley exclaimed. "The ghost children!"

"Ah," Talon nodded, recalling the story she had told about meeting them. "Yes, this is where they came from," he said.

"I still have to help them." Though she whispered this, it carried back to Talon.

"But you need to help Melanie first. She is still alive. The children will still be there many full moons from now."

Kiran flew on, carrying them over more fields, hills and forest. Talon could see the Deadwater Bog to the west, and north of that, a great snowcapped mountain, and to the northeast a thick forest. Kiran headed directly for a craggy range that ran between these two places. "I believe that is the mountain they call Drydican, which makes that thick wood over there the Dark Crystal Forest," he said.

"Why do they call it that?" Ralley asked, her eyes scanning the thick treetops.

"It is said that deep black crystals grow like plants there. Unfortunately, few people have been able to harvest any. Those that have keep them as a closely guarded treasure. I have yet to see one myself."

Kiran shifted, beginning to slow his approach to the rocky mountain range ahead. "And you best not try." His voice grew eerie. "There is great evil there. I assume you cannot feel it, being the humans that you are, but the aura about that place would twist even the gentlest of creatures."

"That is reason enough not to take a peek," Ralley said with a shiver.

Talon too felt a chill in the air, but it must have been the result of finding themselves in the shadows of the mountains. Kiran found a reasonably flat surface to land upon and even discovered a small cave as well. Talon began to wonder if the unicorn had been here before. Veru and Axle caught up in short order, but Axle disappeared among the cliffs.

Veru plopped down at the cave mouth, panting heavily. "My, that was a run!"

"So how much farther to the summoner's tower?" Ralley

asked, sliding off the unicorn, grateful for the chance to stretch her tired legs.

"A day and a half, as long as you are able to continue riding." Kiran folded his feathery wings along his body.

Talon also dismounted. Though he was used to riding horses, he found himself feeling a little wind burned from the speed of their flight. "What now? I am getting hungry and we have no supplies, and how will we keep warm?" Ralley Asked.

"Veru has plenty of fur. I am sure if you snuggle up with him…" Kiran began.

"Absolutely not!" Talon huffed. "I have my cape," he said, wrapping it about her.

Veru's ears flopped. "I am hurt, Talon, I thought we were close friends," he said with mock sadness.

"You keep your friendship over there," Talon retorted, but a slight chuckle escaped him.

He could hear Ralley giggling too. "Well, I'll take you up on that offer," she said, moving over to him and sitting next to him, burying her hands in his furry back.

Kiran's horn flashed, and soothing warmth radiated from him, touching them all. "This shall help you as well."

Talon ended up huddled next to Ralley and Veru despite his earlier protest. There was little to worry about, however, as they all kept warm enough with the light from Kiran. Even as the sun's light faded, Kiran's warm glow continued on into the night. Food was delivered by Axle, who brought several rabbits and even some fruit. Despite appearing highly insulted at such a chore, he said nothing. Talon was able to gather together enough wood to make a small fire and cook the rabbits, but it took much to get it started, relying on old fire-building methods and it died out soon after the rabbits were cooked. They all settled in to sleep, even Axle, though he chose a spot at the edges of the unicorn's heated circle. At first, Talon slept restfully, but sometime in the night, he was awakened by Veru's cold nose on his hand.

"Veru, for the sake of Austia, would you stop fooling around and let me get some sleep?" Talon grumbled.

"I am afraid the Goddess of Mercy has nothing to do with this. It would appear we are going to be surrounded soon if we do not act quickly," Veru replied.

Talon was on his feet in an instant, sword in hand. A fog had rolled in while they slept, but he suspected Veru had something to do with it. Axle was gone and Ralley was still asleep, but Kiran was awake, his ears perked forward, listening. "Who are they?" Talon asked, moving next to the unicorn.

Kiran shifted. "I suspect they are the dark elves from the forest below. They must have seen my light. Veru covered it with the fog shortly after you fell asleep, but perhaps they had already spotted it by then."

"Veru," Talon whispered, "Can you slip through the fog undetected and see how many we are up against?"

Holding his head high, Veru nodded. "Fog travel is my specialty, your Highness; they will not detect me." Veru faded into the fog. Talon was surprised to see it happen, but he trusted the amarill now. Moments later, the wolf materialized from the thick fog. "Five, your Majesty, and they are dark elves. Better wake Her Eminence," he said, pointing his nose to Ralley. "We are in for a fight."

-47-

RETURN TO THE TOWER

He was not quite sure when he had fallen asleep, but Estat woke to the sounds of a fire and the smell of meat cooking on a spit. Melanie was cuddled in his arms, and the past few days began to come back to him as his vision cleared, giving him a distinct view of her face in the gentle glow of the fire. A smile crossed his lips. She was beautiful, kind, gentle and even brave. She had been by his side while his vision was gone, and now she was with him still.

"She is quite a girl," Weiland said in a low voice so as not to wake her.

"Yes," Estat whispered back. "Weiland, Immuraudi, I thank you for all that you have done."

"As long as the safety of this land is your goal, I am at your side, Grand Summoner." He smiled. "And as long as I am at your side, so too is Immuraudi."

The coramira nodded her head. "At the mercy of where this blasted redheaded, pointy eared pain in my tail wills me to go I am afraid," she said, her tail swishing in slight merriment.

Estat eased his way to a sitting position, doing his best not to disturb the sleeping young woman. "And you as well, Malstraun; as always, you are my good friend."

The massive serpent lifted its head, slightly tipped now as the weight of its remaining horn and the lack of the other caused a slight imbalance. "Humph!" he grunted. "You are a pain in my own tail little friend. This blasted horn will take months to grow back. I will be lopsided for weeks, and that is not a very intimidating sight now is it?" he questioned. Though he too was only teasing.

Chuckling, Estat shook his head. "You should all be holding your heads high. You are all heroes, and yet all I get is complaints."

"I would feel far more like a hero had I killed that slimy toad," Malstraun grumbled. His deep voice echoed through the humid caverns.

"We have taken a great step toward stopping him … but there is still much to be done. He already has an army in his pocket. We have to get one of our own before he is able to destroy anything," Estat sighed. "I have to concentrate on the problem for a while. I am certain I will see the symbols I will need." He closed his eyes and sank into a restful position. Malstraun, Weiland and Immuraudi remained silent.

For a while, he saw nothing, though he thought hard about Xenopus. Perhaps if he learned Xonopus' symbols, he could summon him and all would be taken care of. But much to his dismay, the symbols would not come to him. He turned his thoughts to the bigger problem, Xenopus and his army. Suddenly, his mind was flooded with symbols. He had to concentrate … slow them down. He oriented on one of them that he recognized. "Triventalis," he said, and the symbols dissipated as he opened his eyes. "We need to get back to the tower. I have someone to summon," he said and looked down at Melanie. He did not want to wake her, but he could not let everything get out of hand. "Melanie…" he said, putting a hand on her shoulder and shaking her a little. "It is time to get up."

She stirred and opened her eyes, blinking a few times and looking up at him. The smile she gave him then was more beautiful than the ones he had seen before they had fallen asleep. "What? Are we leaving?" she asked in a sleepy voice.

"Afraid so," he said, returning her smile. "We have to get back to the tower."

"Oh, good… I need a bath," she mumbled as she sat up and yawned.

"I think we could all use one," Weiland chuckled.

"You will come with us then?" Estat inquired.

Weiland smiled at him. "Of course I will. I have a village to protect as well you know."

Malstraun slithered out from around the rock. "Very well then, allow me to fetch myself a meal, and we shall begin our journey," he said before slithering away through the caves.

"Good idea. Let us eat," Weiland said, pulling the meat off the fire.

Immuraudi exited the cave along with Malstraun as her appetite was for grass and clover. The rest of them settled for the cooked fowl and a few apples left over from Estat's traveling sacks. Despite all that had happened, they were all in a more cheerful mood than expected. Estat wanted it to last. He listened as Melanie tried to explain to them what her world was like, the music, houses, and something called "sell fones," though Weiland and Estat had little idea what she meant.

It sounded more like her world was filled with magical things, not machines, as she described them. Malstraun returned from his meal, complaining about shark's teeth.

Melanie gapped, appearing awed at his meal choice. "You eat sharks?"

"Every once in a while," he replied with a toothy grin, "Somone has to remind them who is king of the sea."

When all were ready, Malstraun created the portal that would take them back to Estat's tower. Immuraudi carried Weiland through first on the pretense that they could check for danger before the others went through.

They all emerged on the opposite side of the portal safe, much to Estat's relief. They were almost directly on the cusp of the volcano's crater, his great tower still standing in it's center. He stepped up to the edge and knelt down near a flat area of rock. A small summoning circle had been carved here, and he used his fire calling ability to light it aflame. He spoke softly in the magical language, and the rock rumbled, cracked and extended out toward a very large window of the tower. They used this bridge to cross, feeling the heat rising up from the base of the volcano. Malstraun had changed to his human form, making it far easier on the bridge, which probably would not have been able to hold his weight as a Serpent despite its magical nature. His hair was cropped short on one side, and Estat believed this was the human effect of his horn having been broken away. It made him look rather strange, but he chose to ignore it. Like the Black Serpent had said, it would grow back, just as human hair did.

Nothing had changed here, Liquendia had seen to it to keep the demon or any of his minions from entering the tower. It also occurred to him that the demon was keeping the tower under observation. If this were the case, he would now be alerted that they had come here. He was not sure of the implications, but he well knew that Liquendia would not be able to repel a great onslaught of demons by herself. But the symbol he had come up with was the answer: Triventalis. He had summoned it once, long ago. It was a purely informational visit, but Triventalis had been most polite, not minding the summons. It had actually appeared to enjoy the visit.

Estat led them all into the summoning room. Everything but the braziers was undisturbed, as those had been melted down. Estat was not sure how this had happened, but he had an idea that it was the result of Liquendia making sure Xenopus left. "Malstraun, I need more braziers. I care not where you get them; I must have them," he said, and the tall, thin, human form of the Black Serpent bowed with a smile and turned to exit through another of his portals. "Come with me, Melanie. I will need other things that are in my study." She nodded and followed him, leaving Weiland and Immuraudi in the summoning hall. Estat brought the travel bag with him, and when they arrived in his study, he simply put it in a corner next to a pile of books. He quickly gathered everything he needed: chalk, torches, and a red candle. He then took a large tome that had been laying on one of the tables and swiftly dusted it off. He opened it and flipped through the pages until he came to the symbol that he had seen in his vision. A large swirl with a sideways tail, very similar to Malstraun's own symbol, but instead of a bull like head on the tip of the larger swirl, there were three dots hovering over the top of the curl.

"That's it?" Melanie said, looking at the book over his shoulder. "The symbols look so simple."

"Most of them are, but there are some here and there that can try my patience," Estat said with a light chuckle. "This set here is what we shall use," he said, pointing to those symbols used in Triventalis's summoning.

"Others can do what you do though, just by knowing these?" she asked, quite curious about it all.

Estat decided he liked her head so near his own, so he continued to explain. "Not just anyone can do it. You must have the magic within you, be able to draw the symbols perfectly, pronounce the words correctly, know which step to…"

Melanie had begun to laugh and took hold of his arm. "Okay, okay, I get the point. It's a lot harder than it looks, right?"

"Yes, that is right," he said with a chuckle. "There are few like me in this part of the world."

"I thought I was like you. You know, with powers?" she asked.

"Oh, well…not exactly like my own. Your aura is strange, but you are far closer to the powers of the amarill than my own," he said, hoping this would not insult her.

"You mean, like Malstraun?" she asked, sounding doubtful.

"Yes like him, Liquendia, Triventalis." He nodded, closing the book and turning to face her.

She looked a bit confused. "So what does that mean exactly? I can't be an amarill, I don't have other forms like they do… at least, I don't think I do. I come from a place where there is no magic at all."

"Perhaps things work differently there. Magic certainly works here, and perhaps your travel to this world has released it.

You must have had an amarill visit your world, and maybe that one is your ancestor," he said thoughtfully.

She giggled. "That's silly. All my ancestors are dead except for my grandpa and my parents. Aren't amarill supposed to live for thousands of years like Malstraun?"

"They can live that long, but they can also die. Malstraun is not immune to death. He can still die before his time is up just as you or I can. There is always the possibility that he could not have used his power there and died as a result," Estat suggested.

"That can't be right. Xenopus could use his portal to get there. Magic must work in my world, somehow." Her eyes drifted across the room to the globes. "There!" she said suddenly, jumping up. "What about checking those? Can I see anywhere with them? Even into my own past?"

"I…I am not sure. I have never tried to peer into other worlds with them, but perhaps we could try," he said, setting the book aside for now. Looking into her past, her world, was too compelling to pass up. Estat removed the globe they had taken with them and placed it with the others. "Come, set your hand upon the crystal of the past and concentrate on your ancestors, perhaps a name if you can remember one," he suggested.

She nodded and closed her eyes. He wondered at what name she thought of, but he now turned his eyes to the globe. An image of a castle materialized, it was familiar somehow, as if Estat had been there. The image sharpened as it zoomed towards a tall tower in the keep, then to a window. Someone was standing there, staring out into the light of the sun, his face perfectly illuminated. This could not be her world! That was King Sephyron and Castle Aurora! This was *his* world!

-48-

FOREST OF DEMONS

Ralley woke to Talon shaking her. "What, morning already? It's freezing, where did Ver..." she stopped as she noticed everyone was wide-awake. "What is it?" she asked, trying to clear her eyes.

"We are surrounded; get onto Kiran," Talon replied in a hushed voice. His sword was drawn, and he faced into the fog in the direction Veru was staring. The white wolf's head was low and his ears back.

With all that had happened, she decided not to ask questions. Ralley crawled to her feet and struggled onto Kiran's back. Everyone was holding their breath, and Talon held his sword up, half crouched, ready to strike. He lifted his hand as if telling the others to hold steady. She wondered what it was that would be coming through the fog. More monsters?

Talon's hand dropped, and on cue, Veru instantly dispersed the fog, revealing five humanoid figures standing all around them. They were around her size and dark skinned with pointed ears. They wore inky black clothing, and each one had a short sword, the blades were crystalline and as black as onyx. Ralley sucked in a breath, seeing the lack of mercy in their eyes.

They were all a bit surprised as the fog lifted, but their sinister faces recovered faster than she had.

"They have a unicorn!" one of them exclaimed.

"Call for Keshar; we will take the man," another shouted as he lunged forward at Talon.

Ralley watched horrified as the three dark ones closest to Talon came at him, swinging their ebon swords. Another came toward Kiran and Ralley. They all ignored Veru, perhaps thinking him a simple pet and not worth bothering. It was their mistake. Veru lunged at one of those who had chosen Talon as a target. The two went tumbling down the side of the cliff, where Ralley lost sight of them. Kiran turned to face the one that came towards them, lowering his horn menacingly. This caused the attacker to hesitate and rethink his strategy. He swung his blade at the unicorn's head, but Kiran appeared to be no slouch when it came to swordplay. He used the spiral horn to block his weapon like an expert fencer. Ralley had to grip his silken mane tightly as the unicorn shuffled to keep a good distance between the dark one and himself.

She couldn't help but spare a glance in Talon's direction, but he too was handling the remaining two attackers well. Ralley suddenly remembered there was a fifth and frantically began searching the area with her eyes for him. She spotted him some distance away waving at something, or someone, down the cliff.

"I think we are going to have more company!" she shouted.

Kiran and Talon were too preoccupied to spare a glance, but Ralley could see everything from her perch atop Kiran's back. Something was racing up towards them. The signaling dark elf turned and waded into the fray with Talon and his fellows, catching the prince off guard, his black sword slicing Talon's left arm. He yelled out, though it sounded angry rather than hurt, and the Prince swung his sword arm, smacking the opposing blade away from him. But now he faced three opponents, and Ralley became far more worried. "Kiran, Talon is in trouble! We have to do something!"

"Hold on," Kiran replied. At first Ralley thought he meant to wait till he got a chance, but then he reared up on his hind legs, forcing Ralley to grip his mane, her legs clenching his body. She gave a small scream, and Kiran kicked out with his front legs, delivering a double blow with his silver hooves at the elf, who tried to block the first blow with his sword unsuccessfully. The second blow landed square on his chest, knocking him back down the cliff. Ralley could hear his scream as he tumbled down into the brush below.

Kiran spun around to face a new threat that had just come into view. Ralley gasped, surprised. Standing to face them was a great black unicorn, its horn a red crystalline shard that looked just as intimidating as Kiran's. Upon its back was a dark elf like the others; his hair was much longer and like his fellows, it was black as night. The sword in his hand was far longer than those the others carried, and the look in his eyes was cold and frightening.

Fumbling with the pouch at her side, Ralley knew she had to do something, or else this would be the end of her. The stranger saw her going for a weapon and reacted, nudging his steed forward and lifting his sword high overhead. Ralley squealed as she yanked the blade free of the pouch. The huge black blade came down at her in a sweeping arc; she could hear its whistle in the air just before the Blade Beast swung around to meet it. Though the blade was smaller than the other, she did not feel the impact that she was bracing for. Her opponent seemed surprised at her ease of handling his onslaught, and his sword drew back again as the dark unicorn underneath him clashed with Kiran.

The heads of the two equines became a blur as they each tried to skewer the other with their horns. It became an all out sword fight between two great spiral spears. Ralley held tightly with one hand as sparks flew from the horns every time they met. There was a terrible squealing sound as they rubbed together, but there was no way she would let go of either Kiran's mane or the Blade Beast. Kiran danced about, keeping a fair distance between Ralley and the Elvin warrior's sword reach.

There was a cry of pain and surprise from somewhere, and Ralley spared a glance in Talon's direction, fearing the worst. She spotted Talon's bloody sword emerging from the stomach of one of the two he fought, and she gave a cry of relief. Unfortunately, the dark rider noticed this and leapt from the ebon unicorns back, landing on the ground and running towards the prince.

There was no time to shout a warning to him, so she threw her weapon at the elf. He must have seen it coming as he turned and brought his sword up to slash it away. Surprise met his stony face once again when the blade contacted his sword and remained in position as if someone were wielding it. The elf leaned forward, giving his sword more pressure but the blade refused to back down, so he changed his strategy, swinging the sword around him to cast the blade past him. This worked, leaving him free to pursue Talon. Her interference had helped more than she'd expected. Talon cut the leg of his current opponent and turned to face the new enemy.

The two looked evenly matched as this dark elf was taller than the others, almost as tall as Talon himself. Just as their fight began, Ralley heard a shriek from the ebon unicorn and turned to see it rear up and kick out at Kiran's head. He managed to avoid the head strikes, but one of them landed on his neck, and he gave a whinny of pain. Ralley felt the body underneath her jerk sharply from the blow, and she frantically began to look for the blade, trying to mentally shout for it. Out of nowhere the blade, in its bestial form, leapt to the back of the black unicorn.

This moment allowed her to return her attention toward Talon. He was still standing, but something was wrong. Blood covered the black sword of the elf and Ralley cried out as their swords clashed together, an impact that rang sharply from the elf's crystalline weapon. "We have to get out of here! I think Talon is hurt!" she cried, tugging on Kiran's mane.

The black unicorn was now distracted, bucking and spinning to rid itself of the dragon that clung to its back with hooked claws. Kiran spun around and bolted forward, nearly dislodging Ralley at the same instant. His horn lowered as he ran straight for the Elvin fighter, but the elf's light frame allowed him to dodge easily away, this action effectively splitting the two combatants, one on either flank. Kiran swung his horn to meet the crystal sword, and Ralley reached down for Talon. "Hurry! Get on!" she shouted.

Talon easily pulled himself up behind her, one arm wrapping around her to hold tight to the mane. His sword was switched to his right hand, allowing them extra defense against the crystalline sword and its wielder. "What about Veru?" Ralley cried, realizing she had not seen the white wolf since he disappeared over the cliff.

"No time," Kiran dodged back, turning from the dark warrior and racing for the cliff. To their left, a black figure raced after them. It was the ebony unicorn, and it looked furious.

Ralley called out for the Blade Beast, and it raced after the dark creature. Kiran made it to the drop off and leapt out into open air. The ebon unicorn was right on his heels, sprouting black webbed wings just as Kiran's feathered ones emerged. It was prepared to give chase, and Ralley was none too sure if Kiran could fight in the air with two riders upon his back. She reached out her hand for the Blade Beast as it shifted from its dragon form to the blade. It spun through the air after them, tearing into the webbing of the unicorn's wing as it passed and ending up in Ralley's hand, content to be placed back in its pouch. A piercing whinny cut through the air as the pursuing creature skidded to a stop inches from the edge, angrily flailing its injured wing and lashing its horn through the air as its prey escaped.

It was close, but it appeared as though Talon, Kiran and Ralley were safe. Yet Ralley worried now what had become of Axle and Veru, and as Kiran spiraled into the sky and once again headed northward, she began to search the ground for their familiar blur. It was still rather early in the morning; the sun had not yet risen, but she could tell the landscape was becoming clearer. Below was the continuing range of crags, but beyond that, a great forest to the north. "Is that the demon forest?" she asked.

"Yes," Talon said sounding a bit winded. "It will take some

time to get through it, but we should be fine as long as we stick to the skies."

This seemed like a good plan to her, as she was tired of running into things that wanted to kill them. It made her wonder what troubles and dangers her sister was in, and she shuddered to think of it. She had to get to her as fast as possible… but at what cost? Her rushing had almost gotten them killed, and she wasn't so sure that Veru wasn't already dead. Somehow, she had to hope for the best and continue to keep her eye out for him; perhaps Axle had found him and was looking after him now. That made her feel more at ease, but she hoped they could catch up to them on the other side of the Demon Forest.

Talon shifted and gave a slight groan of pain. Ralley frowned, gazing at the journey ahead as she asked, "Are you alright, Talon?"

"I have been better," he admitted, struggling to get his sword back in its sheath. He grunted, and Ralley thought he sounded as if he were in pain.

"You sure?" she asked, trying to turn her head a bit to look at him. Out of the corner of her eye, she could see blood staining his shirt. "Talon?" she asked, more concerned now.

There was no reply, and she felt Talon sliding to one side, the arm holding Kiran's mane loosening. She gasped in alarm as she realized he must have passed out and frantically reached for his arm. But it was far too much weight for her to handle, and Kiran faltered as Talon's body shifted too far to one side, upsetting the wing. "NO!" Ralley shouted as he slid off and his weight yanked his arm right out of her grip. "TALON!" she screamed as his body dropped toward the mountains below.

-49-

Insult to Injury

The wind whistled around him, but his body was free falling through it instead of the forward motion he was expecting. He heard Ralley screaming his name, and that made him open his eyes. This was not the greatest idea, as all he saw was a bevy of rocks and boulders far below to land on. Light began to blur the image of the boulders, and at first Talon had thought that his soul was being pulled out of his body. The light intensified until he cold not see the boulders at all. Instead, he now saw something else rising towards him out of the glow; his whole body slowed as if the light were cushioning him. Then his body contacted a solid form, slightly furry, and the sound of pumping wings filled his ears as the light faded.

"It seems as though I was needed," came a female voice.

Talon struggled some, his stomach wound threatening to make him pass out once again. "Who?" he groaned as he managed to seat himself properly on what he discovered to be the back of another unicorn.

"Worry not; I am Meilea. It seems I have come to save you." the female voice intoned.

Talon righted himself on the equine's back, recognizing the

black and white patterns on the unicorn's body, but this was not Kiran. "You are a unicorn. Where… did you come from?" he groaned, his hands gripping the soft mane.

"I have remained in the meadow with others of my herd until they fled from the evil that grows in the northeast." She let out a whinny, and another unicorn flying high above them answered it.

"Is that Kiran? Is Ralley alright?" he gasped.

"Yes, that is my mate; they appear to be well and are quite glad that you are too. Come, we will land in the meadow and tend your wounds. You must remain conscious while we are in the air, I may not be able to catch you a second time."

Talon responded by gripping her mane tighter. He fought against the darkness of unconsciousness and just as he thought he would not be able to hold on any longer, Meilea began to glide downward toward a large open meadow bordered by hills and a thick forest. In moments, Talon's feet were back on solid ground, and he sank to the grass and laid on his back, watching Kiran as he spiraled down toward the meadow, Ralley peeking eagerly down at him.

When Kiran's hooves touched the earth, Ralley leapt off and raced to his side. "Talon! Are you all right? What happened? Let me see…" She paused as Talon began to laugh though it hurt to do so. "What are you laughing about? I'm serious!"

Talon reached up to take the hand that was reaching for his shirt. "It is almost as if you place me in danger so you may rescue me. It is not supposed to work that way. I should be rescuing you."

She gave him a small smile. "Well I guess it is in the story-books, right? The prince rescuing the damsel in distress, but I

guess I'm no ordinary damsel." She frowned. "I'm sorry Talon…
I…."

"No, Ralley, *I* am sorry. I have been a fool. You are the
Empress, and I should have done as you ordered without question. I should have trusted in you always. I will not make those
mistakes again. I am yours, Ralley." He pulled her hand to his lips
and kissed it softly. He could see her face redden, and it made him
smile, but it was brief, as pain turned it into a frown. He winced.

Kiran and Meilea had stepped towards them, their wings
now gone, but their kindly equine faces peering down at them.
Meilea nuzzled Ralley. "Do not worry for him. We are unicorns, are we not?" Ralley appeared somewhat confused by this
statement, but Talon was quite certain of its meaning. The pair
moved to either side of him and lowered their horns toward his
stomach. Ralley appeared worried, and he watched her reach
out a hand as if to stop them. A gentle glow spread from horn
to wound, and though Talon cringed, waiting for some kind of
sharp pain to signify the knitting of the flesh, it never came. The
glow spread around his body and through his gut, and he felt
nothing but its loving heat.

Moments later, the pair stepped back from him, and Talon
discovered he was able to sit up, feeling like himself again. Ralley
inspected the hole in his shirt that was still caked with blood,
but the wound that had been underneath was healed without
being tender. "Wow! That was awesome!" she said, looking up at
Talon. "You're okay!" she cried, throwing her arms around him
in a tight hug, knocking him back.

Talon laughed and returned the hug with just as much en-
thusiasm, though he did find he was still a bit dizzy. He turned

his head to look at the unicorns and gave them a respectful nod. "Thank you."

"You are most welcome, Prince, but Ralley is the one who summoned me. It is her you need thank." Mielea spoke, and Kiran nodded his head as well.

Ralley smiled, giving a shrug. Talon squeezed her hand. "Thank you."

"We must continue." Kiran said, stepping forward. "Meilea tells me it is not safe here in our old grazing meadows any longer."

His mate bobbed her head. "The evil spreads, and even the Faye of the Moon Tree are hard pressed not to leave their home. We should not remain here for long."

"Faye of the Moon Tree?" Ralley asked. Talon raised a brow and awaited an answer himself. He had never heard of them before.

"There is no time to explain each denizen of the forest. Come, we must hurry." Kiran stepped next to Talon and Meilea to Ralley, bidding them to climb on. Once Talon had helped the Empress up and had slid onto Kiran's back, the two unicorns bolted off through the trees. Talon and Ralley were forced to press themselves against their backs to avoid low hanging branches, but the pair did their best to find the easiest route through the thick forest.

"Why not fly?" Talon questioned the moment he could.

"Too dangerous," was Kiran's explanation. It was good enough, and Talon turned his attention to Meilea and Ralley, who were able to find a far less branchy area to run through as Ralley was able to sit up a little farther. Everything was moving so fast now that Talon was sure they would be through the forest in no time. Their travel took them through miles of forest in a northwest direction. The pair seemed tireless as they galloped on through the maze of trees and they stopped only once to allow them to drink from a stream.

A sudden scream cut through the air, and Talon's head snapped around to look at Ralley. She too peered about in confusion. Was someone else in trouble? "Wait! What was that? Where did it come from?" There were no reins for him to grab hold of and direct the unicorn, nor to even halt him as the pair continued to race on.

"It is the Mortix; they have discovered us," Kiran said, sounding rather calm.

Talon would have put a hand on his sword, but he also wanted to make sure he did not fall from the fast moving unicorn's back. "I thought you said it was safer to travel on the ground!"

"It is. Meilea tells me there are worse things watching the skies now," Kiran said. Talon did not like the sound of that.

"What should we do?"

"Outrun them."

This did not seem like much of a plan, but he could feel Kiran gaining speed, and Talon clutched tighter to the mane, crouching down as far as he could. He kept an eye on Meilea and Ralley as well, but the mare was keeping a steady pace, keeping up with them easily. He could hear the Mortix speeding along beside them and heard their screams from behind. If it came down to it, he would loosen his hold to draw his sword. He thought he saw one pacing them; through the trees to his left, and moments before he realized it, the creature had thrown itself through a bush towards them, its claws and fangs were the first thing Talon saw and the last, as something large and black barreled into it from behind. Kiran plunged on through the trees, not slowing for a moment.

Talon had only just began to wonder what type of creature had gotten the monster when he heard a familiar, and now welcome, metallic howl echo through the wood. Those screams he could hear behind them cut off, leaving the only sound that of the pounding hooves of the unicorns. "It is alright, Kiran, I think we are going to be safe now," he said, unable to conceal his smile. Though Veru could have an annoying habit of smiling at the worst of times, and his brother Axle was no sack of peaches, the two of them were truly proving themselves to be loyal.

Kiran and Meilea soon slowed to a cautious pace, and the two riders were able to relax and loosen their grip, rubbing at their sore hands. Ralley turned to look behind them several times. "Did you hear that? It was Axle," she said eagerly. "I bet Veru is with him. Those two wouldn't leave each other behind, right?"

Talon frowned a bit and gave a light shrug. "I did not see him, but, perhaps you are right."

The unicorn pair kept a steady pace, and Talon too began to wonder if Axle and Veru would even show themselves. Then, out of the corner of his eye, he could see a black motion through the trees. "Axle?" Talon called. The black shadow-like thing slipped through the brush, pacing closer to them.

It was indeed Axle, and his wolfish face appeared just as annoyed as always. "What do you want?" he barked, his ears flattening.

Ralley spoke up first. "Where is Veru? Is he alright?"

Axle growled. "That stupid pain in the tail! He should never have taken a liking to you two! Look where it has gotten him!" he snapped.

Talon and Ralley exchanged worried glances. Had Veru not made it after all? "What has happened to him?" Talon asked, true concern in his voice.

"I busted my fool leg of course," the soft voice of Veru spoke behind them all. "It is to be expected when falling down a cliff side. Cannot say the elf was quite so lucky though. Too bad," he said with a wolfish grin. "And do not mind Axle, he is just concerned for me."

Axle growled in response. "Hah! You should have broken both legs, and then we could go home and stop this foolishness! You are far too slow to hunt as it is."

"I caught up, did I not?" Veru said, calm as ever. Talon did notice a limp in the right foreleg, but Veru appeared to be moving along well despite his handicap.

"Are you going to be alright, Veru?" Ralley asked. She looked as though she would leap off the back of Meilea.

"Certainly. We are fast healers, otherwise I would not have gotten here as quick as I did," he said happily, ignoring Axle as he stalked about with a scowl. "I wanted to be sure and warn you about Ezvex before you accidentally blundered into him. But I suppose it is a bit too late for that now."

That did not sound good, and Talon frowned. "Why is that?"

"Well, because you all got chased right into the middle of his domain. You two better tread softly," he said, his eyes turning to Kiran and Meilea. "He can feel the vibrations."

-50-

HERITAGE

"That cannot be right," Melanie heard Estat say. She opened her eyes and watched the image in the crystal now. It was a very stoic figure of a man staring out a castle window.

"Who is that?" Melanie asked.

Estat gave her an odd look. "Supposedly someone from your past Melanie, if you were thinking of your past, that is," he said, watching her carefully.

"Well, yes, of course I was. The one name that I can remember was the name Sephyron. I suppose it stuck in my mind because of how odd it was. My father only mentioned it a time or two, but didn't tell us much. I guess we never really tried to ask about our ancestors honestly; Father always got upset about it." Melanie shrugged and examined the image. "He does look like dad, but it couldn't be our grandpa, unless he's in some kind of movie or lives in Ireland or something," she said.

Estat shook his head. "No, that is Castle Freewind. I recognize it; I have been there before. The man you see there is Sephyron. He was king there for three lifetimes until he disappeared."

"Three lifetimes?" Melanie asked a bit skeptically.

"Yes, he is the son of Emperor Traeis, who retained the title for over 300 years until the Blade Beast chose a new ruler. After that, Traeis lived in Freewind Castle, ruling as a King there until his son came of age. Then Traeis left into the north, leaving his son Sephyron to be king." Estat turned his eyes back to the image of Sephyron.

"So could Traeis be an amarill then?" she asked, eager to hear more of this world's history, even though she was never much for the subject in school.

"Yes, half, if the stories are true. His father was Clavoyat, an amarill like Malstraun, but nobody knows much about him. He did not care to remain behind closed walls, but many amarill are free spirited in that way. But this does not explain your connection to Sephyron. Their line disappeared many years ago. Only one is left now." Estat still gazed at the image, drawing Melanie back to it as well. The Sephyron in the image was walking away from the window, but the crystal image was following him through the hallways. There was little detail to be made out around him, though she could see people walking past him, bowing or nodding, but the faces were hazy the farther the people were from him.

She frowned. "How do you mean disappear? You don't mean they just went 'poof' and were gone, right?" This idea was silly to her, but in a world like this, it almost seemed possible.

Estat shook his head. "No. They left, or so everyone believes. People most often do not accept change. Every Emperor before had been human, and they liked it that way. But what they do not realize is that the Blade Beast chooses the best Emperor, whoever they may be, human, elf or amarill. When a half amarill was chosen, it caused an uproar in the people. They could not believe that someone who they decided was half demon could ever rule their country. Nevertheless, he ruled it with all the elegance, honor, trust, wisdom and love that any Emperor before him had. After his first full lifetime of rule, the people reconciled with this fact. Most of them decided he must not truly be half demon after all and began to speculate on other possibilities and explanations for his long life and the fact that he never appeared to physically age. He went on to rule lifetime after lifetime without ageing. Even those who felt he was a demon could do nothing. Traeis had the Blade Beast at his side, but after his 300-year rule, the Blade Beast left him. He was given his own kingdom to rule as a King, but many of the people there were afraid of a halfbreed who had been stripped of Emperor status. Fear grew into hate over the years, but Traeis had decided to leave the rule of the kingdom to Sephyron. After he was gone, Sephyron continued to rule the kingdom in his stead, though assassinations were attempted upon him." Estat paused, watching the image.

Melanie too, stared at Sephyron. She was afraid that she would see one of these attempts, or the final one, but King Sephyron wandered through the halls without incident, coming to a large door that he rapped on gently, then after a moment, entered. The room was hazy, but she could make out a large four-poster bed. The room was decked in silver cloth and colorful tapestries. "Who is that?" Melanie inquired, seeing a boy turning to face Sephyron.

"That is Sephyron's son. He was destined to be King after Sephyron, but with the king's disappearance, there was no protection for his family, so they went into hiding," Estat said, sounding rather regretful.

She nodded, understanding that Estat was great friends with the amarill and was an outcast himself. The image of the boy came into far better focus as he approached Sephyron. He was perhaps 12 or so, but his face was so familiar. "What is his name?" She asked.

"Prince Derrin." Estat replied.

"What!" Melanie jerked her hand away from the globe in surprise and the image faded away. "But, that's crazy!"

Estat blinked and frowned at her, not understanding why she was so surprised. "What is?"

"Derrin and Sephyron! I mean…either it's a huge coincidence or there's something way weird going on. Derrin is my father's name!" Melanie turned back to the globe to take a closer look at the boy, but the image was gone, the crystal was blank. "I have to see where he went after Sephyron left. Is that possible?"

He nodded, still staring at her a moment before placing his own hand on the globe. "Allow me, this time," he said, closing his eyes for a moment.

She watched as the crystal swirled to life again. The image was not as sharp as before, but she could see the boy again. The scene had changed. The boy indeed looked like a young version of her father now that she had better opportunity to examine him. The boy that was Derrin raced down the corridor of the castle, passing tapestries that she could not make out, as they were far too blurry. Someone was running with him, an older woman from what Melanie could see. She was wearing a lovely silver dress. It made Melanie conscious of the fact that she was still in her travel worn, mud covered prom dress and would seriously love a bath after all this was over. For now, the prospect that her own dad had come from this world was too interesting, so she watched as her father, and what she could only guess was his mother, raced down a spiral staircase into a darker hallway. Here the woman took up a torch to light their way as they hurried along through a far less decorative corridor.

Estat had opened his eyes and now watched with her as the miniature movie played on. Derrin and his mother finally came to an old wood door that was unbarred and opened. The two went out into the night, rushing to a copse of trees. Melanie couldn't quite make out who the man was that they met among the tall woods, but he was wearing black clothing and had a mass of black hair. Estat leaned closer to the crystal, trying to inspect the figure himself, but it was almost impossible.

"Who is it? What are they doing? Why is everything getting harder to see?" Melanie asked with a frown.

"The crystal is nearly spent; it will renew over time, but we have been viewing for far too long," Estat replied. "It will not last much longer…"

Melanie bit her lip as she watched the mother converse with the dark one while her father stood quietly by. He looked frightened, and every once in a while, he peered over his shoulder at the castle they'd left. Finally, the dark one nodded his head and turned away from them. He spoke and moved his hands in a strange fashion and slowly, a silvery white tear in the air appeared before him, blackness swirling within it as it widened enough for the three to pass through. The blackness spread throughout the image before it suddenly cleared, leaving nothing behind but the blankness of the crystal within the sphere.

"Wait! Where did they go? Who was that?"

"It was Malstraun," Estat said with certainty. "Come. It is time to go and speak with him. He should have the rest of your story," he said, taking his hand from the spent orb. He picked up the book with the symbols for Triventalis in them, tucking it under an arm then pocketed the large red candle and chalk.

Melanie stood and followed him out the door of the study. "Are you sure we should bother him? After all, you have to summon this amarill, don't you?"

"I am certain Malstraun's story wont take long; he should already be waiting for us in the Summoning Hall. I am curious to know what happened."

When they arrived in the huge room, Malstraun was indeed standing amid the braziers that were already lighted and set around the carved symbol on the floor. Weiland and Immuraudi watched from the edges of the cirlce as Estat hurried to the middle of the symbol and placed the red candle there. Then he pulled a piece of chalk and settled into a corner of the star, beginning to sketch out a symbol there. "Malstraun," he began, without looking up. "Where did you take Prince Derrin and Queen Sitanya that night?"

Melanie turned her gaze to Malstraun. He didn't even flinch or look away as Estat spoke the question. He simply smiled and replied, "To a safe place of course. Why is it you view the crystals about such things?" he asked and turned his gaze on Melanie.

"It was for me," she said before Estat could answer. "I think Derrin is my father. I just want to know for sure. Did you take them to my world that night that they left the castle?" She watched as he smiled at her; his yellow eyes, though frightening in his Serpent form, were strangely kind and alluring in his human one.

"They asked for a world away from this one where they would not be found by those who would hurt them. There were very powerful wizards who wished them harm, so a place where magic worked well was out of the question." Malstraun smiled. "I wondered, but I should have known it. Yes, you are the child of Prince Derrin of Freewind, who is now undoubtedly a king by right of age. I guess that makes you a princess."

Melanie couldn't quite believe all this, but Malstraun didn't look like the type to lie about anything. She wasn't sure what she should say, so she turned her eyes to Estat. He gave her a smile and looked back down to his work. A princess in a strange world she knew so little about. "So… what now? What does this mean, and what am I supposed to do? I have lived my life in another world, friends and family and school…" If she came from this world… should she remain in it?

"That, Princess Melanie of Freewind, is something you must decide on your own," Estat said in a tone so low she almost didn't hear him.

-51-

THE TRUE HERO

Veru's warning was taken to heart, and the two unicorns moved with great delicacy across the ground. Ralley noticed that Veru hadn't changed the way he stepped, but Axle, who had continued to follow with them, had. If she had not been so scared, she would have continued to stare at how different these two amarill brothers were. It was slow going, and Ralley wondered if they should have simply continued to run through this Ezvex's domain. "What is this thing we are trying not to waken?" Ralley whispered to Veru.

"Ezvex? Oh, he is just a Multi-headed amarill, really nothing to be too afraid of. We have met him on a few occasions; he is really not all that bad," Veru said with his usual wolfish grin.

"Pfft" Axle scoffed. "Yet another pain in my paw; why, if I had about three more brothers or so, I would tear him limb from limb," he growled.

Ralley decided she didn't want to know what this thing was that Axle estimated took five wolf amarills to defeat. They continued on through the trees, but Ralley heard and saw nothing; in fact, the forest was far quieter than any she had been in since coming here. There were no birds singing, no insects chirring.

Even the trees were silent, no rustling leaves or creaking trunks. She glanced to Talon, and he stared back at her with fearless eyes; his gaze swept back as he surveyed the area. She turned her eyes forward again, feeling the quiet of the wood closing in and suffocating her.

And then, both unicorns and wolves halted their movement at once. Talon's hand slipped to his sword just as the ground beneath them began to quiver. Kiran tossed his head and pranced to steady himself. Ralley gave a small gasp and leaned over Meilea's mane, clutching to it as the unicorn beneath her shifted uneasily.

"Ah, well, we tried," Veru said casually.

Ralley watched as Talon drew his sword. She took the cue and fumbled with the blade pouch. She didn't like having to defend her life; there was definitely no thrill to it, but it was better to fight than be dead. Then something burst from the ground ahead like a volcanic eruption, spraying dirt, leaves, brush and twigs in all directions. The sun was still trying to rise above the horizon, resulting in the creature before them to be a giant silhouette against the little light that showed through the canopy of forest trees. It towered over them, a rather thick body or neck that reminded her of the black serpent Talon had fought, but its head was far more elongated. She held on as Kiran and Meilea backed away from the massive creature that let out a high-pitched roar.

Behind them, two more eruptions shook the ground, and more debris went flying through the air. Ralley turned in the saddle and spotted two more serpentine heads rising from the ground. "Two more!" she cried in dismay. This was just not turning out to be a good day.

"Veru, can you give us some cover?" Talon shouted.

"It will not do much good, I am afraid. Ezvex can feel our vibrations as we move," Veru replied, shaking his wolfish head. Axle had already crouched down, his ears flat to his metallic head, his glittering blue eyes intent upon the larger body.

The larger head moved down towards them. "And what has wandered into my trap? Quite a feast I might say," the creature hissed; its voice was surprisingly quiet for its massive size. "Ah, Axle and Veru. I thought we established that you were not to meddle with my hunting ground."

Before Veru could answer, Axle leapt in front of their group, ears flat, teeth bared. "I did not make any deals with you!" he snapped.

"That is your own fault," it said, its head drifting back some as if it knew that Axle would leap at it. The creature turned his head slightly to the side, one of its glittering black eyes examining Ralley and Talon. "Tell me, who are you two?" it asked.

Ralley wasn't so sure she wanted to let it know; after all, it had said it wanted to eat them. She turned to look at Talon, hoping he had a far better reply. He was sitting up straight in the saddle with his sword ready.

"We are travelers, and we must pass through your domain freely; if you hinder us, we will have no choice but to force our way through," he said, sounding far more confident than Ralley herself.

The creature laughed, which sounded more like a collection of hisses and snorts. "Nobody escapes from Ezvex."

"We have!" barked Axle, leaping toward the thick body, his claws digging in, his jaws opening wide and clamping down at the nearest vulnerable spot.

Ezvex reared back and shook itself much like a dog might after being bathed. Axle was thrown off, but the black wolf rolled back to his feet and charged in again. Veru joined him, leaping up to sink his own teeth into the monster's neck, but Ezvex used his head to bat him out of the air, its speed incredible for its size. Before she knew it, Talon and Kiran charged forward, horn and sword ready to strike. Meilea pranced uncertainly beneath her but did not move forward. Ralley could only guess that the unicorn didn't want to bring her into the fray, defenseless as she was. But this was not true, she had the Blade Beast, though she could never be sure quite how to use it. To Ralley, it was much like a boomerang. Throw it, and it came back eventually. She drew it from the pouch and threw it as hard as she could toward the monstrous Ezvex. It whistled through the air, but the beast saw it coming and ticked its head to the side enough for the blade to pass harmlessly past it.

Disgruntled at the miss, Ralley waited for the blade to return, but something burst out of the dirt just behind Meilea and herself. The unicorn turned in time for both of them to see another serpent head rising from the ground, dirt raining down on them in the process. This made four heads total, and the number was getting to be a bit distracting. Meilea backed away from it as it swung down, its jaws snapping just a foot or so in front of them. The two other heads that had come up before took a few snaps at them as well. There was something about these other heads that was far different from the bigger one, but in all the distraction, she couldn't quite focus on what it was. It was not just that they were smaller either. Apparently they weren't able to move forward through the dirt, which was a good thing for them. Ralley pointed toward an open space where there were no monstrous heads, and Meilea turned to run forward.

They only got a few feet before another head erupted from the ground in front of them. They were now completely surrounded by undulating giant snakeheads. Ralley craned her head around looking for the blade and spotted it coming toward her. She reached out and it came to her hand. "Alright, no more Miss Nice Girl!" Ralley cried, throwing the blade at the base of the smaller serpent head in front of her.

With no way for it to dodge, the blade hit the base of its neck, sinking in and lodging itself there. This is when she discovered that this one did not make any sound. Instead, the expected screech of pain came from the larger serpent. Ralley turned, wondering if this was simply a result of something the others had done to it. The head of the serpent had arched back in pain and Kiran took this grand opportunity to thrust his conical horn into the front of the beast. Ezvex let out a horrendous roar and swung its massive head into the unicorn's flank with such force that it threw both Talon and Kiran into the air and through the trees. Ralley was horrified, but felt she could do nothing as the twin brothers Axle and Veru continued to tear at the larger serpent. Ralley had to get her weapon back. She turned and looked for it, but the serpent before her had disappeared back into the ground.

"Blade Beast! Where are you?" she shouted out, hoping it would speak with her as it had done before. There was no response. Meilea turned underneath her, forcing her to head off toward the beast. "Meilea! What are you doing?" Ralley shouted but the unicorn did not pay her much attention. She neighed angrily and charged Ezvex, her horn lowered and aimed. The beast saw her coming and again began to swing his head toward them. "To your left!" Ralley shouted.

"Hold on!" Meilea shouted, screeching to a halt. There was hardly enough time to grasp her plan, but Ralley was able to catch herself before being flung right over the unicorn's neck. It helped that Meilea kept her head high, as she did so to be sure of Ralley's safety. The head of Ezvex passed in front of them with a heavy whoosh of air. Meilea's head ticked to the side as her horn caught the edge of the monster, cutting a gash in the back of its skull. With its passing, she sprang forward and lowered her horn once again; it sank deeply into the base of the monster. The force of it almost knocked her off again, but she was getting the hang of the sudden stops as she held tightly to the silken mane and righted herself.

Ezvex recovered far more quickly than she would have guessed. She glanced up to see a massive jaw racing down towards them. She only had time to scream.

Something white knocked her from the unicorn's back and toppled with her across the ground, then sprang back to his four paws. Ralley watched in horror as the monster clamped its jaws around Meilea's body and lifted her into the air. Axle came out of nowhere, leaping as high as he could up the back of the serpent body and let out the same loud and powerful bark that had caused the swamp dragon Kurnok to topple from the air. To their mutual annoyance, it didn't appear to bother Ezvex in the least. It threw its head, tossing Meilea and sending her crashing through the brush. The horrific sound of her body hitting a tree made Ralley scream again. This caused Ezvex to focus on her now. It grinned maliciously as it craned its neck towards her.

"Ralley!" came the shout of a most welcome voice.

She turned to see Talon racing towards her, his sword in hand. He skidded to a stop in front of her in a protective stance, his sword raised at the creature.

Ezvex chuckled evilly. "You think that's going to stop me? I am the most powerful amarill of these woods," he snapped at Talon, who blocked with his sword.

Veru smirked. "You do not really believe that do you?" he chuckled.

Then it came to Ralley that she could summon something tougher to help them, but how? She had done it before, right? The giant black serpent that fought Talon, the unicorns.... she had to get help for them. Ralley desperately looked around for some sort of trigger. Her feelings did this, didn't they? She'd cried for help... she'd done it in the blackness after Melanie was taken, when she was angry at Talon, and in the castle so that they could escape.

Yes, that was it. She was angry. Angry at Ezvex for hurting Kiran, Meilea, Veru, Axle and Talon! She wanted him dead. She wanted revenge! Something that was nearby, to get here in a hurry, something powerful and strong! She wanted someone who could save them all.

Then she felt it. A heat that rushed through her body, and instead of fearing it, she embraced it, allowing it to engulf her in its red light. She could see the back of Talon's cape as it reflected her red glow. Her eyes flooded with the red fury, and she fought to stay conscious as she felt herself lift from the ground. Controlling herself took the breath from her, and as the light died away, she dropped to her hands and knees. Slowly, she looked up, praying she would perhaps see the black serpent ready to tangle with Ezvex... but it had not come.

-52-

TRUE CALLING

Talon deflected the snapping head of Ezvex as the monster attempted to swallow him whole. He saw the reflection of Ralley's red glow in the eyes of the beast, but he could not take his gaze away from the battle. Veru charged in again, going after previous wounds made by the unicorns. Axle continued to bite into the back of the neck, appearing quite furious that his sonic attacks were doing nothing. Then, in a flash of red and complicated symbols, Axle appeared to be engulfed, and when the light faded, he was gone. Talon turned to Veru, but he too disappeared in the same red flash. For a moment, Ezvex and Talon were both rather puzzled, but Ezvex began to chuckle. "Looks like your friends have abandoned you. That makes things easy," he hissed, but before the massive monster could come in for another snap, the red light flooded the area and a large circle of symbols flared into existence before them all.

The creature that rose from it was neither Axle, nor Veru, but both. It was as if the two had been fused together by their flanks. No longer two individuals, they were now one large two-headed wolf. They now stood at around three horses high, Axle with his black head and blue eyes along with Veru, his white crown and green orbs. Where the two bodies met, it blended to a shade of gray, complete with a gray tail.

"Axle? Veru?" Talon was unsure if this beast was truly who it appeared to be.

"Did she do this?" Axle barked, the sound of which made Talon want to cover his ears. "This is an outrage!"

"Oh, do not be so sore; we are far stronger when we work together you know," Veru said merrily, giving Axle a quick nuzzle before he could snap at his nose.

"What on Asatiria has happened to you?" Talon called, not quite understanding what was going on.

Axle's ears flattened as always, but Veru turned his head toward Talon, peering at him over Axle's neck. "Oh, worry not; this is really our true form used when we are able to agree with one another, and you can imagine how often that happens," he chuckled.

"Oh, be silent!" Axle snapped. "Might as well make use of it and get this over with!"

For a moment, Talon wondered if he would see Axle's half leap forward and drag Veru's half along, but the two moved as one and lunged forward. Ezvex hissed angrily, and two more heads burst from the ground to intercept them.

Talon began to wonder where all these extra heads were coming from. As he looked around him, he noticed the others had gone. He turned back just in time to see two more of them burst from the ground around Axle and Veru, and the largest of all of them, Ezvex, sank back into the ground, leaving the two headed wolf to fight the smaller ones.

The ground quaked underneath him, and Talon could not

help but wonder what Ezvex was planning to do. He could even hear angry hisses and screeches from below. Then, exploding out of the ground and showering him in debris, Ezvex was now between him and Ralley.

"You want to play dirty? So be it!" Ezvex grinned, showing his jaw full of teeth. He turned towards Ralley, who seemed to still be somewhat dizzy and opened his maw wide.

"You leave her alone!" Talon shouted, charging forward and thrusting his sword into the base of the Serpent. This only made him pause a moment or two and chuckle, then his head descended upon Ralley. "NO!" Talon roared and wrenched his sword free, charging forward just as Ralley turned up to see what was happening and opened her mouth to scream. It was cut short as Talon shoved her roughly aside and thrust his sword up into the upper jaw of the huge beast. For a moment, all he could see was the darkness of the beast's cave-like mouth. Teeth surrounded him on all sides. Were Ezvex to close his mouth now, Talon would surely lose his legs, but the sword would also rise into its head. A screech burst from the depths of the ama-rill's throat, but Talon refused to loosen his grip on his weapon.

He then felt his feet leave the ground, yet he clung to his sword. He found himself kneeling on the lower jaw as the head became level. The long red tongue of the serpent curled around his waist and began to pull him inward. Talon refused to budge, planting his knees and holding the sword for his life. He could hear Ralley screaming below. He had saved her from this fate. If his strength gave out and the creature swallowed him, he would have no regrets. She was more important to this world than himself; she alone would rule this land the way he had never intended to do. Only now could he see the error of his own ideas of rule. No wonder the Blade Beast had not chosen him; he had to realize that his people were more important than his own selfish goals.

"And now that you know this, you have become the Emperor I have been waiting for!"

The voice in his head took him by surprise and almost made him lose his grip on the sword. He renewed his effort to keep from being swallowed and felt the presence in his mind overpower him. He closed his eyes and could feel it, the Blade Beast, wedged somewhere far below him. He reached for it and felt himself inch forward toward the darkness of the throat. At once, the Blade Beast obeyed his command, wrenching free of its location and spinning towards him, eager to be in his hand. Sliced through a barrier and he felt it nestle into his palm. Ezvex jerked, issuing another scream. Talon opened his eyes to see a great bleeding hole in the lower jaw where the blade had cut through to reach him.

The world began to tilt wildly. Talon held on with what was left of his strength as Ezvex tried to shake him out. Desperate, he threw the Blade Beast into the throat of the angry serpent.

The monster shuddered around him, but another scream did not come. Again it violently tossed its head, and this time, dislodged Talon's sword, sending the blade and him flying from its jaws and into open air. He felt he would hit a tree at any moment, but something snatched him from the air and landed with a light thud. Talon looked up to see a great white furry mouth clamped around his cloak, lowering him to the ground before it tore the fabric. The head of Axle was growling, glaring at the mass of bloody writhing heads that they had been fighting before. Ralley threw herself into him, hugging him tightly and crying.

Ezvex flailed weakly and began to withdraw into the ground, the other heads doing the same. Talon reached out, calling to the blade that nestled somewhere underneath the earth. It burst through the ground and returned to his hand. They heard a great groaning sound, and the ground shuddered once more… then all fell silent.

Ralley's sobs subsided, and her light brown eyes peered up at him. "I'm sorry, Talon, the Blade Beast stopped talking to me, I couldn't find him and…."

Talon wrapped his arm around her and pulled her up to him, kissing her soft lips to quiet her. He then pulled away and smiled. "I made a big fool of myself all this time. I was angry that you had everything I wanted; I just had to realize that I was not ready for it yet. When I did, the Blade Beast came to me." He held up the blade that rested quietly in his hand.

Ralley smiled up at him, her eyes sparkling with tears. "So, he won't talk to me anymore? I'll miss him, but he is in the right place now," she said.

A soft sigh escaped Veru as he observed them. Talon ignored him, but he could see Ralley's face reddening. Axle scoffed. The giant two-headed wolf began to shrink, and white light flared around Veru while darkness consumed Axle. Light and dark battled with one another until it separated and the white and black faded out, leaving behind Axle and Veru in their previous wolf forms, no longer attached.

"Finally!" Axle barked. "Now, can we get back to the mound? I have had enough of all this!"

Veru trotted over to them and nuzzled Ralley. "Of course not; they need to get to the tower, and I want to make sure they get there safely."

Axle growled, but this time, he did not fade into the surrounding trees. He lay down, crossing his front paws and laying his head on them, grumbling and looking off to the trees.

"Oh! Kiran! Meilea!" Ralley cried. She turned and began to search for the two unicorns, Talon following after. They discovered them only a short distance away, Meilea lying in a small mossy patch as Kiran stood over her, turning his head towards them as they arrived. "Oh no! Is she…?" Ralley asked, running to them.

Kiran nuzzled her. "I have taken care of her; she is just resting. We are a bit magically worn, but we should be able to transport you through the rest of the forest."

"Are you sure?" Talon asked, gazing at Meilea, as she lifted her head and rolled into a sitting position.

"I am certain, Emperor Endrayen," Kiran said with a bow of his head, his horn dipping low. Meilea also dipped her head to him respectfully.

Talon was taken by surprise to be called such. He lifted his hand that still held the blade, looking at its shining and somewhat scaled surface. Ralley smiled at him and removed the blade pouch, handing it over to him. "Here, Emperor; you're going to need this."

He smirked. "Just call me Talon," he said, taking the pouch and slipping the blade into it. He slid the strap over his head and let the blade rest on his hip. "We have a sister to rescue. When Meilea is ready, we mount up!" he commanded.

With his words, Meilea slowly pulled herself to stand. Ralley ran to her but hesitated. "Only when you're ready," she said.

Meilea lowered herself to allow Ralley an easier time of getting on. "I am."

Talon cleaned his sword in the moss, sheathed it, and swung onto Kiran's back. He turned to look at Veru and Axle, who had chosen to plod after them when they went to look for the unicorns. "Scout on ahead. Find us a safe path out of this place and to the Tower of the Grand Summoner."

"Certainly, your Majesty," Veru said with a sort of sweeping bow of his head.

"Call me Talon; it is what I prefer my friends to call me," he said while smiling and looking from Veru to Axle.

"As you please." Veru's wolfish grin grew wider than he thought was possible. He spun on his hind legs and bolted through the trees to the north. Axle gave Talon what he decided was a glare of approval and sprang after his brother.

He chuckled and turned to Ralley. She was now settled on Meilea's back, beaming a beautiful smile back at him, one that he decided he wished to see more of. He would defend her more than ever now, even though she was no longer Empress. As the two unicorns began to gallop through the trees side by side, he began to wonder what other adventures he would continue to have with this foreign girl. When they passed through a small clearing in the trees, Talon caught a glimpse of the Tower in the distance and began to hope that it was not as dangerous as it appeared.

~53~

TRIVENTALIS

Continuing his work, Estat chose not to meet Melanie's gaze, though he could feel it burning holes through him. He had hoped that she were not royalty. He had hoped that she would want to stay here, with him, but that was impossible now. If she stayed in this world, she would be taken back to Freewind as their princess. So things would return to normal for him. Or would they? He did not have an apprentice anymore and was not sure he could trust anyone else in that position again. Moving on to the next symbol, Estat could feel her eyes follow him. Did she wish him to make the decision for her?

Malstraun's deep voice cut through the silence. "It is quite simple, really. I can take you home now if you wish it. Then again, you are a princess here, and there are responsibilities. I have never been one to follow the rules, though, so it is not as though Estat or I would reveal your birthright."

"And I do not tend to involve myself in human politics." Weiland added.

Estat finished the symbol and looked up at Melanie. She fidgeted with the tatters of her dress, looking down at the floor, then up to Malstraun. "I can't go home now. My sister Ralley is out there somewhere. I can't leave her behind."

"Hmm… sister?" Malstraun crossed his arms and brought one hand up, tapping his chin in thought. "Ah yes, of course. The young girl traveling with the Prince, I should have known it. Too many distractions, I suppose. Ah well, she travels with good company."

"You saw my sister?" Melanie asked hopefully as she clutched Malstraun's shirt. "Where was she? Was she all right? Can we get to her?"

"She was a long ways south when she summoned me. She appeared fine at the time, but no; I doubt she is in the same location. I could try and find her again, but it would take some time. If she is traveling, as I assume she is, then it will be even more difficult."

"We have no time to search for her," Estat said, returning his gaze to the next symbol that he had begun.

"What do you mean? We have to make sure she's still alright!" she said, a small amount of panic in her voice.

Estat continued the symbol, not answering her till he had finished and moved on to the final one. "Malstraun, you said she travels in good company?" he asked, not looking up.

"Indeed, Prince Talon Endrayen and the amarill twins Axle and Veru," he replied.

Pausing in his work, Estat gazed up at Malstraun. "The twins? That is odd, but perhaps not unusual." He considered this a moment, then returned to finishing his chalk work.

"Why would a Prince be helping my sister?" Melanie asked.

"Perhaps because they have discovered who she really is," Weiland suggested.

Estat nodded. "If you are a princess, and she is your sister, then she too is a princess. This could be a good thing. If they are traveling north from Degrail, perhaps they are coming to fight the demon as well."

"Or to find me," she said.

Estat stood from his finished work and made a final observation. When he was satisfied, he stepped to the red candle, spoke a few words of power, and lit the wick. It flared up with a bright red glow, and he stepped back out of the circle. "Everything is ready. Stand back, Melanie, Triventalis is large enough to fill this room from top to bottom."

She did as he asked, hiding behind Malstraun. Estat took a deep breath and began to speak the arcane language of magic. As he did so, he lifted his hand and spread his fingers. The red flame on the candle began to dance gently as if in a slight breeze. As Estat's voice grew more commanding, the flame bounced and twirled, and with a burst of red light, tendrils leapt from it and onto the etchings of the star. Within moments, the entirety of the symbol was aglow with dancing red firelight that swirled around the braziers and turned their flames crimson. Estat withdrew his hand, his voice leveled but remained authoritive as he called out Triventalis's name, summoning him through time and space to come to their aid. The symbols came to life, stretching and glowing red, trying to escape the confines of the star.

Estat did not expect to be interrupted during his chanting, but he could sense the presence of Malstraun stepping close to him and leaning toward his ear. "I sense both demon and amarill approaching the tower. What will you have me do?" he said in a whisper.

Continuing his concentration on the summoning, Estat frowned. The process would be complete shortly, but he could not be interrupted, or he would have to redraw the symbols, and that would take far too much time than they apparently had. "I must complete this summoning," he whispered back, wondering if they were simply trying to keep the urgent news from Melanie. "Wake Liquendia."

Malstraun bowed to him, though Estat had never found the formality necessary, and left his side. Weiland leapt to Immuraudi's back. "We shall return to the outside and be your scouts." He spoke quickly and in moments they had left the tower. Estat suspected Weiland too had sensed the approaching threat.

The star and symbols flared brightly and danced about as the entirety of the symbol lifted off the ground. Triventalis would be here shortly, though he would likely resist at first. No amarill liked to be interrupted while they slept, especially not this one. The tower suddenly shook, and Estat did his best to keep his concentration and footing under such a quake. Speaking of waking sleeping amarill...

Melanie moved closer to him, and when the room quaked again, she carefully slid a hand into his. "Wh... what's going on?" she asked, her voice squeaking with fright.

He continued to watch the symbol, speaking a few more arcane lines to the summoning before answering. "It is just Liquendia. Do not worry about it. I am sure she is just a little grumpy from being re-awakened so soon."

"What's that sound?" she asked, her voice still shaking.

Estat had not noticed any unusual sounds besides that of the crackling, dancing fire and the groaning of the tower with all the quakes, but now that she had mentioned it, he listened more carefully to hear a strange wailing noise that was slowly getting louder. He did not answer her question; he had to finish the job of the summoning. He spoke the last few words needed, and the fires rose as one to the roof of the hall, creating a red column of flames. At that moment, there was a massive impact against the side of the tower somewhere above them. Rocks crashed down from above, and Estat felt Melanie give his arm a rough jerk, throwing him to the side where he stumbled and hit the floor. A large chunk of the hall's roof landed only an arm's length from his feet. His eyes turned upward to see smaller pieces of debris still falling from a massive hole where the roof of the room met the wall.

"Are you okay?!" Melanie cried, frantically inspecting him for injuries. "I'm so sorry, I had to…"

"I am fine, Princess, thank you; you saved my life yet again." For a moment their eyes met, and he gave her a smile. It quickly faded as he turned to look at the summoning circle. His concentration was ruined; he had failed. The column of red flames had turned to a thick red fog that spread throughout the room and began to dissipate. Light from the hole in the upper wall lanced through the hall and illuminated the red cloud. "Xenopus is here; there is no more time to try again," he said dejectedly.

"Look out!" Melanie screamed, pointing into the fog and tugging on him to get him on his feet.

When he did find his feet and managed to back up, he saw the reason for her alarm. A head rose out of the red haze, followed by a second, and then a third. The heads were rounded like that of a sheep, and a single smooth horn protruded from the backs of each head. The eyes were very large and the color of onyx. As the miasma cleared, it revealed the long necks of each head that merged into the same bulky mass that was its body. The hide looked much like that of Malstraun, though it was a deep tan color. Its great tail uncurled from around it as if it had just gotten up to stretch itself. Its four legs ended in four toes that each had a claw on them the size of Estat's arm. "Triventalis! We did it!" he shouted, looking to Melanie, his eyes wide with the triumph.

He wanted to laugh aloud as he saw her widened eyes and her mouth agape. "Th... that's... T... Trivenwhatsits?" she stuttered. She attempted to step back even further.

"Yes, it is; do not be afraid. He is here to help." Estat turned to face the three headed amarill. "My friend, there is not much time, but I will explain what I can. A demon has been called to this world and has brought a small army from the netherworld. I am sure you know what will happen if we do not stop them as soon as possible." The three heads turned to him as he spoke and nodded in unison at his last statement. "They besiege my tower as I speak..." As if on cue, the tower shook with another impact. "Please, friends, I am in need of your help."

"You have it," said three voices at once. Melanie jumped back as the sound reverberated off the walls as one.

Estat smiled and turned. "Come... you and I must get to the top of the tower. It will not be safe down here anymore." She did not argue and hurried on after him as he led her up the set of stairs just outside the summoning hall.

"How's he supposed to get out of here? I mean, he's huge! He's stuck inside there...."

"I assure you, he is not stuck, and he is going to be our defense." They continued up through the rooms, sticking mostly to the stairs. The tower shook violently as they went, sometimes making them stumble into the walls. Estat held her hand firmly, not wanting to let her fall. They said nothing until they finally arrived in the observatory, then Estat spoke several words of opening and revealing. In answer to his magic, the ceiling and walls became transparent, allowing them to see everything around them at this height.

Melanie gasped and spun around. "You can see everything from here!"

Estat did not much like what he saw. Blackish creatures surrounded the entire volcano. "This cannot be right! There are far too many of them!"

"Well, it's not like you could count them while we were at the cave. There were tons of them," she replied, now looking to the monsters below.

"No, there is far more now than there were...." A great crack was heard in the air, and the tower shivered. Melanie jumped into his arms with a scream. Accompanying the sound was a flash of light somewhere below them, and a bolt of lightning shot out from the middle of the tower and into a grouping of monsters huddled on the lip of the volcano's crater. Some in its direct path disintegrated, others caught fire, and a few seemed not to notice it. He was not sure how much of this black tide Triventalis, Malstraun or Liquendia would be able to hold back. They were powerful amarill, but the demons were so plentiful, they would overrun them all by sheer numbers. Then he caught sight of a creature rise up among the others. It appeared much like a great grizzly bear with massive fangs and spiky fur.

"What is that?" Melanie cried.

"Amarill," Estat said darkly. With both sides holding such powerful creatures, the advantage went to Xenopus and his numbers.

~54~

Journey's End

Ralley felt as though a great weight had been lifted from her shoulders. She was no longer the Empress, and so, no longer responsible for so many people and duties. Nobody would expect anything of her here anymore. She was free to continue looking for her sister. The best part was that Talon had become the Emperor and was still determined to see her safely to her sister. Kiran and Meilea kept up a speedy pace through the trees. The twins, Axle and Veru, raced in wolf form on either side of them like an honor guard. She was surprised that Axle had not disappeared into the trees again as per usual. He explained that this was because they were so prone to getting into trouble that he was forced to stay close and keep an eye on them.

It was not long before they came away from the trees and the mountainous region was the only thing ahead of them. Rising out of it all was the top of a great tower. There was little else to see, and Talon waved them onward. "We need to get up into the mountains and take a better look," he said.

"I hope she's still there…" Ralley said, staring up at the top- most spire of the tower as it slipped away from view the closer they got to the mountains.

Talon touched the blade. "Is she?" he asked. It took her a moment to realize that he was speaking to the Blade Beast as she had done. She had to admit she truly missed that. After a moment, he nodded. "She is, but she is still in danger. We should get there as fast as we can."

"The moment we reach the higher cliffs, Meilea and I should get a good enough height to jump. Then it will be smooth flying to the edge of the crater," Kiran's musical voice informed them.

"Good idea; let us hurry," Talon replied.

Ralley wondered what they would face within that tower. Was Melanie trapped inside? Perhaps being held prisoner? If so, who was holding her, and what had they done to her? They were so close, and Ralley found herself getting restless, wanting to rush in and rescue her. But shouldn't they form a plan? "Veru, didn't you say there was some kind of summoner that lived there?"

"He is a hermit, really," Veru said with a nod. "But a powerful summoner from what I have discovered."

"I suppose we are going to find out," Talon said. "Flying will be our quickest route there, but that also means we might be detected by him. I cannot be sure what he is capable of." Talon appeared troubled now. She figured he too had not thought of the implications of what they would be up against.

"We need a plan," she mumbled as the unicorns climbed the rocky area.

Axle growled, "Who needs a plan? Just go in there and tear him apart!"

"Oh yes, just rush in, kill the Grand Summoner and when you find him to be innocent, you can roll in your guilt," Meilea snorted, sounding irritated.

The black wolf growled but said nothing. Meilea was right. What if he was innocent? She had a serious doubt that that was the case, seeing as he was holding her sister prisoner. "I guess we will just have to knock on the front door and ask," she said sarcastically.

Veru ignored the sarcasm as he turned and gave her a bright wolfish smile. "Of course," he replied.

Talon shrugged and nodded. Ralley blinked at him in surprise. "You're not serious, are you?"

"Why not? We have few other options. We will just have to be ready for any type of attack. Besides, we will be easily seen flying there, but Axle and Veru will be on the ground, and perhaps, if they are not seen, we will have some type of edge if they try a surprise attack," he said, nodding to the twins.

"Sounds fine by me," Axle growled.

She wasn't sure it was a good idea, but she kept quiet, feeling it was no longer her place to put in a forceful opinion. When they reached the top of the rugged crags, they paused for a meal. Veru went through the brush and scared up a rabbit while Talon made a fire. From this vantage point they could all clearly see the volcanic crater with the tower rising from it. "Do you think he will see the fire?"

"Too far to tell," Talon said, gazing off in its direction. "If he was looking, maybe, but I doubt he even knows we are coming for her."

She nodded her agreement, and the two of them quietly ate while the unicorns grazed on the meager patches of grass between the rocks. The twins hunted for their own rabbit. Ralley watched Talon for a moment as he ate. "What will happen to me after we find my sister? I mean ... how do I get back home?"

Talon blinked at her, wiping his chin with a sleeve and setting down his share. For a moment he said nothing, just looked at her as if he wasn't sure what he should say. Then he cleared his throat. "Well, it would be mostly up to you. If you come from the mainland, then it would not be a problem to…"

Ralley shook her head. "I don't think I come from the mainland, Talon. I think I was summoned here. Like the creatures I summoned before. They lived somewhere else, but I brought them here. It reminds me of when my sister was taken. There was a big portal thing, and we were dragged through it. It brought me here, to this world."

"You are saying you come from somewhere completely different, then?" he asked.

"Yes. I think so," she said. "But I don't know how to get back there, unless… well, I guess unless someone summons me there. So… I think I'm stuck here," she said. Ralley felt as though she should be crying. She would never be able to go home, right? She should be breaking down. Instead, she felt as though she could live with it. She looked up to meet Talon's blue eyes.

"Ralley… I am sorry. I do not know how to get you back to wherever you came from, but if you cannot go back… then…" He hesitated, glancing at the ground for a moment before meeting her eyes again. "Then I want you to stay with me… at Castle Degrail," he added.

Ralley's heart skipped a beat, and she crawled forward to throw her arms around him, hugging him tightly. "I would love to! Thank you!" That's what she wanted, to stay here, with Talon. She felt his arms around her in moments, and they sat there for some time until she heard Veru chuckling. She sat up and turned to look at him.

"My my, I leave you two alone for a moment… perhaps I should leave for a while longer?" he asked with a sly grin.

Ralley reddened and lowered her head to hide it. Talon cleared his throat. "Er… no Veru, you may remain. We should get going."

"Right," Ralley agreed, jumping to her feet and walking towards Meilea. Veru chuckled in his merry way and sounded a soft howl.

Moments later, Axle joined them, licking blood from his muzzle. "What? Going already? Very well, let us get this over with," he grumbled.

In short order the two returned to the backs of the unicorns, and in one frightening leap, they left the ground behind as the pair spread their feathered wings and rose up above the mountains. Again the world was laid out like a quilt before them. The thick forest of demons was at their backs, and ahead was the intimidating spire of the tower. After a moment of clinging to Meilea's mane, she relaxed enough to look around a bit more. The forest wrapped around to the east of them, as well as to the west, though the trees were not quite as thick in that direction. Far north, beyond the tower and its mountains, was a thin strip of blue. Was that an ocean? She'd always loved the beach and began to wonder if a beach in this world was any different than in her own. She resolved to discover that once this whole mess was over with.

As the wind whistled past her ears and she hunkered back down again to shield herself from the cold, Meilea banked closer to Kiran. "What's going on?"

"Something ahead… near the ground," she said, tilting her nose as if to point at it.

Ralley carefully leaned to the side to look down past Meilea's neck. Some distance ahead, there was movement on the ground. "What is it?" she asked curiously. Being so high up on the back of a unicorn, she felt far less concerned about anything lurking about on the ground. Then again, she knew that Axle and Veru were pacing through the mountains somewhere below them.

"Not sure yet … but I do not like the look nor feel of it," she answered.

Frowning, Ralley felt fear creep into her again. So much had happened to impede their progress. They were so close now… what could keep them from their goal other than the Grand Summoner himself? Meilea gently tossed her head. "Hold on!"

With barely enough time to get her grip, Meilea rose sharply higher. "What is it?" she shouted above the sudden flurry of wind around her.

"They are demons. We must get some height, or they will discover us too soon. Kiran thinks we can make a fly for it. We must pray that the Grand Summoner is innocent, for we will be trusting him to allow us inside."

"Wh… what? Wait a minute!" Ralley shouted, glancing to the rising unicorn a short distance from them. Talon glanced her way, but his face appeared determined. Suddenly, the plan didn't seem so great. "What about Axle and Veru?" she shouted, looking below once again, trying to find the white streak that dodged through the crags.

"They are amarill, and they will make their own way. It appears they know these mountains better than you think."

It occurred to her that Meilea had been keeping an eye on the twins herself. Ralley nodded slightly and clung to her until the unicorn leveled out and began to glide upon the wind once again. Far below, she could see a mass of moving creatures, though they were too high up for her to make out any specific details. "Alright," Meilea said, turning her equine head slightly to eye her. "Hold on, we are going to dive in."

"Oh, gosh! Wait… what are we doing?" Her eyes scanned ahead to the tower. It still looked pretty far away, but she could see no place for two unicorns to land upon its peaked top. "I don't think this is a good idea …." she began. But she realized it was far too late as the two unicorns dove through the air as one. Burying her face in Meilea's mane, she screamed. There was an awful roaring sound, and she felt her stomach do a flip-flop.

There was a sudden jolt as Meilea flared her wings to slow them, and before she could protest about their tactics, a large section of the tower opened up, revealing a way inside for the two winged equines and their riders. In the next moment, Ralley caught sight of something that made her heart want to leap out of her chest.

-55-

THE FALL

Melanie wasn't sure what impact the Amaril on the side of the Demon would have, but she was sure it wasn't good for them. "What are we going to do?" Before he could answer her, Estat glanced up to the sky. When she turned to look for herself, Melanie couldn't quite believe her eyes. Two great winged unicorns were flying toward them. Estat must have immediately sent some kind of magical, unseen message to Liquendia to open the tower's roof as she could see the transparent shimmer of the wall as it slid open. She had to assume that unicorns brought friends since Estat didn't hesitate to allow them in, though she could see two riders. She watched in amazement, their wings spread out around them to slow themselves enough to make a softer landing as they flew in. She didn't recognize the blond haired man sitting on the back of one of them, but as her eyes turned to the second rider she screamed out in joy. "Ralley!" She watched the unicorn settle to the floor and fold its wings.

"Mel! You're here! And you're alright!" Ralley shouted back, sliding off the unicorn's back and running to her.

The two hugged each other, ignoring the shudder of the tower as another blast hit it from somewhere below. "Just look at you! I can't believe it! This just proves that all this wasn't a dream after all, right?"

Ralley nodded, smiling up at her. "You're a complete mess! Are you alright? Who's that?" she asked, now seeing Estat standing quietly behind her, one of his tomes tucked under an arm.

Before Melanie could answer, Estat had stepped forward toward the man who had been riding the other unicorn. "I am the Grand Summoner, Estat," he said, bowing low.

"I am Emperor Talon Endrayen of Degrail," the man said formally, nodding his head.

"Emperor?" Melanie asked, turning to look at the man. He was pretty good looking, too, with his blond hair, blue eyes. Her sister had a princess' escort for certain. "Ohmigosh! Ralley, I have something to tell you, we're …." But she was interrupted by a blast that threw them to the floor. The unicorns were the only ones who managed to keep their feet.

"The battle does not go well. Emperor Talon, we are in need of help, or else this world is finished."

"I am not sure what I can do, but I will try. You must tell me what is going on here," Talon said, picking himself up off the floor. Talon held his hand out to Ralley, helping her up, just as Estat did the same for Melanie.

"My former apprentice has released Xenopus, a demon that is ready to destroy our world. He has readied himself an army, and they will consume everything in their path, starting with your entire kingdom," Estat explained.

"Is that all?" Ralley said, clutching Talon's arm. Judging from her expression, Melanie realized that Ralley had been through plenty of trouble herself. She wanted to hear all about it, but of course, now was not the time.

"It is enough," Estat said, his voice calm despite the battle raging outside. "Those amarill on our side may not be enough. Xenopus has many lesser demons and has persuaded some amarill to his side. His numbers and powers are great."

Talon frowned, but nodded. "Then I shall fight. I am Emperor, and so, I am responsible for keeping my entire kingdom safe. According to the gods who created the Blade Beast, that kingdom stretches from the northernmost beach all the way back to Degrail and the floating island."

"I'm fighting too!" Ralley said, still holding Talon's arm.

This surprised Melanie. It was as if her little sister had suddenly grown up, and perhaps she had. Melanie herself felt far more assertive, more mature. This world, their true home, had changed them both. "I will, too," she added.

"No… you should stay here… it is safer," Estat began, but Melanie shook her head.

"No. I can help, my powers can heal, and in a battle that means I play a big role, right?" she asked, taking Estat's hand. "Please, I can help."

Estat nodded, taking her hand with his own. "Yes, you are right…"

"Healing?" Ralley asked. "You have powers too?"

Melanie turned to Ralley. "Too? Sounds like we need to catch up on some sisterly conversation."

Ralley nodded. "I can call to things, like the unicorns, and once, I summoned this big giant…" The tower shook, and Malstraun rose up around the side of the building and slid in through the open part of the roof, his body surrounding them as he stared down at Estat. "Oh crap, I did it again!" Ralley said, staring up at him in awe.

Malstraun looked as though he'd gotten into a fight with three-dozen cats. He had cuts all along the length of his serpentine body, and several of them were deep. "Liquendia has cast lava down the volcano's sides. She is keeping ground creatures from approaching while Triventalis keeps flying monsters back. However, we cannot hold them back much longer."

"Help has arrived," Estat said with true hope.

Malstraun glanced over the newcomers. "The prince and the Summoner?" he asked. "I suppose they shall do," he said and somehow, shrugged, though he didn't have shoulders.

"Summoner?" Melanie asked, looking to Ralley.

She gave a weak smile and nodded a bit. "I guess so... I thought I summoned that thing again," she said, pointing to the Black Serpent.

"Thing? I am Malstraun," he grunted indignantly. "The Black Serpent, Master of the Void, Destroyer of Ships..."

"And you are missing a horn," Estat finished calmly. "It is time we fought back. Make them pay for that," he said, smiling up at the Serpent.

Malstraun gave him an evil grin, showing his rows of teeth, his yellow eyes glittering like a hungry lion. It was almost enough for Melanie to throw herself screaming from the tower. She couldn't imagine one of those demons being able to face the Black Serpent and still keep its courage. Despite all that, she still couldn't quite feel sorry for the nasty beasts, not after all she'd been through.

Estat stepped over to Ralley. "You are a summoner, then?"

"She is," Malstraun said before she could reply. "But not like you."

"She has the blood of Traeis flowing through her veins. I can understand that her power to summon is unlike my own in many ways. But if that is true, then perhaps together we can finish this battle." Estat held his hand toward Ralley. "You will help me?"

Melanie smiled as she met her sister's eyes. "You can trust him," she said, nodding.

"I know," Ralley replied, taking Estat's hand. "But... who is Traeis?"

The tower shuddered with another blow and for a moment, everything was still. Then, the entire observatory floor began to tilt, and Melanie felt weightlessness for a brief moment.

"The tower is lost, everyone out!" Malstraun bellowed.

One of the unicorns leapt toward Talon, who gripped Ralley about the waist and hauled the two of them upon its back. The second unicorn managed to half flap, half glide toward Estat. He reached out and grabbed Melanie about the wrist and pulled her to him, as the floor fell out from under their feet. In moments the unicorn was underneath them and spread its wings wide. There was a bit of a jolt as the two came in contact with her back, then a heavy feeling as the unicorn lifted them out the open observatory roof and into open air. Melanie wrapped her arms around Estat's waist as she peered below them. As they rose higher, she could see the entire top half of the tower as it fell away into the molten lava below. Part of it still stood, and she could see the floor of the summoning hall and the star within a circle etched upon it. But a massive crack had split the symbol, and there was no sign of Triventalis.

Melanie felt horrible for Estat. The tower had been his home. Within the volcano she caught a glimpse of Liquendia swimming among the lava. She turned her head to gaze at the creatures milling about around the base of the volcano. They screamed, howled and roared in triumph at what they had done. She could feel her anger boil. Malstraun had managed to spring free of the tower as it toppled near the volcanoes edge and now battled his way through the throng of creatures. What would they do now? Where could they go? A black cloud of beings was flying towards them, and they didn't look at all friendly. She could see two of them clearly as they flew after them. One had a pair of grotesque bat wings, a long whip-like tail and a short, thick neck with a fat snout. The other didn't have wings at all, yet it flew towards them just as easily as the other. Several tentacles wriggled around it, making snapping noises, and it had a round body with green eyes scattered around it randomly. With a simple and familiar flourish of his hand and a sharply spoken word, flames shot from Estat's fingers and engulfed the many-eyed creature.

It made a sharp squealing sound, though Melanie wasn't sure if it had a mouth. It hovered a moment and then plummeted down to the throng below. Estat repeated this with the second creature, but the flames did not affect it in any way. It simply barreled forward, barking like an angry mutant dog. Melanie even saw its glittering teeth as it got closer. She gripped Estat tighter as he spoke a new word and worked his hands into a new gesture. This time, lightning shot from his fingers. The creature roared angrily but continued on its course. Just as Melanie thought it would plow into them, the unicorn pulled its wings in and tilted forward, causing them to suddenly speed downward for a moment before it re-spread its feathered appendages and climbed back into the air, effectively dodging the creature.

It howled in anger, and Melanie turned her head to watch as it continued chasing them. She could see the other unicorn as it flew some distance to their left. Several creatures were chasing them as well, but to her relief, Talon was keeping them at bay with his strange throwing weapon. It flew from his hand and seared off wings, cut through necks and sliced through tails. They were too busy to notice the one following them. Melanie glanced back at the creature and realized it was gaining on them. "Estat!" she called over the rush of the wind.

He turned to see the demon, but turned his head forward again, and she heard a blast of fire leave his fingers. This made her peek around him to see the mass of monsters flying towards them from ahead.

"Hold on tight!" the unicorn called. Melanie felt Estat hunch over, one of his hands gripping her arm, and she tightened her already tired limbs around him. The unicorn tilted upward this time, climbing above some of the demons, a few of them being battered by her hooves and letting out angry yelps. She felt she might fall, and though she wanted to squeeze her eyes shut, she checked for the one behind them. Not seeing it, she felt a wave of relief wash over her, but in the next instant, she heard its roar as it descended from above and bit into her back. She screamed in pain and let Estat go, reaching around to pull the teeth from her flesh as the weight of the monster tore her from the back of the equine. She elbowed the beast as hard as she could and must have hit something tender, as it released her. She realized too late that the only thing underneath her was a sea of demons far below.

-56-

LAST CHANCE

It was not easy to see anything that was going on around her. Ralley's vision was marred by various flying demons that were too horrible to describe. Talon kept them all at bay with the Blade Beast as it flew from his hand, stabbed through the enlarged eye of one beast, and returned like a boomerang. She was amazed at how much control he had over it when she had felt barely able to use it. Just when she'd thought that Talon had taken care of the last monster, several more swarmed in around them.

"Do not let them escape!" came a thick booming voice from below.

Ralley turned to see who, or what, it was that had spoken, but then she heard Estat yell out Melanie's name, and her eyes shot over to Meilea. Melanie was gone, and Estat yelled out again, but this time it was not a name, but a strange word. Ralley followed his gaze to the falling form of her sister. She was horrified as she watched Melanie tumbling toward the surging throng of terrors below, some even spotting her and reaching up into the air, pushing others aside so that they may be the first to get her. Estat's words had evoked a strange wind that lifted

Mel back into the air. But Ralley wasn't sure how long it would last. "Talon! We have to do something!" she screamed, letting go with one arm to tug on his sleeve and point. Where were Axle and Veru when she needed them?

Something tore through the throng of monsters below, a red creature looking much like the unicorns, though far more petite and frail. Upon its back was a young man smattered in blood from head to toe, and his expression was fierce yet beautiful. The crimson equine flew up to meet Melanie as she began to fall once again, the wind magic dissipating underneath her. She watched, horrified, as the bloodied rider caught her and the equine faltered with the weight, then righted itself and slowly lifted into the air to fly next to Meilea. Ralley was relieved to see that everyone had smiles on their faces, and she let out the breath she had been holding in, realizing this stranger must be a friend. Multiple monsters still circled around them, but now they kept a fair distance, not wanting anything more to do with the Blade.

"STOP THEM!" shouted a deep, sinister voice.

Ralley turned to see a massive toad-like demon leaping into the air after them; his legs had so much strength that the single leap carried him up almost level with them, and great green tentacles lashed forward but came up just inches too short, and he dropped back to the ground, landing on five or six smaller demons who barely had time to make a sound before they were crushed. "Hurry!!" Ralley shouted, nudging her knees into Kiran's sides. The next leap, he would have them unless they moved faster. She could even now see the beast getting ready to launch himself toward them for the next assault.

Then there was a horrible sound like rolling thunder that vibrated the very air around them. Every eye turned to the crater of the volcano as creatures began to screech and howl in fear, scrambling over one another to get away. Lava burst up from the inside of the cone, rocketing into the air like a water fountain and then raining down upon anything settled around the outer cone and its base. Demons trampled over each other to get out of the way of the lava flow as it swallowed up hundreds of them. Ralley had to turn her eyes away, and though she was high in the air and quite a distance from the volcano itself, she could still hear the screams of the dying. A tentacle came from behind, wrapping itself around Kiran's leg. With one powerful jerk, all three were hauled backwards and down as the huge froggish monster descended back to the ground.

Screaming, Ralley tightened her legs around Kiran's body and her arms around Talon. The Emperor turned to the side, throwing the blade behind them and severing the tentacle. With the sudden release, Kiran faltered, trying to regain altitude. Ralley could turn her head just enough to see the furious toad swing a second tentacle in their direction. "To the left!" she shouted. But it was too late, the tentacle slapping against Kiran's flank, stinging his leg. The unicorn let out a squeal and began to drop rapidly toward the throng of monsters below. Ralley screamed out the unicorn's name, but she was certain the wind carried her voice away as it roared passed her ears. Moments before contact with the ground, the feathered wings of the equine spread out on either side of them, and there was a gut wrenching change of direction. The three of them swooped back up into the air like a yoyo, catapulting back into the sky before they slowed to a complete stall, the unicorn beating his wings, allowing them to rise further and level out into his previous glide.

Ralley's eyes watered, and she could see nothing for a time. "Kiran?" Talon asked, leaning forward. "Are you alright?"

"I shall need a very long nap," the unicorn replied, sounding calm, though huffing from the exertion.

She could feel Talon turn a bit. "Ralley?"

"My leg hurts..." she said, though both of her legs were numb from trying to stay on Kiran's back.

"Mine too. It looks like the toad is not following," he said.

Ralley wiped her eyes with a sleeve and turned a bit to watch. The Demon was squatting some distance back. "Good..." She began, but did not finish. The monstrous toad was opening its mouth, and within it was a swirling black and red energy. "What is it doing?" Somewhere far ahead of them, she could hear her sister yelling something but couldn't make out what it was. Then a sound brought her eyes back to the demon. The strange swirling light in its mouth shot out towards them. Again Ralley found herself squealing, her head unable to think clearly as she looked death in the face once again. As one, both Ralley and Talon brought their hands up as if to block the blast from themselves. The blade spun out behind them, and a red flair of shifting symbols within a star appeared with it.

Things happened in slow motion for her as she watched a black blur leap from the symbol and the blade shift to its beast form in the air, webbed wings outspread. Finding something solid to stand upon, the black creature settled precariously on the Blade Beast's back. It was Axle. He puffed out his chest, taking a deep breath and as the blast came upon them, Axle let out an ear shattering metallic bark that thundered through the air. Its sound waves sent shocks through their bodies as they retreated, and the effect of the blast from the demon was staggering. The waves of sound could easily be seen as the black and red energy was effectively turned back on itself then dispersed in all directions, raining down around the frog demon.

Ralley let out a burst of laughter at having escaped death yet again, Talon joining in. The Blade Beast turned, Axle still on its back, and flew after them. "I fail to see how any of this could be funny!" Axle barked indignantly. "You had better find a way to get all four of my paws back to the ground, you hear me?"

This only made them laugh harder, relief washing their bodies of the stress they had been under. Ralley could no longer see demons below them either, only forest. The flying creatures were hesitant to follow them, allowing them to slip farther away. Ralley was confident that if they had truly wanted to test them again, Axle would simply use that strange bark of his to knock them from the sky. "Where is Veru?" she asked Axle after her laughter had died away.

"We were doing what we do best, hunting demons, until you decided to pull me away to save your skins!" he growled.

"Thank you, Axle," Ralley said, truly sincere.

Axle's rage faded some, though he refused to drop that look of annoyance. Meilea drifted closer to them along with the strange red equine with the redheaded boy. Estat turned to them. "We must veer to the right and follow the river there. If the demons follows us, we must not lead them into the forest."

"Why? What is in the forest?" Talon asked.

"Weiland's people, wood elves, peaceful folk. If we lead them down the river, there is a meadow. Fly quickly, and we might have enough time to open a portal with Ralley's help."

Talon glanced back to Ralley and she nodded to him. He returned his gaze to Estat. "Alright… Kiran?"

"I can make it; do not worry about me. I know the meadow they speak of. Let us hurry," the unicorn replied, turning to follow the river they had indicated.

"What about Melanie? Is she alright?" Ralley called.

Estat turned to her as she rode upon the back of the red creature. When he looked back, he appeared quite worried. "We must hurry; her injuries are deep, and Weiland cannot heal her up here."

She nodded, and they rode on in silence for some time, following the river as it met another, widened and cut its way through the thick forest. With every passing moment, she could swear that Melanie slumped lower and lower. Estat was watching her too, exchanging glances with the red unicorn's rider, Weiland. Axle began to grumble about being let down, but the Blade Beast was determined to keep up with them, refusing to be sidetracked. Finally, Estat pointed ahead to a patch near the river where there were no trees. To Ralley's relief, the three equines glided down to it and landed safely within the tall grass. Axle jumped from the Blade Beast and headed to the river, the Blade Beast returning to its weapon form, then back to Talon's hand. Estat immediately slid down from his mount and hurried over to help Melanie down to the ground. Talon in turn held his arm out for Ralley. The moment her feet touched the grass, she raced to her sister's side.

"Mel! You okay?" she asked, inspecting the deep wounds in her back where the demon had caught her. They were still bleeding, and Melanie was tired and weak. "Maybe you should lie down…"

"Ralley, I'm so glad that were here together… I was really worried…" Melanie said.

Weiland also dismounted and came to her. "Do not worry, Ralley. I think, with the help of these unicorns, we can help her," he said smiling.

"Thank you, Weiland," Estat said. He lowered her to the ground and kissed her forehead. "Please rest for now." They exchanged smiles, and Estat stood to face Ralley and Talon. "We must summon Triventalis again. But this time…." He turned to Ralley. "This time you must do it. You will be able to hold him here without a circle, yes?"

"W… well… I guess so…." she said timidly. "But I don't know exactly how…"

"Time grows short; you will have to learn quickly," he said, looking to the sky. "They are coming."

~57~

Make A Stand

Talon had mixed feelings about what Ralley was about to do. Granted, the last two creatures she summoned had not attacked him. She looked scared, and he watched as Estat began to explain to her about symbols. He fingered the sheath where the blade rested and then turned his eyes to the sky. So far, he saw nothing, and he hoped it remained that way. The short rest would do them all a great bit of good. The unicorn pair moved close to Melanie, who peered at them with wide eyes. The Elf kneeled down with her and put a hand over her, beginning the work of healing, his hand glowing in unison with that of the unicorn horns.

"There are rumors of a small village of elves in the south, but they were said to be the last left in this land; how is it you have come so far north?" Talon asked softly, not wanting to disturb the healing, but his curiosity of the world around him was too great not to ask.

"We have heard of and had a small amount of contact with them, but no, I am not of their tribe. We have lived in these northern parts since the Great War. This is our home, that one is theirs. We understand that they are at war with humans there to protect their land."

Talon raised his brows. "I had not heard of this..."

"Few know, as the humans there keep it a secret," he said, nodding slowly, his eyes still watching Melanie.

Frowning, Talon wondered why they would do such a thing and what other things had been hidden from his father when he was Emperor. "What of the elves? Why did they not speak to the Emperor and tell him what is happening?"

Weiland frowned. "We are all hesitant to enter the cities of men. We wished only to live in peace, and so over the years have become almost a myth to you. Some of the tribes have gone away across the sea to other lands to live and thrive, away from those who hate or fear us. Some, like us and like the elves to the south, wish to remain. They will fight honorably to protect their land, but they would not risk entering the kingdoms of men. I am sure they fear that you will not help or will simply turn them away."

Talon nodded. "I understand." He turned to the sky again, thinking this over. Weiland was right. The elves would likely be frowned upon. *But that will change.* Talon thought.

"Are you ready?" Estat's voice carried over to Talon, and he turned in time to see Ralley nod.

"I suggest we move to the top of that hill; it will be easier to defend against ground attack." The others agreed, and carefully, Talon and Weiland carried Melanie up the slight incline. This vantage would be best, though not as easy to defend against those that would likely come from the air. Talon moved over to Ralley and put a hand on her shoulder. "Will you be alright?"

"Uh... I think so," Ralley said. She sounded doubtful, and that made Talon worry.

"Is there anything I can do to help?" he asked, watching her eyes. She met his, and a small smile came to her lips.

"Be here for me?"

Talon smiled. "That, I can do," he assured her. Her smile brightened with his words, and she straightened. Their eyes lingered on one another's for a long time, then a sound, like the screams of one who was dying horribly, cut through the air.

"They have spotted us," Axle growled, returning to them and looking up to the sky. Talon followed that gaze and caught sight of one of the flying eyes circling above.

"Talon, we need you to buy us some time!" Estat shouted above another scream from the wretched monster.

He only nodded back in response, drawing the blade from its sheath. Keeping the flying monsters at bay from the sky would not be too hard, but if the land beasts caught up, he was not sure how long he could hold them off. Then there was Xenopus. He was not at all sure what would happen when he showed up. For now, he was content to do his best with what was laid before him. He threw the blade in the direction of the creature flying above. It spotted the object and screamed once more before bolting back over the trees and out of sight. The blade hung in the air a moment or two before dropping back to Talon's waiting hand. "We are about to have company…." he began. There was a small quake under his feet, and in the distance… the terrible noise of crashing and the crack of trees as they were uprooted or simply thrust out of the way. "Lots and lots of company," he finished, stepping back towards the others.

Axle leapt to his side and faced the forest, his ears flat, his teeth bared and giving off a strange echoing growl. "What is the matter, Emperor? Are you afraid?" he taunted.

"No," Talon said, bringing himself under control, though his hand gripped the blade till his knuckles where white.

A large form came to his other side; it was Kiran. He lowered his head so his horn was brought down like a lance. "Nor am I."

"Then let us buy some time with their blood," Talon said. It was then that the first few demons burst through the trees. These first were smaller than many of the monsters they had seen; their size and speed allowing them to arrive earlier than the others. Most of them appeared to be forms of grotesque hell-hounds with teeth that seemed far too large for their heads to carry them. Blue fire poured out of their eyes, and thick smoke blasted from their nostrils and mouths at every breath.

Talon stood his ground, the blade in his hand, throbbing and almost squirming to be released. He turned his head only slightly to look back at Ralley. Their eyes met in that brief moment, and he could see her fear. He turned to face the onslaught again. Talon would fight till his last breath to protect her. He cast the Blade Beast out, his thoughts directing it, watching it fly straight as an arrow toward its first victim. It pierced through the horrific creature and continued on to strike any other creature that crossed its path. Beside him, Kiran lunged forward as one of the hounds raced closer. The coral horn dove into its chest, and it let out a piercing cry. Another one behind the first bounded over the back of its dead comrade and clamped its jaws into the nape of Kiran's neck. Talon called the blade back to him, wishing he had his sword. The moment the blade touched his fingers, it changed so quickly that Talon almost dropped it in surprise. It had become a long sword; its blade was unlike anything he had seen. The balance was perfect, and the hilt held the symbol of the Blade Beast.

He smirked at the blade in his hand. "This is more like it." He wasted no more time and thrust the new weapon into the head of the beast on Kiran's neck. The moment it dropped, he turned, having no time to be sure the unicorn was all right. Axle had raced forward, tearing at the throats of the dog-like beasts and moving from one to another, never pausing to be sure of the kill. Talon rushed forward after him, swinging the Beast Sword through one demon after another. Talon could feel it cut through them as if they were simply apparitions. Their numbers seemed endless as yet more of them spilled from the trees. Now there were a few other types of demons with tentacles and multiple eyes coming toward them. The rest of them were catching up.

Talon could already feel his muscles complaining, but Axle barked loudly, "Stop playing around and get serious!" The black wolf was being swarmed by many of the tentacled beings, their limbs wrapping around every available extremity.

Talon let out a yell as he charged into the fray, swinging his sword through one of the creatures that had hold of Axle's back legs. It screamed loudly, making Talon wince as he brought the sword up for another demon. From somewhere to his left, a tentacle wrapped about his wrists, disrupting his swing and then throwing him off balance as it pulled him away. As the creature dragged Talon toward itself, he let loose a bit on the sword until it was level with the monster, and he lunged forward, plunging it into the creature. The moment the tentacles loosened, he spun around and charged back toward Axle in an attempt to free him of his predicament. He had completely lost sight of Kiran as the monsters thickened and surround them. Talon quickly sliced his way through several of the creatures to get to Axle. The black wolf had his jaws clamped upon one demon dog's throat while two others were biting and clawing at his back. The first to die was the one that had held Axle's legs, the blade cutting it down without mercy. The two hellhounds turned on him now, lunging forward, their jaws wide. He brought the sword around in an arc, cutting through the head of the first. The second beast clamped onto his shoulder, and he was thrown to his back with the force of its body weight.

He struggled to get the sword into a position where he could thrust it into the hound's side, but it planted a clawed paw on his sword arm, pressing him to the dirt. It let go of his shoulder and went for his throat, and Talon knew he was done for as the bloody jaws descended. At that moment, two golden hooves rammed into the hound's head, sending it flying into the air with a loud crack. When Talon got back to his feet, he gave a quick nod to Kiran, then surged forward again toward Axle, who had managed to tear the throat out of his latest victim. The three had little time to recover from the last moments of battle. Talon could see several more hounds bounding towards them, nearly upon them, with yet more vicious monsters emerging from the trees.

"Cover your ears," Axle growled. He took a deep breath, and let loose a bark that would have made the blast of a volcano jealous.

Though Talon's ears were covered the sound was deafening. He felt it through his whole body and was knocked to the ground once again. This time when he got up, he could hear nothing and felt slightly disoriented. He tried to call out to Axle and Kiran, but he could not even hear his own voice. His vision was also slightly blurred, but he was able to find Axle still standing where he had been. Then a ringing came to his ears and he shook his head, trying to be rid of it. When that too cleared, he could hear Axle growling. "What... happened?" he asked, hearing his own voice, though it sounded distant and disconnected.

"I stopped playing around," Axle lifted his nose in the air in an arrogant manner.

When Talon's vision cleared, there was a horrendous scene before him. Those creatures that had been close to Axle had been blasted back into the ones behind them. Many of them were in gruesome shape, bleeding from their ears, missing eyes, and a few were missing their heads. For a moment it appeared to be over, but slowly, like sap, more demons oozed from between the trees ahead. "Got enough in you for another of those?" Talon queried.

"No," Axle growled, taking up a defensive stance against the emerging army.

Something above caught Talon's eye, and he looked up in time to see the massive body of the frog-like demon Xenopus descend, landing atop the ruined bodies before them. "Did you think you had gotten away?" his booming voice questioned. Xenopus let out a throaty laugh. "There will be no escape, even if you were to have slipped between the cracks. There will be nothing left after I am finished."

"We shall see!" Talon shouted. Though his shoulder sent pain through him every time he moved his arm, he gripped

Kiran's mane and threw himself onto his back. The unicorn knew what Talon wished, and he charged forward, horn lowered at Xenopus. The demon laughed at their effort, but Talon remained set in his course. There was no turning back now, and even if he could, he would never forgive himself if anything happened to Ralley. The demon swung its arm down at them to swat them away like flies, but Talon was ready and stood up on Kiran's back, lunging at the arm as it came at them and bringing his sword down like an axe. It cut through just as easily as it had any of the other demons, and Xenopus roared in anger. Landing on the ground, Talon felt the sting of a whip-like object across his back. The force of it threw him along the ground, and he rolled several times before stopping. He opened his eyes, but immediately regretted it as all he could see was the webbed foot of Xenopus as it came down toward him.

-58-

THE STRUGGLE

Ralley had done her best to listen to what Estat was telling her, but her thoughts were on Talon. She kept glancing over to him as he battled the demons alongside Kiran and Axle. When Estat pulled her attention back to the book he held open, he pointed to a symbol that looked like it had three heads coming off a circle with a tail.

"Picture this in your thoughts when you begin your summoning. You must think only of this, or you will not get the proper beast," he warned.

"Right…" she said, nodding slightly, but she turned her head to see Talon again just in time to hear the thunderous bark of Axle. Though they were some distance away, her hands flew to her ears along with Estat, Weiland and Melanie. She had to tear her eyes from the gruesome scene afterwards, looking back to Estat, who had dropped the book to protect his ears.

"Hurry, Ralley! Do it now!" he shouted, even though she was standing right in front of him.

She was a bit stunned, and it took a moment for his meaning to sink in, realizing that he wanted her to summon Triventalis now. Ralley gave a hesitant nod and closed her eyes, taking her hands from her ears. She had to think hard about the symbol he'd shown her. For a time she wondered if she would pass out again, like she did when summoning the Black Serpent. *C'mon.* She told herself. *Talon needs my help.* She tried to think harder. She could barely remember what she was supposed to be doing. Thoughts of Talon in danger kept interfering with the image she was trying to think of. She opened her eyes a moment to glance over at Talon, and her brows flew up in surprise. The huge toad had arrived! What now?

"Ralley!" Estat shouted. "Concentrate!"

She didn't look back to Estat, though, and she gasped as Talon was thrown to the ground. "TALON!!!" she screamed, and when she tried to race forward, Estat caught her arm.

"Wait!"

She screamed again as Xenopus lifted a foot to crush him. She had to help him! At the edges of her vision she could see the red haze again. Bursting forth from the ground appeared the summoning circle, and rising from it was Malstraun, the Black Serpent. Without hesitating, he lunged forward, his remaining horn bearing down, and launched himself into Xenopus' side, knocking him off balance and saving Talon from being crushed. Ralley sank to the ground, relief washing over her along with a dizzying weakness. Weiland and Estat were at her side in moments, and she could hear Melanie struggling to get up.

"Ralley!" Estat said, trying to keep her upright. "Malstraun is in bad shape, he cannot do this by himself. You must summon Triventalis with whatever you have left!"

Soothing warmth crept into her as Weiland held her opposite arm. "Come now, you must not rest yet, there is still much to do."

The slight heat made her sleepy, but it also helped to clear her head. She could see the others still fighting for their lives; even Veru had finally broken from the trees ahead and joined them, though his silken white fur was stained with blood. She glanced to Talon, who was getting back to his feet. Axle stood close to him, fending other creatures off to protect him. She had to do something, or they would all lose this fight. Finally, she felt Melanie's hands on her shoulders. "Ralley... you can do it! I know you can!"

Nodding, Ralley closed her eyes again, glad her sister was up and about, but knowing that if she couldn't do this, they would all die. Everyone was tired, wore out, and had used up every bit of power and strength they had to fight these demons. Not only would they die, but everyone else who called this world home would, too. She had traveled from one end of this kingdom to the other; the beautiful landscape, Talons mother, Regence, the nice Innkeeper and his family. She couldn't let them down; she needed help. They all did. She let that desperate feeling grow while thinking of the symbol Estat had shown her in the book. She could feel the power rise in her, and she took hold of it. When she opened her eyes again, she was seeing red. Before she lost it in her excitement at being able to pull it forward on her own, she let it loose. In the open expanse in front of them all, a red circle and star spread out and rose into the sky, leaving behind a great three-headed beast.

"You did it!" Estat cheered.

Ralley giggled weakly and watched the world spin, her legs no longer holding her up on their own.

"Help me, Melanie," Weiland said, hovering somewhere

beside her. "I know you are weak too, but we must keep her conscious for now."

Ralley could feel her sister's hands sending the same strange warmth through her, and it did indeed keep her aware enough to see what was happening. Xenopus was battling Malstraun, but this time, was attempting to rend his other horn from his head. He had paused at the appearance of Triventalis, and the three-headed amarill didn't waste a moment. Ralley watched as the head to the far left, its eyes a milky white, lifted its chin high and opened its mouth. Thunder shook the very air around them as lightning shot from its throat, arcing through the air with smaller ones flicking about in random patterns. The bolt struck Xenopus in the chest and threw him back to crush several demons crowded behind him.

Relieved, Ralley watched as Malstraun shook his head and roared at the fallen toad demon, ready to continue the fight. Talon was back on his feet and brought the Blade Beast around, ready to continue the battle. There were still far too many demons, and more continued to emerge from the trees every moment. She heard Talon shout for Kiran and the others to retreat back behind Triventalis. "There's just too many..." Ralley moaned as the small group struggled to get back to them. Triventalis shifted its body, the head to the far right; it's eyes like Onyx, lifted its chin and opened its jaws like the other. From this one's mouth emerged a black substance that fired straight out over the heads of the retreating party and slammed into the creatures that pursued them. The moment it touched ground, it spread like black ooze, covering everything that came in contact with it. The demons howled, growled, screeched and roared in confusion and then pain as the strange substance ate away at them like acid. Ralley wanted to close her ears and eyes as many of them melted away but she refused to do so till Talon, Kiran, Axle and Veru made it safely back to them.

"Above us!" Melanie cried, pointing to the sky.

Shadows fell over them all, and Ralley looked up in time to see hundreds of flying demons zeroing in on them. "Triventalis!" she shouted, pointing up.

This time it was the middle head that reacted, its eyes a shade of gray. It tilted back and gazed at the demons above, taking a great breath, the body of the huge amarill swelling; then gray smoke billowed out of the nose moments before it opened its jaws. A thick smog rose from its gaping mouth, accelerating into the air, where it spread out like a swelling rain cloud. The flying demons that came in contact with it began to cough and choke as they breathed it in and quite suddenly they fell from the sky, gasping for air. Those who did not die from the fall alone lasted only a few moments more before suffocating. Some dodged around the smoke cloud and dove at them. Talon turned to face the onslaught, Kiran on his left, Meilea and Immuraudi stepping up to his right. Together they formed a barrier of horn and sword that caused the horde to pull up and away to try and circle around for a better impact.

Ralley heard a loud crash and turned to see Malstraun struggling to rise up from colliding into a grouping of trees. "Think you are winning, do you? Your little amarill summoner will not be enough!" Xenopus croaked.

The trees parted and snapped like twigs as a huge creature came into the clearing. It looked like a grizzly bear, but its size was three times greater. Its claws and fangs were far longer than any bear she had ever seen, and its tail was similar to a scorpion, except with fur.

"Oh crap, can't I un-summon those?" Ralley asked hopefully.

"Only if you were the one to summon them," Estat said.

"Fine, then I'll summon it!" she shouted.

Weiland frowned and shook his head. "You cannot summon them all Ralley; you hardly have the strength to stand even now."

The bear-like amarill barreled forward towards Triventalis, and the two massive bodies collided. Though Triventalis' four legs had been firmly planted, the furry beast had driven him back several feet, its claws tearing great gashes into the earth. The three-headed amarill used the horns on the backs of their heads to bludgeon the attacker, but it did little good; the monstrous bear-creature didn't stop. Its wicked hooked claws dug into Triventalis, gouging out flesh and blood. Ralley was horrified, feeling a great heavy weight of blame on her shoulders for having brought the poor amarill here to endure this. She had to stop it somehow.

The hoard of demons could now slip past the two embattled amarill and again came towards them. Axle and Veru launched themselves into the fray without a thought, causing some of the demons to scatter. Those who tried to plow forward were engaged by Talon and Kiran. Meilea and Immuraudi hung back, trying to keep an eye on the flying demons, but they were not the only threat coming in from the sky. Ralley heard Melanie gasp. "What's that?"

Ralley followed her gaze to see a massive creature, wings outspread and casting great shadows over the battle taking place. The wings were feathered, but the body was scaled. Its head was like that of a horse with two great goat horns and a whip-like tail. It must have been an amarill like the other, but before she could ask Estat, something bursting from the nearby river caught her attention. Its skin was sleek, and it had tentacles like a squid. Despite its water bound appearance, it dragged itself ashore and made its way across the meadow towards them. "This is not good," she said, turning to Estat.

"There are powerful amarill helping him…" Estat said, his voice in awe.

The one flying over the battlefield landed, its sharp splayed hooves kicked out at Kiran, who was already distracted by a group of multi-eyed demons. The hit made him stumble and squeal in pain, making Ralley cringe. The squid creature was getting closer to their little band, and Immuraudi was the first to stand in its path. The resulting standoff was short lived, and the amarill brought four tentacles forth to entangle the equine. The coramira, nimble as she was, could not avoid them all, and one wrapped around her foreleg. Weiland was at her side the next moment, leaving Ralley standing on her own despite her weakness.

Ralley was startled by another clap of thunder and heard a deafening roar from the Bear-like amarill. It retaliated with a bone crunching impact to the onyx-eyed head of Triventalis. A demon hound caught Talon's arm, and he yelled out in pain. Immuraudi squealed in agony. Estat called out a spell. Melanie screamed. They were loosing. There was so much noise that Ralley had no time to think about her next action. She had only to act.

- 59 -

FINAL DECISION

Talon dispatched the hound with the blade, slicing clean through the demon. The Blade Beast continued to guide his hand, giving him a strange boost of strength and will that allowed him to continue the battle, though he knew it was taxing his body to its limit. He almost did not notice the red haze that fell over the meadow and the eyes of the approaching demons, but it soon became too much to ignore. When even the demons held their positions, Talon turned his attention to the top of the hill. Ralley was glowing red from head to foot, her eyes closed in a deep trance, her feet floating off the ground and her hair blowing about with a wind that came only from her. He turned his gaze to the field to see where the newly summoned amarill might show, but found instead that the red symbol appeared beneath the three newly arrived amarill enemies. Yet more confusing, the symbols also surrounded Axle and Veru, and the pair vanished into them.

"What is going on?" Talon shouted.

His question was not directed to anyone really, but he heard the Blade Beast answer him. *"She turns the tides. Look."*

Indeed, as Talon watched, the three evil amarill turned away from the defenders and advanced instead upon Xenopus. A new symbol appeared as well, re-depositing Axle and Veru onto the meadow as their combined, two-headed wolf form. The twins then advanced on Xenopus, bounding over the lesser demons. Xenopus must have realized he was now in dire trouble as all the demons that had been fighting them turned about and ran to his aid. Talon spun about and raced up the hill to the others.

"STOP!" Estat shouted at Ralley. "You will kill yourself!"

The plea caught Talon off guard. "Ralley!" he called desperately at her floating form. Her eyes were now open, and she was watching the ensuing battle. Talon spared a glance to Xenopus, but he could barely see the giant reptilian demon among all the amarill that surrounded him. Malstraun looked haggard but was managing to join the fray. Triventalis was slowly making his way over as well, not wanting to be left out despite his injuries. The crowd of lesser demons attempted to distract the larger amarill, but they all moved as one mind with claw, horn, teeth, flame and tentacle. As a result, Xenopus gave a horrendous roar of pain and defeat. The first indication that Xenopus was no more was the sudden scattering of the demons as their controller's life was destroyed. The second was the behavior of the amarill as they turned to give chase to the demons, slaughtering any they could catch.

Talon turned back to Ralley, and there was a pained expression on her face. "Stop her!" he shouted at Estat. Before the Summoner could do anything, Ralley's red glow dissipated, and she dropped; Talon caught her before she hit the ground. "Ralley are you…" But she was unconscious, no, she was not breathing! "RALLEY!" Talon shouted at her, shaking her as if to wake her from sleeping. Melanie rushed to her side. She looked weak from her recent injury, but aside from her tattered dress, there was no sign of a wound. Talon gave her a desperate look.

"Oh… Ralley! I won't let you die! I can do this!" she cried, putting her hands to her sister's torso.

Estat reached out to her, but his hand hovered inches away. He wanted to stop her from exerting herself, but he must have known that neither Melanie nor Talon would allow him to. He turned away instead, shouting for Weiland, the unicorns, anyone who could heal. Talon turned his eyes back to the lifeless young girl still in his arms. He refused to let her go, feeling that holding onto her body would somehow keep her spirit here.

Tears stained Melanie's cheeks as she held back sobs. Talon could never know what it was a healer felt when putting their hands upon death. Melanie's face twisted in concentration, and it was as though her body sent a magical pulse into her lifeless sister. Ralley's body jerked in response, and for a moment, Talon thought she was alright, but she fell limp once more. He glanced to Melanie. She would not look at him, only to her sister, and again the pulse leapt from her hands to Ralley's chest. Once more her body jolted, and once more there was no life. "Again!" Talon shouted.

"But Melanie…" Estat began.

"AGAIN!" Talon repeated.

Melanie appeared not to hear either of them. Tears continued to trickle from her eyes while she fought to send another pulse through. She screamed out, and the sound was both angry and sorrowful. The resulting pulse threatened to throw Talon back. It was only his love for Ralley and his stubborn nature that held him in place. Estat, however was knocked to the ground, and Weiland, who had just come to the top of the hill, staggered back.

Ralley's eyes popped open, and she gasped, struggled, and then settled back, closing her eyes, but breathing. "Ralley?" Talon said, his voice calming. Life had come back to her; she had returned though she was still terribly weak.

"I did it," Melanie whispered. She lifted her gaze to Talon and his blood stained arm, then to those who were just down the hill. Malstraun slowly slithered along the grass, blood pouring from hundreds of wounds. Triventalis, all three of its heads hung low, was sluggish to move its legs, and its huge body was marred with giant claw marks. Even the unicorns did not escape injury. The beautiful Meilea sported teeth marks all over her legs and back, while Kiran had a bad limp, favoring his left foreleg. Even Weiland and Immuraudi were limping and bloody from horrible wounds.

Estat got back to his feet and crouched down to her. "Melanie..." he began, but was unable to put his thoughts into words. He must have known what she was thinking as she examined everyone.

"Ralley found her power; it's time I found mine," she said to him. "I can do it," she added, feeling confidence rise with her voice.

Estat breathed deeply and took hold of her hand. "I believe you," he said with a gentle smile.

She returned his smile and took up his free hand with hers. Closing her eyes, she called up that power that she had so recently come to know so well. It came to her so much more easily than ever before, and though she could feel her own body tiring of the use of such powers, she would not let it go. Instead she allowed it to grow inside of her. The need to help everyone around her was all she needed to fuel it until she couldn't hold it any longer. Like the bursting of a balloon, she released it out into the very space around her, letting it latch on to those with injury, spreading out to touch Triventalis and Malstraun as well. She continued to call and feed this power through her, acting as a sort of conductor, healing the worst of the wounds, aches and pains of her newfound friends. When the flow of power was exausted, she felt herself tip forward. Estat wrapped his arms about her, and when she opened her eyes, she was looking up at him. "See, I knew I could do it… I… knew it…" she mumbled.

Estat only smiled at her, and it was all she needed.

When Ralley finally opened her eyes, she was overjoyed to see that Talon was staring down at her. At first, she wasn't sure she would be able to move, but somehow she managed to lift a hand to touch his cheek. "You're, real right?" she asked, not quite recognizing her own voice.

He chuckled. "Of course, I thought I lost you. You and your sister, your powers are incredible," he said, shaking his head.

"Is… everyone okay?" she asked, trying to look around her now.

"She healed them… all of them," Talon said, helping her to sit up. "Everyone that was here. We lost sight of Axle, Veru and the other amarill that you turned. They chased the demons into the trees."

Ralley could see Melanie in Estat's arms. "Mel!" She half crawled to her from Talon.

"She is alright," Estat said, smiling to her. "She is very weak. She will need much rest."

Melanie turned to grin at her. "Ralley, you have a boyfriend!" she said with a light giggle.

Ralley smirked at her. "So? Looks like you have one, too, but I approve this time."

Melanie paused and blinked at her. Her face reddened, and she turned to Estat, who smiled back at her. "More than just a friend... if you would have me," he said softly back to her.

"Oh! You mean, like, marry?" she asked, her eyes widening at him.

Estat smiled back at her, nodding. Looking ready to faint, Melanie was caught in her reply.

"What is wrong?" Estat asked, frowning a bit.

"What about.... home? I mean... not here, but back in our own world? I... love you, too Estat. But, will we have to go back?"

Before he could answer her, Axle and Veru ascended the hill. Ralley's hold must have faded from them as they were now apart from each other. "Enough of this mushy foolishness!" Axle barked. "At least there are more interesting things to hunt in the forest now, demons intent on human flesh. Way to go, heroes. Things will not get so boring around here, thanks to you," he huffed as he trotted off.

Veru stepped up to Ralley. Though his coat was matted and

bloodied like Axle's, he was still beautiful. "That is his way of saying thank you. He is also not very good at goodbyes. Do not worry; lesser demons without a leader are easier to handle than those *with* one. Besides, the other amarill took care of most of them, anyway. The others will not take long to hunt down."

Ralley smiled. "It's okay. I love you guys, too." She giggled and turned to look for Triventalis, but he was gone as well. Melanie's thoughts about having to go home troubled her. "Will I ever see you guys again?" she asked, turning back to Veru.

The amarill gave her a wolfish smile, green eyes glittering as he looked from her to Talon. "Yes, Ralley, I think you just might." Without explanation, he turned and hurried off after Axle, the two disappearing into the trees.

An equine nose nuzzled her back and she turned to face Kiran. "You too?" she asked.

"You know how to call us if you ever need us again," the unicorn said.

"But how will we get Talon and everyone back to their kingdom without you?" Ralley frowned, wanting them to stay.

"I can take you wherever you wish to go, Ralley," Malstraun said, slithering up to them. Melanie's healing must have been amazing, as his horn had also grown back.

"Wherever I want?" Ralley asked thinking for a moment, and then she smiled. "I know exactly where I want to go. Malstraun, we have a few stops to make."

-60-

HOME

Regence sat in the finely decorated prison to which he had been consigned. The tiny window let in some of the light from the evening. He wondered, as he had since they left, what Talon and Ralley were doing, how they fared. He had been well taken care of as the Queen had promised, though she had angrily questioned him at the disappearance of his comrades. He politely informed her that while he was still a prisoner of her castle, they would keep her secret. The rest of the men confined in the room with him were quiet as well until one of them yelped in surprise at the appearance of a dark portal. They all reached for swords that were not with them and backed away instead. Emerging from the portal was Talon and a man dressed in black who looked oddly familiar. "Talon! What in Asatiria are you doing here?" Regence asked, waving the men off and rushing to him. They clasped wrists in greeting and patted each other on the shoulder.

"It is Emperor Talon, but I suppose Talon will do," he said with a wink. "And I was simply coming to rescue my sword master, of course!" he replied. "It is good to see they have taken good care of you, your up and about! Oh, this is Malstraun," he added, indicating the dark man with him. "He will be taking you and the men back to Degrail. I need you to prepare for our arrival... there is much I need to tell you, but it will have to wait, so much to do," he smiled.

Regence chuckled. "Emperor? I think you have grown up since you escaped, and you have plenty to explain. Until then, I am at your command, Emperor."

It had been days since anyone had seen his daughters; Derrin sat staring at the TV. No matter how long the news channel stayed on, the only thing they ever said was that they were still missing, and today, there had been nothing. The story had grown cold, and there was nothing left for them to go on. Derrin's shoulders slumped, and he turned the power off on the TV. His wife peered up at him with a frown. He had told her everything once, about where he came from and why he was here. She was a wonderfully patient woman and understanding. She believed him, after he had proved it, and was the first to suggest that perhaps their daughters had gone to wherever it was he had come from. He had done his best to reason out why they couldn't. He only knew of one creature that could have taken them back, and the two had been on friendly terms enough that he didn't believe that theory.

"I'm going to bed," he said with a miserable tone.

No sooner had he taken his first step than the house shook with the arrival of a portal that spread out in the living room. He spun to face it, stumbling back toward the couch. He heard his wife scream, and her hands gripped his arm as she scrambled to him. A dark figure stepped from the swirling mass, very tall, dressed in black with ebony hair. "Derrin," he said, bowing his head slightly in greeting.

"Malstraun?" Derrin spoke, his voice uncertain.

"Good to see you again; you have visitors." He stepped aside, and Derrin's eyes caught on the portal. Could it be? Was it them?

The next to emerge was a princely figure, dressed in travel clothes that were stained with blood and dirt. His hair was a golden color and very long, tied behind him. "King Derrin," he said, bowing low to him. This made Derrin's eyebrows rise. He had not been called King when he left; he had only been a prince then. He respectfully bowed his head back to the man, assuming him also very important. "I am Emperor Talon Endrayen of Degrail," he announced, formally introducing himself before stepping aside from the portal.

"Emperor!" He bowed deeper this time, pulling his wife down as well.

"What are you doing?" his wife asked, pulling back from him. "Who are these people?"

"Forgive my wife; she is not of our world…" Derrin began, but was interrupted by a third figure that came in from the portal.

This man was also tall, almost as tall as Malstraun, appearing as young as the Emperor, his long white hair was in disarray, and his blue robes were a disaster, though he appeared well enough. He too bowed to Derrin. "I am the Grand Summonder, Estat Valoren, keeper of the tower," he said, apparently having no kingdom status.

Derrin nodded a greeting to him as he too, stepped aside. He was becoming agitated. Where were his daughters? His heart was slowly sinking again, fearing bad news. That's when they stepped through, the two of them, together, hand and hand. Melanie, his eldest, wearing what once must have been her prom dress, though it was mere rags now, and Ralley was dressed in royal traveling clothes that appeared well traveled in. His wife cried out, and despite the presence of the portal and strangers, she ran to them, taking them in her arms. Derrin slowly came forward, not sure what to think of where they had been all this time. He too hugged them, relief, excitement and wonder catching him. He didn't quite notice the portal close until he let them go. "I have so many questions, and it looks like you all have a most exciting story to tell me." The two girls looked to each other, then gave him broad smiles.

Ralley and Melanie explained their own parts of the story; Talon, Estat and Malstraun were quiet unless they asked for any details. Her father took it all well and even appeared to be envious of their adventures. Their mother looked like she was going to be sick, but accepted their tale nonetheless, adding in tiny gasps here and there. It was late in the evening by the time they finished. "Dad..." Ralley began. "Um, Talon... he..."

Talon stood from the chair he had been sitting in and faced her father. He bowed low to him. "King Derrin, I ask for your daughter's hand in marriage," Talon said, still bowing. Ralley fidgeted and looked from Talon to her father. At first he was surprised, but then he lowered his head thoughtfully.

Her mother's eyes popped open, and she turned to Ralley. "Marriage? But … but you're only…" She turned to face Ralley's father again. "She's only…"

Ralley's father put a hand on her arm. "That is quite enough, Reena," he said softly. "Ralley is not a child, and in the world we come from, she is old enough."

Mother settled back down to the couch, a look of bewilderment and protest in her face. Her father stood and put a hand on Talon's shoulder and let him straighten. "Emperor Talon, I would be honored to know that my daughter will be Empress. All I ask is that I am able to return home as well." He turned to look at their mother. "Reena, you too."

"What? But…" She was at a complete loss for words, looking somewhat shocked. Her eyes fell on Melanie. "What about our other daughter?" she asked. "We can't leave her…"

Now Estat stepped forward and bowed to them both. "King Derrin, I regret to say I am not of royalty, nor do I own a kingdom. I am but a summoner that lives far in the north and am even partly to blame for the theft of your daughters; however, I love Melanie with all my being. I would give up all that I am to have her at my side."

Sudden tension was brought to the room. Ralley could almost feel the emotions all around her. Melanie was the worst of them all, peering nervously at their father, fearing a refusal. The ringing of the Blade Beast in sword form echoed in the quiet room. All eyes turned to him as he lifted it in front of him. "Estat, you have sacrificed much already. Your apprentice, your voice and sight, your home and even risked your life to set things right again. Kneel Estat." When he had done as Talon asked, the Emperor lowered his sword from one shoulder to the other. "You are deserving of a far grander ceremony than this, but rise now, Lord Estat Valoren, Grand Summoner of Asatiria." Talon waited till Estat rose before returning the sword to his scabbard. The motion was like the gavel of a judge, finalizing the status.

Derrin smiled and turned to Estat. "I would be honored to know that my eldest daughter is a Lady of the Grand Summoner of Asatiria," he said.

Melanie squealed and jumped forward, hugging her father. This seemed rather out of place for all the formality that was going on, but everyone in the room, even her mother, laughed.

A few phone calls, some preparations and several hours later they were all standing before a great portal. Malstraun stepped through and disappeared without hesitation. Estat lifted an arm and Melanie took it, a suitcase in her other hand and wearing a fresh summer dress. Together they stepped through. Next were her father and mother; the two were hefting suitcases, and only her mother appeared to be nervous. Together, they disappeared through the portal. Ralley giggled as she heard her mother squeak at that first step. Ralley turned to Talon with a smile. "Are you sure I'll be a good Empress?" she asked.

"I was a fool to ever think you could not be." He kissed her softly, and then offered his arm. Together, they stepped into the void.

www.ingramcontent.com/pod-product-compliance
Lightning Source LLC
Chambersburg PA
CBHW030544020726
47494CB00005B/1475